This book is dedicated in memory of Lieutenant Jacqueline (Jacquet) Melvin, Naval Flight Nurse, USN and all the other members of "The Greatest Generation." Through their unselfish efforts and sacrifices, our freedoms, values, and great nation were preserved.

CHAPTER 1

Unfulfilled

March 11, 1945

With the constant reminder of death all around him, Michael felt that if he died and went to hell, it would not be any worse than where he was now. Between the un-ending explosions, the excessive heat, and the stench of corpses left to rot in this godforsaken island, he no longer had any fear of dying. He figured that he already served his time in purgatory, and he might go straight to heaven for his efforts. Hearing the desperate pleas of the gravely wounded calling out, "corpsman," he thought of joining in their chorus but decided to save his breaths, not knowing how many more he had left. Besides, those Navy Corpsmen who might be lucky enough to escape being hit by a sniper's bullet were stretched too thinly for the tasks at hand. Despite exposing themselves to enemy fire, they would try to provide aid and comfort to those suffering from the devastation that only the horrors of war could bring to the human body. Often it was nothing more than injecting morphine into a mortally wounded Marine and then moving on to the next one. Although it was not necessarily a part of their medical training, they would often tell those bleeding out that they would be okay, knowing that it was not true. By virtue of a jagged piece of shrapnel embedded in his chest, courtesy of an unseen Japanese mortar, Michael could now feel his warm blood beginning to pool against his skin. The cotton twill fabric of his uniform was no longer capable of absorbing any more of the precious fluid escaping from the gaping wound that savagely violated his body. The once sage-green color of his uniform shirt, having been saturated with his blood, was unrecognizable.

The training he received in boot camp had instinctively kicked in, and for what it was worth, he ripped open the packets of sulfa he carried with him and poured the contents into his wound. He wondered if his efforts to fight off infection were nothing more than a waste of time since he would most likely bleed to death anyway. He tried to reach for his rifle, but the force of the explosion had thrown it clear of where he was lying. It probably did not matter anyway since it was most likely damaged by the blast, just as his body was. Yet that training made him want to fight on to the very end. Even if Michael could never get his revenge against the individual who fired the mortar, he would like to take as many of that Jap's buddies with him as possible before he would die.

As he lay there, he grabbed some of the black-colored sand upon which his wounded body was resting. Clenching the sand in his hand, he raised it slightly and let it slowly slip between his fingers, letting the fine particles fall back upon the hard volcanic rock that was everywhere. As his nostrils filled with the pungent smell of sulfur that seeped out of the ground, he wondered if the sight of the falling sand were the last visual memory he would have of this life. His mind conjured up the image of sand steadily falling in an hourglass. As his bright red blood continued to leak out of his body, he could not help acknowledging the inevitable outcomes of the two.

Michael wondered if his entire life would flash before him, but even having lived just twenty-three years, there were still too many past events to remember and so little time to do so. What he had experienced just in the past few years was more than most people would encounter in a lifetime. He felt cheated, wondering what he had done to deserve this, yet he harbored no ill feelings or regrets. No one had forced him to enlist. It was his choice. Although, at this moment, he could not help but wonder if it was the right choice. Like most of his fellow Marines, he always thought that it would be the other guy who would not be going home. Michael did not feel sorry for himself, but he thought of his family and how they would feel as they received the telegram from the War Department informing them of his untimely death.

Not knowing how much time he had left, his thoughts were now of his lost opportunities, and tops among them were Cindy. At first, he wished that she could have still been 'his girl,' but then he was grateful that she was not. It would not be fair for her to suffer the grief that would accompany his demise. Still, after all these years, he was never able to erase the image of her precious face, smiling lovingly at him as they were planning their lives together. A future that neither one of them could have thought of ending in such a manner. He thought of her photograph that he constantly carried with him and how he took great care to ensure it surviving the war. But the fact that the thin and fragile photo might endure while he did not was just another cruel irony that he had to accept.

Still feeling the sand clinging to his bloody fingers, his mind drifted off to another place and another time. That place had also presented challenges and hardships, but he would have gladly changed places given the opportunity. He fought hard to remain conscious, but his weakened body was losing the fight. As his eyes began to close, he heard the sound of approaching footsteps as the soles of their boots were grinding against the sandy surface of this volcanic island. He thought of grabbing his KA-BAR combat knife from its sheath, but he was too weak to fight anymore and too much in pain to care. As he lay there, quietly awaiting his fate, his last thoughts before losing consciousness were of that other more peaceful time and place.

CHAPTER 2

Friends

March 20, 1930

The several inches of snow that fell belied the coming change of seasons across the Oklahoma Panhandle. Despite the blanket of snow that made everything look pristine and clean, the picturesque image it created would be short-lived. The afternoon sun was getting higher each day as spring was rapidly approaching. A flawless blue sky had already replaced the sullen-gray skies of this morning's surprise storm. Unobstructed by cloud cover, the warming rays of the sun had already started to melt the snow. Within a couple of days, if not sooner, the barren fields that lay dormant throughout the winter would be completely exposed to the elements. For the past years, that had not been a bad thing. Ample rainfall and rich soil had contributed to excessive planting that reaped the fertile earth's benefits. For the countless farmers that made this region their home, farming was a way of life and not a science to be studied. After all, that was the concern of the state agricultural colleges. Besides, any worries about changing planting methods or rotating crops never mattered previously. And it certainly did not put food on your table or cash in your pocket to pay the bills.

Large corporate farms were not typical in this region, whereas family-run farms were both familiar and numerous. Within these family businesses, it would require all family members to chip in to do their part. Almost always, it worked out that the older children would share increasingly higher work responsibilities. School worked around planting and harvest schedules if that was even an option for the teenagers in many families. With winter over, other than the winter wheat planted last fall, the new planting season would soon begin in earnest.

All in all, it was still a good and satisfying life, albeit not a particularly prosperous one. While you did not receive cash riches, there was a sense of pride and accomplishment in realizing that you had accomplished something at the end of the day. Seeing the results of your labor provide food and sustenance and knowing that your family would eat well because of those efforts made for easy sleeping at night. Life on the Oklahoma Panhandle made you grow up quickly, which was not necessarily a bad thing. Still, it was good to be young and carefree.

Michael and Cindy were fortunate to be both young and carefree, as much as possible for anyone their age growing up in or around Goodwell, Oklahoma, during the Great Depression. But despite the economic hardships that bore so heavily on everyone's lives, the strong faith of the community and the family values instilled upon the residents from their births made it an excellent place to raise a family.

Born just months apart, they had known each other all their lives, as limited as those lives had been so far. Growing up in similar wood-frame farmhouses, they could see each other's house from their bedroom windows. Cindy was the only female among the six Smith children, so she was influenced and protected by her older brothers. It would come as no surprise that she exhibited traits that might best describe her as being a tomboy at this stage of her life. She would be much more likely to be wearing a layer of dirt on her face from roughhousing with her brothers than she would be wearing a frilly dress. Still, when the occasion came that required a fresh-washed face and putting on that frilly dress, her natural beauty was evident even at this tender young age. With her auburn hair and sparkling hazel eyes, in years to come, there would be no doubt that this tomboy would transition into a lovely young woman. But even with the accelerated growing up from living on the farm, this would still be many years away.

By comparison, Michael Johnson was the youngest boy of the five Johnson children, but he was born between the birth of his two sisters. Being the younger sibling of both his brothers and one of his sisters, he benefited and suffered from having that distinction. As a result, he would learn about life from what his brothers would impart to him. These facts of life were not what you could learn from a school textbook. Yet, at the same time, having an older sister helped to temper the rough masculinity that he would naturally acquire from his older brothers. Michael was also a good-looking child. His bright blue eyes, along with his impish grin, would often serve him well in getting out of trouble. Even at this young age, he realized that no matter what he may have done, neither his parents nor siblings could stay mad at him for very long. He had not realized it yet, but for that matter, neither could Cindy.

Besides attending the same small schoolhouse that served their community, they attended the same church and went to the church's Sunday school. It would come as no surprise that when growing up, they would be best friends. They shared so many things in common. But their world was limited to the immediate area where they lived. Since hospital births were rare to residents of this rural county, both of them slept each night in a bed that was no more than twenty feet from where they were born. They had neither the occasion nor the reason to travel outside of the confines of Texas County, Oklahoma.

As he bent down to tighten the shoelaces of his well-worn leather shoes, Michael looked down at the fresh layer of snow and saw the long dark shadow of the young girl that was standing beside him. The angle of the late afternoon sun had stretched her shadow to nearly three times her actual height. Standing back up, he took one quick step and shouted, "I'll race you to the Miller's mailbox."

"Not fair, Michael. You cheated," she shouted back. Then, as she started to run after him, her reddish-brown ponytail began bouncing freely in the brisk cold air.

"What's keeping you?" he shouted back, as he was now turning around to watch his friend trying to make up lost ground.

"Michael, stop running. You know I can't keep up with you." Chasing after him, she laid down a parallel set of footprints that traced his imprints in the previously undisturbed snow.

"Come on, Cindy, you're such a slowpoke." Michael was now back-pedaling, keeping an eye both on her and the Miller's mailbox. He would slow down just enough to tease her into thinking she might close the gap and reach the mailbox ahead of him, but he would at the last minute reach out and touch the mailbox just seconds before Cindy would get there. Doing this would surprise neither of them, as this scene would replay itself countless times over the years, always ending the same way.

"Maybe the next time I'll let you win," Michael would say with a smile, knowing that he probably would not.

"Maybe you wouldn't have to if you didn't cheat," Cindy scolded him while punching Michael in his arm.

"Wow! That hurt," Michael said, feigning injury, then adding, "You hit like a girl."

"I am a girl," Cindy yelled back, her rosy red cheeks showing the effect of the cool winter breeze.

"You could've fooled me," Michael said, taunting the eight-year-old.

"I hate you, Michael Johnson," she responded falsely while picking up a handful of snow and trying to shape it into a snowball as quickly as possible.

"What are you going to do?" her classmate said defiantly. Then he quickly added, "Go ahead and try to hit me. Go ahead. I dare you. I double dare you."

Never the one to back down from a dare, let alone a double dare, Cindy let the snowball loose with the best over-the-arm throw she could muster and hit Michael squarely in his face. The force and accuracy of Cindy's throw caught Michael by surprise as he recoiled from the impact. His face now splattered with snow, Michael could feel the warm trickle of blood that was now flowing from one of his nostrils.

"Ouch!" he shouted, more from surprise than the actual pain of his bruised and bloody nose.

Seeing the blood on Michael's face, Cindy rushed over to aid her friend, taking a handkerchief from her coat pocket and handing it to him.

"Here, hold this and keep your head back," she said, now feeling sorry for her actions and showing remorse not usual for someone that young.

"It's no big deal," Michael said, wanting to seem more mature than the eight-year-old boy that he was.

Brushing off the snow from a discarded wooden crate, Cindy said, "Here, let's sit down until the bleeding stops." Then looking at the blood-soaked handkerchief, she added, "I'm sorry, Michael."

"Okay," was Michael's simple reply, feeling more embarrassment than resentment.

Once they were able to continue walking, they began to talk about their hopes and aspirations. Although they were both brought up in families that were multi-generational farmers, neither of them wanted to follow in their parents' footsteps. Michael would talk about the far-off places they learned about in school. He would enthrall Cindy with his stories of how he would travel to these places when he would be older and no longer have to live here in the Oklahoma Panhandle. At the same time, Cindy would tell Michael of her desire to be a nurse when she grew up. She loved the idea of helping people, much like she just helped Michael with his nosebleed. Of course, that she was responsible for it was conveniently left out of the conversation. Having hopes and dreams was essential for children everywhere, but they were incapable of realizing how difficult it would be to escape from their present lives at their tender young ages. Unfortunately, neither one could know what the future might have in store for them. In retrospect, not knowing the future might be a blessing.

CHAPTER 3

Nightmares

December 3, 1934

They would not usually appreciate the early season snow as much in prior years, but it was a welcomed change since it put a pure white blanket over the layers of dried dirt and dust. The cloudy skies that brought the snow had all but dissipated as a cold front moved into the area, bringing with it brisk northwest winds. Walking to the bedroom window, Sarah looked out at the surreal image of their farm that had turned into a winter wonderland. The clearing skies allowed for a nearly full moon to glow brightly above the white landscape as it was rising from the east. Only a few thin veils of clouds were passing quickly in front of it. The reflected brilliance from the hidden sun enabled the moon to shine upon all that was within its sight. The combination of the moon's low angle and the white ground provided for long dark shadows of the farm's buildings and fences.

"Philip, come look," Sarah asked of her husband.

"What is it?" Philip inquired, having just put on his nightshirt.

"It's just so beautiful," she answered.

"You mean like this place used to be," Philip responded somewhat cynically.

Sarah did not respond, nor did Philip expect a reply. They both knew what he meant, and it pained them greatly to acknowledge the events of the past years outwardly. Instead, they each carried their concerns inside them, and they persevered as well as they could. It was the right thing to do. Besides, they had no other choice.

"Come. Let's go to bed," Sarah said, fully aware of the burden they each carried. But Sarah was also mindful of the hidden demons that her husband had within him. And these demons were much deeper and more disturbing than the problems brought on by the long-lasting drought. Unlike the lack of rain, which would not last forever, this problem would not be capable of ending with a change in the weather. As much as it troubled her that Philip carried this added weight, it upset her even more that she could not do anything to help him. But unfortunately, the demons he had inside him would never leave his consciousness. Even worse, they would often surface at night when he was alone in his dreams and most vulnerable. Sarah would pray that tonight might be different, but she doubted if that would be the case despite the great faith in her Lord.

As they both crept into bed and got comfortable under the quilted comforter that would keep them warm tonight, Sarah reached over and turned down the light on her nightstand.

"Goodnight, Philip," she said, hoping that it would be true.

"Goodnight, Sarah," Philip said in reply. Then, before turning onto his side, he added, "You're a good woman. I love you."

"I love you too," was her simple reply, as her concerns would keep her from falling asleep right away.

It had been over sixteen years, but to Philip, it could have just as easily have been just sixteen minutes. Because for him, time had not healed old wounds, especially wounds of the soul. Philip was a brave man. More than that, he was a hero. The medals tucked away in his bureau's drawer were testimony to that. But he feared these nocturnal demons because he was unable to defeat them. They would manifest themselves differently, but their theme was consistent. They were cowardly because they hid in the one place he could not fight them. But cowardly or not, they would be relentless, and they had a powerful ally, his dreams. Trying to fight their collaborator would prove fruitless, so Philip closed his eyes and fell asleep, expecting the worse.

It might have been hours, or it might have been just a few minutes after they had each fallen asleep when it started. Philip was experiencing chills, but it was not from the cold night air. Instead, it was from a chill that was emanating from deep inside him. His eyes were closed, but he saw things anyway. It would be the same story, not always the same, but always similar enough. All the essential elements would be there, but not always in the same or proper order, as dreams had a way of presenting real-life events illogically. Yet, it had a way of making them seem so logical at the time.

It began as it had so many times in the past. Philip was marching with his unit to the ship that would take him and his regiment to France. Proudly wearing his Marine uniform, he stepped sharply to the sound of a band playing one of John Philip Sousa's military marching songs. Crowds of people were cheering and clapping as the loud horn of the ship blasted its salute. From among the onlookers, someone threw a bouquet of roses which Philip caught. But then he would focus on a woman seated in the crowd who was not cheering. Instead, she was crying as she held a dying Marine, his bloodied head cradled on her lap. Soon, a policeman stopped traffic to let the parading Marines pass by, tweeting his whistle while smiling at Philip. Then, the officer thrust his arm forward, staring grimly at Philip as he once again tweeted loudly on his whistle.

Philip found himself breaking ranks from his unit and began to walk towards the policeman. As he did, the police officer was now wearing a different uniform, that of a U.S. Marine Corps Captain. The officer began shouting at Philip to climb out of a trench, blowing his whistle to signal the attack. Suddenly, Philip found himself back on the battlefield at Belleau Wood, just as he was there in 1918. Although it looked the same, like the rest of his dream, specific details had changed. As he and the other men of his battalion began to advance towards the heavily defended German lines, the sounds of machine guns firing, as well as the mortar and artillery explosions, were deafening. As the enemy's fire was cutting down his fellow Marines, he found himself running barefoot across the area called no man's land. By now, Philip was sweating in his dream and real-life as he began squirming in his bed. Still deep in his dream, Philip found himself stopping to put on a pair of combat boots from a fallen Marine. But then, the voice of Marine Corps First Sergeant, Dan Daly, winner of two Medals of Honor, yelled out to him and the others, saying, "Come on, you sons of bitches, do you want to live forever?"

Philip began charging forward again, stopping briefly only to fire his rifle. Soon he and his fellow Marines were becoming entangled in barbed wire. As Philip stepped carefully through the sharp metal spines, he watched as those around him were falling victim to the relentless German machine guns or a sniper's well-placed shot. It was now that he realized he had charged into battle not carrying his rifle but that bouquet of red roses. Philip continued running forward as more and more of his comrades and friends were dying about him. Finally, somehow, he made it to the enemy trenches, confronted by a young German soldier, charging at him with the pointed edge of a bayonet.

Had Philip been able to, he would have seen himself beginning to thrash wildly about in bed. Droplets of sweat were now dripping down his forehead and onto his face. But still caught up in this nightmarish rendition of his actual combat experience, the disturbing dream continued. Philip now found that his bouquet had turned back into his trusty M1917 Enfield rifle. Equipped with his fixed bayonet, Philip charged at the German, thrusting his bayonet into the young man's chest. As he withdrew his bayonet, dripping with the fresh red blood of the dying German, he looked into the man's face, only now it was his face. As he was now lying there dying, he looked up to see the German standing over him, laughing hysterically, holding the bouquet. The young soldier then knelt beside Philip and placed the flowers on him, apologizing in perfect English and telling him it was time to go. "Go where?" Philip demanded of the German but received no reply. Then, in the bat of an eye, Philip found himself back at the dockyards where he had been marching to his ship. Only this time, he was lying across his mother's lap as his unit continued parading by. She whispered into his ear, "Philip, it's time to go."

"Go where?" he began shouting, over and over again. Then, finally, he felt a woman's hand gently stroking his brow.

"It's alright. It was just another nightmare," Sarah said, trying to reassure Philip.

As strong as he was, the former battle-toughened Marine and hard-working farmer allowed himself to nestle in his wife's loving arms. As he slowly allowed himself to fall back to sleep, his last thoughts before drifting off were of his dream and him cradled in his mother's arms, still wondering where it was he was supposed to go. Had he been able to interpret his dream better, Philip might have realized that perhaps it was time to go home and to leave the nightmare of Belleau Woods forever behind. Of course, how to do that was the problem.

Satisfied that her husband had fallen back asleep and was no longer experiencing the disturbing nightmares that were occurring all too frequently, Sarah slowly released Philip from her embrace and rolled over. As it was now Sarah's turn to fall asleep, she thought of a disturbing secret she kept from her husband. Sarah did not want to burden him with any additional concerns and worries. Because she felt his existing burdens were already exerting a toll on his mental and psychological well-being, she kept this recent fear to herself. Lately, it was not just Philip who was having recurring nightmares. Sarah was experiencing her own. But unlike Philip's dreams of past events, her dreams were of things yet to come. She could only hope that these dreams were not of some yet-to-be-filled prophecies. Her grandmother had told her years ago that the women in her family had a special gift of sometimes foretelling future events. Thinking now of her grandmother's words, Sarah thought it might be better described as a curse if they were true. Because in her dreams, she saw visions of war and destruction. Sarah would hear the cries and screams of people in agony as fires and explosions were happening around them. Then, as if that was not disturbing enough, she would slowly recognize the voices of some of those crying out. They were the voices of her two younger sons, Matthew and Michael.

It would take several more minutes before Sarah would fall back to sleep. As she was still lying there awake, she once again prayed to God to protect her family from past and future trials and hardships. Taking comfort in having implored the Good Lord for his help, Sarah finally was able to close her eyes and join her husband in sleep. Meanwhile, the continued serenity of the rising moon, reflecting upon the snowy landscape just outside her window, belied the less than peaceful world events that would soon affect all their lives.

CHAPTER 4

Black Sunday

April 14, 1935

As it had happened so many other times, the dry, sand-like dirt had managed to find its way into Michael's shoes. Their leather creases had numerous cracks, and they were as dry as the arid land they were treading upon. Just normal walking would kick up enough of the dusty material to annoyingly settle between his inner-sole and his brown wool socks that his mother had knitted. Sitting cross-legged on the dirt path that would eventually lead them home, he took his shoe off and slowly turned it upside down. He watched silently as the sandy particles slowly streamed out of the shoe and back onto the earth beneath it. Then, after replacing the shoe on his foot, he duplicated his actions for his other shoe. Watching him the entire time was his thirteen-year-old companion, who stood by patiently.

Ironically, it had been so dry for so long it was in sharp contrast to how their town got its name. When the Chicago, Rock Island, and Pacific Railroad was being built and would cross the Oklahoma Panhandle, stations would follow based on the steam locomotives' ability to have water. If there were no water, there would be no sense stopping there. So instead, the railroad would continue drilling wells. As they continued to look for a sufficient water supply, the railroad would often drill dry wells. But if they were fortunate enough to hit a good well, then a station would follow. Inevitably, towns would spring up along these railroad stops. Goodwell was one such town named for the 'good well' the railroad was using.

Standing once again, Michael wiggled his feet, trying to position them in the shoes correctly. Then, looking at his life-long friend, he said, "Remember back when we didn't have all of this dryness and dust." It was asked as a question, but it sounded more like a statement from the insightful thirteen-year-old. Cindy took it as a statement, and instead of answering him, she simply nodded her head in agreement. They both fully realized that the dust was not the problem. Instead, the problem was what was causing the dust. But if the collective minds of all the agricultural experts and the local and federal politicians could not solve the problem, what could two young teenagers do.

A short distance away, the other members of the Johnson and Smith families were also heading back to their respective homesteads. Although it was a couple of miles from their homes to the church they all attended, they would make this weekly pilgrimage by foot. At nineteen cents per gallon, gasoline was expensive and needed more for the tractors that would till the land. Besides, compared to a day's work in the field, these Sunday strolls were a walk in the park. Both families were second and third-generation farmers and lived nearby to each other's tracts of land. They were of pioneer stock, and they were a proud and God-fearing people. They were honest, hard-working, and devoted to their families, as were most of the residents of this small but close-knit community. Their ancestors had moved there as squatters in 1886. It was then that the part of the territory known as No Man's Land was declared public domain. It was self-governed by the settlers and was named the Cimarron Territory. It had continued by that name that until Oklahoma filed for statehood in 1907. For all practical matters, the Panhandle should have been part of Kansas. The U.S. Senate and the House of Representatives passed bills assigning the land to Kansas, but President Grover Cleveland never signed the bills into law.

Although the Smiths and the Johnsons lived as good neighbors, during the span of nearly half a century and with dozens of descendants, there would always be some instances where persons and personalities would clash. So it should not have come to any great surprise that the current generation of Johnsons and Smiths would be different. Some friction and petty jealousies were inevitable with the five young Johnson siblings and the six young Smith siblings. But there was never any hostility. On the contrary, and for the most part, there was much harmony and friendship between the two families.

Of more concern to them and the entire region was the ongoing multi-year drought devastating the farmlands. Mother Nature may have been to blame for the lack of rain necessary for their crops and livelihoods. But over-farming of the land had equally contributed to their demise. While politicians and agriculture experts would debate the merits of the farmers' roles in contributing to the problem, the concerns of families like these were much more fundamental. For them, it was the question of how to survive yet another year of diminishing crop yields and the loss of income from those crops to survive financially.

Having tied his shoelaces, Michael began walking again. By his side, as so often in the past, Cindy was matching his strides with every step he took. Michael did not mind walking with Cindy. Instead, he enjoyed it. However, things had changed recently for both, and their lives would never be the same because of these changes. Even if they tried, they would have been powerless to prevent what was happening. The first change was the child's natural progression into adulthood, while the second was the weather. No one ever had a good reason to attempt stopping the former, while everyone lately wished they could stop the latter.

Cindy was transforming from the tomboy friend he had grown up with into an attractive young teenager. Besides the noticeable physical changes, she was also maturing emotionally. Michael was also changing physically. His voice seemed to be nearly an octave lower, and he was discovering the other hormonal changes to his body that came with puberty. But as it was with boys, Michael lagged behind Cindy emotionally. In time he would catch up, but for now, there was a disconnect in their relationship. For the first time, Michael had difficulty conversing with Cindy. He felt awkward being with her, and he did not know why. He had always liked her, and he had enjoyed being with her. But that was when they were best friends growing up as kids. Now things were different. But he was not yet able to fully understand the reasons why he liked her so much. At times it was as if he felt intimidated by her newly acquired maturity. He felt like he was awkward in her presence and probably not worthy of being with her. Maybe because of her new maturity, Cindy seemed to understand Michael's issues. She also realized that she liked him a lot, but unlike Michael, she understood why. Fortunately for both their sakes, Cindy had also learned to be patient. Besides, she knew that they had their whole lives ahead of them.

They were all within several hundred yards of their homes when they first began to notice something ominous. What moments ago was a warm and sunny Sunday afternoon had now become something both dangerous and threatening. The sky was turning darker, and a strong breeze was picking up from the northwest. Winds on the Panhandle were not uncommon, but this somehow seemed different. It carried with it a sense of foreboding, almost as if there was something evil about it. The church's pastor had previously spoken of the Judgement Day prophecy from the bible, and his words were now echoing in Michael's mind. As the winds grew more robust, the entire group looked to the northwest and froze in their steps.

Since the drought had begun, dust storms were often occurring. As annoying as they were, the residents of the area had learned to live with them. It was a daily ritual for many to sweep off the dirt and dust from their front porches. Over time, the storms had acquired many names, such as dusters and black blizzards. The region's residents had adapted to the inconvenience out of necessity, but they were not appreciative of doing so. Yet, they all managed to somehow coexist with the wrath that nature bestowed upon them. But this time, it was different. Even before it happened, they all began to experience a sense of something menacing. That sensation was soon followed by a sudden chill that began to run up and down their spines. The cold was undoubtedly due to the rapidly falling temperature, but the hairs on their exposed skin started to tingle and stood out also.

Whether it was from the static electricity in the air or their body's instinctive reaction to being frightened, it did not matter. For those caught in its path, the threat was now genuine. It was no longer a feeling of apprehension; instead, the Smiths and the Johnsons were now fully aware of the evil about to envelop them. Heading towards them in a south-southwest direction, with winds of up to sixty miles per hour, was a rolling black mass. This sinister-looking, five-hundred-foot-high wall of darkness appeared to devour everything in its path. Ahead of the encroaching storm, hundreds of ducks, geese, and other birds were desperately trying to avoid being swallowed up by the vicious, ruthless, and lifeless squall. The static electricity created by the dust storm was powerful enough to knock a man down.

They began to walk faster, but against the backdrop of an advancing and threatening wall of darkness, they began to realize the futility of it. Michael and Cindy watched as blue sparks began leaping off a nearby barbed-wire fence. The crackling sound created by the electrically charged air was now barely audible as the storm drew nearer. As the winds were starting to howl, it was apparent to any people on the ground that they could not outrace the swirling, angry black clouds. Having no shelter available to them, they did the best they could do. As the other Johnson and Smith family members began to lie prone on the ground, Michael took Cindy's hand and led her to a narrow ditch that ran parallel to the dirt path. Although Michael may have had perplexing emotions about Cindy, his concern for her safety and well-being had not faltered. He had her lie face down as he then shielded her with his body. "Keep your eyes closed," the thirteen-year-old implored her, worrying more about her safety than his own.

While Michael and Cindy were trying to protect themselves from the stinging sand and dirt being driven into their exposed skin by the sixty-miles-per-hour winds, trying to breathe normally without ingesting the sandy particles became impossible. As the billowing clouds of dirt, dust, and sand overran the area, daylight turned to darkness. At times it was so dark they could not have seen their hands in front of them. But, of course, to look would have made their eyes vulnerable to the sandblasting effects of the storm. Michael would have had his jacket to cover Cindy's face and head if it had not been a warm spring day. But not having that as an option, Michael tried to protect her using his arms and hands. His gallant efforts would prove to have been largely successful, but not without his exposed face taking the brunt of the storm's fury.

Eventually, the worst of the Black Sunday storm had passed, but not before an estimated three million tons of Oklahoma topsoil had been picked up by the storm and blown away. That was as much soil that an entire army of excavators had removed to dig the Panama Canal. Even more impressive was that this occurred in just one day, whereas it took seven years to excavate the canal. Cases of pneumonia in the affected areas would increase dramatically from the inhalation of the dust, while painted objects were stripped bare by the corrosive effects of the blowing sand. The residents would feel the immediate effects of the storm for days, but the long-term effects would last well into the end of the decade.

Finally feeling that it was safe enough, Michael stood up and looked around. One by one, he saw the other members of their families come into view as the visibility slowly improved. An eerie silence was now evident as the winds began to diminish. The honking of the fleeing geese was no longer evident. No longer to be heard were the crackling sounds of the storm's static electrical discharges. No conversations were heard as they stood in silent awe at the magnitude of what they had just experienced. Instead, the sounds of people coughing were now noticeable. It was not a loose phlegmy cough, but a dry hacking cough resulted from ingesting sand and dust into the nose and throat. Michael also heard another sound, which may have been drowned out earlier by the storm's fury. It was Cindy quietly sobbing. She was still lying face down on the ground as he bent down to lift her. As he held her shaking body, she held tightly onto him in return, not wanting to let go. He assured her that everything would be okay, wondering if that was true. But one thing was true. From this day on, Michael had finally caught up to Cindy. Michael was no longer the emotionally confused immature teenager. Michael was now well on his way to becoming a man.

CHAPTER 5

The Hay Bailer

July 29, 1935

Compared to when all planting, harvesting, and other farm work was done by hand, the invention and implementation of mechanical devices to do these chores were welcomed by farmers everywhere. Growing and producing greater yields per acre benefited the consumers while making life easier for the farmers. Still, like all things mechanical, farm machinery was not immune from the occasional, if not regular, breakdowns and malfunctions. Disruptions like this would happen on all farms, but it was even more true of the smaller family-run farms in challenging times such as now. These farmers would lovingly tend to their devices, always trying to coax another year or two of usefulness before relegating them to the scrapyard. But, of course, this fondness of their machinery would sometimes resemble more of a love-hate relationship. Today would not be an exemption to that example.

"Hey Paul, what are you up to?" Michael asked of his older brother.

"I'm trying to fix the damn bailer," Paul responded, speaking of the hay bailer that was now refusing to work.

"Don't let Ma hear you say damn. She'd wash your mouth out with soap," Michael said with a concerned look.

"I think I am old enough to say damn," the sixteen-year-old emphatically stated as he struggled to get the machinery working.

"Why won't it work?" Michael followed up on his last line of questioning.

"If I knew the answer to that, then maybe I wouldn't be wasting half my day trying to fix this piece of crap," Paul answered, hitting the aged machinery with his wrench out of frustration.

"Can't Pop fix it. He always did in the past?" An inquisitive Michael asked.

"Sure, Pop can fix it, but he expects me to be able to do these things now. Maybe one day I may be running this or my own farm, and I will need to be able to do these things," Paul replied, wondering if it would have been easier just to admit his failure and have his dad fix it.

"Can I help?" Michael asked.

Not that he didn't want his brother's help, it was just that he didn't need his help. But Paul appreciated the offer and was glad to see that Michael had finally taken an interest. Of all the Johnson boys, Michael seemed the least likely to spend his life as a farmer. He and that Smith girl, Cindy, would spend most of their time talking about traveling to different places, faraway places, and foreign lands that most people from the Oklahoma Panhandle would never visit in their lifetimes. But Michael was young, and Paul wondered if Michael had shared any of those same thoughts and hopes when Paul was Michael's age. Paul might have let these thoughts linger if not for the current problem at hand, a broken stationary hay bailer.

The principle was simple enough. Once the gasoline engine was running, a series of belts, gears, and hinges would allow a rectangular piston made from woodblocks to forcibly compress the hay into a hopper, allowing it to take on the shape of a bale ready for tying with wire. It was still a tiresome job, as the hay would have to be gathered from the field and brought to the bailer. Then the hay would have to be thrown into the hopper, only to keep repeating the process. But none of this would matter if Paul was not able to get the machine functioning properly. Finally, the old engine kicked in, and all the moving parts were functioning normally. Hearing the engine running again elicited a gratifying smile from Paul and a look from Michael that exhibited a sense of pride in his older brother's accomplishment.

"Pop would be proud," Michael said while still beaming at Paul's success.

"He'd be a lot prouder if I got all this hay bailed today. Here, you said you wanted to help. Go grab a pitchfork and start moving that pile of hay over here so I can get it baled before Ma calls us for dinner."

As Michael was sticking his pitchfork into the untidy mound of hay and throwing it at Paul's feet, Paul would grab as much as he could and stuff it into the hopper before the wooden plunger came down. Their actions went on as the two brothers proved to be an effective team. The repetitive motions of each were now fully synchronized as if they could perform their combined tasks automatically. Not requiring their total concentration allowed them to talk as two brothers might while getting completed another essential chore of the farm.

They were close to finishing when Paul, whether through error or fatigue, missed throwing most of his hay cleanly into the hopper. Not wanting to disrupt the timing of the routine that he and Michael had successfully established, he quickly picked up the pieces of hay that fell short of the hopper and attempted to push it back in before the heavy wooden piston came back down. Michael had his head down, grabbing another load of hay for his pitchfork when he heard Paul scream. It was so loud that both their mother in the house and their father two hundred yards away had heard it. The sound of it had instantly brought back those horrible nightmares that their father had suffered on so many sleepless nights. Knowing that something terrible had happened, but not knowing what it was or who it had happened to, he began running towards the area near the barn from where the cry emanated. At the same time, his worried and frightened wife, Sarah, started running from the kitchen with her flour-covered apron still tied around her waist.

While the machine was still running, its piston still systematically going up and down, Michael saw Paul holding his bloodied and mangled right hand. With all the force that the machinery could apply, it had crushed Paul's fingers, pinning them between the piston and the hardened wood base that lay beneath it. Michael stood there, shocked and not knowing what to do. Paul was also shocked as he looked down at his hand in disbelief. Their mother was the first to arrive, and after the initial shock of seeing the damage inflicted upon her son, she tore off part of her apron and began to wrap it around Paul's hand in an attempt to stop the bleeding. She momentarily stopped as Paul yelled out in pain but continued, knowing she needed something to stop the hemorrhaging. Soon, the white flour that had covered the apron was now a bright red from Paul's blood.

When their father arrived, he said nothing, as was often the case, but he began to utilize the same first aid training he received as a Marine who had fought on the battlefield at Belleau Woods. He improved upon the bandaging that his wife had initiated and began barking orders to Matthew, who had just arrived, telling him to get their pickup truck. Michael, feeling useless, did the only thing he could think of helping. He shut off the machine, at least ending the continuous sound of its noisy engine, a sound that now had become both annoying and threatening.

As Matthew pulled up with the truck, Philip led Paul into the cab and had Matthew join them. As they pulled away, Sarah stood next to Michael. She was now mindful of the unsettling emotions that were troubling him. With a trail of dust rising behind the speeding truck, Rebekah and Grace stood watching from the porch of their family's house, not knowing what happened exactly but still aware of the significance of it.

Philip knew from his experience on the battlefield what type of medical care and treatment Paul would need. Due to the severity of the injury, driving into town and bringing Paul to Doc Willis would not be enough. All the good doctor could have done was not that much more than they had done already. With that knowledge in mind, Philip would head north across the state line into Kansas. There was a small hospital in Elkhart about 45 miles away. It was not much, but given the circumstances, it was the best that they could do. So with Philip behind the wheel and Matthew keeping compression on Paul's bleeding hand, they raced to the hospital, driving over roads either poorly paved or not paved at all. If nothing else, compared to the injuries of his fellow Marines, Philip was confident that Paul's injury, as devastating as it was, would not be fatal. But his greatest fear was whether or not Paul would lose the loss of his right hand. Only time could tell. But ironically, time might also prove this tragedy to be a potentially life-saving event, as fickle as fate could be.

Paul had passed out from the pain when they finally arrived, and his face was pale and sallow from the loss of blood. Acting quickly, Phillip carried Paul from the truck and rushed him into the reception area, just as Matthew pushed open the door ahead of them. It was a small hospital, and it would not have been the top choice for a severe trauma injury such as what Paul had suffered, but it was better than any other options Philip had. His prior military training had served him well, as he acted quickly and decisively, but that would only go so far. The fate of his son's hand, as well as Paul's overall future, would be determined by what a small team of doctors and nurses in rural Kansas would be able to do.

Philip had seen much more trauma than one person should have to see in their lifetime. And much of it was horrible beyond belief. But although the overall comparison of Paul's injury to what Philip saw on the battlefield might not seem all that bad, it was far more disturbing as a father. Even though Philip kept trying to convince himself that there was nothing that he could have done to have prevented the accident from happening, as a parent entrusted with his child's safety, he felt that he had somehow failed in that responsibility.

As he and Matthew sat in the small waiting room, the image of Paul's crushed hand, and his son screaming in pain, repeatedly played in his mind. Then, Philip began thinking back to a past instance when he had carried a severely wounded Marine over his shoulder, dodging bullets at Belleau Wood. Philip never knew if that Marine had survived, and Philip often wondered if his action that day had made any difference. Philip hoped that it had and that wounded Marine might someday be able to help someone, just as he had aided him. As they waited for word of Paul's condition, Philip wished for the same degree of faith that his wife had, hoping that it would somehow make things better. But he also was facing the stark reality that was before him. Still, Philip managed to seek God's help in the only way he knew how. Never one for knowing or saying the correct prayers or verses from the bible, he did what he always did when he sought divine intervention. He spoke directly to God. It may have been too informal and not how Sarah would do so, but it helped him on the battlefield at Belleau Wood. He would now hope that it would help again, not for himself and his fellow Marines this time but for Paul.

Had he had his pocket watch with him, Philip would have been looking at it often, seeing how much time had elapsed.

Instead, he checked the elapsed time on the large round clock on the waiting room's white wall. In this instance, time was not an ally. Philip understood that the longer Paul was in the operating room, the less likely there would be a favorable outcome.

With so much attention being paid to Paul's injury, and rightfully so, Philip realized that he had not considered the effect this was having on Matthew. While Philip was driving them to the hospital, Matthew cradled his brother while applying constant pressure to his mangled and bloody fingers. Looking at his son sitting beside him, he now sensed the fear and worried look on Matthew's face. He also noticed for the first time Matthew's blood-soaked coveralls. Philip knew it would be relatively easy for Sarah to remove the bloodstains from Matthew's clothes. But it would be much more challenging to remove that same image from Matthew's mind.

Finally, a doctor walked into the waiting room. He would have been quite good if he had been a poker player, as his expression did not indicate what he was about to say. He was wearing a white lab coat stained with Paul's blood. Still expressionless, he walked to where they were sitting. Philip and Matthew both stood up and anxiously waited for the doctor to speak.

"Mr. Johnson, your son suffered severe injuries to his hand. Unfortunately, several of the bones of his fingers were crushed so badly that we had no choice but to amputate two of them completely. We also had to amputate one other finger partially. If you could call it such, the good news is that we could save his thumb and index finger, so he can still do many of the more important things. Holding a pen, a knife, or a fork should not be a problem. Other tasks or functions might prove to be more challenging, but all things considered, it could have been worse."

"Can we see him?" Philip asked.

"In a short while, you can do so. Right now, we are transferring your son to a room. We gave him a sedative, and he will be experiencing pain. We also gave him penicillin to help fight off any infection."

"When can he go home," was Philip's next question.

"We will need to monitor him for any infection, and he did lose a significant amount of blood, but he should be okay to leave in a few days. By the way, you and your son did the right thing by bringing him here right away. If you had waited, gangrene might have set in. Then, he might have lost his entire hand instead of just those fingers."

Philip put his arm around Matthew and breathed a sigh of relief. It was not good, but he knew it could have been a whole lot worse.

"The nurse will be out here shortly and will bring you to see him," said the doctor before turning away.

"Thank you, Doctor," Philip shouted back as he and Matthew once again sat down. Now his thoughts were of Sarah, Grace, Michael, and Rebekah, who were at home and utterly unaware of Paul's condition. With home telephones a luxury few families back home could afford, the Johnson's house would be no exception. Being unable to communicate by phone, any fears and worries those at home had would not be addressed until he and Matthew returned home later this evening. He did not look forward to telling them the worst of the news, but they were a strong family, and like so many other challenges, they always found a way to survive. With God's help, they would do so again. Then, in his own way, Philip's simple prayer of thanksgiving was a simple, "Thanks, God."

CHAPTER 6

The Photo

September 20, 1939

Despite the constant work and effort needed to successfully run a farm, even the most hardworking farmers would find it necessary and refreshing to take a little time off to enjoy the various county and state fairs each year. Most counties had their fairs or exhibitions. The simplest would consist mainly of livestock competitions and contests for the best pumpkin pies or homemade jams. A few might have a small midway comprised of vendors and concessionaires selling their wares or offering games of chance. The more prominent and better-attended fairs would also have in their midways assorted rides. For the small price of an admission ticket, you could ride something as tame as a carousel or as thrilling as the Ferris wheel. Named for its inventor, George Washington Gale Ferris, it was first designed and built for the 1893 Columbia Exposition in Chicago. While sitting on the bench-like seat, the rotating vertical wheel would raise you and your companion slowly to its apex, affording its riders a never-before-seen view of the surrounding fairgrounds.

To go to one of the larger fairs would be, for most farm families, the equivalent of a family vacation. First and foremost, provisions would have to be made for the livestock to be fed and taken care of, very often by neighboring farmers who would remain at home. Once they took care of that, deciding what kind of food to bring would be next. Eating out would usually entail stopping along the side of the road. Then, they would partake in devouring whatever goodies they packed in their wicker picnic baskets. If the distance traveled were to be significant enough, arrangements would be necessary for inexpensive overnight accommodations. The keyword being affordable. If possible, free accommodations staying with either friends or relatives was even better.

It was not so much because of the difficulties of the past decade, as it was despite it, that the neighboring Johnson and Smith families decided to go. None of them had gone on anything closely resembling a trip like this. Financial considerations would still impose limitations. Travel distance would impact time away, as well as the cost of gasoline for their trucks and cars. The big state fair held each year in Oklahoma City would have been their first choice, not just for its size but also for 'Sooner' pride. But at a distance of 273 miles each way, it was not feasible. Less than half the distance was the Amarillo, Texas, Tri-State Exposition. Held each September for the residents of Texas, Oklahoma, and New Mexico, it was a good option. Compared to rural towns such as Goodwell, Amarillo would appear to those Panhandle visitors as a bustling metropolis. With a population of 50,000, it was one hundred times the size of Goodwell.

The day they all left, Michael and Cindy would have preferred to be riding together, but logistics and Cindy's family dictated otherwise. Even though the two families got along well enough, being the only daughter seemed to make Cindy's parents more protective of her than usual. This attention was especially true of her father. Despite generally approving Michael as her suitor, Reuben Smith could not overcome his fatherly distrust of anyone hoping to win his daughter's heart. His deep religious beliefs, combined with his embracement of Victorian values, made him suspicious of not only Michael but also of his daughter. Despite being a third-generation 'Okie' herself, Reuben's wife, Eunice, seemed to disapprove of anyone from the Panhandle dating her daughter, complicating matters for the young couple. Perhaps due to her own narcissistic and unfulfilled wishes for a better life for herself, Cindy's mother would have difficulty accepting Michael as anything more than just a childhood friend of her daughter. Had it been up to her, Eunice would have gladly moved to California years ago. It was only because her husband refused to give up on the land that was his family's home since his parents first settled there 53 years ago that they were still here.

They left their homes in a caravan consisting of three vehicles. Philip and Sarah sat in the cab of the family's pickup truck with Rebekah. At the same time, Michael, Matthew, Paul, and Grace got as comfortable as possible in the cramped bed portion of the vehicle, using the canvas valises containing their clothing as cushions and backrests. Similar arrangements were in play for the eight members of the Smith family. However, they had the advantage of being spread out in their truck and the old Model-T Ford that their family had owned. Despite being just two months shy of her seventeenth birthday, Cindy sat with her parents, the object of her father's watchful eye. The ride to the Exposition would take nearly four hours, stopping only to either fill up the gas tanks or taking time to grab a bite to eat.

Cindy and Michael looked forward to those stops, as it allowed them to be together. When it was time to have lunch, they all parked along the side of a country road that bordered what had previously been a large stream. Due to the lack of rain, its diminished water exposed the large rocks that dotted the stream's bed. As the families exited their vehicles, the members of the two families began intermingling with each other. In part to exchange conversation and see what other culinary delights the other mothers and wives had prepared. The power of food, enhanced by a healthy appetite, was a force of nature greatly underestimated. The aroma from one of Sarah's apple pies was even seductive enough to distract Reuben's attention away from Cindy.

Seizing the opportunity, Michael and Cindy each grabbed something to eat and began to explore the picturesque countryside. With the rest of their families pre-occupied with the lunch offerings spread out before them, the young couple finally had some private time. As they approached the water's edge, Michael took Cindy by the hand as he carefully led her across the stream as they used the large rocks as stepping stones. Once on the other side and well out of sight of their families, Michael held Cindy in his arms, telling her he wished he could do this forever. Cindy, her eyes now looking lovingly into Michael's, said how she always hoped for that to happen. Sensing that a moment like this did not happen that often, Michael pulled Cindy closer and kissed her on her lips. Cindy did not pull away but instead, let their lips linger and took full advantage of enjoying the moment. It should have come to no surprise to either of them, as this moment was nearly seventeen years in the making. But on this September day, at an unmarked roadside somewhere in Texas, Michael and Cindy were able to express their true feelings for each other. Despite being life-long friends, their relationship had now evolved to that of young lovers. Some might say it was just a case of typical teenage hormones, but they both knew otherwise. Michael knew that from this day on, Cindy would always be his girl. Whereas for Cindy, this just confirmed what she had believed would be the case ever since she was a youngster and first tried on her mother's bridal headpiece and veil. She dared not tell Michael previously of her feelings, but now she felt both relieved and happy that it was out in the open. They kissed several more times before heading back to the group. Although still teenagers, today, they felt like they each matured into a loving couple.

When they rejoined the others, Cindy was glad to see that her father unnoticed her absence. But her relief was soon shattered when she caught the suspicious look on her mother's face. Her mother had not only been aware of her absence but also took note of the blushing of her daughter's cheeks that did not exist before Cindy and Michael sneaked away. As they got back into their respective vehicles, no one spoke of this, but Cindy could not avoid sensing the tension in the air as she sat in the car with her mother and father. Michael, on the other hand, reclaimed his spot in the back of the pickup. As he sat there for the rest of the trip, he smiled as he replayed the earlier events in his mind. He probably would not have been smiling nearly as much if he had been aware of Cindy's situation.

For many farmers from the Oklahoma Panhandle, where seeing sixty or seventy people at church services on Sundays was a lot, the crowds that packed the midway at the Exposition were something to behold. Masses of people strolled about in a seemingly haphazard fashion, their eyes straining to take in as much as possible of the colorful scenes that surrounded them. Besides the unique visual offerings they were experiencing, the midway sounds were even more alien to the everyday quiet farm life they were accustomed to hearing. Heard loudly above the combined conversations of hundreds of sightseers like themselves were the voices of the various barkers and hucksters. Each one was extolling the virtues of the products or services they were selling. The sounds of a horse-drawn, steam-powered calliope playing repetitive and robotic tunes added to the festive atmosphere. Nearby, a brightly decorated carousel made countless rotations, stopping only to allow a new group of riders to hop onto its colorful wooden horses. Its calliope was adding to the cacophony that only a carnival atmosphere could create. Riders lucky enough to be on horses on the outer edge of the carousel would have a chance of grabbing the elusive brass ring. If you earned that honor, your reward was an additional free ride. Passersby would hear the loud shrieks of riders at regular intervals on some of the more thrilling rides and attractions. When first hearing the seemingly terrifying cries, the visitors would look towards its origin with wonderment. But after hearing it over and over again, it would soon become nothing more than background noise, and it would no longer cause any curious stares.

The Expo was not just a feast for the eyes and ears of the crowds making their annual pilgrimage, as the unique odors of the midway were evident also. As the Johnsons and the Smiths continued exploring the fairgrounds, they experienced the distinctive smell that only freshly popped corn could have. It was in contrast to the delightful aroma of the various homemade baked pies sitting on tables lining the busy street. Their proud bakers were hoping to tempt the crowds to taste and purchase their products. Other booths and concessions would offer up other treats and delights. Many of these were familiar, as they were staples of what was cooked or baked back home. But it was still interesting to see all the various interpretations of these food items.

Not all the smells and aromas were as pleasingly enjoyable as the families walked towards the farm animals and livestock exhibits. The all too recognizable odors quickly brought them back to reality. No longer were the displays strange and unique, but they were now experiencing much of what they lived back home. Yet, all in all, it was a pleasant and exciting diversion from their drab lives back on the panhandle.

Cindy and Michael were probably enjoying the day more than the others. Not only were they enthralled by the excitement and spectacle of the exposition, but they were also doing it as a couple. For them, they did not just see all these new sights, but they were making memories. More importantly, memories that would last a lifetime. There was a special thrill that came with enjoying these experiences as a couple. But although they walked together as closely as they could, the young couple realized that they were under the watchful eyes of both Cindy's mother and father. Tempting fate and daring to bring greater scrutiny to their budding relationship, they took a chance. Cindy confronted the issue head-on, thinking that even her strict parents could find it hard to imagine any moral harm befalling their daughter with so many people around. With her brothers fully occupied with the livestock shows and knowing that neither her father nor her mother would want to go on any of the rides that the fair had to offer, she made her bold move.

"I want to go on the rides. Do you want to come?" Cindy asked her parents, already knowing what the answer would be.

"That's not our thing," her father replied, speaking for his wife also.

"Then you won't mind if I go with Michael," she said, quickly adding, "At least he will be there to keep an eye on me."

Not wanting to wait for their answer, she joined Michael, who just told the same thing to his parents, but without anywhere near the worry of their reaction. Then, while still under the watchful eyes of her parents, she and Michael slowly disappeared into the crowded midway. The bright sun and brilliant blue sky matched well with the bold new future that lied ahead for the two of them. It was as if all the years that they spent growing up together, first as neighbors, then as childhood friends and classmates, and now as a young couple in love, had all been channeling them to this point in time. Now, lost among the countless strangers around them and no longer under the scrutiny of her suspicious and overbearing parents, they joined hands and continued the journey they were on. It may have been just hours since those kisses by the stream, but for them, it seemed like a lifetime. They had turned a new chapter in their lives, and the book that would chronicle their life together, they were just now beginning to write. They each had to wonder what the following chapters would be. But if today were just a small sample, then the rest would have to be even better. But for now, it would be enough to enjoy the present and make the most of each day.

No matter where you are or what you are doing, a second is still a second, just as an hour is still an hour. But today, with Cindy at his side walking hand in hand, time had raced by quickly. The bright sun would soon be setting in the western sky above the flat expanse of the Texas prairie. They both had lost track of time, having conversed about just everything. Not that their talking to each other was by any means new or uncommon. They had spoken thousands of hours together throughout their lives. But this was now different. They talked with a common purpose, and they talked to each other for the first time as a couple in love. It was not just an infatuation but a meaningful love that had finally blossomed after years of nurturing their friendship.

Cindy was shocked when she realized how long it had been that she and Michael were apart from their families. It was not just the time factor since she had been away from them countless times as a child growing up. If it was not school, it might have been playing with Michael. But this was different because of the circumstances. They went to the fair as a family. But she was now separated from them with her life-long friend, who was now so much more. But despite the curious looks and questions that she would probably encounter, she did not care. For the first time as a young adult, she never felt more alive or more confident of what she wanted in life. Everything she had hoped and wished for had come true. And the reason for it was standing beside her, holding her hand and making her feel like a woman.

They both had brought with them money they had saved up for the trip. Having spent most of it on food and rides, they had just enough left for two more things before they would attempt to reunite with their families. One would be a repeat ride on the giant Ferris wheel, only this time at night. But first, while the late afternoon rays of the sun were still shining brightly, a photograph would be taken.

They had earlier passed a photo booth while exploring the many concessions that filled both sides of the midway. A photographer would take your picture and have it printed for a small fee, providing the purchaser with a personal and lasting souvenir of the exposition. Having no other photograph of the two of them and cameras still a luxury for panhandle farmers, they decided to take their picture. With his Speed Graphic camera fixed on its tripod, the photographer positioned Cindy and Michael on a pre-determined spot. As he got behind the camera, he told the happy couple not to move. Satisfied that they were in focus, he instructed them to say cheese. It would not have been necessary since the couple was smiling all day. Still, they made sure they looked their best for a momentous occasion such as this since there was just enough money for the one picture. The Speed Graphic was an excellent camera, but it was capable of just one photograph at a time. After depressing the shutter button and hearing the distinctive click, Cindy and Michael relaxed as the photographer removed the two and one-quarter inch by three and one-quarter inch film sheet from the camera. As he gave it to an assistant to develop, Michael and Cindy stood off to the side, anxiously waiting for their photo. A short time later, the assistant exited the make-shift darkroom, holding the freshly developed picture in his hand. Eager to see themselves together, they jointly held the black and white photograph in front of them. It was hard to tell if they were more excited about having the photo or the reason for taking it.

As they were walking back toward the Ferris wheel, they both realized the dilemma they faced. There was just one photo, but only one would be able to have it. Michael, being the perfect gentleman, immediately offered it to Cindy. Cindy was appreciative of Michael's offer, but she had a better idea. Seeing a booth nearby selling hand-made quilts and pillows, she walked over to the middle-aged female proprietor sitting behind it.

"Excuse me, but could we perhaps borrow a pair of scissors from you," Cindy asked, warmly smiling while hoping that she guessed correctly that the woman should have one.

"Why, of course, dear," the woman replied, thinking of her granddaughter.

As the woman began to reach over the table to hand Cindy the scissors, she asked, "If you don't mind me asking, what do you need it for?"

"We're going to cut this picture in half, so we each have part of it."

The woman examined them closely, and recognizing the love in their eyes that they had for each other, offered this solution. "I might have a better idea," she said, holding onto the scissors and asking to see the photograph.

Curious about that idea and not feeling afraid of what the woman might do, Cindy handed the photo to the lady.

"I can sense that this picture is very important to the two of you," she stated, seeing both Cindy and Michael nodding their heads in agreement. Then, still looking at the young couple, she went on, "As a constant reminder that just as the two of you are both unique and special, both halves of this picture should also be." She carefully proceeded to cut the picture in half, but not in a straight line. Instead, she made random zig-zag cuts that turned the photograph into a two-piece jigsaw puzzle.

Holding each piece in her hands, she said, "Not only will you each have a permanent reminder of the other, but should circumstances ever occur where you are to be apart, just as these two pieces will only match up with the other, so shall the two of you."

Cindy and Michael stood there quietly, stunned by the eloquent and heartfelt words they just heard. Then, recovering from their momentary silence, they each thanked the lady as she handed each of them their half of the photograph. The nice lady with the warm smile may have been selling bed linens and such, but she could have given any of the so-called fortune-tellers that dotted the midway a run for their money.

Cindy put half of the photo into her handbag, while Michael folded his portion and put it in his wallet, careful to make sure the fold did not crease the image of Cindy's pretty face.

"Come on. We still have time," Michael said, looking at his watch and leading Cindy to the direction of the Ferris wheel.

Almost running, they weaved their way through the still crowded midway, wondering if their families might see them. But, not caring, they continued until they reached the big steel wheel. Holding the few coins they still had left in their hands, Michael took enough to cover the cost of the ride. After handing the money over to a young man in a small wooden booth, he received their two tickets and got in line. They were excited as they waited for each seat to move into position to offload the old riders and take on the new ones. When it was finally their turn to board, they climbed in, sitting together as the operator took their tickets and pulled a safety bar down in front of their laps. Then after the wheel made several more quick starts and stops to change passengers, he pulled a large lever engaging the gears.

As the gasoline engine began to power the wheel's rotation, the steel structure began to creak as it came back to life. Now, snuggled together in the cool night air, Cindy and Michael enjoyed the view as the giant wheel began to rotate. As colorful as the fair was during the day, it took on an almost mystical appearance at night as thousands of electric lights illuminated the midway and its various rides. The wheel completed several more rotations before stopping to let the passengers get off. At one point, they sat motionless at the high point of the wheel. They looked out over the glittering midway, being entranced by its romantic appeal. His arm around Cindy, Michael turned and kissed her as they had done earlier today along the roadside. She kissed him back, not wanting the moment to end. But then, suddenly, the wheel lurched as it once again began turning. When their seat reached its exit position, the operator raised the safety bar, and they got off. Now, the task of finding their families and explaining their long absence would be challenging. But thinking of what they had accomplished in just one day was enough to keep those other worries in perspective. Today was indeed the first day of the rest of their lives.

When they were finally back home, alone at night in her room, Cindy took half of the photo from her handbag and looked at it. On her portion of the jagged-edged picture, she saw Michael standing, his arm around a missing companion. Cindy wished that they would never grow apart, and she longed for the day when just like the two parts of the photo coming together in perfect harmony, they would do so. Cindy wondered if Michael would be looking at his half of the picture, and she hoped that he wished the same thing she had. Finally, Cindy made a silent vow to herself that she would keep and cherish the photo forever. That would be the easy part. Keeping it from the prying eyes of her family would be more challenging. But for now, clutching the photo tightly against her chest, she would fall asleep for the first time knowing how it felt to be loved.

CHAPTER 7

Rituals

September 27, 1939

There were no such things as alarm clocks when you lived on a farm. However, nature had its way of preventing anyone from sleeping too late by letting them know when to get up. If the constant crowing of a rooster were not enough, then the morning rays of the sun would shine brightly into any bedroom that faced east. Even if neither of these incentives was enough, then the smell of bacon and eggs whiffing its way upstairs from the kitchen would certainly aid in getting even the heaviest sleeper up and around. This natural alarm would soon be followed by hearing their mother's call that breakfast would soon be ready.

Even though Michael would be going to school shortly, it did not give him a pass on performing his daily chores. First, like his brothers before him, he would have to collect the eggs from the hen house and spread the chicken feed for the hens to eat. Then, Michael would pack the eggs in crates, setting aside just enough for their own consumption. Finally, after cleaning out the henhouse, he would be ready to walk the two miles to the schoolhouse. Later, one of his brothers would load the eggs into the back of the family's pickup truck, ready to be brought into town and be sold at the farmers' co-op. The income was not much, but it was necessary since the yield from the wheat, corn, and sorghum crops was virtually non-existent.

"Breakfast's not going to wait all day," their mom shouted, just as three hurried sets of feet came running down the stairs. The noise of Michael, Matthew, and Paul's muscular bodies pouncing upon the wooden steps, reverberated throughout the otherwise quiet farmhouse. Shortly after that, they would hear the more discreet creaking of the aged wood as their sisters stepped less violently upon the steps. As Rebekah and Grace joined their brothers at the long rectangular table, they waited as their parents sat down, each at opposite ends. Michael was seated next to his mother, which was within striking distance, which did not bode well. Being both hungry and forgetful, Michael reached across the table to grab some of the juicy strips of bacon that his mom had just put out.

"Where are your manners?" she lectured Michael while smacking him in the back of his head. Michael, more embarrassed than hurt, quickly dropped the piece of bacon back onto the tin plate.

"You know we don't eat until we've said grace. I swear I don't know what you are thinking about half the time." At that, all seven members of the Johnson family held hands as Mrs. Johnson led them in prayer. Had Michael been looking at his father, he would have seen him shaking his head yet displaying a look of understanding. His father had just begun to reach for a stack of pancakes when he saw his wife's reaction to Michael's lack of manners. Michael's dad also had many thoughts race through his mind this morning, and he hoped God would forgive him for his lack of attention to the morning ritual of saying grace.

"Oh Lord, we thank thee for our bounty that you have graciously provided. We pray that you, in your divine mercy, deliver us from this drought. And let the rains fall once again from your heavenly kingdom," then quickly adding she said, "And forgive Michael for his temporary disrespect, and forgive me for saying I swear. Amen."

Having gotten that daily practice out of the way, they all began to grab their food from the plates Mrs. Johnson had set out on the table. Philip looked over at his wife and forced a slight smile, but they both knew the difficulties they were facing. Still, Sarah was a woman of strong faith, and she felt that having survived this long, they might be able to endure until the drought, now in its ninth year, would finally be over. Although a man of faith also, Philip was more realistic, which meant he was also more pessimistic. Philip watched with dismay as so many of the area's farms ceased operating. Their families were giving up and leaving Oklahoma forever. He watched in disbelief as entire families left most everything behind, taking with them just what they could fit in their family's beat-up old cars or pickup trucks. It may not have been the same as saying grace, but Philip Johnson felt it was probably the right time to pray. In silence, he asked the Lord to spare them from suffering the same fate.

One advantage of getting up early was that it provided the time to get your chores out of the way. The added morning time allowed Michael the opportunity to go to school on time. After eating a hearty breakfast of farm-fresh and farm-grown groceries, the three Johnson brothers would complete their required daily tasks. Rebekah and Grace also had to pitch in and help in the operation of the house and the farm. The youngest of the family, Rebekah, was expected to help her mother with household and kitchen chores, while the same held for Grace, but at a level commensurate with her older age.

While Michael was finishing up his job in the henhouse, Matthew worked on their old tractor, trying to get one more season out of it. He was good at working with mechanical things, and he had a knack for fixing engines. Had he not been committed to working on the family's farm, he could have been successful as a mechanic working in town. But as it happened, the 'could haves' and the 'should haves' did not always work out. Paul also seemed to be wasting his talents. Although he had no formal training, he was a talented artist, despite the accident with the hay bailer that cost him two fingers on his right hand. Not being able to afford art supplies, he was limited to sketching with just pencils. But his drawings showed both an artist's eye and the natural technical skills necessary for capturing and putting images on paper. Unfortunately, even in better economic times, the opportunity to make a living as an artist was virtually non-existent on the Panhandle. So ironically, Paul, the artist, was today whitewashing the sides of their shed.

Having completed his chores, as he did every weekday morning, Michael stopped at the fence post that held the Smith's mailbox. While he waited, he played with the red metal flag that alerted the postman that outgoing mail was ready to be picked up. It was not the most exciting thing to do, but it passed the time as Michael waited for Cindy to meet him. Then, alerted by the creaking sound of her front door opening, he put the flag back into its proper position and turned his attention to the house. As he watched her quickly running towards him, he thought of all the times they met this way and walked to school together. They had been best friends since they could barely walk, and now, after all these years, Cindy was his girl.

Whether it was because they had always been together or because they always looked happy together, people would comment on how the two of them were the perfect couple. It would be hard to argue against either of those two reasons. They did seem well suited for each other. And they were always smiling when they were together, despite there being so little to smile about these days. And in a small town like Goodwell, where everybody knew everybody, it was well known that they had grown up together.

It also did not detract from the perfect couple notion that Cindy was exceedingly attractive. Had she not grown up on a farm in Oklahoma, she could have been on the cover of Glamour Magazine. Cindy certainly had the physical attributes necessary for being a model. Her complexion was nearly flawless, and her warm hazel eyes seemed to sparkle, especially when she smiled, which was often. Adding to the overall image was her naturally curly, auburn hair that fell just above her shoulders. Even her clothes, which she would wear as a country farm girl, could not hide her perfectly proportioned body. Michael matched her as well as any boy in the county could have. Tall and robust, the result of helping with the strenuous farm chores, he had piercing blue eyes and an honest and engaging smile. His tanned complexion fit well with his sandy-blonde hair. When standing together, they looked like they belonged on top of a wedding cake. It was a foregone conclusion by most folks that they would one day be married.

With Michael being just seventeen and Cindy being two months shy of it, marriage was not a topic discussed in any great detail. But lately, they had been considering the possibility of it. There were no definite plans, but it was more a general acceptance that they would wind up together. It made sense, mainly because they had been together in some relationship for the past seventeen years. Besides, they were in love, at least as much as seventeen-year-olds could be. Since they first kissed on that fateful day last week when they were going to the Tri-State-Exposition in Amarillo, the idea of them one day getting married was genuine

to both of them. Not to anyone's surprise, Cindy had been thinking about the possibility ever since she and Michael first shared a
peanut butter and jelly sandwich when they were five years old.
Now, with graduation less than a year away, it was time to start
making plans about their futures with or without marriage. But,
of course, there was a world beyond the Oklahoma Panhandle,
and that world would ultimately impact any plans they might
make. That world, to complicate things, was not at peace across
both oceans. To make it through another day of school and be one
day closer to the rest of their lives was the main thing on both
their minds.

That night back at Michael's house, his father had tuned
the radio station to the Columbia Broadcasting System's evening
news. Edward R. Murrow was reporting live via short-wave radio
from his office in London. Now, even here in Oklahoma, there was
an increasing interest in the war across the Atlantic. First, they
had heard of Germany's invasion of Poland. And now they would
soon hear of Poland's surrender to the forces of The Third Reich.

Meanwhile, France and England's entry into the war was in
its fourth week. Naturally, these events sparked the interest of all
those listening. However, Matthew seemed to be listening to the
news the most intently of all the Johnson men.

"Do you think we will join the war?" Michael asked to no one
in particular.

"Roosevelt would be a fool if we did," his father replied.

"You were there in the Great War. Why are we still fighting
in the same places?" Paul asked his father.

"Damned if I know," their father said with annoyance. Then
before leaving the room, he added, "They just never learn."

"Japan and China have been at it for years. That can't be
good. But at least our Navy will keep those Japs away from us. Did
you know that we keep most of our Pacific Fleet in Hawaii, at a
place called Pearl Harbor? Beaches, palm trees, and hula girls. That
has to be a sweet deal," Matthew offered, seeming to know more
than expected.

"Don't let Ma hear you talking about Hula girls," Paul
chipped in.

"What's a hula girl?" Rebekah asked as she was walking through the room.

"Nothing. And don't go asking Ma either," Matthew quickly responded.

"Why the sudden interest? You never cared about these things before?" Michael asked of Matthew.

"There's nothing wrong with wanting to broaden my knowledge. But, unfortunately, I didn't get a chance to finish high school like some people," Matthew said, looking directly at Michael.

"Hey, don't blame me," Michael shot back, standing up and walking towards Matthew.

"I'm just stating facts. I can't help it if you don't like it."

"Yeah, well, maybe you might like these facts," Michael said, advancing closer to Matthew, who had also stood up.

Paul put an end to any further argument as he quickly stepped in between his two brothers, telling them, "Just because I'm missing two fingers doesn't mean I still can't whip the both of you."

Saying that broke the tension in the room as Michael and Matthew began playfully messing up Paul's thick crop of hair.

Unfortunately, the tension in the rest of the world would not be so easily lessened.

CHAPTER 8

Rain

October 1, 1939

The aging John Deere tractor, its engine struggling to make it past yet another day in the field, continued the now nearly senseless plowing of what had once been fertile farmland. Despite the roar of the howling winds, the sound of the distinctive green and yellow tractor could still be heard at the farmhouse several hundred yards away. As its plow turned over the arid soil, it created small clouds of dust that hugged the ground. It followed the path of the steel-wheeled tractor, as did the acrid black smoke that pulsated out of its vertical exhaust stack. Neither would linger long, being dissipated by the strong southwesterly winds that whipped across many area's farms. The devastating effects of the long-lasting drought were noticeable everywhere. It had become such a way of life, those still living on the Oklahoma panhandle would wonder if they might ever again see any meaningful rain.

Standing on the wooden porch of their two-story house, Sarah Johnson looked out over the forty-acre farm that had been her home since she married Philip twenty-one years ago. That was soon after his return from France. Just like her marriage vows, the farm and the life it provided would be both for better or worse. In the beginning, it was better, as there were good years. Early on in their marriage, it seemed as though Sarah was as fertile as the land had been, bearing five healthy children. She was always a devout Christian and a woman of faith. Sarah thanked God for his blessings upon her family. And she bore him no ill will when she suffered a difficult pregnancy that resulted in the loss of their sixth child. Sarah also accepted as God's will her subsequent inability to have any more children. Thinking now of the uncertain times, she could not help but wonder if having had more children would have necessarily been a good thing.

Even during the beginning of the economic hard times that plagued the nation, they could still grow enough crops to support their family and provide a small income. In addition, their children were all growing up to be decent, hard-working, and God-fearing adults. She and Philip had much to be proud of for their accomplishments. But now, with the future of their farm uncertain, they were seeing and experiencing the worse. Having to turn her face away from a fresh dust cloud blowing in her direction, Sarah silently worried just how much longer the family could hold out in its losing battle against the weather.

Sarah walked from the porch and into the parlor with no let-up from the driving dust, still looking out through the wood-frame window. It desperately needed a fresh coat of paint, but so did most of the house. After a decade of what the newspapers and radio stations had labeled "The Great Depression," she wondered what was so great about it. Although a wise woman, her limited schooling would not understand the underlying economic reasons that caused it. Their farm and lives were far removed from the problems on Wall Street and in Washington, both geographically and politically. Yet those events that took place half a continent away were impacting not only her but, more importantly, her family. If that were not enough, the past year's combination of bad weather, poor planting techniques, and just bad luck had contributed to the affected region now being called the "Dust Bowl."

Once again, this year's fall harvest fell far short of what was needed, and she could not stop thinking that the plowing under of what remained of their crops was nothing more than a waste of time and gasoline. For as far as the eye could see, there was nothing but rows of wilted corn stalks, with dried-up ears of corn that were not even half their usual size. Next spring, there might not be enough money to buy the seeds necessary to plant next year's crop with no income from the corn. Their other crops did not do well either under the scorching summer sun with little or no rain. Their hay production would be barely enough to feed their livestock, let alone having any surplus to sell. Thinking back to Paul's tragic accident with the hay bailer, Sarah thought that maybe having less to throw into its hopper might not be a bad thing. The fact that they managed to survive this long was some-what of a miracle. Despite being a woman of great faith, Sarah had often been tried and tested during the past eight years, ever since the series of droughts began in 1931.

The dust was now inches deep everywhere. But it was not the dust that you would generally find under the bed. Instead, it was fine particles of dried-up dirt that had once been topsoil suit-able for growing. When picked up by the prevailing winds that had swept across the Great Plains, billowing clouds of dust had frequently blocked out the sun, turning the sky black, and turning day into night. Unlike her criticism of the word 'great' to describe the depression, Sarah could appreciate the news' description of these storms as black blizzards. Since that big one on Black Sun-day over four years ago, these would continue regularly. These winds had carried what had been once part of the Oklahoma Pan-handle to east coast cities such as New York and Washington. Even ships in the Atlantic Ocean would find their decks covered with a thin layer of dust.

If the winds were driving the dust clouds east, it had the opposite effect on the local residents, forcing them west. Many of their neighbors and friends had finally surrendered to the bleak future and stark reality they faced each day. With little or no hope and no viable income, they would pack up and leave. More often than not, it was to California, where they hoped for a new life and a new beginning. She hoped and prayed that they would not be-come one of them.

Through the whirling clouds of dust, kicked up by the repetitious act of plowing, she could see Philip sitting atop the tractor. He and the tractor were silhouetted against the quickly setting sun about to disappear below the flat Oklahoma horizon. However, her gaze diverted when Shep, their family dog, began barking. She watched him running down the winding dirt road that linked their farm to the single-lane, dirt and gravel road that connected the many neighboring farms. Coming towards the house was Michael, who, upon seeing Shep, ran to greet him also. With his tail wagging, Shep leaped up onto the teenager, and as Michael bent down to pet him, Shep began licking Michael's face.

"Good boy, Shep," said Michael, as he was rubbing both sides of the dog's neck, having to reach beneath the dog's thick coat of sable and white hair. Michael continued walking towards

the house in a straight-forward path while Shep ran a more cir-
cuitous route, running circles around him as they both edged
closer to home. As he approached the house, Michael saw his
mom through the window and waved, eliciting a similar response
from her. Then, with the winds temporarily subsiding, his mom
walked back outside to greet her youngest son. As Michael walked
up the creaky wooden steps to the porch, he slid the knapsack
off his shoulders and let it drop to the weathered wooden planks
below. The weight of several heavy schoolbooks contributed to
the loud thud that ensued.

"Hi Ma," he said, repeating what he had told her each day
after coming home from school for the past twelve years.

"And how was school today?" his mom asked as she did
every day also. Before he could answer, she followed with, "Did
you and Cindy get together again?" She was sure she already knew
the answer since school ended more than two hours ago.

"We did hang out in the gym after school. There were discussions by some of the students of possibly asking the school if
we could use it for some type of dance." Michael now waited for
the expected look of consternation on his mom's face. He was not
disappointed.

"You realize that there has never been a dance in all the
years the school has been there. Besides, you know we all talked
about this, and you know how most of the community feels about
it. It's just not what we do, and it certainly isn't proper," Michael's
mom spoke, admonishing him.

"I know we did, but what can be so bad about dancing?
Most of the country dances. Things are so depressing around here.
People want to have some fun. That's why all those roadhouses
are popping up," Michael offered as a rebuttal.

"You should know by now that this is not the rest of the
country. And for the idea that dancing is fun, I don't believe Pastor Simmons would call it that. Besides, even if the school held
a dance, do you honestly think that Cindy's parents would allow
her to go?"

His mom paused a moment before continuing. "There's
about as much chance of that happening as a snowstorm in
July. Her parents feel even more strongly about this than we do,
especially Rueben, her father. He would never agree to have his

daughter participate in some immoral public display. Her mother, Eunice, would never allow you to take Cindy dancing either, although probably not for the same reasons. Lord, forgive me for saying unkind things about her, but that woman has some strange thoughts on things concerning her daughter's future. Besides, how do you know how to dance anyway?"

"Cindy and I, along with a few of the kids, have been practicing after school at the Davidson's. They have a Victrola set up in their barn, and their parents don't mind. They have a bunch of cool records, all the latest hits. And it's fun to learn. Besides, I don't see how dancing is immoral."

"It is immoral because it leads to other sins of the flesh. I think that the Davidsons are a bad influence for encouraging such behavior. I don't recall ever seeing them at our Sunday church services. There's talk around town that they're agnostics."

"Then, maybe we should all be agnostics," said Michael, not really sure what an agnostic was.

"Michael Johnson, you hush your mouth. You were raised better than to say something like that."

Rather than continue arguing with his mother, Michael just turned away and walked into the house. He realized he would have had a better ally in this discussion had he spoken with his father first, but even then, his mother would usually overrule his father in matters like this. Eventually, Michael realized the current futility of debating this further and rejoined his mother on the porch. When he walked outside, the expression on his mother's face was not so much of a surprise that he came back, but more of a surprise that it took him so long.

"I'm sorry, Ma. It's just that times are changing. I didn't really mean what I said," Michael said apologetically, if not one-hundred-percent truthful.

Sarah never held a grudge against any of her children. Instead, she reached out to hug Michael, who reciprocated with outstretched arms. In instances like this regarding family squabbles, having a short memory was a good thing.

"Well now that you're home, go check with your dad to see if he needs any help, then you can wash up and get ready for dinner." His mom knew that there was little for him to do, but it was a ritual that she demanded of her sons. Then she added, "We have creamed chicken on biscuits. Oh, and some stewed tomatoes. Your sisters picked them fresh today."

Michael winched at hearing about the tomatoes since they did not look that great on the vine, the effect of the minimal watering, and the constant dust.

"Okay, Ma," Michael shouted back as he headed towards his dad, who was finishing up with the day's plowing.

"Oh, by the way, when Paul gets back from the general store, tell him I need the flour right away. Otherwise, you'll be missing fresh hot biscuits tomorrow morning at breakfast. I had to use the last of it for tonight's dinner.

Because of her religious beliefs, Sarah felt she needed to stay the course about the practice of dancing in public. Still, even she would sometimes find herself tapping her foot to the rhythm of the Big Bands that came over the family's radio. Maybe it was the infectious nature of the music that seemed threatening to her. But if the music could sway someone like her, then what about Michael. Even worse, she thought, what about Grace and Rebekah. She was determined to put her foot down on any such dancing. And it would not be the same foot that was keeping up with the beat of Glenn Miller's "In the Mood."

As Michael left the house, Shep was following after him, his tail wagging back and forth. As the winds began kicking up the dust again, Michael fixed a bandana around his face, shielding his mouth and nose from the airborne particles. It provided some protection from inhaling too many irritants, but it did nothing to protect the eyes. Michael squinted to minimize the amount of dust that would get in his eyes, but he could still see his father pulling the tractor into the barn. In past years, the tractor would be outside. But to do so now would result in the tractor's green and yellow enamel paint being stripped away by the continuous sand-blasting effect of the blowing sand and dust. As his father shut the tractor's engine off, Michael walked in through the open barn doors.

"Hi Pa, Ma said for me to see if you needed anything done," Michael said, looking around and realizing that there would be no need.

"No," his father said, also looking around and coming to the same conclusion.

"Did your brother get back from town yet?" It was now his father's turn to ask a question.

"No, not yet," Michael answered, having not seen the pickup truck.

"Well, if he's not back soon, he'll be late for dinner."

"Ma said it'd be ready soon,"

"I hope your Ma isn't making creamed chicken again," his father asked, looking at his son for a reaction.

"Don't kill the messenger," Michael said, then laughing and getting a displeased look from his father's gruff and now disappointed face.

Just then, Shep, who had been lying near Michael's feet, quickly turned his head toward the outside road, giving two quick barks. Then he sprang up and ran outside.

"Paul's here," his father said, also hearing the recognizable sound of the family's pickup truck bouncing along the rough-surfaced road.

As they were leaving the barn, Michael met his brother while their dad waited by the open doors of the badly weathered building. As Paul stepped out of the truck, he stooped down to rub Shep's neck and back, causing the dog to roll onto the dusty ground, wanting the same attention for his belly. When Paul had finished scratching Shep's belly, the Collie stood back up and shook himself off. But unlike when he would have been wet, and droplets of water would come flying off his dense fur, this time he released a small dust cloud that briefly hung in the air.

"Too bad we aren't able to do that," Paul remarked as he brushed his jacket and dungarees with his hands to remove some of Shep's dust that settled on his clothes.

"Hand me the flour. Ma wants it as soon as possible. I'll run it up to the house while you and Pa unload the rest of the truck," Michael said as he took the fifty-pound sack and threw it over his shoulder. As he headed up to the house, Shep ran ahead. Although knowing where Michael was going, the dog would still look back occasionally just to make sure.

As Michael delivered the flour to his mom, Paul helped his

dad put away chicken feed sacks and large steel cans filled with gasoline for their tractor.

"Hopefully, this will last a while," the father said while pulling the barn doors closed. "Come on, let's go eat. Your Ma's making creamed chicken again," he said, smiling at Paul.

Back at the house, Sarah was putting tonight's dinner out on the table with the help of Grace and Rebekah. After the men had all washed up, they all sat down and began to say grace. Just when Sarah would get to the part about delivering us from this terrible drought, she paused. At first, she was not sure, but then the others had heard it too. It was not much, and it had been a while, but there was no doubt. God would no doubt be understanding of them interrupting their saying grace. After all, they would all swear that it was in answer to their prayers. They all quickly got up from their chairs and ran out onto the front porch. Looking to see if it were real, they then ran out onto the lawn and looked up to the heavens as tiny droplets of rain fell onto their faces. Rebekah had her mouth open, trying to capture as many drops as possible. Even Shep was taking part, running around the group and barking up at the skies. Soon it began raining heavier, and the group all moved back inside. Back at the table, they once again joined hands and said a special prayer, thanking God.

There would soon be other rains, and the decade-old drought would officially come to an end. Of course, it would still take some time to get back to normal, and the excessive mud that would result from the rains would create its own set of problems. But it was a start, and for the first time, there was the belief that the new decade soon to arrive would be a good one. At least, that was the hope of all concerned. But for now, after a decade of despair, things on the Oklahoma Panhandle were starting to look better. If only that could be true for the rest of the world.

CHAPTER 9

Dancing

October 2, 1939

"What is this we hear about you dancing after school at the Davidson's.

"Why is this such a problem?" Cindy asked, annoyed and wondering who had snitched on her and how they knew.

"We will not permit our daughter to be on public display, especially in some den of iniquity, dancing to immorally suggestive music," her father answered.

"I don't think that "Moonlight Serenade" by Glenn Miller is suggestive, nor do I believe that the Davidson's barn is some den of iniquity," Cindy replied, shaking her head in disbelief.

"And I suppose that you would be doing this dancing all by yourself and not in the arms of the Johnson boy," her mother quickly added.

"Would you rather I would be doing it with a perfect stranger?"

"Watch your tone, young lady. You know exactly what I mean," her mother shot back.

"I'm seventeen years old. Next year I'll be eighteen. I could get married without your permission."

"Then you and your husband, whoever that might be, can dance together. But it won't be in public, and it's not going to be now," her father said, reentering the conversation.

"What about them?" she said, pointing to the interested audience of her five older brothers, some of whom suddenly became uncomfortable. "Do you think they never danced?" At that comment, three of them slowly left the room, leaving only Jake and Caleb.

"I would hope that they would have the common decency not to put on such a vulgar display in public," her father sternly answered as he looked over at the two remaining brothers and wondered where the others had gone.

"So then it's okay if I do it in private. Maybe I should dance in the bathroom. Or how about the hayloft?" Cindy said, raising her voice.

"That's it, young lady. Go to your room," her father said, having the last word in the conversation for now.

Cindy, now in tears, stormed out of the living room and ran upstairs to her bedroom. At least here, she would have the privacy of being alone. Having her own room was one advantage of being the only girl of the six children. She wondered if Michael had the same experience telling his parents, especially his mother, the same thing. She was frustrated. All Cindy wanted to do was dance. She considered herself a 'good girl,' and she did not believe either she or dancing was immoral. Cindy could not understand what the big deal was. She and Michael would hold hands if they were walking, so what if they held hands to the music? Their feet would be moving in either event. How would dancing in public be any worse than kissing in private as far as the moral issue? She and Michael had kissed many times since their first kiss last month, although she doubted that her parents knew.

The surprise rain that started last night had since ended. Cindy took a sweater from her dresser and threw it on. Walking downstairs, she passed her parents, who were discussing their previous conversation.

"Where are you going?" her mother asked.

"Maybe I'll check if we got any mail. Besides, maybe I need some fresh air."

"Maybe you need a fresh attitude also. And I'm not going to be waiting on you for dinner either," Cindy's mother snapped back.

Passing Jake, she exchanged looks with him that were not indicative of sibling love. He had been siding with his parents lately with regards to the topic of dancing. She thought maybe if he had a girlfriend, he might think differently. As Cindy left, she let the house door slam shut to emphasize how she felt about everything. She would check the mailbox, but before she did, she had a more important stop. If Cindy cut across the fields, it would have saved about five hundred yards and five minutes, but she opted for the road and dirt path that led to Michael's house. Approaching the Johnson's house, she saw Matthew outside.

"Hi Matthew, is Michael around?"

"Hi, Cindy. He should be out by the barn."

"Thanks. Is that a new haircut? It looks good," she asked.

"Yeah. I had my Ma cut it short. I like it this way. You look pretty good yourself,'" he said with complete honesty.

"Thanks, but you'd better not let your brother hear you talking like that. He might get jealous," Cindy said with a coy smile on her face.

"Jealous of what? Everybody knows that you two will always be together. Nobody else would stand a chance having either of you."

"Maybe so," she said smiling. Then, as an after-thought, she said, "You look very military with that haircut," as she headed toward the barn.

Michael had seen Cindy coming. He was expecting her arrival, having heard her and Matthew talking. He put down a large canvas sack he was carrying on the ground, then he began walking to her.

"Hi, what's up?" Michael asked, surprised but happy to see Cindy.

"I had to get away. I had an argument with my parents about our dancing. It didn't go very well.

"That's too bad," Michael said, holding Cindy's hand.

"I just had to talk to you." She said, glad to feel his hand holding hers.

"I'm glad you came over," he said while looking to see if anyone was around. Satisfied that they were alone, he embraced Cindy and kissed her softly. She held the kiss and then slowly withdrew her lips from his.

"I needed that," she said.

"Me too. I can't wait until the day we can do so much more," Michael said, thinking about what that future might be.

"That will be nice," she thought, also thinking about their future.

"But what are we going to do about the dancing?" Michael asked.

"If I continue to go, I'll be going against my parents, but I can't let them control my life forever. I love them, but I love you also."

"More, I hope," Michael asked with a sly grin on his face.

"Of course I do, but they are my parents, and I don't like upsetting my father with his health issues. Doc Willis said that my dad had something called a heart murmur."

"Well, he looks as strong as an ox to me. And he's got a grip like a vise. I've felt it," Michael was flexing his hand as he said it.

"Yes, but my parents are a lot older than yours. He was almost your father's age when I was born."

"So, does that mean we don't go?" Michael asked.

"I guess not," Cindy said, sounding dejected.

"Well, my Ma wasn't exactly keen about the idea either. And she kind of warned me what your parent's reaction would be."

"So, you won't be mad at me if we don't go?" Cindy asked, hoping that Michael would understand.

"Of course not. Have I ever been mad at you in all these years?"

"Probably not. But what about that time I gave you a bloody nose with the snowball I threw at you?" Cindy asked.

"Maybe just a little. That had to be, what, ten years ago. I'm surprised you still remember that."

"It was more like nine and one-half years ago, and I remember everything about us," Cindy said, still holding Michael's hand.

Michael leaned in and kissed Cindy once again.

"I've got to get back," Cindy said. "My parents are probably already wondering where I am, and they probably imagine the worst. But they are my family."

As Cindy walked away, she would keep looking back at

Michael, waving at him when she did. Michael stood outside the barn, waving in return and watching her until she was no longer in sight.

Despite having had limited exposure and experiences beyond Goodwell, they believed that the issue that confronted them was not prevalent throughout the nation. Although technically a border state, dancing in Oklahoma and other states in the south had a checkered past over the years. For those who belonged to particular religious affiliations or were inclined to adhere to strict puritanical or Victorian standards, dancing was still considered immoral and improper, if not downright prohibited. The belief held by these individuals was that it led to other social evils and sins involving drinking, gambling, and sex. While among other more socially progressive and younger individuals, it was a means of entertainment, self-expression, and an opportunity to blow off steam. With its increasing popularity, and because such extremes existed throughout the state, the establishment of for-profit dance halls had been popping up. If the local schools, churches, or civic groups did not provide an outlet for those wanting to dance, then, as always, some enterprising entrepreneur would take advantage of the opportunity to provide the service. These establishments had many names, such as honkey-tonks or roadhouses. The latter often sprang up on country roads outside the city limits and free from any zoning restrictions or ordinances. These dance halls would also provide food and drinks, especially those of the alcoholic variety. These businesses would attract people from neighboring 'dry' counties or states, adding to their clientele being looked down upon by the locals.

Adding to the growth of public dancing as an accepted form of social behavior was the increasing popularity of big bands such as Glenn Miller, Bennie Goodman, Artie Shaw, and the Dorsey brothers, Jimmy and Tommy. These dance bands played a new type of music, one not meant to just sing along with the lyrics, but rather to enjoy the melody and dance to it. Although they often featured vocalists to sing with the band, it was more for the arrangements and orchestration of the band's instruments that added to their admiration. These bands were very popular with the younger generation, mainly when they played upbeat music that created a dance style that was much more athletic than traditional slow dancing. These better-known bands would go on tour, playing to sell-out crowds in the major cities. Still, in rural America, smaller and lesser-known bands would be tasked with providing a similar experience at the local roadhouses. Yet, in the end, whether it was the jitterbug, where one partner would swing and throw the other, showing what some considered was too much leg of the female partner. Or a slow, romantic dance where the partners held each other so close that their two bodies came together as one; it did not matter. Because for those opposed to such public displays of latent sexuality and romance, it was considered taboo. Because of these beliefs, those future events would significantly alter the course of Michael and Cindy's lives.

CHAPTER 10

Grace

September 22, 1940

Michael had just got back from walking Cindy home from school and began the short walk to his house. It had been nearly a year since they first entertained the idea of dancing. The two life-long friends had become somewhat of an item, and the talk around town, and the high school, was not if they were to get married, but when. With Michael soon to turn eighteen and Cindy only a few months behind, they would each be able to be legally married without parental consent by next spring's graduation. It had been a topic that they had spent much time discussing. There had been no formal proposal from Michael, nor was there any official engagement. It was just that there was general agreement between them that they would one day get married and spend the rest of their lives together. Other than the physical love, marriage would not be that different from their lives up to now. They had been friends for as long as either one could remember. In Reality, they were not just friends, but best friends. They played together, they went to church together, and they went to school together. Seeing them together was not a surprise. Not seeing them together would have been.

Of course, there were many more hours each day when they were apart than when they were together. Chores, school work, and family responsibilities would understandably keep them apart. But whenever there was free time for social inter-action, they were a couple. As they each grew older and began the process of maturing into adult bodies, the nature of their relationship would evolve as well. In what could only be considered inevitable, their long-lasting friendship had eventually turned into love. It certainly was not love at first sight. Their first sight would have gone back to their early ages as toddlers. And it was not as if one day, each of them had an instantaneous revelation of what their friendship had now become. Instead, it was a slow and steady progression that crept up on them but without any surprises.

As Michael neared closer to the family's house, Grace took advantage of a clear and sunny day to hang up the family's wet laundry outside. Seeing Michael, she smiled at her younger brother. Grace was usually smiling, even on wash days. Besides, what she was doing now was easy, having already completed the hard part. Despite her young, fresh complexion, her hands and knuckles appeared much older, having experienced the harsh reality of washing clothes manually.

Having seen the Johnson women doing it, Michael was glad that his farm chores did not include doing the laundry. Having to fill two large galvanized tubs, one with hot soapy water for washing and another one with clear water for rinsing, might seem simple enough. But then, spending the next couple of hours scrubbing the dirt out of the family's clothes would not be easy, especially when it came to the men's work clothes. All the added dust on everything did not help either. Yet, none of the women ever complained while they kept their hands submerged in the hot dirty water and rubbed the clothes against a corrugated steel washboard. When the item was eventually clean enough, they would rinse it in a tub containing fresh water. Often, they would have to dump out the dirty rinse water and refill it, pumping water from the well. They would continue these repetitious actions until the last piece of laundry was clean. Only then would they be able to remove their hands from the dirty water, the harsh effects of the lye soap evident on their tender hands. For Michael, having to clean out the barn or the henhouse was now seeming like a much better option. Having this behind her for the day, Michael better understood why Grace was now smiling.

Michael was glad that he had an older sister. Not that he liked her better than Rebekah, it was just that it was easier for him to talk to her. Michael would always speak to his brothers, but some things required a female's perspective that neither Paul nor Matthew could provide. He hoped that someday, Rebekah might feel the same way about talking to him, as he was able to speak to Grace. But for now, Michael needed advice, and he sought it from his older sister.

"I need to talk to you about Cindy," he said, bringing up the reason for this conversation."

"Don't tell me there's trouble with you two love birds."

"No. Well, yes, actually, but not with Cindy. It's more about her parents," he said, trying to explain the problem.

"Go on."

"She's almost eighteen, and they still treat her like she's thirteen. And me, they look at me like I'm some sort of bad guy who's going to hurt their daughter."

"How does she feel about it?"

"She doesn't like it, but she's afraid to upset them. I know she loves me, but she's still a part of that family, and you know how close they are."

"Tell me about it. I dated Cindy's brother Joshua once."

"I never knew that."

"I don't think anybody knew except him and me. And of course, now you. It was just one date. I was sixteen, and he was nineteen. He took me to the movies in Guymon. It was just one time. I didn't tell Ma and Pa, figuring they might not approve, with him being older. But he was so worried that his parents would find out, he drove me nuts. The whole time he kept looking over his shoulder. He lived in fear of his father. Plus, I think Eunice is even worse than her husband."

"But what was he worried about? You weren't their daughter."

"It didn't matter. It's that whole morality issue that drives that family. They were probably worried that I would be the one getting their precious son into trouble. Little innocent me, can you believe that? That's why they're so hung up on the dancing thing. To them, dancing and doing anything outside of marriage is a big no-no."

"So, what do I do?"

"What is it you want to do, Little Brother?"

"I want to take Cindy out on a date, something special for her eighteenth birthday. I'd like to go dancing. I need ideas, and I need a woman's point of view. It wouldn't be the same asking Paul or Matthew. Although Matthew did mention a roadhouse that he had gone to a couple of months ago."

"I might be able to help you, but it might be a little daring. Are you up for it?"

"Tell me what it is, and I'll let you know."

Having finished hanging the last piece of wet clothing on the line, Grace put her arm around Michael, and as they were walking, she said, "What do you know about Sonny's?"

CHAPTER 11

Matthew's Decision

October 27, 1940

"Hey Michael, do you have a few minutes?" Matthew asked out of politeness since he would bend his younger brother's ear in any event.

"Sure, what's up?" Michael replied, putting his pitchfork down.

Michael sensed that something was up, as Matthew did not answer right away. If that was not enough of a telltale sign, the worry lines now creasing his forehead were a dead giveaway.

"You always wanted to travel and see the world, right?

"Yeah, and I still do, hopefully with Cindy one day."

"Well, I want to do that also, except I don't have a Cindy as you do."

"You never seemed to have a problem finding a date," Michael stated, but it could have also been a question.

"You and Cindy have been together forever, and you probably always will. I'll bring someone to listen to music and go dancing, and maybe to have a good time, but that's not the same."

"So, what are you saying?" Michael asked.

"What I'm saying is I don't have the ties to this place that you do. For what my relationships consist of, I can do that anywhere and in places more exciting than here."

"Okay, I get that. But what's your point?" Michael asked, accepting much of what Matthew had said but knowing this was not at all about him and Cindy.

"I want to leave," Matthew said, sounding both excited and

relieved at having said it.

"Leave and go where?" a surprised Michael asked.

"Everywhere and anywhere. I want to see the world. I want to see something beyond the flat plains of the Oklahoma Panhandle." Matthew was now talking excitedly.

"That's easier said than done. What would you do for a living? It's not like you had a great education. I mean, you're good with mechanical things and such." Michael wondered if he was laying it on too heavy, but he felt that he was just honest.

Before Matthew could answer, Michael continued, "How come just now? I never heard you talking about this. I was always the one saying I wanted to see the world, not you."

"That's why. I knew Ma and Pa would have expected you to leave the farm one day, but I didn't want to burden them with the possibility of losing the both of us. But even though things are getting better, there's still not as much work as there used to be. And if things do pick up, maybe Grace's new beau could help out, and Pop's still young enough, so it really got me thinking," Matthew explained, hoping for support from his kid brother.

"What does Paul think? You told him, didn't you?" Michael asked.

"I couldn't, not since that accident with the hay bailer. Paul's stuck here. He'll do okay on the farm, but he doesn't have the options that I have with his injury. He'll find out soon enough, but I feel bad telling him. That's why I'm telling you."

"If you're asking me if I'm okay with you leaving, then the answer's yes. But why do I think that my opinion really doesn't matter? What is it that you're not telling me?"

Taking a deep breath, Matthew paused before answering Michael's question.

"Remember when we were driving to Guymon a couple of weeks ago, and there was a recruiter from the Navy by the county courthouse? Well, I went back to talk to him, and one thing led to another. The next thing I know, I enlisted. I leave in two weeks. I'll be going up north to the Great Lakes Naval Training Station in Illinois. Then after basic training, I'll probably be assigned to a ship somewhere."

Michael was shocked but also happy for his older brother.

He was also surprised and a bit melancholy that it would be Matthew and not him leaving to see what lies beyond the borders of Oklahoma. But Michael realized that he would have that opportunity with Cindy one day, but now he wondered if Matthew's leaving would alter his plans.

"So, what do you think?" Matthew's inquiry snapped Michael back from his thoughts.

"I think that's great," Michael said as he hugged his brother, feeling more than a little envious. "But how are you going to tell the rest of the family?" he asked.

"That's why I need your support. I will need you to help convince everyone that I am doing what's right for me. I was never meant to be a farmer, and neither were you. We had no choice in the matter; we were born into it."

"You know Pa will be the hardest, and not just because of the farm. He never really talks much of his war experience, but having been in the Marines, maybe he'll understand. Maybe you should sit down and talk to him first. If nothing else, he would respect you for doing that, not that he has a choice."

"You're right. I'll do it after dinner. Pa's always more relaxed after gobbling down Ma's dessert."

"We better get back to work. These stalls aren't going to clean themselves," Michael stated as he picked his pitchfork back up and began scooping up the remaining layers of hay from the ground. As Matthew walked out of the barn, Michael's thoughts were now of Cindy. Matthew was right. She was always a part of his life, and he could think of nothing that could ever change that.

As much as he tried not to show it, it was apparent to everyone that Matthew's thoughts were somewhere else besides sitting down with the family for dinner. It was even more obvious to his father, as of all the people seated at the table, it was with him that he most tried to avoid direct eye contact. It was a good thing that Matthew was not a poker player because his tells were obvious. When dinner was finally over, and after everyone finished his mom's dessert of blueberry cobbler, he asked his father if he could have a word. Sensing that it would be more than just a word, and with an early frost making for a chilly evening, the elder Johnson grabbed his coat and asked Matthew to join him out on the porch. Matthew did likewise and looking out over the expanse of their farm, his father spoke first.

"So what is it, son? I know there's something on your mind." Not one to beat around the bush, Philip Johnson was not a man of many words, but he made the most of each one when he spoke.

"There's something I need to tell everyone, but before I do, I wanted to talk to you first," Matthew said, as cold wisps of vapor emanated from his mouth.

"Am I the first?" his wise father asked, having seen Matthew making frequent eye contact with Michael throughout dinner.

"I may have talked to Michael," Matthew offered sheepishly, being inaccurate about the 'may' portion of his explanation.

"Let's not stand out here in the cold any longer than necessary. Tell me what's on your mind."

Matthew took a deep breath and exhaled, causing an exaggerated cloud of vapor to exit his mouth before answering his father's question. "I joined the Navy. I enlisted a couple of weeks ago. I leave in two weeks."

There was an awkward pause as his father said nothing. Philip Johnson was staring over the farm that they struggled to maintain during the hardest of times. Matthew had no idea what his father's reaction would be, nor would he know what words he might say. Finally, his dad broke the silence. "Have you given this enough thought? We are at peace right now, but there are storm clouds on the horizon."

Matthew was relieved that his father's first question was not about the farm but rather about a parent's concern for their son's safety. He was glad thinking that this question would be easy to answer. "Yes, I have," he responded.

"Son, have a seat," his father said, pointing to one of the old wooden chairs that were on the porch. He did not have to say so, but this conversation would not be short. Quite the contrary, it would be the longest that his father had ever spoken to any of his children. Like his son earlier, Philip Johnson also had to take a deep breath before talking, causing his exhaling to create a cold vapor cloud that rivaled the size of his son's.

"You know I was in the Great War, as it's called. But there was nothing great about it. I joined the Marines because it was the patriotic thing to do, plus I liked the thought of the girls seeing me in my uniform. It probably was what made your mother become attracted to me. I liked the brotherhood that I shared with my fellow Marines. We felt like we were invincible. Going off to France was going to be the adventure of a lifetime. I felt so proud as we marched off to our ship that would take us across the Atlantic. It was probably the best time of my life so far. We got to France, and even before we went to the front lines, it was as if we were heroes. The young French women would run into our ranks, randomly kissing as many of us as they could. Their mothers would hand us flowers while their fathers would toast us, holding glasses of wine up high in the air. I was so proud. Proud of my unit. Proud of being a Marine. And proud of what I had accomplished. But that soon changed."

Matthew sat there, mesmerized by every word his dad spoke. The entire time his father's gaze never once turned away from looking out over the farm as he continued his story.

"When we got to the front, the reality of war quickly set in. There was no glamour. There was no glory. There was just agony. The sights and the smell of death were everywhere. The pungent odors of rotting corpses filled your nostrils. The trenches that were our homes were filled with mud and water that soaked our feet and our shoes. If there were not scores of rats running around trying to steal our food, we had to live with the scores of dead rats that seemed to be everywhere. Our food, when we could get it, was cold and ill-tasting. We couldn't shower or bathe, and we reeked of body odor. We lived in constant fear of enemy artillery shells and mortars that would come hurtling down towards us from the sky. If they exploded within our ranks, they would turn what had once been your best buddy into small fragments of unrecognizable flesh."

Matthew continued to listen intently, not feeling quite as comfortable sitting down as he had been at the start of the conversation.

"We had to carry gas masks since we were under constant fear of gas attacks. Those that didn't get their masks on in time would suffer from the painful and deadly blisters that the mustard gas would cause in their throats and lungs. Even for those lucky enough to have their masks on, they would have blisters forming all over their body as the gas would soak into their woolen uniforms. We would fire our rifles at an unseen enemy, not knowing whether or not we hit our target, wondering whether or not we would be killed likewise from an unseen bullet, fired by the same unseen enemy."

"As bad as it was in the trenches, it was even worse when the order came to attack. We ran across no man's land, exposing our bodies to a hail of machine-gun bullets. Bullets capable of having your body cut nearly in half. We would fight our way through barbed-wire entanglements and watch helplessly as your best friend next to you would die from a headshot that came from a sniper's bullet."

"But perhaps the worst and most haunting was having to kill or be killed. Seeing the look of disbelief on your opponent's face as you would plunge your bayonet into his chest is something you can never forget. Then you come to realize that he was probably just doing what he was told to do, just as we were. He would likewise have been someone who also did not fully understand the reasons why we were fighting there in the first place."

While his father paused briefly, Matthew began squirming a little, not feeling at all comfortable. But he still listened intently, leaning closer towards his father.

"When we got home, the government promised us bonuses. A bunch of fellow veterans marched on Washington fourteen years later, demanding that they pay us the rest that they had promised. With the depression forcing so many people out of work, they hoped that a massive show of support might cause the Government to advance their payments. You were just twelve years old when the government used the police and our troops to disperse the demonstrators. They had tanks and cavalry clearing the makeshift camp and burning it to the ground. The general who was in charge of this operation was Douglas MacArthur, who is now the Army's head honcho in the Pacific, a place where you could be heading. So if you're thinking of getting any great rewards for your service, you could be setting yourself for a disappointment."

Matthew sat there stunned. Not only at what his father had said, but hearing him speak so much about something he never talked about previously. While his father had been looking out at the farm the whole time he spoke, Matthew realized that his father's mind had been back at another place and another time.

"Pa, looking back, would you have done it all over again, knowing what you know now?" Matthew asked, eager to know but soon to be surprised by the answer.

For the first time since his father began speaking, he turned to face his son, and looking straight into his eyes, Philip said, "You would think that it would be easy to answer. The truth is it's not that simple. They said that it was the war to end all wars. A part of me believed that. I had probably hoped that I might be able to help create a safe and peaceful world, where my children would not have to fight in yet another war and suffer what I had to endure. Now, the world is at war again, and my children face the same decisions I had to make. Although you will not face the same threats I had fighting on land, the horrors of war will be the same in the Navy. Instead of a bullet, it might be the shell from an enemy battleship or the torpedo from a sub you never saw. But in the end, it's the people who suffer and die. I doubt if you are looking at it this way, but perhaps your reason for enlisting might be no different than mine was. Besides, I know you, and I know the type of person you are. You are both strong and determined, and I think you have already made up your mind. I just want you to be aware of what might be."

"Thanks, Pa, I have, and I hope I make you proud."

"You already have, Son."

It was exactly two weeks, just as both Matthew and the United States Navy had said. Having no luggage of his own, he was using an old, embroidered satchel that had belonged to his grandmother. Matthew managed to stuff it with everything needed for his new career. Although, any clothes that he had packed would see little use once he received his Navy uniforms.

His mother had accepted his leaving, but acceptance was not the same as embracing it. Unlike that conversation they had two weeks ago, his father was stoic and had very little to say about it, to no one's surprise. But despite any misgivings he might have had, he could not hide the pride he was feeling. Of course, Paul would miss him, but he seemed conflicted about his feelings, probably wondering if his life would have been different if not for the accident. Grace, more aware of the overall situation in the world than her younger sister, was more concerned for his well-being but managed to hide it well. Meanwhile, Rebekah thought it was neat to have a sailor in the family.

Michael, more than the others, better understood why Matthew had chosen this path. Although he did not wish to join the Navy or any other military services, he did envy the sights and places Matthew would see. But even the Navy, at this point, did not know what those might be. His assignments would all come to be after Matthew finished his basic training.

Matthew, if he had his preference, was hoping for a Pacific Fleet assignment. Despite the ever-increasing threats from the war-mongering Japanese, the travel brochures he had seen of Hawaii were highly alluring. For someone who had spent his entire life on the Oklahoma Panhandle, much of it during the worst drought on record, anything with water sounded good.

They had all piled into the family's pickup for the drive into Guymon. A bus would take him to Kansas, where he would transfer to yet another bus that would bring him to Chicago. Matthew would then have some time to take in the sights of the nation's second-largest city before hopping on yet another bus going to the Naval base.

As they all exited the front cab and the rear bed of the truck, his mother handed him a paper bag containing a sandwich large enough to last him at least the first half of his journey. His father gave him three one-dollar bills, hoping that would tide him over until he received his first paycheck, a whopping twenty-one dollars a month. Even Cindy had gone with them, sharing a Hundred-pound, canvas sack of chicken feed to sit on in the back with Michael.

They stood on the corner, exchanging any last-minute conversations with Matthew before the Greyhound bus would arrive. Then, hearing the distinct sound of the bus's engine, they turned in unison to see it coming down the street. As the sleek silver bus with its rounded edges pulled to a stop, they all began to say their goodbyes. When the bus driver announced that he was leaving in five minutes, the urgency in saying those goodbyes increased.

"Do us proud, son," his father said, being the first to say

goodbye and also being the most brief. But a lengthy handshake, followed by a firm hug, spoke volumes.

"Love you and make sure you write," Grace said, unsuccessfully fighting back the tears as she kissed him on his cheek.

"Bye, Matthew. Can I come and visit you when you get your big boat?" Rebekah asked as he lifted her in his arms, her knowing neither the Navy rules nor the fact that the Navy did not call their ships' boats.

"You take care of yourself. You won't have me around to fix your problems." Paul said, still not believing he was leaving.

Cindy was next. Throwing her arms around him, she said, "I'm going to miss you."

"You take care of my kid brother over there. But if you ever get tired of him, give me a call. You know what they say about sailors." Matthew said with a wink of his eye.

Now looking at Michael, they threw their arms around each other, holding their embrace. "You better come home when you can. It's not going to be the same here without you," Michael said.

"I know. I'm going to miss you too," was Matthew's simple reply.

Finally, patiently waiting near the open door of the bus, Matthew's mother stood quietly. Of all the Johnson's, only she knew of the terrible toll that the last war had taken on Philip. She was praying that Matthew be kept safe and spared from any such ordeals should war break out once again. "Maybe you'll be stationed somewhere nearby," she said, knowing it most likely not to happen.

"I'm going to miss you, Ma," he said softly. Then, trying to end the goodbyes by being upbeat, he added, "I'm sure the Navy cooks can't hold a candle to your cooking."

"In or out, mister," the now impatient bus driver proclaimed.

Walking onboard, with his satchel in one hand and his sandwich in the other, Matthew found an empty window seat, and after putting his bag away, he sat down. He pulled the widow up and waved goodbye as the bus slowly pulled away. He watched as long as he could as they all waved goodbye until the bus was out of their sight.

The ride back to the farm covered the same distance as coming here, but the trip seemed to take twice as long and was much quieter, as each took time to reflect upon seeing Matthew off. Matthew's long trip would seem even longer, as he would alternately long for the happy memories of the past while anxiously anticipating the new life he was beginning. Only time and fate would decide which of these would dominate his thoughts going forward.

CHAPTER 12

The Birthday

November 1940

Michael had been planning it for several months now. He had heard about it from Matthew initially, but even Grace had suggested it, thinking that it might not be a bad idea. Of course, his mother and his father would not have necessarily agreed. The thought of going to a roadhouse would not have even been an option not that long ago. But being eighteen inferred certain adult privileges, and he had already reached that plateau, and soon would Cindy.

One such establishment, named Sonny's, had opened up north of town, near the state-line. It had already gained popularity among those adults who could drive their cars or trucks to escape the restrictions imposed upon them by their parents or society. Although greatly condemned by local officials, church leaders, and parents concerned with their children's moral values, it continued to thrive. The stories circulating about the romantic and often immoral activities were partially accurate, but they also greatly exaggerated these events. The result was that these rumors and half-truths added to its desirability, giving it a larger-than-life image. Michael was one to buy into that image. However, it was not the drinking that got his interest. It was the overall excitement of the live music and dancing that enticed him.

Of course, there were the romantic and often sexual activities rumored to take place out in the parking lot. The privacy afforded by the steel body of a car or a truck's cab gave many couples the opportunity and freedom to explore their newly found sexuality. Cindy was a good girl, and there were limits to not only what she would do but what he might ask. But Michael would not be above attempting to cop a feel should Cindy let him.

The hard part would be convincing Cindy to go to Sonny's. Today, after school, when they would be sitting on Cindy's porch, he would try.

"Come on. It'll be fun. Matthew had gone there right before he left and said it was great," Michael was telling Cindy.

Michael was doing his best to convince her to go to the road-house. It would be her birthday, and he wanted it to be remark-able. He had just walked her home from school as he had done every day since they were kids. Checking to make sure no inquisi-tive ears were eavesdropping as they sat on the porch, Michael continued their private conversation.

"And did Matthew tell your mom? I can't imagine her being happy with that."

"Well, no, of course not. But do you tell your parents everything you do?" Michael asked in rebuttal.

"But that's different," she said, not knowing if it was.

"Is it? Besides, it's not every day you turn eighteen," he pleaded, without wanting to sound desperate.

"I don't know. Remember what happened when we were simply dancing in the Davidson's barn. I don't think it's worth the trouble," Cindy answered, referring to the arguing she had with her parents over it.

"But you'll be eighteen," he reiterated, quickly adding, "You could even get married without your parent's approval."

"I think that would cause fewer problems than going to the roadhouse," she stated, knowing her parents' position on busi-nesses serving alcohol and encouraging dancing. "Besides, it's common knowledge of what goes on in the parking lot."

"That's probably over-blown anyway, just a few guys exag-gerating. But would that be such a bad thing?" Michael asked, al-ready expecting the answer that he knew would be forthcoming.

"Michael Johnson, you know my position on that. There are just some things that will have to wait for our marital bed."

"But not all of them," Michael replied, smiling coyly.

"Shush your mouth. What if my parents heard you? They're still suspicious when we went to the expo, and that was over a year ago. But a gal might not be opposed to some serious necking if it was with the right fellow." She replied, also smiling coyly.

Cindy's parents had not heard them, but her brother Jake had, just as he was walking around the side of the house. Curious, he stayed out of sight and began to eavesdrop on their conversation.

"I don't care if they heard me. It's not your mom and dad who I am in love with," Michael said as he held Cindy's hand.

"I know, but they are my parents, and I have a responsibility to them also."

"I can accept that, but not if it comes at the expense of our happiness," he said, now holding her other hand also.

"I'm sure we can find a way to make it work. There's nothing that says a wife cannot love her mom and dad, as well as her husband," Cindy responded with a smile.

"Are you saying that you will marry me?" Michael asked.

"I don't know. You're going to have to ask me first. But then a gal can't wait forever," Cindy answered.

"Yeah, but a guy needs to be able to support his wife and family first before he can ask."

He did not need to say it, but times were still hard, and there were still families giving up their farms and leaving for good. Even Cindy's family had been toying with the idea for the past several years. Had it not been for the stubbornness of her dad in not wanting to give up, they might have left years ago. Her dad's stubborn behavior in all matters had been a constant irritant with Michael, but he was grateful for his reluctance to leave. The thought of Cindy moving away would be too much for him to bear.

"Well, just don't wait too long. I'm not going to be young forever," Cindy said, joking.

"What about your dream of becoming a nurse? How does that fit in with all of this?" he asked, wanting to hear her answer.

"About the same as your wish to travel and see the world. You never really wanted to settle down here."

"We both know that there's no real future here unless you

want to spend the rest of your life as the wife of a dirt farmer. As long as you are with me, it doesn't matter where we are. You can be a nurse anywhere," he stated, hoping that someday it would be true.

"But what about your family? Now with Matthew having gone off and enlisted in the Navy, that leaves just you and Paul. And besides, Paul has just one good hand after that horrible accident. Your Pa needs help running the farm."

"Paul does just fine with that hand. At least we don't have to worry about him going off to enlist like Matthew," Michael replied, thinking of the irony.

"I need to go to nursing school first, and that's not so simple and easy. But first things first." It was a simple statement to a complex problem.

"At least you are not expected to help run your farm. You have five brothers to do that. That's more than enough. They don't need you." Michael was stating the obvious, but it helped to make his point.

"But my Ma needs help. Besides, they're older than your parents, and my Pa can't do as much as he once did. Doc Willis told him that he needed to take things slower. I can't go off to some nursing school and leave them. Not now."

"Your mom will be just fine. Besides, to be honest, she gives me the willies. It's always like she's giving me the evil eye."

"Now you're the one exaggerating, although she does treat me different than the boys. It's like she expects more from me but doesn't say why. Even naming me when I was born was different. Everyone in my family has names from the bible except me. She said mine was from the storybook Cinderella. It's like she wants me to marry a prince. Besides, she's been having a tough time here like everybody else. So please go easy on her," Cindy asked.

"Okay. We can talk more about this later. But you still haven't answered my question about going to the roadhouse."

"Michael Johnson, you are nothing if not persistent. You certainly know how to wear down a girl's resistance. I want to go dancing, and the idea of going to the roadhouse is exciting. But I make no promises of anything else," she said, thinking over the possibilities in her mind.

"So that's a yes?"

"Call it a qualified yes. But my family can never know. You promise me that."

"It's a deal," Michael proclaimed happily, unaware that it was an impossible promise to keep.

"Where are you going?" Cindy's mother asked on her daughter's eighteenth birthday.

"Michael's taking me out to celebrate, probably over to Guymon to see the new Disney film, Fantasia. It just came out, and it's supposed to be a combination of animation and live-action. A bunch of the kids from school saw it and said it was good," Cindy told her mother, feeling bad about having to lie.

"I would have thought that you'd rather enjoy having your birthday cake here with your family?"

"I can do that later when we get back. Besides, Michael's my boyfriend, and I want to spend my birthday with him also."

Cindy had not noticed, but her father was paying much closer attention than usual to her discussion with her mother. His everyday stern look was even grimmer as he eyed his daughter suspiciously while Jake stood off to the side.

Soon, the sound of the Johnson's pickup truck pulling up to the house could be heard, followed shortly after that by three quick knocks on their house door.

"That must be Michael," Cindy shouted as she ran to greet him.

She wanted to hug him, but knowing that any display of affection would not go over well with her parents, she just smiled and said hello. Besides, there would be a much better opportunity for that later. Michael did not waste any time in getting Cindy into the truck. He never felt comfortable under the watchful eyes of her parents, and he was excited about the evening's prospects, even if it were only dancing and some much-anticipated necking. He was just hoping that Cindy would stick to her end of the deal.

They pulled into the parking lot of Sonny's. It was not so much of a parking lot but more of just an open field. What remained of the grass had been trampled down due to the many vehicles that had visited the establishment. In makeshift rows lining the highway, scores of cars and pickup trucks were parked perpendicular to the roadway. Most cars and trucks were empty as their occupants were dancing and drinking the night away inside the rowdy building. The sound of a jazz band was blaring out the open windows, as well as the telltale odor of tobacco. Some of the vehicles had occupants, although, in most of them, the inhabitants were horizontal and not readily visible without closer inspection.

Looking at the crowds of people entering the roadhouse, many of them much older than she and Michael, Cindy was beginning to have second thoughts. Although now, at eighteen years of age, she could legally be served alcohol but never having any, she was hesitant about trying it. And, not being a smoker, being in a room filled with cigarette and cigar smoke was less appealing. Still, the sounds of the band and the prospect of finally dancing on a wooden floor instead of the hay-covered dirt of the Davidson's barn were enticing. But she felt it necessary to build up her courage, and what better way than to be held by the only person she had ever loved.

Snuggling up against Michael, she asked, "Can we sit here and wait a while before we go in?

"Sure, whatever makes you feel comfortable," he replied, sensing her hesitancy.

"Thank you," she said as she turned to kiss him, appreciating his understanding.

As they pulled into the parking lot, Rueben Smith and his son Jake were unsure whether they wished to find Michael's truck empty or occupied. If unoccupied, it would have meant that his daughter had already entered the roadhouse and was probably cavorting about on public display. Yet, had they been in the truck, God only knows what manner of salacious behavior might have been going on. It would all depend on their timing and whether or not they were too late. Rueben pulled into an empty space and parked their truck. Since so many vehicles looked the same, especially at night, he decided it would be better to search for them on foot. He and Jake exited the truck as Reuben already began clenching his fists.

After first disturbing, then apologizing to several other couples in similar-looking trucks, they finally spotted the black 1923 Ford pickup they came looking to find. Inside the cab were the silhouettes of two people. They were still upright, but they were engaged in what Reuben believed were acts of passion that might lead to sexual activities. Cindy was visible through the large rectangular windshield even in the dark as they approached the truck. Both Reuben's temper and blood pressure began to rise as he saw what appeared to be his daughter beginning to unbutton her blouse. With his large veins on his neck and forehead noticeably bulging, he moved to the passenger side door and pulled it open, yelling at Cindy as she sat there stunned by his presence and actions.

Jake had gone to Michael's side of the truck and began yelling at him and threatening him with both fists. Cindy's father had now managed to grab his daughter's arm and began dragging her out of the truck. Michael tried to intervene but was unable to prevent Reuben from pulling her out of her seat. As Michael slid out Cindy's side, Jake came running around from the other side, still cocking his arm back in a threatening manner and yelling at Michael. Cindy, with her partially opened blouse beginning to slide off her shoulder, continued struggling, trying to free herself from her father's firm grip. Seeing his daughter's bare shoulder, Rueben became even more furious as he continued to drag her away from the vehicle.

Meanwhile, Cindy's reactions and her emotions were visibly strained and divided. As a family, she loved and respected her father, as well as her brother. But Michael, she loved on an entirely different level. It was a love not based on family ties but a passionate love that exceeded that between a father and daughter or a brother and sister. She was in the middle of a conflict between two opposing sides. Having to choose one instead of the other would not be something she cared to do. She realized that nothing good could come of this, but it was Michael with whom she wanted to spend the rest of her life.

Cindy could see the rage in her father's eyes. A fury that she could not fully comprehend. She understood his desire to protect her from what he thought were immoral and harmful acts, and for this, she was grateful. They were, after all, a family. A loving family that she grew up in during her first eighteen years. But it was her life and not his. She was here voluntarily. It was her own choice, and despite her being Daddy's little girl, she was now a woman and had a right to make the choices that would affect her life from now on. Unfortunately, with both her dad and Jake being old school and set in their ways, she could not see an easy answer to her dilemma.

By now, the commotion had attracted the attention of several couples, as heads were popping up among the occupied vehicles. Despite the loud music and noise emanating from the roadhouse, the yelling still managed to draw the attention of at least one of the building's bouncers. He walked out from his post near the door to see what was going on. Seeing that it was far enough away from Sonny's and feeling satisfied it was no longer one of his concerns, he walked back inside.

Michael had focused his attention on Cindy and had lost sight of Jake. Jake, however, had not lost sight of Michael. He was coming around the back of the truck and seeing Michael advancing towards his father and sister; he pulled his right arm back and was ready to strike at Michael. Just as he was beginning to throw his punch, Cindy screamed out a warning to Michael. Michael turned around in time and dropped down to one knee, avoiding Jake's swing as the powerful right hook caught nothing but air. Recovering quickly and his attention now focused on Jake, Michael sprang to his feet and drove his shoulder into Jake's midsection as if Jake were a tackling dummy on the football field. Jake immediately fell back and was temporarily immobilized, as he had the wind knocked out of him.

Cindy's father saw what he thought was his unconscious son lying motionless on the dark and poorly lighted ground in what had now become a series of unending and needless escalations. He immediately let go of his daughter and advanced towards Michael, holding his fists up high in a threatening manner.

"You did this. You brought this upon my family," Reuben cried out, moving closer to Michael with each word.

"Pa, no!" Cindy shouted, imploring her father to stop.

"God will punish you for your sins, and I will uphold my daughter's virtue," Reuben shouted at Michael, adding, "May he have mercy on you."

Michael was back-tracking as much as he could until he

could go no further, finally coming to rest against an expensive roadster with out-of-state license plates. With the altercation having spilled over to this neighboring vehicle, its male occupant jumped out, openly brandishing a handgun tucked into his waistband. Seeing this, Michael quickly moved away from the car while Cindy's dad continued to follow him. Satisfied that his expensive vehicle would not be damaged, the man stepped back into the car, happy to be just an interested spectator.

As Jake was finally recovering from having the force of the impact expelling the air from his lungs, he slowly began to move, but his father did not notice his movements. Still thinking the worse regarding Jake's condition and still seething with hatred for Michael's influence over Cindy, Reuben again raised his powerful arms and prepared to strike at Michael's head. With a massive effort, Reuben unleashed a powerful but wild swing that Michael would avoid. Michael could have thrown a few punches in return, but the last thing he wanted to do was strike Cindy's father. But her father did not share Michael's non-aggressive stance. He was obsessed with inflicting physical harm upon Michael, and his face evoked images of a man possessed. Once more, he raised his large hand, but before he could swing it forward, he felt a hand grab his arm from behind. Obsessed with just one thought in mind and wanting no interference, he swung blindly at the person behind him, striking the soft face of his daughter. Cindy instantly recoiled from the impact and fell to the ground. Seeing what he had done, Reuben let his arms fall to his side, and he dropped down to his knees, looking up to the heavens and asking God's forgiveness.

As Michael rushed to Cindy's aid, her father clutched his left arm with his right hand. Michael was now kneeling beside Cindy, gently cradling her in his arms. Having been more stunned than injured by her father's blow, she began to sit up on her own, surveying the situation. At first, Cindy saw Jake unsteadily standing as he was still recovering and confused at what had just transpired. Then she saw it. It was the sight of her father; his arms folded tightly across his mid-section as he doubled over and slumped to the ground. His last look on this earth was staring directly at Cindy, silently asking for her forgiveness.

"Pa!" she screamed as she crawled over to where his still body now lay.

Jake was now making his way to the side of his stricken

father, kneeling beside him and urging him to wake up.

"No. No. This can't be," Cindy kept repeating, her earlier screams now replaced by softer cries of anguish.

As tears began freely flowing down Cindy's face, Michael stood silently, not knowing what to say or do. Whatever his hopes for this evening were, none of this would have been part of it. Through no fault of his own, his girlfriend's father lies dead, just a few feet from where he stood. It was of little solace that the previous aggressiveness of Cindy's father and brother was no longer an issue. As Jake began to lift his father and carry him to their truck, Cindy tried to help carry the load. Michael attempted to help, but Jake quickly rebuffed his offer and was now accusing Michael of being responsible for the death. As Reuben was lying dead in the truck, Michael went over to Cindy and held his sobbing girlfriend in his arms. They embraced for several seconds when Michael attempted to kiss Cindy on her cheek. With her emotions in turmoil and having suffered a tragic personal loss, she broke off the embrace and began striking Michael repeatedly on his chest.

Her tears turned to anger as she told Michael, "I hate you."

Michael just stood there, taking her abuse as she said it over and over again. Then, Cindy's anger diminished as quiet sobs of pain and anguish replaced it, as each successive "I hate you" became softer and softer until they ended completely. The silence was soon interrupted by Jake, who was now jabbing his finger into Michael's chest, saying, "You are responsible for all this. I will make sure you pay for what you did to our family."

Michael did not reply. He thought that in time, Jake's words would just be idle threats. Of course, Michael would have no way of knowing what future threats might come from another member of the Smith family. But for now, he could do nothing but stand and watch as Cindy joined Jake as they drove away, bringing their dead father's body back home.

CHAPTER 13

The Funeral

November 29, 1940

There is no such thing as good weather for a funeral. Even the brightest, clear blue skies would not have been able to overcome the sadness and the pain that resulted from the ending of someone's physical life on earth. Still, it seemed rather appropriate that the weather was both dismal and depressing. The cold rain falling from dark and bleak overcast skies matched the feelings of the many family and friends standing alongside the plain wooden casket. Ironically, the rain that was adding further frustration to the event at hand would have been a welcomed sight many times over the past decade.

The mourners had followed the casket from the church that Reuben Smith had attended all his life to the same patch of land that contained the remains of his parents. The two simple grave markers would now be joined by a third, as they all would spend the rest of eternity interred here, underneath the shade of a large cottonwood tree. However, there would be no shade today, just heavy droplets of rain falling from its leaves and branches onto those huddled beneath it.

Pastor Simmons would say some appropriate words before Rueben's sons began lowering the casket into the rectangular hole they had dug previously. The onlookers would bow their heads, occasionally nodding in agreement with the eulogy. Yet, few, if any, would remember anything that he said after just a few days. The Smith women were dressed in black, as were the other female attendees. The black veils that Eunice and Cindy wore could not hide the tears that flowed down their cheeks. Eventually, their tears would join with the raindrops that were dampening their faces. Finally, the mourners heard a few soft sobs as the

pastor spoke the last words. But then, the painful cries of a grieving widow penetrated the previously subdued ceremony.

As the other mourners now proceeded to walk away, the
Smith family stayed at the gravesite. One by one, Pastor Simmons
extended his condolences, shaking their hands while holding his
wet bible in his other hand. Then the Smith boys each began
shoveling dirt from a pile alongside the grave onto their father's
casket. The soil had become mud from the constant rain, making
the difficult task even more challenging. Finally, with nothing left
to do, they all began the slow walk back to their farmhouse, where
various homemade dishes were prepared for the hungry mourners, courtesy of friends and neighbors.

Michael would be the only mourner who could not join with
the others. His absence was noticed and understood by those who
had been aware of the circumstances involving Reuben's death.
While all the others were standing outside as a group, Michael
was observing the funeral from afar. Using a parked pickup truck
to shield himself from being seen, he watched the services, wondering what he could have done to have prevented all this. He
watched with probably as much sorrow as that experienced by
the deceased's family. It was a different type of grief. It was the
pain of not being able to be with Cindy at this time. It pained
him not to be able to console and comfort her. But what hurt him
the most was the realization of what would happen next. Reuben
Smith had been the force that kept his family here throughout all
the struggles for all his faults. Now with him gone, it was a foregone conclusion that they would pack up and leave for California,
as many others had. As difficult as it would be, he had to see Cindy.
Although he wanted to believe that she did not blame him for
what happened, the issue loomed large on both their minds. They
needed to talk. It obviously could not be here or now. He had a
plan, and he hoped it would work.

As Cindy was walking, she began to scan the surrounding
area, hoping to see Michael. She had not spoken with him since
the tragic incident the other night. It was not an easy decision.
Seeing Michael at this time of sorrow would have put a terrible
strain on her relationship with her mother and brothers. She
hoped that Michael would understand and realize that it was not
her decision to ban him from attending the funeral. She accepted
his absence since he could not have been able to offer his con-

dolences personally. Yet, it would have been comforting if he was somehow there, even if it had to be at a distance. She had just about given up hope when she caught a glimpse of his head as he was hiding behind the fender of an old black pickup. She saw the remorse in his face and longed to be in his strong arms. Despite her genuine sorrow at the loss of her father, she managed a hint of forgiveness as they exchanged glances. Looking around to make sure no one saw either Michael or her looking at each other, she returned her gaze to the area near the pickup truck, but Michael was no longer there. In keeping with the rollercoaster ride of emotions that had plagued her the past couple of days, she was confused, scared, and experiencing all sorts of mixed feelings. She desperately needed some love and stability in her life. And as always, that would need to be Michael.

Although it was clear that Michael was not welcome at the Smith's residence, the rest of his family had no such restrictions. There had been much happy social interaction between the two families over the years. With his family in attendance at the funeral luncheon, they would have access to Cindy. Since Grace had been friends with Cindy over the years, their talking should not raise any alarms. Knowing this, Michael had written a note for Grace to pass on to Cindy.

With so many people inside the house, the overflow crowd gathered on the porch. They were waiting their turn to walk up to the bereaved family, standing at the end of a receiving line. Once they had offered their sympathies, they would move onto still another line, this one leading to the spread of the various hot and cold dishes that covered the large dining room table. Then, holding their plates, they would mingle among the crowd, managing to take bites of their food as they spoke with one another. As was the case in instances like this, the people paying their respects would gather around and talk about the deceased, often relating a humorous anecdote or story. Sadly, most people could not remember much humor or lightheartedness in Reuben's life. In a cruel twist of fate, Reuben died much like he lived his life: angry, bitter, and failing to accomplish his goals. When there was no longer a need to receive their guests formally, the Smith family members separated, each going their separate way.

Choosing a time when there were no watchful eyes on

Cindy, Grace went to extend her condolences once again. Then as she held her hand, Grace passed the note to Cindy. Correctly guessing what it might be, Cindy took the folded note and held it tightly in her hand without looking at it. Cindy waited a few minutes, then excusing herself to the other guests, she went up to her room. Closing the door behind her, she unfolded the note and began to read it. Michael wanted to meet her tonight. He would wait until everyone had gone to bed, and then he would wait for her at her family's barn. Cindy tore up the note and went back downstairs. Recognizing that her curious mother noted her absence, Cindy was cautious as she searched for Grace. Finally spotting her across the room, Cindy, while still under the watchful eye of her mother, got Grace's attention and gave her a simple nod of her head. Understanding that the message was received and acknowledged, Grace nodded back to Cindy.

Later that afternoon, back at their house, Grace relayed the information to her brother. Satisfied that at least he would have the opportunity to explain his actions, he began to think of what he would say. Other than that night outside the roadhouse, he had no contact with Cindy. Now, with her leaving Oklahoma a real possibility, it was more important than ever that they speak. Not knowing what other opportunities they might have, his words tonight had to be perfect. Practicing what he would say, he began pacing about his room, repeatedly speaking the words until they would flow smoothly. The creaking sound of the old wooden-plank floor became more noticeable to anyone sitting in the parlor directly below his room. He was interrupted by a knock on his door. Grace had been sitting in the parlor and could not avoid noticing his walking back and forth. He opened the door and invited her in.

"How are you holding up?" she asked.

"Okay, I guess," he answered without any conviction in his voice.

"You know it wasn't your fault." She offered to try to ease any feelings of guilt that Michael had.

"Maybe so. But none of this would have happened if I didn't bring Cindy to the roadhouse." Michael finally stopped pacing and sat down on the edge of his bed.

"If that's the case, then I should have some responsibility also. You did come to me for advice, and I thought going there was a good idea. Sometimes bad things happen, and we have no control over them. Cindy's father had a bad heart. If he didn't die then, it would have happened eventually." Grace thought she had made some valid points as she sat down next to Michael.

"The bottom line is that it happened then, and it happened because I had made the decision to bring Cindy there. It all falls on me."

"When I saw Cindy earlier and gave her your note, I could see in her eyes that she still cares for you. Nothing's changed."

"If only that were true. Everything's changed, and I can't undo it, even if I tried. The best thing in my life may soon be out of my life," Michael said, the moistness in his eyes now evident.

"Have faith, younger Brother. Think of all that this family and hers have dealt with and survived. God will find a way."

"I just hope and pray that his way is also my way."

As he and Grace got up, she hugged him. Before leaving the room, she turned around and said, "Good luck tonight."

"Thanks," was the only thing Michael could think of saying.

After Grace had left, Michael walked over to the heavy, old oak chest that held his clothes. Pulling open the top drawer, he took his wallet out. Opening it up, Michael removed the photo of Cindy, hoping that the two would come together, just as the woman had told them nearly two years ago at the Tri-State-Exposition in Texas. Regardless of what happens tonight, he swore that this picture would never be out of his reach. He just hoped that the same would be true for Cindy.

Darkness had long since crept over the flat farmlands, causing the still overcast skies to look even darker. With no moon and no streetlights anywhere insight and most home lamps already turned off for the night, the world around the Johnson and Smith homesteads appeared as black as coal. On farms everywhere, entire families were either asleep or about to go asleep. There was no such thing as staying up late when you lived on a farm. Yet, there would be at least two exceptions to this throughout Texas County this evening. Like a modern-day Romeo and Juliet, Michael and Cindy were awaiting their nighttime rendezvous. Lying in bed but fully clothed and his eyes wide open, Michael was listening to the silence of the night. The rain of earlier had ended along with the sound of it falling upon the roof above his bedroom. He tried to look at the time on his pocket watch but could not see it due to the absolute lack of light.

Believing enough time had gone by, Michael got up and walked downstairs as quietly as possible. The almost total darkness was a minor hindrance to maneuvering about, as he could feel his way around the house's interior. Stepping outside and into nearly four inches of mud from the earlier rain, Michael realized that he would need a light to guide his way to Cindy's house. He grabbed an oil-fired lantern and, striking a wooden match against the side of the matchbox, he lit the wick. With the light now to guide him, Michael began walking to meet Cindy, still replaying in his head what he would soon be saying.

Less than five hundred yards away, Cindy was anxiously looking out her window. She was following the tiny point of light that grew larger as it also drew nearer. Cindy could not yet make out the face of the person carrying it, but she knew it had to be him. Unlike Michael, she was in her long nightshirt, afraid of what might happen should her mother come into her room and find her fully dressed. Cindy would put on her warm flannel robe when it was time to meet up with him. As the person carrying the light turned up the muddy path to her house, she put on a pair of shoes and grabbed her robe. Putting it on, she tiptoed down the stairs and carefully opened the front door. As Michael drew nearer, she could make out his face, distorted as it was by the uneven light of the lantern. When they were about fifty feet apart, she stepped off the porch and ran to him, showing no concern for the several inches of mud she was sinking in. He would have picked her up in his arms and carried her, but with the lantern still in one hand, they had to settle for his one-armed embrace. Any concerns he might have had about their relationship were not warranted as she kissed him softly yet passionately. They remained silent as they continued walking the muddy path to the old barn. The barn was far enough away from the house, so they would not be heard or seen.

Once inside, Michael set the lantern down safely, and once

again, they embraced. After several more kisses, Michael spoke first. Despite all the practice and memorizing what to say, he forgot his script, but more importantly, he spoke from his heart.

"I am so sorry. Can you ever forgive me?" Michael asked, desperate to hear Cindy's answer.

"Of course, I forgive you. I'm sorry for what I said the other night. I didn't mean it. I hope you believe me." Now it was her turn to wait for the answer she also desperately sought.

"Of course I do. How could I not? I would never want to do anything that would hurt you. I still feel horrible about what happened," Michael replied, giving her the answer she wanted.

Michael led Cindy to a bale of hay, where they each sat down, his arm around her shoulders. Then, Cindy's face took on a more worried and troubled look. Noticing the change in her demeanor, he asked her what was wrong. Taking time to answer his question, she finally spoke as a tear began flowing from her eye.

"I have bad news, terrible news. Tonight my Ma said that as soon as possible, she's putting the farm up for sale, and we're moving to California."

"That's not good, although I expected it. But it might take a while to find a buyer for the farm. That could take months, maybe longer," he said as he wiped the tear from her smooth cheek.

"No," she interjected, then adding, "She said she's not waiting. She wants to get away from the memories of this place. She said they could wire her the money when they find a buyer. Besides, my father had mortgaged the farm so many times there's probably little or no value here anyway."

"I don't know what I would do without you," Michael said, thinking that they had known each other for their entire lives, the last two years as romantic partners.

"Me neither." Then, before kissing him once again, she said, "I love you. I have always loved you."

Michael would have answered right away had he not been caught up in the excitement of Cindy's soft lips melting into his. Finally, he spoke, "I love you more than anything. We will somehow figure it all out. I will never let you out of my life."

"I don't want to leave, but maybe you can join me in California. You always wanted to travel and see the world."

"Yes, but that was with you. Why can't you stay." It was a question that needed asking but not an easy one for Cindy to answer.

"If I did, where would I stay, and what would I do."

"You could stay with us. You could stay with me. We could get married." Michael just realized that he had proposed to Cindy, and he liked the sound of it.

"That would force you to stay on the farm forever. What kind of life would that be? If I can go to nursing school in California, then I'll have a real job, and you can move there, and then we could get married."

"Did we just propose to each other?" Michael asked.

"I guess we did, but let's make it unofficial for now. There will be plenty of time for that. But it does sound nice."

"We have so much to plan and do but so little time to do it," Michael said.

"But we can make it work. I know it won't be easy, but it won't take forever either. But right now, let's enjoy the moment for what it is. And for the next few days or weeks, we will make the most of each day." Cindy was sure of what she said.

The cool, night air was beginning to affect her, as she had not dressed as warmly as Michael. "I'm cold she said,' as she rested her head on his shoulder.

They snuggled closer together. Michael took his jacket off and offered it to Cindy. She thought about it but declined, opting instead to kiss Michael. As they pressed their bodies together, the cold she had experienced was gone, as the warmth of passion surged through their bodies. Still kissing each other passionately, Michael removed her robe and slid the hand that was on Cindy's shoulder across her nightshirt, resting it on the side of her warm and supple bosom. Rather than repel his hand away, she encouraged him by taking his hand and placing it directly over her breast. Whether it was from the heat of the moment, or the coolness of the evening, even with the soft flannel material of her nightshirt covering it, Michael could not help but notice and feel the firmness of her stiff nipple. Michael carefully laid Cindy down across the large bale of hay. With emotions running at light speed, he began to pull her nightshirt up over her narrow waist.

With only her panties now covering her nearly naked body, they continued intensely kissing as Michael started to unbuckle his trousers. She allowed his hand to discover the smooth skin of her thighs when she suddenly broke off the kissing.

"No. I can't do this," Cindy shouted, half crying and surprising herself as she pulled her nightshirt down.

"What's wrong?" an equally surprised and disappointed Michael asked.

"It's just not right. Not now, not this way. I have dreamed of doing this since our first kisses on the way to the Exposition, but not like this," she stated emphatically, putting on her robe as she spoke.

"I'm sorry. It's just that I love you so much," Michael said, not knowing what else to say

"I love you too, but I want to do this on our honeymoon after we are married. Not before. And especially not like this on a bale of hay." Then standing up and walking towards the door, wearing her muddy shoes, she added, "I'm sorry. I truly am. I wanted this as much as you, but...." she couldn't finish the sentence. "I have to go back to the house. Please don't be mad at me. I do love you. I hope you still love me." Cindy was sobbing uncontrollably as a disappointed and embarrassed Michael led her back to the house.

Before she walked in, she turned back to Michael and threw her arms around him once again. "Forgive me, I hope you can understand?" she said as she kissed him tenderly on his cheek. More from shame than anything else, Michael was at a loss for words and failed to respond to Cindy's request. Hearing nothing, she closed the door behind her. She paused a moment before she headed up to her room, unsuccessfully trying to fight back her tears. With the door now closed, Michael began the slow and lonely trek back to his house, angry at himself for failing to say anything. He did love her, probably more now than ever. And Michael did understand, but he now wondered if or when they might ever be together again. The confusing events of this evening would keep him awake most of the night, but in the end, he took some solace in knowing that they still loved each other, and he vowed he would do whatever was necessary to keep them from drifting apart. But he wondered if these were the last memories they would have of each other. The possibility deeply troubled

Michael.

Before Cindy returned to her room, she quietly passed her mother's bedroom, and hearing no activity, she felt confident that her mother was sleeping soundly. Entering her room, Cindy removed her muddy shoes and laid them beside her bed. She was also confused over the events that just happened, but unlike Michael, the stress of the long and emotionally charged day proved to be too much, and she fell off to sleep rather quickly. Had she been awake, she might have heard her mother quietly opening the door to her room, holding a small oil lamp. The light coming from its wick was bright enough for her mother to see the fresh mud that coated Cindy's shoes. She would have also been able to see the rage in her mother's face. At least for now, it was better that she slept.

CHAPTER 14

Farewells

December 14, 1940

Despite thinking it could not be any worse, it was even worse than he thought. When he was finally awake after a restless night's sleep, Michael was rubbing his eyes, hoping it was nothing more than a bad dream. Hopeful as he was, that notion was facing the harsh reality of what was to be. He had been dreading this for the past two weeks, hoping for some miracle that, unfortunately, would not be forthcoming. Michael laid in bed wondering if some magical words could be said to make it all go away. Sadly, he quickly realized there were none.

Had he ever doubted how much he cared for Cindy, those doubts were gone as the pain of her leaving was heavy on his heart. He knew now what he had always known. Cindy was such an essential part of his life. Now, the thought of her not being involved in every aspect of his being was tearing him apart. Their dreams and desires were blown away like so much of the Oklahoma topsoil during those terrible drought years. He blamed himself, but that was neither fair nor satisfying. There was too much hurt to assign to just one person and just one event. But when everything was said and done, he alone felt responsible.

Her leaving would have been terrible under any circumstances. But, that it came about because of her father's death, which he was at least partially responsible for, just made things worse. Now, mainly because of Cindy's mother and her brother Jake, he was not even allowed to be at their house to say his goodbyes. Instead, like a thief in the night, he had to sneak up to their house last night and toss pebbles at Cindy's window to get her attention. Hearing the sound of the tiny stones striking the glass, Cindy quietly crept downstairs to meet Michael as they simply held each other tightly in their arms, saying nothing, as there were no words to ease their misery. Cindy cried first as Michael tried to remain strong, but then, even he could not hold back the anguish that had been building up inside him. Finally, not fearing what she might think of his manhood, Michael began sobbing uncontrollably.

The sudden appearance of a lamp followed by the sound of the front porch door opening would make their final moments together even worse. Suddenly, Cindy's mother appeared menacingly in the doorway, interrupting their goodbyes. As her mother began yelling at Cindy, Jake appeared and once again began threatening Michael. Though Michael's tears had long since stopped flowing, Cindy was now crying even more as her mother began pulling her away. Michael half-heartedly tried to intervene, not wanting things to escalate any more than they had. But Jake stepped between Cindy and Michael, jabbing his finger into Michael's chest as he had done at Sonny's parking lot, the night that his father had died. Michael stood there in disbelief as Cindy disappeared out of sight. Not at all what he wanted, the last face he saw that night was not Cindy's, but a vengeful Jake's, as they stared each other down. Finally realizing that nothing good would come of this, Michael turned around and left. As he walked away, he kicked violently at the dirt path, sending up portions of the still muddy ground.

Walking back into the house, Michael ran into Grace, who had not yet fallen asleep. With her window opened slightly despite the cold night air and facing the Smiths' house, she had heard the distant sounds of Cindy's heartbreaking cries. She had walked downstairs and was waiting for Michael.

"I couldn't help but hear. I am so sorry," Grace said, almost apologizing.

"It sure as hell didn't go well," Michael said, and not apologizing for cursing.

"I wish there was something I could do." Grace offered but knowing there was nothing.

"Thanks, that means a lot," Michael said, his eyes still red from earlier.

"This will not stop you two from getting together. It may seem bad now, but in the end, things will work out. Fate cannot keep the two of you apart. Your lives have been entwined with each other since you were babies. So please, Little Brother, have faith that things will work out."

Grace put out her arms and accepted Michael's embrace as he once again began crying. Then, continuing her empathy for her brother, Grace also started shedding tears as she felt the pain that Michael was experiencing.

Now, after re-living the sorrow of last night, Michael had to get up and face the reality of today. He would be dressed and waiting when the Smith family would be leaving. Their travels would require them to drive right past his farm. Even cranky old Eunice Smith, or her annoying son Jake, could not prevent him from standing alongside the road when they would pass by. Besides, Michael had concocted a plan. And with the help of Paul, Grace, and even Rebekah, it just might work.

Paul was with Michael, ready by the family's pickup truck waiting for the signal from Grace, who was upstairs by her bedroom window. Meanwhile, Rebekah had positioned herself two hundred yards away in the cornfield, having a direct line of sight to the Smith's house and barn. As the Smiths began loading themselves into their old car and truck, already overflowing with everything they would bring with them, Rebekah watched diligently, waiting to see which vehicle Cindy had entered. Then, with the pre-planned signal of one wave of her scarf for the car, or two waves for the truck, Rebekah played the role of a modern-day Paul Revere. Watching for Rebekah's signal, Grace anxiously awaited until she saw Rebekah wave her bright-red scarf just once. Then, running down the stairs and past the surprised looks of her mother and father, Grace ran outside and shouted "car" to Michael and Paul as loud as she could.

With his adrenalin surging, Michael hopped into the truck with Paul as they drove towards the road that passed their house. As they approached the end of their dirt path, Michael hopped out and hid behind the old John Deere tractor they had left there while Paul turned onto the road. He drove a little bit further to a spot with quite a bit of mud from the recent rains. Then Paul stopped the truck and began alternately going forward and backward, just enough to create a deep rut in the roadway. Satisfied that it was enough, he got out of the truck and waited.

Michael watched patiently as the Smith convoy was approaching. The truck was leading the way, with the old Model-T right behind. Then, seeing Paul and his truck stuck apparently in the mud and blocking their path, the two vehicles slowed to a stop.

"What's wrong" shouted one of the older Smith brothers as he stuck his head out the truck's window.

"I got stuck in the mud. Can you help?" Paul shouted back.

"You get in and drive while we push," said Caleb, Cindy's oldest brother, as he and the other three from the truck began pushing.

Making sure their efforts would fail by alternately stepping down sharply on the brake pedal, Paul shouted, "We need more help."

Hearing that, Jake exited the car he was driving in with Cindy and their mom. As Michael watched Jake join his brothers in what would be a nearly impossible task, he waited for the right time. Then, sensing that it was now or never, he slipped away from his hiding place and slowly approached the car. With Cindy's mom's suspicions focused on the delay up ahead, Michael could catch Cindy's attention as she looked around, also suspicious of what was happening. Seeing Michael crouching behind the car, she almost yelled out his name but was able to keep her composure.

"I'm just going to step outside while they push Paul's truck out of the way," Cindy told her Mom.

With everyone else's attention focused on the theatrical drama playing out before them, Michael grabbed Cindy by the hand and led her back to the tractor. Safely out of sight, but knowing their time together was limited, he spoke quickly.

"Cindy, I love you, and I always have. I'm sorry for everything, but I promise to write every day." Before he could finish, he was interrupted by Cindy.

"I love you too with all my heart. I will write to you each and every day, and I will always carry my half of our picture where ever I might be."

"I promise you the same," Michael said before taking Cindy in his arms.

"We will be together again," Cindy said before kissing Michael.

Not knowing how much time they had, and more importantly not knowing how long it would be before they would be able to kiss once again, they made the most of this opportunity. Had they been able to, they would have continued doing this forever, but they did not have forever. Cindy's mom was now turning her head, wondering where Cindy went, while even Paul could no longer keep five able-bodied men from pushing his truck forward. Seeing that his plan was drawing to an end, Michael kissed Cindy one more time as he swore his undying love for her. Then, as their hands slowly separated and they said their goodbyes, Cindy walked out from behind the tractor, giving one last look to Michael. Michael gave a brief wave as she returned to the car, just as Jake was getting back also.

"Where did you go?" her mother asked.

"I thought I saw a baby goat that might have gotten loose, but it was gone by the time I got there," Cindy said, having to think quickly.

With Paul's truck now out of the way and parked on the side of the road, he waved a thank-you as the small convoy passed. Today and the ensuing months would not have been what Michael would have wanted, but at least his plan worked, and that brought a smile to his face. Meanwhile, the same smile appeared on Cindy's face. It would be a long trip and ride to California, but at least Cindy would be able to smile and think about what had transpired today.

Having felt better about seeing Cindy yesterday, Michael went into town early this morning, making his first stop at the town's post office.

"Good morning Mr. Peterson," Michael cheerfully said to the postmaster standing behind the counter.

"And a good morning to you, Michael. How can I help you today?"

"I need some stamps," Michael said as he reached into his pocket and removed a handful of coins.

"It looks like you are planning to send a lot of letters

to someone," Mr. Peterson replied. He was fully aware of both Michael's life-long relationship with Cindy and the fact that she had just left Goodwell for good with her family.

"Yes, I will," said Michael, as he was spreading his coins out on the counter.

Having counted twice, Michael pushed the assortment of nickels, pennies, and a solitary dime toward Mr. Peterson.

"I believe that's sixty-nine cents. That should buy me twenty-three stamps," Michael said, doing the math in his head at three cents for each first-class stamp.

Taking the change and counting it, Mr. Peterson proclaimed, "That's correct. Would you like the Pony Express commemorative stamp? We still have a supply of those."

The stamps were celebrating the 80th anniversary of the Pony Express. It was a mail service that used relays of horse-mounted riders, who would deliver the mail between Missouri and California. So much was through territories that were open frontiers, similar to what Cindy and her family were now experiencing.

"That'll be fine," Michael answered, just happy to be getting any stamps that will get his letters to Cindy.

Carefully tearing the stamps along their perforation, Peterson counted out twenty-three commemorative issue stamps and handed them to Michael. Before carefully folding the postage stamps and putting them in his billfold, Michael took brief notice of the orange stamp, depicting a Pony Express rider in full gallop.

"Thanks," Michael said as he walked away, stopping first to look at the map of the United States that was on the wall.

Michael was anxious not only to write to Cindy but also to receive her first letter. He had his first supply of what he hoped would be many stamps for equally as many letters. But all Michael could do right now was wait. Until he heard from Cindy, he had no address to send his letters. It was just yesterday that she left, and Michael wondered where she might be. Looking at the map, he knew that they had some long and arduous miles ahead of them. Long before getting to southern California, they would have to cross all of New Mexico and Arizona, much of it desert. But, at least at this time of year, they would not be contending with the oppressive summer heat.

     As he walked down the street to meet up with Paul, who was at the general store, he began estimating how long it might be before he heard from Cindy. He realized that she could probably write to him before he could write back to her. If she wrote a letter, she would not have needed a permanent address yet. She could just drop it off at a post office in some town they were passing. At least he might be able to hear from her relatively soon. However, he knew that she would not get any letters from him until she would have an address for Michael to write back to her. That could take weeks, depending upon how quickly her family would get settled once they reached their destination. He had so much to tell her, but for now, he would have to wait. Michael was becoming impatient, but he had no control of the timing, and he could not do anything to speed the process up. He was looking forward to when he could utilize those stamps he just bought. Then, thinking about the image on the stamps, he was hoping that the mail would get through as quickly as it did when the Pony Express delivered it.

CHAPTER 15

Letters

December 1940

As he had done every day for the past week, Michael was keeping both an eye and an ear out for old Ben Jacobs and his noisy 1925 Chevy pickup. Each day around noon, Ben would be passing the entrance to the Johnson's farm in his duties as the area's rural mail carrier. If he had any mail for the family, he would stop at their mailbox attached to the top of an old weathered fence post. Then, as he had been doing since before Michael was born, he would open the hinged door and insert any letters into the rusty metal box. Of course, it was not every day that they would get any mail, but Michael hoped that today might be an exception.

Michael was in the barn when he first heard Ben's truck. It had just passed the vacant property that had been Cindy's farm. Michael's hopes ran high as he stepped outside, watching Ben slow down as he approached their mailbox. Ben saw Michael and waved to him as he began his slow and methodical routine. Michael waved back as he saw Ben inserting something into the mailbox. Before Ben was able to pull away, Michael was already running to retrieve the letter. When he arrived, he lowered the door and removed one single piece of mail. Turning it over, he was elated to see a postmark from Gallup, New Mexico. Cindy had mailed it three days ago. Michael rushed back to the barn, and sitting on a hay bale, he carefully opened the envelope and began reading.

December 14, 1940

My Dearest Michael,

By the time you receive this letter, we will probably be in Cali-

fornia. Obviously, I would much rather be with you in Oklahoma, but the sooner we get settled, the sooner you will be able to write back to me, and we can start making our plans for the future.

This letter is the first opportunity I had to write. We drove to Santa Rosa, New Mexico, where we are spending the night. We had hoped to make it to Albuquerque, but the drive is slow, and we did not want to drive at night, as the roads are so dark it is hard to see. Even now, it is so dark, but an oil lamp is enough for me to see what I am writing. Tomorrow I will try to drop this off at a post office we'll pass along the way. With any luck, you will receive it in a few days.

Just eight hours ago, we were together, but it seems as if it were a lifetime. I miss you so much already. I think it's because it will be a while before I can be back in your strong arms. I was so glad that we had those precious moments together. My mother asked where I had gone. I told her I was looking for a baby goat that I thought I saw, but I am unsure if she believed me. It does not matter, as I don't care what she thought. Please thank Paul for blocking the road, as I would have been a basket case had we not been able to say our goodbyes. As I write this, I have to be careful not to be seen by my mother or Jake. I long for the day when this will not be necessary, and we will be together forever. I have the photo of you, and I was just looking at it, thinking how our lives changed that day. I wish our lips were once again joined, and I miss holding your hand. I feel ashamed to say it, but a part of me wishes that I had not stopped you last week when we were in the barn. But it is probably best that we wait. I want to be your girl, but I also want to be your good girl. Besides, we will have so many opportunities for that in the future. "Our future," I like the sound of it.

It is getting late, and we will be leaving early tomorrow morning. We hope to make it to Flagstaff, Arizona, before nightfall. I will write again soon.

Love always,

Cindy

Michael folded the letter and put it back in its envelope. He felt a sense of satisfaction knowing that Cindy had held and touched this same paper and envelope. It was not much, but for now, it was the best Michael could have. He wanted desperately to respond to her letter, but he knew that was still not possible. For now, Michael was glad to have heard from her. He was wondering when that next letter would come.

He did not have to wait long, as old Ben was delivering another letter the next day. This time, Michael was at the house when Ben inserted the letter into the mailbox. Michael ran out the front door, not even waiting to put his jacket on. Then, retrieving the envelope, he ran straight up to his room. As Michael sat on his bed, he carefully tore the envelope open, not wanting to rip Cindy's letter. Then, as he did yesterday in the barn, Michael began reading.

December 15, 1940

My Dearest Michael,

Today we are in Flagstaff on day two of our journey. There is a post office not far from where we are, so I will drop this off tomorrow. Again it's a slow and tedious ride, especially with you not here to talk to. Yesterday there were few words said as I sat in the car with Jake and my mother. So today, I convinced John to switch places with me, and I sat in the truck with Caleb and Joshua. It was not as bad, but I think they would have preferred to have had John there with them.

I still miss you so much. I look at your picture every chance I get. I can't believe it has only been one full day that we have been apart. I can only imagine what this must be like for you since you probably read this several days later.

The weather was generally warmer than back home. Much of our drive was through parts of the desert in the Southwest. But today we started seeing some mountains, some of them quite high with snow near the top. It looks so much different than the flat plains we were used to seeing. Here in Flagstaff, it's pretty cool now.

If all goes well, we should get to one of the work camps that are still around. They are not supposed to be nearly as busy as they were a few years back. This place will be just temporary until we find ourselves a place to live and find jobs. There are many farms where we are heading, and they say they are busy and are hiring help. So if nothing else, my brothers should be able to find work. My mother says she could take a job as a housekeeper. After all, it's something she has done all her life. As for me, I still would want to one day be a nurse, but only if it allowed us to be together. I am sure that you could find something worthwhile to do here and one day we could be married. But, of course, I am not asking, and you will still have to be the one to propose to me.

On a sad note, I just remembered something that we hadn't thought about before. With everything else going on, we just forgot, but this will be the first Christmas that we will not have seen each other. Even when we were just kids, we still got to be together, even if it were just for an hour or so.

I have to go. I hear my mother calling for me. Stay safe and be well.

Love you always,

Cindy

Michael was now feeling melancholy, as he too had forgotten all about not being together at Christmas. He also wished that he had gotten her some gift to have given her. Not only a Christmas gift but a going away present also. The truth was that with all the years they had known one another, they never exchanged presents. Much of that had to do with growing up during a depression and having very little money, but he still felt terrible that there could not have been one thing he could have gotten her.

This time Michael was ready when Ben pulled up to the mailbox.

"Got another letter for you today. What's that, three in a row?" Ben asked, already knowing the answer.

"Yep. Just keep them coming," Michael said, hoping that it would be true.

"If you ask me, I think a certain someone is mighty sweet on you," Ben said, laughing as he pulled away, honking his horn twice for emphasis.

Michael returned to his room as he did yesterday. Getting comfortable, this time, he sat on the floor with his legs stretched out and his back up against the wall. Opening the envelope, Michael paused before taking the letter out. Then, as he brought it up to his nose, he took a deep breath, hoping to breathe some of the same air that Cindy had sealed into the envelope. It was not much, but it did make him feel closer to her. Then, unfolding the letter, he began reading.

December 16, 1940

My Dearest Michael,

Today we finally arrived here in California. I am not sure exactly where we are, but the last signpost I saw said Barstow. The weather is beautiful, and it certainly looks like the pictures we used to look at in school. It was amazing to drive past miles of farmland growing rows upon rows of lush, green crops that went for as far as the eye could see. It's no wonder so many people have moved here. It's like the movie you took me to see last year, "The Wizard of Oz." Remember when everything was in black and white, Dorothy stepped out of the house, and the picture turned to technicolor. That's what it's like between the Panhandle and here. I think you would love it here.

I do miss not being able to get your letters yet. Have you been busy writing them? Will you mail them all at once, or one at a time. I don't care as long as I get them. But more than your letters, I miss you.

I had a terrible dream last night. It was so horrible it pains me to write about it. I dreamt that we were apart, and I forgot what your voice sounded like. I pray that that never happens. When I woke up, I was so scared that I immediately took out your picture and looked at it, thinking of all that you said the last time we were together. But then, I was comforted because, in my mind, I could hear your voice. A voice that I hope I can listen to soon in person.

We are staying here, but it still will not be a place for you to send me your letters. That will have to wait just a little bit more. Please don't be angry, as I am sure that I am just as upset as you are.

Are you saving my letters? I think it would be nice if we had them to read years from now when we're old and gray. We could even read them to our grandchildren. Oh, did I tell you? We're having lots of grandchildren. And the boys will be handsome, just as their grandfather would be. But, of course, we'll need our children first. But at the right time, I'm sure that can be arranged, and I'll be more than happy to do my part.

Well, that's all for now.

Loving you always,

Cindy

As Michael finished the letter, he placed it with the other two and secured them together, placing them in his dresser drawer. He had also thought it was a good idea to have something to show their grandchildren someday.

CHAPTER 16

Opportunity & Hardship

December 1940

Although it was not something they would have wanted, Reuben Smith's untimely demise made the family's ultimate move to California easier than it would have been years earlier. Had he not resisted the idea so vigorously, they may have left at a time when "Okies" was a derogatory name for the large number of migrants coming from Oklahoma. The peak years were in 1937 and 1938, and those refugees of the dust storms and the droughts that contributed to it endured many hardships and widespread discrimination. Dorothea Lange's famous photos graphically portrayed the struggles these families faced in the various farm labor camps. In addition, John Steinbeck's best-selling novel written in 1939, "The Grapes of Wrath," opened the nation's eyes to the plight of these displaced families. Although now, one year after its publication, conditions had drastically improved. Jobs were more available, and the economy was improving, as the nation was coming out of the economic depression of the prior decade. The movie version of the book had come out earlier this year, but ironically none of the Smith family had seen the movie. Even if they had, considering the circumstances under which they decided to move, it would have been unlikely that it would have swayed their decision.

Like so many others before them, their travel followed U.S. Highway 66, commonly referred to as Route 66. Now, however, the sight of their over-loaded car and truck on the highway was not as common as it would have been a few years earlier. It was not only displaced farmers who migrated west to the "promised land." Nearly half of those who moved to California during the past ten years were from urban areas and had decent-paying, blue-collar jobs before the depression hit. Like the farmers, they too were seduced by the seemingly limitless opportunities that California offered. Another misconception was the idea that the migrants were all "Okies." While many were, large numbers of former residents of Texas, Arkansas, and Missouri also sought the deliverance from economic hardship that California seemed to offer.

Those seeking blue-collar jobs would soon find themselves gainfully employed while earning a respectable wage and enjoying a satisfactory lifestyle. For those former farmers seeking agricultural work, they too would find ample opportunities in the lush farmlands of the San Joachim Valley. But these families seeking a better life were not always welcomed with open arms by native Californians. In fact, in many jurisdictions, the opposite was true. In 1936, The Los Angeles Police Department established a border patrol unit nicknamed the "Bum Blockade." With orders from the city government, the special detail was at major railroads and highways. Its purpose to turn back any non-residents who lacked apparent means of support. Even as recent as last year, the District Attorneys of the counties most affected by the influx of migrants from the dust bowl states brought charges against their own residents. Their crimes were attempting to help their relatives move into California.

Fortunately for the members of the Smith family, their timing worked out well. The following year the U.S. Supreme Court would issue a landmark decision. In Edwards v. People of State of California, the court would decide that states had no right to mitigate interstate travel. But even before that would happen, all seven members of the family would find gainful employment. However, it would cause the family to be divided geographically for the first time.

Cindy's four older brothers, doing what they do best, would all be hired by local farmers. However, it was a different story for Cindy, Jake, and her mom. Cindy was still hopeful of becoming a nurse, requiring living near a hospital with a nursing school. Jake had become disinterested in the family's farming business and was exploring other opportunities. And, although their mother was no stranger to manual labor on a farm, her current age and skill set made her better suited as a housekeeper. Presented with the prospect of seeking employment in an urban environment, they narrowed their choices down to two, Los Angeles and San Diego. Cindy and Jake initially favored Los Angeles for its greater size. But having come from rural Oklahoma, their mother, despite her lofty ambitions for her daughter, felt somewhat intimidated by the city's sheer size, thinking San Diego would be a better fit. Had the Smith family been a democracy, Los Angeles would have won. But it was run as more of an autocracy, with their mother at the head. So despite being outvoted two to one, it would be San Diego that the three now set their sights on.

With the family now split up, all had some tearful goodbyes as they began their new careers and lives. Like how they had left Oklahoma, the four older brothers had the pickup truck, while Cindy, Jake, and their mother kept the old Model-T. Neither Cindy nor Jake could have known at the time just how impactful their mother's decision would be on their lives.

Cindy would have many more letters to write to Michael, but she would soon have a new address to give him. Then, she would look forward each day with anticipation to receiving the latest letter from Michael, just as he had been doing. These letters that would go back and forth helped to bridge the many miles that separated them. Besides being kept informed of each other's lives, they would rely upon these letters to preserve and strengthen their love for each other. In time, reading these letters proved to be just as important as looking at each half of the photograph they each kept. If asked, both would have agreed that it was no substitution for actually being together. But it was the best that they currently had. And no one could deny the impact that the simple act of expressing yourself in writing could have. So, despite their physical separation, nothing could ever come between them as long as they had their letters.

CHAPTER 17

Return Letters

January 1941

Michael finally received the letter he was hoping for. He had been getting letters from Cindy regularly, but it pained him not to respond to her. Besides keeping Michael apprised of what was happening in her life, the outpouring of love that Cindy put into every letter brought warmth to Michael's heart. Now, he would have the chance to tell Cindy just how much she meant to him. Cindy's latest letter included her new San Diego address. Grabbing a fresh sheet of paper and pen in hand, Michael sat down as he began thinking of what he would write. Finally, satisfied with what he was about to say in words, he put his pen to the paper and started writing.

January 3, 1941

My Darling Cindy,

I am so happy to be able to write to you finally. I have received all your letters and have followed your route on an old map I had found. It's so strange that you are only inches away on the map, yet you are so far from me.

California sounds nice. I can't wait to hear more about San Diego. Have you been able to see the Pacific Ocean yet? Is it as blue as its pictures? I guess you and Jake will be living together with your mom, at least for now. Hopefully, that is not a problem for you. I wish it could be me instead of them who were with you. But hopefully, one day soon, we can somehow make that happen.

Christmas was last week, and it was not the same without you. I can't believe that it's 1941 already. Matthew is still in Illinois at the naval base there. He said that Lake Michigan is unlike any lake he had ever seen. Matthew said it looks as big as an ocean, and you cannot see the other side. He had hoped to be home for Christmas, but that didn't happen. It is too far and takes too long to travel since he would only have a three-day pass. So it was strange for him not to be here also.

I got you a Christmas gift. I won't tell you what it is, but I hope you like it. I've been earning some extra money helping Mr. Randall at the general store, so I thought it would be perfect when I saw it. I bought it right away, and I had it shipped once I got your new address. I hope you like it.

Grace says to say hello. Paul and Rebekah also. They were all in on my plan the day you were leaving. I'm so glad it worked, and I got to hold you in my arms. At night when I go to bed, I think about our last kiss. I can't wait until we can do it again. I guess I am also glad you stopped me that night in the barn. As much as I wanted to that night, I think now that our first time deserves something more memorable than doing it on a bale of hay in a smelly old barn. Just think, once we are married, we will no longer have to wait. But you are so worthy; I will wait as long as it takes.

I will write every day until I run out of stamps or ink. I'm just kidding. I have an ample supply of each to last me until Valentine's Day, which is not that far off. I hope you have success with getting into nursing school. Once I know that Paul and my father can run the farm without me, I will make plans to move to San Diego to be with you. Until then, we will have to keep writing to each other.

Getting your letters and knowing that you care enough to write makes me feel good. I hope you feel the same way. I cannot imagine what it would be like if either of us stopped writing to one another. But that will never happen.

Tomorrow I will be at our mailbox, waiting for old Ben Jacobs to bring me your next letter. Until then, I have your picture to look at each day. I hope that tonight when I go to sleep, I will dream of you. Better still, I wish I dream of us. I hope that after you get and read this letter, you will also dream of us.

Love,

Michael

After that letter, they continued to exchange letters daily. Of course, if the mail were late, the one not receiving their daily letter would feel disappointed and a bit concerned. Still, they soon became accustomed to the occasional break in their daily routines of reading each other's letters. They both knew that it might not always be possible to write every day, but as long as the following letter would eventually arrive, it would all be good.

After many more letters to Cindy, Michael composed yet another.

January 15, 1941

My Darling Cindy,

I was so relieved to have finally received your letter of January 9th. It only just arrived today, but I was glad to hear that all is well. I guess we cannot always depend on the post office to deliver on time. Maybe tomorrow I will get multiple letters from you. Not hearing from you since your last letter that I received three days ago had me worried and concerned. I think we best prepare ourselves for gaps like this. There might even be some days when you will be too tired to write at night, especially now that you took that job at the cannery. I know it's not what you wanted, but I understand the need to have something, and hopefully, it will be only temporary. It sounds like hard and tedious work.

I, too, have been busy. I picked up more hours at the general store, and with my farm chores, I am usually beat when bedtime comes. So please forgive me in advance if I somehow fail to write once in a blue moon. I promise I will never make it a regular practice. The extra money I'm earning working at the store I am putting away. When the time is right, I will have the money to pay for moving to San Diego and joining you.

Right now, it's snowing. And with the ground frozen, it will be good not to see all that mud we had. But, I still am amazed by what you wrote in one of your previous letters when you described the weather on Christmas day. By the way, your pile of saved letters keeps getting bigger.

Matthew finally finished his training, and he got to come home for a few days before shipping out. You're not going to believe where they are sending him. San Diego! He's on the USS Enterprise. It's a large aircraft carrier, and it's at the navy base in San Diego. He said he would try to look you up when he gets there. So I gave him your address. Now I will have two people to see when I come out.

I was glad to hear that your mother got a good job. The family she's working for sounds nice. They also must be pretty rich from the way you described their house. I was surprised to hear that Jake still doesn't know what he wants to do. I hope he's not freeloading off you and your mom. I know he's your brother, but we never got along that well, and after what happened with your dad, I know he hates me. That's okay as long as you never hate me.

I had sent you that gift I had previously mentioned. Did you ever receive it? I sent it nearly three weeks ago. Hopefully, with the delay in our letters, you already got it. I won't say what it is in case it didn't come yet. I want you to be surprised.

I know I say it over and over again, but I miss you so much. My heart aches to be with you. At least we have our memories to keep us company until we can once more be together. When I get to hold you once again in my arms, it will be the happiest day of my life.

As always, I love you, and I miss you so much,

Michael

As their letters traveled back and forth, the delays in the mail would sometimes throw their timelines out of whack, as each would be asking the other about future events that were now history. But their letters still kept them connected when conversing by telephone was not a viable option with Michael still living on the farm.

Of course, as much as Michael wrote to Cindy, she wrote to him also.

January 19, 1941

My Dearest Michael,

First, let me say thank you so very much for my Christmas present. I got it today. It took quite a while to get here, but at least I have it. It is perfect. It is just the right size, and I will put it away until we can share it together. I can picture it sitting on the mantel over our fireplace. Did you notice that I said, "our fireplace?" I can't wait until that day comes. It was so sweet of you, and it was very thoughtful. The frame is beautiful, and the inscription, "True love is forever," is perfect. When we are finally together, we will piece the two halves together as we become one, just like that lady told us at the fair.

It was so good reading your last letter. At least it got here quickly. That is excellent news about Matthew. He must be so excited. I have some good news to tell you also. Remember the family that hired my mother to do their housekeeping? Well, their son is some bigwig doctor at a large hospital here in San Diego. My mother told him that I was working at the cannery, but I wanted to become a nurse. Guess what? He tells my mom that I could do better than work at the cannery and that he would see if he could get me a job at the hospital. It would just be doing clerical stuff. But here's the great news. He said that maybe he could see about me getting into nursing school. Of course, I would need to meet him, and he would need to see me, kind of like an interview. But can you imagine me possibly going to nursing school? I know how excited you must be for me. That's another reason for you to hurry up and come out here.

So much has happened in the last month. It's been crazy, but at least now, things seem to be falling in place. Even Jake may be putting his life together. I had mentioned to him about Matthew, and now Jake's talking about joining the Navy. Think about it. Maybe soon, I might have both a brother and a brother-in-law in the Navy. But, of course, as long as I have you as my husband, nothing else matters. But as I have always said, I'm not asking you to marry me. You are still having to get down on one knee and propose. I think you already know what my answer will be.

I will cut this letter short, as it was a long and tiring day. Hopefully, you will get it soon.

As always, I will always love you,

Cindy

With their letters continuing to crisscross across the country, each of them would sleep well tonight. It was always a good feeling knowing that you are loved. Neither one could imagine it being any other way.

CHAPTER 18

Changes

January 22, 1941

"Is that what you are going to wear?" her mother asked, disapproving of her daughter's choice of clothes.

"Yes. What's wrong with it?" Cindy asked, somewhat surprised by her mother's sudden interest in her wardrobe.

"Well, you want to make a good impression. So you should wear something nice."

"This is something nice!" Cindy replied.

"I thought that you should wear something better."

"I don't have anything better. And why all the concern about what I am wearing. It's just a meeting about a possible job. He will either accept me for who I am or not," Cindy said, referring to the doctor.

"I'm sure he'll like you, but it wouldn't hurt to look your best."

"I'm not trying to impress him with my appearance. I just want to make a good impression about the hospital job and possibly getting into nursing school.

"Of course, but it wouldn't be a bad thing to impress him. He's good-looking, brilliant, wealthy, and he's single. Did I mention that his family is one of the wealthiest families in San Diego? You do realize you could do a lot worse? If you play your cards right, who knows what could happen."

"Play my cards right? I'm going to a job interview, not a poker game. Besides, I already have a boyfriend, or did you forget?" Cindy said indignantly.

"How could I. The two of you send each other letters every day. What do you see in him anyway? He'll never amount to anything. He can't even afford to come here and visit you."

"I love him, and we will one day be married. He told me so."

"And when will that happen? I don't see a ring on your finger."

"It will happen. Michael has to make sure his family's farm can get by without him. Do you remember what it's like working on a farm? Or has working with a bunch of stuffy rich folk made you forget?"

"Don't you get fresh with me, young lady. I am still your mother."

"Then, why don't you start acting like one," Cindy replied, as she was getting angry.

"Don't forget who killed your father. And don't think I didn't know about you sneaking off with him the very night we buried your father. I saw your muddy shoes that night. That Johnson boy probably ruined you for any other possible men, and he made me a widow."

"He didn't ruin me, that night or ever. He respects me too much. And Pa's death was a tragic accident. You are just too blinded with hate to see the truth. Now, if you'll excuse me, I have a meeting I need to go to," Cindy said as she stormed out of the room.

Across town, Dr. Andrew Cauldwell was just leaving a meeting with the hospital board of trustees. As Chief Surgeon, it was necessary to attend the meetings chaired by his father, Jonathan Cauldwell, MD, retired. Their name was well known not only at the hospital but also throughout San Diego's society circles. But it was not the Cauldwell family who earned a spot near the top of San Diego's inner circle, but rather it was the Prendergast family, of whom the elder Cauldwell had married into. Andrew's mother's family had ties back to the Pilgrims who landed in Massachusetts. Over time, they migrated west before settling in California. Along the way, they turned a family-run vegetable farm into a multi-million-dollar food and grocery store business. Ironically, Cindy's brothers who stayed north working on the farms coincidentally worked for one of the Cauldwell family's subsidiaries. As Andrew was walking toward the elevator, he glanced at his watch.

"Damn," he said to one of his colleagues, "I promised my mother I would do a favor. I have a quick meeting. It shouldn't take too long, but you go ahead, and I'll meet up with you at the restaurant."

Entering the elevator, he pressed "L" and waited for the steel doors to slide shut. As the elevator doors opened, he walked into the lobby and walked directly to the woman seated at the information desk.

"Hello, Doctor Cauldwell," she said smiling, "How can I help you?"

"Hi Joan, I'm supposed to meet a Miss Smith. I told her to check in with you when she arrived."

"Yes, doctor. That's her sitting over there," she replied while pointing at Cindy.

"Thank you," he replied as he walked to where Cindy was sitting.

"Miss Smith? I am Doctor Cauldwell. I believe our mothers had arranged for us to meet."

"Yes, doctor. And please call me Cindy," she said as she stood up and extended her hand.

Cindy was dressed much simpler than the other women that Andrew saw daily, but Cindy looked radiant.

"Please, if you don't mind coming with me, I have an office where we can talk in private. It's awkward trying to do that here in the lobby."

"No, I don't mind at all." Cindy walked with the doctor, thinking that her mother was right about one thing, he was good-looking.

They entered an office with a nameplate on the door with the engraved inscription, Dr. Andrew Cauldwell, Chief of Surgery. The doctor offered Cindy a seat, and then he walked behind a huge oak desk and sat down in an over-stuffed, brown leather chair.

"So, I understand you are possibly interested in becoming a nurse."

"Yes, that is correct. It has always been a life-long dream."

"Well, as you may know, Pacific General has an excellent nursing school. Is that something you might be interested in?"

"Of course, if that were possible," Cindy exclaimed.

Now smiling, Andrew said, "Let me worry about that." But, as he said it, he could not keep his eyes from looking at Cindy's pretty face and attractive shape.

"I also understand that you are currently working at the cannery over on the west side."

"Yes, I have only been there a short time, but the pay isn't too bad."

"It's up to you, of course, but if you want, I can get you a job in the accounting department. It's just simple filing, but it pays more than what you're getting at the cannery. So you can start Monday if you want."

"Even though I just started there, shouldn't I give them two weeks' notice?" Cindy asked.

"No, that won't be necessary," Andrew said laughing, "My mother's family owns the cannery where you work. So we'll take care of everything."

"Then, Monday it is. Thank you, Doctor Cauldwell," Cindy said as she got up from her chair.

"Please, call me Andrew. After all, both you and your mother are working for us. So it's almost like we're family." But, then he quickly added, "Well, at least socially it's Andrew, but for proper professional decorum, here at the hospital, you should still address me as Doctor."

"Yes, Andrew, I mean Doctor, I understand. Thank you."

As Cindy left the office, she was unaware of it, but the doctor was undressing her with his eyes. Instead, she was focusing her attention on how her outlook had taken such a dramatic turn for the better. In a little over a month, Cindy had gone from bleak and unknown prospects to a promising future. Nevertheless, she could not wait until she got home to write to Michael and tell him the good news.

Meanwhile, Doctor Cauldwell was heading to meet his colleague for lunch. As he entered the posh restaurant, he was greeted by the hostess, an attractive young woman who instantly recognized her frequent patron.

"Good afternoon Doctor Cauldwell. And how are you today?"

"Thank you, Karen. I am very well, and I must say I like your outfit. It most certainly flatters you," he replied while winking his eye.

"Well, thank you, Doctor," the hostess said, then she added, "Doctor Barnes is already here," as she led him to a private table near the rear of the restaurant, still blushing from his last comment.

"So Andrew, tell me about your meeting," his friend asked, having just taken a sip from his drink.

"It went quite well. I think this young woman has great potential," Cauldwell answered, as a server was bringing him his usual glass of Cabernet Sauvignon.

"Is that great potential for the hospital, or you?" he asked with a quizzical look on his face.

"You know me well enough, Robert. What do you think?" Andrew said as he took a sip of his expensive wine.

When Cindy finally returned home, their apartment was empty. With no one else to share the good news, she took advantage of the opportunity to write to Michael, undisturbed by either her Mother's prying eyes or curious looks from Jake. Sitting at the kitchen table, she began to write.

January 22, 1941

My Dearest Michael,

I have great news to tell you. I am so excited but at the same time sad, knowing that you cannot be here with me to share my good news. I went to meet with that doctor I told you about in my last letter. I did not have my hopes too high, especially since my mother set the whole thing up. But it went very well. He was so friendly, much nicer than I thought for someone so important and also so rich. Did I tell you his family is one of the wealthiest in San Diego? Anyway, he offered me a job in the hospital's accounting office, which is much better than working at the cannery, and I'll be making more money. I might be able to buy some nice clothes for a change. It's so much differ-

ent here in a big city than back home on the farm. But he also said he would help get me into their nursing school. Other than you being here with me, that is the best thing that could happen.

I just heard Jake coming in, so I will stop writing. I'll mail this as soon as possible, and I'll write another letter later with more details.

Loving you always,

Cindy

She was just folding the letter when Jake entered the room. She noticed that he looked like he had something he wanted to say but did not know how to say it.

"Do you have a minute?" he asked.

"Yes, of course," Cindy responded.

"I've been doing a lot of thinking lately about my life and what I want to do. I realize that I am not cut out to be a farmer," he paused, trying to phrase his next words properly.

"I don't see me working in a factory or a cannery like you are doing. And I certainly don't have the education for some fancy office job." Jake paused again as he was gauging Cindy's response to what he was saying.

"I've been talking to some sailors I saw down by the harbor the other day. They got me thinking, and I went to talk to a recruiter downtown. I haven't signed any papers yet, but I think I want to enlist." Now he stopped talking as he waited for Cindy's reaction.

"Are you sure that's what you want?" she asked.

"I do. I really do."

"Then, that's what you probably should do."

"But what about Ma? What if she disagrees?" It was his turn to ask a question.

Cindy took a deep breath, then she said, "Jake, we may not have had the best relationship, especially lately, but you are family, and I do care about you. You are twenty-one years old. You can vote in the next election. You are a grown man capable of deciding the course of your life. It doesn't matter what Ma thinks. I am certainly not going to let her dictate what the rest of my life will be. I have my future ahead of me, and I know what I want."

She detected some irritation on Jake's face, knowing the strained relationship between him and Michael, but he accepted what she had said.

"Thanks, Sis. I was hoping you'd understand. I may need your support when I tell Ma."

"Just remember, that's a two-way street," she said.

"Okay, it's a deal," he said as they briefly hugged.

Across town in an exclusive residential neighborhood, Eunice Smith had gotten off the second of two buses that brought her to within two blocks of the Cauldwell residence, where she worked as a full-time housekeeper. She was extremely fortunate to have gotten the job. It was initially only a temporary position to fill an unexpected vacancy. Still, the combination of Eunice's obsessive cleaning habits and her tell-it-like-it-is personality hit it off with Andrew's mother, Margaret. There may have been some latent commonality between Eunice's old-fashioned Southern Baptist views and Margaret's puritanical ancestry.

Eunice had finished her duties for the day and was preparing to leave when Margaret approached her.

"My son Andrew had called, and he said that his meeting with your daughter went well."

Eunice was surprised at Margaret's comment about the meeting and her knowledge of it that fast. Not accustomed to having a telephone, she still found it odd to have information pass on that quickly. But looking about the massive house with its expensive furnishings, she quickly realized that she should not have been surprised.

"I'm glad to hear that. Cindy is such a sweet girl," said Eunice.

"She is also quite attractive. Andrew was very enthusiastic in describing her to me. Do you realize that my son is considered by many to be San Diego's most eligible bachelor? So any praise from him should be considered worthwhile."

"I have met Andrew, and he is indeed both charming and very handsome. My daughter would do well to be able to date someone like him," Eunice responded, as both women gave approving glances to each other.

As Eunice sat on the buses returning home, she became more and more fixated on what Margaret had said. The thought of Cindy winding up with Michael gnawed at her insides. He was not worthy of her. She deserved someone better, someone more educated and definitely better off financially. Eunice had not yet realized it, but California had changed her, not her personality as much as her values. She was now willing to put wealth and status above her daughter's true happiness despite her previous and extreme moralistic ideology. She could not stop thinking about how it would be to share in the financial well-being that would come from Cindy being with Andrew. Cindy was now no more than a means to achieving that financial independence. She was now willing even to sacrifice her daughter's virtue if that were to become necessary, as long as it was with Andrew and not Michael.

But she quickly realized that as handsome and charming as Andrew was, Cindy still loved Michael. It sickened Eunice to think of the time Cindy wasted writing back and forth to Michael. So, as her bus continued its route through the streets of San Diego, she sat wondering what she could do to change Cindy's mind. But then, a devious smile appeared on her face as she sat there, nodding silently to herself.

CHAPTER 19

Deception and Lies

February 4, 1941

After coming home from her job at the hospital, Cindy went to their mailbox and anxiously opened it up, hoping for Michael's latest letter. She was not disappointed, as she saw it waiting there. Cindy took it and went back to the house they were renting. In the privacy of her room, she began reading it.

January 31, 1941

My Darling Cindy,

I received your last letter of January 28th. I can't believe that you have finished your first week at your new job. I am glad that you enjoy it. Doctor Cauldwell seems very nice. It's nice that he takes the time out of his busy schedule to come to check in on you so often. It was also nice that he took you out for lunch the other day. I have to admit that first hearing of it, I did feel somewhat jealous, but I understand, as you had said, that it was to discuss you entering nursing school. Perhaps I should have been more envious than jealous that your life is coming together. I still long for the time that we will be together. If he can get you in the next class this spring, that would be great.

I am still working the extra hours at the general store. Interestingly, I get to talk to the customers, and many are people we have known all our lives. They all say to say hello, and they ask how you are doing. I tell them that you are doing well and how proud I am of what you have accomplished in such a short period. Although It may have only been a short time, not being with you seems like an eternity.

Oh, guess who came into the store the other day, Betty Miller. I'm sure you remember her. She and her family were among the first to leave for California, but they didn't care for it, and after all these years, they came back. And get this, they bought your old farm, and now they will be our new neighbors. Betty was asking about you, wondering why we were not together. She said she always thought that you and I would get married. I told her that we hope to be able to do that eventually. We laughed when she brought up that Valentine's Day in first grade. That was when you got jealous of her because you found out that she had given me a Valentine card before you did. I can't believe that was just about twelve years ago. Now she's all grown up like you and me, and her life has gone full circle moving back home. She said to say hi, and she wishes you the best. I remember she was always nice. Of course, not as nice as you.

With the Enterprise still in port, Matthew said he might pop by unexpectedly one day. He already has your address, but with you working, it might be hard to catch you at home. So if you don't mind, maybe I will give him your work address, and he can meet you for lunch one day when he's free. I think that would be nice.

The whole family says to say hello. They all miss you, but not nearly as much as I do. I have to admit it's hard being apart, but at least we have our letters. I honestly don't know what I would do without them. I anxiously await your reply. Just knowing that you eagerly await mine also makes me feel good. Who would've ever thought that a mail carrier like old Ben Jacobs would be an essential part of our love staying strong? Tonight, as always, I will look at your picture. Until I have you beside me, that'll have to be enough.

Love always,

Michael

Cindy put the letter on her bed and walked to the kitchen, curious about dinner. Her mother passed by Cindy's vacant room and saw the letter lying on the bed. Seeing that Cindy was in the kitchen, her mother picked up the letter and began reading it. When she was about halfway through, she got an idea. It would work well with what Eunice had earlier thought about on the bus. If she was right, this seed of an idea might grow to be the cause of Cindy finally breaking up with Michael. Feeling excited about her plan, she placed the letter back down on the mattress and exited the room.

The next day at the Cauldwell residence, Eunice saw Andrew. Engaging him in conversation, she told him that Cindy kept saying what a handsome man he was. And if he played his cards right, she might be interested in going out with him. Of course, these were blatant lies, but to a man of tremendous ego and conceit such as Andrew, these were enticing words for his ears.

"Of course, I find her equally attractive, but doesn't she have a boy back home in Oklahoma that she's committed to?" he asked, thinking that it really wouldn't matter if he wanted his way with her. After all, something like that never stopped him in the past.

Eunice was waiting for the opportunity to make her move, and she took full advantage of it.

"Home is no longer back in Oklahoma for Cindy. She's delighted living here in California. As for being committed to each other, how much could that be when they are a thousand miles apart. And as to having a boy back there, that's just it, Michael's just a boy and not a successful and distinguished man such as you. She may be saving herself for him, but if you ask me, she's wasting her time. She would make quite the catch for the right man."

Hearing Eunice say that "Cindy was saving herself" had the desired effect that she had hoped. Had Andrew any scruples, he might have been suspicious of Eunice acting more like a madam of a brothel than that of a caring mother. But having none, he was more than glad to set his sights on Cindy. Had Eunice been the slightest bit aware of Andrew's reputation, she should have known that any conquest of Cindy's virginity would not result in marriage. As much as he found Cindy desirable, Andrew was in no rush to give up the playboy life and get married. Especially to an "Okie" who was below his social status.

Still, as workable as Eunice's plans and goals were, she would first need to drive a wedge between Cindy and Michael to have any chance of succeeding. Their letters kept their love strong, but she knew she had to do something to disrupt that. She would start as early as tomorrow when the mail would come. But she also knew that by itself, that would not be enough. She would need the help of a big lie, and reading Michael's most recent letter to Cindy, Eunice knew what that would be.

The following day, Doctor Cauldwell was walking to his office when he met Robert Barnes, M.D. Andrew was busy, but he would always make time to talk with his friend.

"Robert, I have an early morning meeting in a few minutes, but I have time for a chat. Come join me," as they entered Andrew's office.

"That's fine. I only have a few minutes myself. After that, I have to prep for my 9:00 a.m. surgery," Robert said as he sat down across from Andrew.

"So, what's on your mind?" Andrew asked of his friend.

"I wanted to know if you were able to get the Board to consider my department's budget request?"

"Yes, but they are still undecided. I'll let you know when I hear something definite."

"Well, hopefully, they act soon. We're already starting to lose patients to Mercy Hospital. By the way, on an entirely different subject, how are you doing in your pursuit of that girl you hired?"

"The Okie? It's odd that you asked. Her mother had a bizarre conversation with me at the house. She basically offered her up to me. She said that she would be available soon. I'll give it a few weeks for her to break up with her boyfriend back in Oklahoma."

"Why do you even bother? You have more women willing to jump into bed with you than you can shake a stick at. What's so special about this one?" Robert asked, wondering why.

"I'm not quite sure. The young woman is obviously attractive, and I think the shapely body she's hiding under her current wardrobe would look much better with the proper clothes. But I think it's just her wholesome and innocent personality that is so appealing. Bedding her is more of a challenge than most of the other women I date."

"But you don't foresee any long-term future with her, do you?"

"Of course not. After a couple of months, all the pedals would have fallen off the rose. Then, she would be no different than all the rest. So then, why would I bother to keep her?" Andrew said as he looked down at his watch.

"You know you are incorrigible. And what about her mother?" Robert asked.

"She's just some itinerant housekeeper my mother hired. Why I don't know, but she's crazy enough to think that not only would I marry her daughter, but that I would have her as my mother-in-law. Could you imagine having her at the country club's next formal ball? But, of course, after I get what I want, both will no longer be of any use to me. Then, her mother will be my mother's problem."

Andrew looked once again at his watch and announced, "I have to get going to my meeting, and you need to prep. I'll see you at lunch."

Robert got up first from his chair and waited for Andrew to join him as they left the office. As they were in the lobby, Cindy walked in, on her way to work. Seeing Andrew, she changed her direction and walked over to him.

"Good morning Doctor Cauldwell. Isn't it a lovely day? I want to thank you again for getting me the job. I really like it," Cindy said, flashing her genuine and infectious smile.

"I'm so glad it worked out. And it is a lovely day. By the way, this is my colleague, Doctor Robert Barnes. He is head of the Orthopedics Department, and he also teaches part-time at our nursing school."

"It is so nice to meet you, Doctor Barnes," she said, now smiling sincerely at Robert.

"The pleasure is all mine," he replied, seeing what Andrew saw in her, but feeling sorry for what may lie ahead for the unsuspecting young woman.

"You'll have to excuse us both," Andrew said, looking once more at his watch.

"I understand. Thanks again, and it was very nice seeing you," Cindy said while looking at both of them.

As she walked away, Robert looked at his friend and said, "You are a scoundrel," shaking his head as they went their separate ways.

On the other side of town, Eunice had not yet left for her housekeeping job. With Cindy now working full-time and having a longer commute, Eunice would be able to go after Cindy had left in the morning and return home before her at the end of their day's work. Eunice walked outside the small house they were renting and looked into the mailbox. Inside was a letter that Cindy had written waiting to be picked up by their mail carrier as he would make his rounds. Eunice removed the letter and pushed the little red flag back down. Walking back into the house, she was undecided as to whether she should dispose of the letter. For reasons known only to her, Eunice decided to keep it for now. She found an empty shoebox and placed the letter inside. Then, standing on a kitchen chair, Eunice hid the box on the top closet shelf behind other boxes. Satisfied that the first part of her plan was successful, she then left the house. As she was walking to the bus stop, she was smiling, wondering what it would be like to have a daughter marry into such a prominent and wealthy family.

Later that day, arriving home well in advance of Cindy, she checked the mailbox and removed a letter that had come from Michael. Then, once again, as she would do many times in the next month, she placed it in the shoebox she had hidden on the top closet shelf.

When Cindy got home, she immediately went to the mailbox, hoping to find the latest letter from Michael. Not seeing any, she was disappointed, but this had happened several times in the past, only to receive it a day or two later. However, her disappointment would grow greater as this scenario would replay itself repeatedly during the next few weeks. A troubled Cindy would become both worried and concerned from not hearing from Michael, much to her mother's delight. Meanwhile, similar concerns would soon be taking place in Oklahoma.

CHAPTER 20

Why?

March 1, 1941

It had been over three weeks since Cindy's last letter. Had either of them had phones, then it would have been a simple matter of calling the other to see what had happened. But just as much as Cindy was troubled and confused about the sudden lack of writing, Michael was too. He could not stop wondering what had happened. Michael would repeatedly read her last letters, looking for any clue or indication of what went wrong. He carefully dissected each and every word, looking for some hidden meaning, but found none. Michael did wonder about that doctor who was helping her. They did have lunch together, but how could a single hour sharing lunch be more meaningful than all the years he and Cindy shared. It just did not make any sense.

At first, he would wait for old Ben to drive by, hoping he would stop at their mailbox. Michael would call out as he passed, asking if Ben might have forgotten to stop. Ben would shake his head, feeling sorry for the recipient of so many past letters that now surprisingly ceased. Eventually, Michael would only make one trip to the mailbox at the end of the day. Finding either no mail or just other mail not from Cindy, Michael's face would show the toll this was taking. Even at his part-time job at the general store, customers would note Michael's solemn appearance. In the beginning, they would ask how Cindy was doing. But after seeing the sad and dejected look on Michael's face, they would no longer ask.

Even Betty Miller noticed the change in her new neighbor. At first, she would ask Michael how Cindy was doing, and she would watch his face light up as he would begin describing in detail what Cindy had written. Now Betty felt sad for her former school classmate. She had seen him slowly digress from being someone happy and full of life to someone that was now just trying to get through another day.

At night, Michael would take out Cindy's picture and stare at it. First, he would think back at all the happy memories they shared. Then he would wonder what changed. The thought that something terrible could have happened to her frightened him, but so did the possibility that she was fine but had just lost interest in him. He could not decide which was worse, as he hated the prospect of either scenario being true.

As he was up in his room, he would write two letters tonight. The first would be easy. The second would be the hardest thing he would have ever written. Grabbing a sheet of paper, he started the first.

March 1, 1941

Matthew,

I hope you are okay. I know you were thinking of coming home for a visit when you start your leave in a couple of weeks, but before you do, I need a big favor. I haven't heard from Cindy in weeks. I don't know what is going on. I had given you her addresses at home and work previously. I need you to try and find her, and if you can, ask her why she stopped writing. I need to know. It's driving me crazy.

Thanks,

Michael

The following letter would be tough to write, but it was something that Michael knew he had to do. With a fresh sheet of paper, Michael chose his words carefully, knowing that these words may well be the last words he will have ever written to Cindy.

March 1, 1941

My Dearest Cindy,

At least, I hope that I still deserve the right to call you that. Unfortunately, I have not heard from you in three weeks. During that time, I had written you each day, just as I had every day since you left.

Not being able to know why is making me crazy. I fear that something horrible may have happened to you. If that is the case, not knowing saddens my heart. I hope that you are well, and I will still eventually hear from you.

I have asked Matthew to try to reach out to you. If he can contact you, please let him know why you stopped writing.

I am also fearful of the possibility that there might be another reason for you not writing. Maybe you no longer care for me, the way I care about you. That this might be the case saddens me also, especially not knowing why. If I did anything wrong, I am sorry. If I didn't do something I should have, I am sorry for that also.

If you receive this letter, please let me know which of my fears are actual. As much as I hope that it is not the latter, I would prefer it for your safe being and happiness. Despite what you think of me or how you feel about us, I would rather you be happy without me than me being sad not having you.

This letter will be my last letter to you. I will not trouble you with any more. Again, I hope to hear back from you, but if not, I will try to understand. No matter what, I will love you forever, and you will always be my girl.

Love, Michael

After finishing Cindy's letter, Michael sealed it in an envelope addressed to her. He would mail it tomorrow when he would be in town, not knowing if she would receive it or if she even cared, again wondering which were the lesser of the two evils. Finally, Michael would go to bed tonight wondering if he would ever have the occasion to write her name again. But before he would try to go to sleep, he took out her picture. Looking at it, he just said one word, "Why?"

Eunice observed her daughter's reaction with each passing day of not receiving any letters from Michael. It continued to progress to annoyance, frustration, worry, concern, and now complete bewilderment from what began as a mild disappointment. Like Michael, Cindy started questioning what, if anything, she might have said or done to upset Michael. And like Michael, despite all her soul searching, she could not think of anything.

Seeing now how disturbed Cindy had become, Eunice felt it was time to go for the kill and finish off their romance once and for all. Since sneaking a look at Michael's letter last month that mentioned Betty Miller and how Betty's family bought their old farm, she had devised a lie that would seal Michael's fate for good. Like an ace up her sleeve, she kept it handy, ready to use at the right time. Considering Cindy's now fragile state, this was the time.

"Another day with no mail from the Johnson boy, I see," her mother said gleefully.

"No, and his name is Michael," Cindy shot back.

"Well, if you ask me, it looks like he's lost interest in you."

"Why would he. There would be no reason," Cindy answered.

"There might be a perfect reason, and it's right next door to Michael, living in our old house," her mother said, baiting Cindy.

"What are you talking about?"

"You remember our cousin Bertha who lives in Guymon, well I got a letter from her a couple of weeks ago. I didn't want to mention it at the time because I didn't want to upset you. She heard about our old farm now owned by that Miller Family." Eunice paused, having to sort out the fact from the fiction as she continued her bogus tale. "So, she drove over to Goodwell and was driving past the farm when she saw your Michael with that Betty Miller girl. They were walking hand-in-hand and looking mighty cozy when all of a sudden they began kissing. She watched as they went into the barn. When they hadn't come out after a while, Bertha finally left. You of all people should know what can go on in that barn, muddy shoes and all," lied Eunice, except for the fact about the muddy shoes.

"I don't believe it. Michael isn't like that," Cindy replied.

"All men are capable of that," her mother said, seeing that she was making progress by the look of concern on Cindy's face.

"And why are you telling me this now?" Cindy said as she was getting more upset.

"Because I was worried how you would react to hearing this. I didn't want you to be upset," Eunice said deceitfully and trying her best to portray herself as a caring mother.

Cindy was now both heartbroken and confused. Her heart did not want to believe what her mother was saying. But what the cousin reportedly had written did seem to explain why the letters stopped.

"Maybe she was mistaken by what she saw. It might have been Michael's brother, Paul. From a distance, they look alike," Cindy said hopefully.

Not wanting Cindy to have doubts, Eunice added rather convincingly, "That's what I had thought. But then I got another letter from Bertha the next week, and she said the whole town was talking about Michael and Betty and what a nice couple they made."

"Can I see Bertha's letters?" Cindy asked, now crying.

"I'm sorry, Dear. I threw Bertha's letters out."

"I hate California. I wish we never came here," then, after a pause, Cindy said, "I wish I never met Michael."

Cindy ran to her room and slammed the door shut behind her. Her mother was now smiling, seeing that her plan had worked. Tomorrow she would pass the word to Andrew that Cindy would soon be his for the taking. Eunice would continue checking the mail for the next several days, finding just one letter from Michael. Curious, she opened it up and read it. Seeing it was Michael's last attempt to write to Cindy and seeing that Cindy would write no more, Eunice did not need to check the mailbox daily for their correspondence. She thought of destroying the confiscated letters she hid in the closet, but Eunice took evil delight in possessing them, almost as if they were trophies of her fiendish success.

Jake had just come in as Cindy had run to her room. Hearing her sobbing, he knocked on her door.

"Go away. I do not want to hear any more of what Bertha had written."

"Cindy, it's Jake. I don't know anything about Bertha. Can I please come in?"

Jake did not get a response, but not hearing a no, he slowly opened the door, finding Cindy lying on her bed.

"What do you want?" she asked between tears.

"I just want to help, but I don't know what happened."

Cindy explained everything as Jake stood there listening. Jake had not left Oklahoma being on the best of terms with Michael. There was still bad blood between them, but Jake had come to terms with his father's death, realizing it was just a tragic set of circumstances. His actions that night were in Cindy's best interests, or so he thought. But now he realized that whatever disagreements he had with Michael, his sister apparently loved him, and now she was hurting. And it was once again because of Michael. His initial reaction was one of satisfaction, knowing that Michael and Cindy would no longer be a couple. But seeing how she was reacting to the news, a part of him wished that they could still be together if it meant his sister's happiness. He was not sure what he could do besides offer support. As Cindy began to sit up, he put his arms around her and told her everything would be okay. He did not know if she believed it. Why would she? He was not sure if he could believe it himself. Not knowing what else to say, he sat there with her in silence, hoping somehow to console her.

After Jake finally left, Cindy never came out of her room the rest of that night. Before going to bed, she took out the picture of Michael and threw it in the trash can. Then, crawling under the covers, she cried herself to sleep, failing to turn her light off. Jake was on his way to retiring for the evening when he noticed her light was still on. Walking into the room, he saw Michael's picture in the trash can. He was unsure why he did it, but he took it and placed it on Cindy's dresser. Then, shutting the light off, he whispered, "Good night Sis, maybe you might want to keep this."

When Cindy woke up the following day, she had hoped it was all just a bad dream. But after realizing that it was not, she saw the picture back on her dresser. Thinking that it was fate, she picked up the picture and looked at Michael. Then before putting it back, she whispered to herself just one solitary word, "Why?"

CHAPTER 21

Rebounds

March 9, 1941

Eunice wasted no time getting the word to Andrew that Cindy was "ripe on the vine and ready to be picked." But, blinded by her lust for the opulent lifestyle she witnessed each day as a housekeeper, she failed to see that neither she nor Cindy would ever fit in with the long-range plans of Andrew Cauldwell. But for all her poor judgment, Eunice was right about one thing. Cindy was the perfect candidate for a rebound relationship. Falsely convinced that Michael had now lost interest in her and may have fallen in love with Betty Miller, she might just fall for the right guy who could sweep her off her feet. But, of course, how that might happen, San Diego style might not be at all that Oklahoma-bred Cindy would be expecting.

When Cindy showed up for work today, she wore a new outfit that she could buy with her first paycheck. It was not only her first paycheck from Pacific General Hospital, but it was her first-ever. She felt as if she had been emancipated and was now a grown woman capable of living independently. Putting on her new clothes, Cindy felt slightly less hurt from the whole breakup ordeal. She thought of herself as a new woman. When Cindy passed her reflection in a window, she stopped to look at what she saw for the first time. Wearing a blouse and skirt that helped to show off her youthful shape, she looked at the stockings on her legs, thinking how far she had come from her days on the farm. But whether she knew it or not, those same farm values would stay with her. Before turning away from her reflection, she wondered what Michael would have thought of her new image.

Andrew, if nothing else, was not a procrastinator. He had a reputation with the ladies, and he did not get it by failing to act.

Andrew had positioned himself in the main lobby, waiting for Cindy's arrival. When he saw her walk in, even he was surprised. She looked lovelier than ever, and it only made him more determined to add her to his list of conquests.

"My, aren't you looking pretty today," he told Cindy, as he made no effort to hide the fact that he was looking her up and down.

"Why, thank you, doctor. It's a new outfit," Cindy said proudly.

"Let me walk you to your office," Andrew said as he put his arm around Cindy's soft shoulder.

"I was wondering if you wouldn't mind having lunch with me. I enjoyed your company when discussing your working here and the possibility of getting into our nursing school. We can discuss those things again if you like, but I very much would want to get to know you better as a person. At the risk of seeming too presumptuous, I would like to think of this lunch as more of a date than just another work-related meeting. I do hope that you would do me the honor of being my guest at the Hanover Room. They have an excellent menu, and I personally know the chef. Besides, you look so attractive; I must admit my desire to show you off." Andrew was smiling and pouring on the charm, waiting for Cindy's answer.

"Well, yes, and thank you. I would be glad to join you for lunch."

"Fantastic, I will meet you at your office. And should we be delayed getting back, do not worry about it. I will speak with your supervisor before we leave. It is a five-star restaurant, and the food does take time to be properly prepared and served."

"Wow!" was all Cindy could think about as she entered the filing room.

Seaman 3rd class, Matthew Johnson, had just begun his annual leave with good news. The Navy approved his transfer request. After returning from leave, he would be reassigned to the Pacific Fleet, Pearl Harbor, and more specifically to the USS Enterprise after completing some radial engine repair and maintenance courses. His mechanical aptitude tests had shown him to have promise as an aircraft engine mechanic. After the hands-on training, his assignment would be to a specific plane crew, where it would be part of his responsibility to keep the plane airworthy.

As he was packing up his belongings, he had to take care of a promise he had made before hopping on the bus that would be the start of a long road trip back home. After receiving Michael's letter the other day, he wrote back promising to look up Cindy and find out why she stopped writing. Armed with the two addresses Michael provided, he decided to stop first at her work address, hoping to catch her there. If that did not work out, then he would try her at home. He did not look forward to having this conversation with Cindy, but he was obliged to do it for Michael.

It was already past the regular lunch hour when he arrived at the hospital. Having only the address, he stopped at the information desk inquiring about which department Cindy worked at in the large medical center. Then, still wearing his Navy uniform, the good-looking Matthew caught the attention of Cindy's co-workers when he entered the filing room.

"Yes, can I help you, Sailor?" A smiling young woman asked while a co-worker hastily put on some fresh lipstick and tuck her blouse into her skirt to enhance her figure.

"I hope you can. I'm looking for Cindy Smith," Matthew asked as he looked about the room.

"She's not here. She should be back soon. But, quite frankly, she's late," she replied, looking at the clock and thinking that it was not fair that Cindy had this seaman asking for her also.

"Maybe I'll just wait out in the lobby," he said.

"Would you like to leave a message?"

"No thanks, that won't be necessary."

Just then, one of the other young women walked up to Matthew, saying, "If she's dumping you for her new doctor friend, I might be available. You can always find me here."

Michael was taken back, not by the woman's brashness which he found flattering, but by her statement. Did Cindy have a new boyfriend? He owed it to Michael to find out.

"Thanks for the info and the offer, but I'm shipping out after this," he said, smiling back at the young lady.

"Too bad. But good luck with Cindy," she said as he left the room.

"Good luck with Cindy," what did she mean by that? Matthew found a comfortable chair and sat down as he pondered these thoughts, clearly viewing the hospital entrance.

Several blocks away, Cindy and Andrew had finished eating. If Andrew wanted to impress Cindy with food, he was highly successful.

"That was the best beef I ever ate. What was it called again?" Cindy asked.

"Chateaubriand," Andrew said, feeling good about his menu selection.

"A girl could get used to eating like this," Cindy said, not realizing the implications that went with her statement.

"Well, we'll have to see what we can do about that," Andrew said, trying to hide his satisfaction.

"What time is it?" Cindy inquired.

"Two-fifteen," the doctor replied, looking at his watch.

"I can't believe it's that late. I should have been back long ago."

"That's not for you to worry about, remember?"

As they walked back to the hospital, Andrew decided to up his game a notch, seeing how well lunch went.

"There's a formal dance at my country club next weekend. I would love for you to be my date."

"I would love to go, but I wouldn't have anything that nice to wear," Cindy said, apologizing.

"Nonsense. After you get off from work, meet me at my office. My mother uses a dress shop just down the block that has exquisite gowns. Let them fit you with one. It will be my gift to you," Andrew offered, knowing that this would indebt Cindy to him even more.

"I can't allow you to do that. It's too much." Cindy responded.

"No, I insist. I want you to be the most beautiful woman there." So at least he was truthful about one thing he said today.

They were about to enter the hospital lobby when he went with the clincher. "Oh, there's one more thing. I have great news. I spoke with the nursing school director, and they are accepting you into their spring class, which begins next month."

Just as he said it, Matthew saw Andrew and Cindy coming inside. Matthew had stood up and was about to walk over to them when Cindy threw her arms around Andrew, thanking him for getting her into nursing school. Matthew could not hear what she said, but he felt that her actions spoke louder than her words. He would renege on his promise to Michael that he would ask Cindy why she stopped writing. He felt that any explanation she gave was meaningless considering what he just saw. Added to what her co-workers had said earlier, he was sure that Cindy and her new doctor friend were dating. Matthew waited until Cindy was out of sight, then he left the building. As he was heading back to the base for the last time, he began thinking that his long trip home would now be even longer, as Matthew would try to think how he would break the news to Michael.

For a road that for most of its 2,448 miles was nowhere close to any navigable waterways, let alone an ocean, the last thing Matthew would have thought was that another member of the U.S. Navy had an indirect role in creating the highway. Yet, in 1857, Navy Lieutenant Edward Fitzgerald Beale was attached to the Army's Corps of Topographical Engineers. Under orders from the War Department, he oversaw building a wagon road from California to New Mexico. The government had been considering camels as pack animals in the hot and dry desert of the south-western United States. His job was also to test the feasibility of using camels for such a purpose. Although the camels were proven to be hardy and well suited for their intended use, the subsequent outbreak of the civil war hampered the experiment, and the idea of a U.S. Camel Corps came to an end nine years later.

Nearly a century later, Seaman Matthew Johnson was riding along a stretch of highway that was part of that original wagon trail. He was looking out the window as the bus continued its journey east along Route 66. Matthew would wake up to sights dissimilar to what he had last seen before dozing off in between catching a short nap. Now that it left the heat of the low-lying southwest desert, the bus had been slowly and steadily climbing in altitude when it approached Flagstaff, Arizona. There, he saw the winter snows covering the higher elevations of nearby Mount Elden, rising to 9,301 feet above sea level.

Other than the commercial establishments that lined the sides of the highway in the more heavily populated areas, most of the trip involved long stretches of undeveloped lands. Matthew's attention turned to the inside of the bus, with nothing new or unique to see outside. He would look at the other passengers and try to guess what the purpose of their trip was. The bus had been about half full since he left the naval base back in San Diego. Many of the original passengers were sailors like himself. Their numbers had steadily declined with each stop the bus made, as his fellow passengers would exit having reached their final destinations. Others, mostly civilians, would later get on or depart, providing for an ever-changing mix of passengers, each with their specific reasons for traveling.

Matthew's original reason for traveling was to take advantage of his accrued leave and make a visit back home to Goodwell. Unfortunately, it would be quite some time before he would again have this opportunity. When he would report back to San Diego, he would fly out on the next available hop to Pearl Harbor. Then he would join the USS Enterprise for what he hoped would be a satisfying deployment. But now, he was carrying the added burden of having to report on his failed attempt to speak with Cindy. He did not bother to send a letter to Michael outlining what had occurred at the hospital two days ago since he would most likely arrive at the family farm before his letter would. In some respects, he wished he had been able to have Michael find out about it before his arrival. At least then, the initial shock of the news would have been over. But now, it would be up to him to give Michael the sad news that Cindy had apparently moved on and was dating someone else.

Meanwhile, back in San Diego, Cindy was already taking the next steps to move on. After work, Andrew took her to the dress shop, and as promised, he had her fitted for an evening gown that would be the envy of any San Diego socialite. As the seamstress was taking straight pins from her clenched mouth and using them to temporarily adjust the fabric to conform perfectly with Cindy's shapely body, Andrew looked on approvingly. Even Cindy, seeing her reflection in the three-paneled mirror, had to pause and think if this was just all a dream. Finally, when the seamstress had tucked in the black satin fabric in all the right places, she looked to both Cindy and Andrew for their approvals. After receiving nods from both, she escorted Cindy to a three-piece privacy panel where she awaited the removal of the gown from Cindy. After putting her street clothes back on, Cindy walked out from behind the panels.

"You looked fantastic!" Andrew exclaimed.

"Thank you, the gown is amazing."

"You make it look better when it's on you," Andrew said.

"This is like a fairy tale come true," Cindy said, hugging Andrew.

"You'll look even more lovely when I get to show you off at the country club."

"There is a small problem. I probably should have said something sooner," Cindy said, now feeling embarrassed.

"And what could that possibly be?" inquired Andrew.

"Coming from where I grew up, there wasn't much opportunity for dancing. So I only got to try out a few steps, and I'm not very good. I don't want to embarrass you."

"That's not a problem. You will do just fine. Besides, there are other things that we can do besides dancing." Andrew was now smiling.

"I really cannot thank you enough," Cindy said, not fully appreciating why Andrew was smiling.

As they left the shop, Andrew turned to the seamstress and said, "She will pick it up no later than Friday. Please bill this to my mother's account."

"Yes, of course, Doctor Cauldwell," she said as she was putting the gown aside, awaiting alterations.

"Thank you again, Andrew," Cindy said as she started to walk to her bus stop.

"Where are you going? I have my car. Let me drive you home."

"I don't want to be a bother," Cindy said.

"Nonsense. I insist. It's parked right up the block."

Seeing Andrew's 1939, ruby-red Cadillac Lasalle convertible, Cindy had to stop to admire it. It was a far cry from the beat-up old Model-T that brought her to California.

"It's a beauty, is it not?" Andrew asked, but it was more as a statement than a question.

Opening the door for Cindy, she stepped in, still admiring the car. After he got in on the driver's side, he started the powerful engine and pulled away. Cindy could not help but comment on how comfortable the seat felt as they drove to her home.

One thousand miles east, Matthew was squirming in his seat, not nearly as comfortable as Cindy was in her drive home in Doctor Cauldwell's luxury convertible. His naps were restless, not only from the unforgiving rigidness of his seat but from the worry of breaking the news to his younger brother. The bus ride was long, but it would soon be coming to an end. When the bus finally pulled up to his stop, Matthew grabbed his seabag and exited the bus. As he walked down the narrow aisle, he stopped briefly to smile at a small boy who had been waving to him earlier. Then, he said goodbye to the driver and thanked him as he stepped down from the bus.

Andrew had pulled up to the small and modest home that Cindy, her mom, and Jake were renting. Seeing the exterior in dire need of a paint job, Andrew cringed at the prospect of having to live in such inferior housing. He thought how odd it was that someone as attractive as Cindy could live in such a place. But as distracted as Andrew was by her home, he quickly focused back on his game plan. He had successfully gained her confidence, and he was winning her over with his good looks, charm, and abundant wealth. Despite Cindy's enduring qualities that would make her a great wife and long-term companion, Andrew had only one thought in mind: it had nothing to do with marriage. To Andrew, Cindy was no more than the next in line of women eager to satisfy his immense ego and fulfill his sexual needs. The fact that she was both innocent and vulnerable did not matter. Besides, the thought of being with just one woman, especially an "Okie," was repelling to him. He was fantasizing about what it would be like having her beautiful body to ravage, especially since her Mom had told him that Cindy was still a virgin. He wondered whether it would be weeks or months before he would tire of her and move on to his next conquest, but right now, he thought that this Saturday would be the time for him to make his move.

"We're here," he said gleefully.

Acting as the gentleman he was not, he walked around to Cindy's door and opened it.

"Don't forget to pick up your gown. I will be picking you up here at six o'clock sharp on Saturday." He said, holding her hand as he helped her out of the car.

"I will definitely be ready." Then, Cindy said, "Thank you," as she kissed Andrew on his cheek.

"You are very welcome," Andrew replied, thinking that he better get a lot more than that on Saturday after spending all that money on her gown.

As Cindy opened the door to the house, she looked back at Andrew and waved goodbye, wondering if this would turn into something promising. But, unfortunately, the sudden thought of Michael momentarily dampened her expectations.

The sun was as high in the sky as was possible for a late-winter afternoon. Since Matthew's family had no way of knowing which bus he had taken leaving San Diego, his expectation that there would be someone waiting there to greet him was low. But he still searched the vicinity, hoping to catch a glimpse of either the family's pickup truck parked nearby or the smiling faces of either Michael, Paul, or his dad. Seeing neither, he slung his navy seabag over his shoulder and began walking in the direction of his childhood home. Fortunately, in a town where nearly everybody knew one another and seeing a man in uniform walking along the side of the road in need of a lift, it was not long before he heard a car slowing down as it approached him from the rear. Turning around, he recognized Ben Miller. Michael had written to him and had mentioned that the Miller's had bought the Smith's old farm. Sitting next to him was an attractive brunette that he failed to recognize.

"Need a lift, Sailor?" Ben asked, not immediately knowing it was his new neighbor.

"Thanks, Mr. Miller. I sure do," Matthew said appreciatively.

"Matthew Johnson, is that you? I didn't recognize you at first. So what's it been, about seven years," Ben Miller said, looking at how much Matthew had grown.

"I reckon it has been about that long. I heard from Michael that you bought the old Smith farm."

"Couldn't take the California lifestyle. The weather's great, but there's still something about this place that made us come back. You remember Betty," he said, indicating to his daughter.

"Sure," Matthew said, not wanting to admit that he didn't. She had obviously changed dramatically since she and his brother Michael had been classmates.

"Good to see you again," Betty said, thinking how much he had grown also.

Betty had always thought that the Johnson boys were a good-looking bunch. And now, a grown-up Matthew in uniform did nothing to change her opinion. But thinking back, she never had a childhood crush on Matthew as she had with Michael and even Paul, who was three years her senior. Of course, with Michael and Cindy being friends all their lives, she had never really considered the possibility of having a romantic relationship with Michael.

"How is Michael doing? I heard Cindy is living in San Diego, not far from the navy base. Have you been able to see her? Betty asked, more than just a little bit curious and knowing about how Michael's mood had changed.

"She's doing okay, I guess. I suspect she's moved on in her life," Matthew offered, thinking that this was almost a rehearsal for what he would soon be telling Michael.

Matthew's lack of follow-up and the awkward silence that followed told Betty more than just the words he had spoken.

"Here we are," Ben said as they pulled up to the entrance to the Johnson farm.

"Thanks for the lift. It was good seeing you both," Matthew said as he grabbed his seabag from the back and once again threw it over his shoulders as he began walking the final three-hundred-feet to his house.

"Tell Michael I said hi," Betty shouted as her dad was driving away.

Matthew's mother was the first to see him. After the initial hugs, she stood back to get a better look at him in his uniform. Then it was Grace's turn as she came out of the kitchen. Matthew had barely finished embracing her when Rebekah ran up to him and jumped into his arms, kissing him on his cheek.

"Your Pa, Paul, and Michael are out by the barn. I'm sure they must have heard you coming," his mother said.

Matthew walked outside to see the male members of the family coming to greet him. That included Shep, who was barking as he ran up to him. He knelt as he rubbed Shep as the family dog licked Matthew's face in return. Michael had been running and was the first to hug Matthew. Paul soon followed, and after a brief hug, they shook hands, Matthew instantly remembering that accident, as he felt just three fingers on Paul's right hand. His father was the last to greet him but not any less happy than the others. After yet another warm embrace, like his wife earlier, Philip took a couple of steps back to get a better look at his son in uniform. Matthew detected what he thought was some moistness in his father's proud eyes.

As they all were heading into the house, Michael pulled Matthew aside. Michael could not wait to ask the question, the answer of which had been troubling Matthew for the past couple of days.

"Did you get to see Cindy? What did she say? Why no more letters?"

It turned out to be not one but three questions. But they all required the same answer. Finally, Matthew put his arm around Michael and stopped walking. Michael looked at Matthew with increasing unease as he waited to hear the answers to his questions.

Taking a deep breath, Matthew began. "You're not going to like what I'm about to say, but I didn't talk to Cindy. I didn't need to. I went to see her at the hospital and ask as you wanted, but...." Matthew stopped in mid-sentence, finding it hard to continue.

"But, what?" Michael demanded to know.

"She's got a new boyfriend. They seemed pretty close, and she looked happy. She's moved on with her new life, and as much as I hate to say it, Little Brother, I think it's time for you also."

"No. That just can't be. Not even a letter to let me know. I can't believe it."

"I saw it with my own eyes," Matthew said, feeling horrible for having to have said it.

Michael walked away slowly and went up to his room alone. Inside he took out the picture of Cindy. Part of him wanted to tear up the photograph into tiny pieces and throw it away. Yet another part of him could not bear to part with it, no matter what the circumstances were. The latter won out, and he put the picture back, still there to be looked at each night. At dinner, Matthew mentioned that the Miller's had driven him to the farm and that Betty Miller had grown up to be a beautiful young woman. Both of his brothers took an interest in his comments. Michael, in particular, thought back to when Betty had given him that Valentine card before a six-year-old Cindy had the opportunity to have given her card to him first. He remembered how jealous Cindy was at the time. All these years later, Michael was now the jealous one, jealous of someone he did not know. Maybe Matthew was right, he thought. He did not want to give up entirely on the hope of winning back Cindy. But if Cindy had moved on with her new life, maybe it was also time for him. Michael made a mental note for himself to stop by and see Betty first thing tomorrow morning.

CHAPTER 22

Exposed

March 14, 1941

In 1882, a group of wealthy men from the social elite of Boston decided to establish a club that would provide activities for them and their families in a cordial yet fraternal organization. It was unlike the typical downtown men's club that was popular in the major cities. In its pastoral setting, with trees and expansive lawns, the family could enjoy activities such as tennis, horseback riding, and dining. However, the clubs remained exclusive, as members would be by invitation only. Even with its goal to provide for the entire family's enjoyment, participation on the golf course could be enjoyed only by the male members. There, men could still be men and discuss things that were best not said in mixed company. So, just four miles from the center of Boston, in the suburb of Brookline, Massachusetts, The Country Club of Brookline became the nation's first country club. Now, on the opposite coast of the United States, four well-to-do men from San Diego's elite were carrying on in that same tradition.

"Nice drive," Dr. Andrew Cauldwell said to one of three other members of his foursome.

"Thanks, but it took me eighteen holes before I got a decent tee shot.," said the player who just hit.

"Now watch this," Andrew said while teeing up his ball. Then, looking down the lush green fairway, he added, "Caddie, give me my two wood."

Taking his time to address the ball, Andrew went into his backswing, and at the right moment, he swung his club down in a smooth arc, making full contact with the dimpled white golf ball. Continuing with his follow-through, he was facing forward as he picked up the flight of the ball, watching it easily out-distance his opponent by a good twenty yards.

"I give up. I don't know how you do it. You must have a magic touch," said another member of their group.

"If you think this is good, you should watch me tonight at the gala. I'll be there with this hot, young "Okie." Just eighteen years old and waiting for the good doctor to make his move," Cauldwell said, boasting, as he handed his club to his caddie.

"Can't you speak more than two sentences about non-medical things without having to make a sexual reference? So give it a break," said Doctor Robert Barnes, the fourth member.

"Is someone envious, or perhaps jealous?" Andrew asked mockingly.

"Envious of your lifestyle? I think not. Jealous of the young woman you are planning to deflower. I think not also," replied Robert.

"You never minded hearing of my exploits before, if I remember correctly."

"Yes, but now that's all I hear about, and frankly, Andrew, enough is enough," Robert shot back.

"Why do you care about her. What's she to you?"

"I have a daughter who's going to be eighteen in two years, and when I think of that sweet innocent girl you're bringing tonight, I can't help to think, what if that was my Veronica? Cindy, is that her name? She's not like most of the others you dated. She's not used to being with someone like you. So you should break it off."

"I hope not until I had a chance to use it," Andrew replied as he grabbed his crotch, feigning injury and earning laughs from the other two golfers.

"I'm leaving," Robert said with disgust as he turned away from the last green and started walking back to the clubhouse, his confused caddie running to catch up.

Cindy had hung the hanger over her bedroom door. Then, stepping back, she looked at the ankle-length gown admiring its classic design and the quality of its material and craftsmanship.

Cindy allowed herself the luxury of imagining what it would be like to live in a world where clothes like this were the norm and not the fantasy. But, unlike her mother, she was not jumping ahead to any conclusions or even optimistic hopes about any future she might have with Andrew. He was well-educated, polite, extremely well-bred, and wealthy. And he seemed to have a knack for knowing what to say at the right time. She instinctively began comparing him to Michael but soon realized that the only thing Andrew lacked was that he was not Michael.

She had been excited all week at work, looking forward to tonight's big date. It would be so unlike anything she had ever experienced previously. Before this, the most elaborate dates she had gone on with Michael were to the movies. Of course, she was not counting their failed attempt to go to Sonny's Roadhouse that tragic and eventful night. Thinking back, she realized the part that fate had played getting her to this point. Had her father not died that night, they probably would never have moved, and she would still be in Oklahoma dating Michael. She wondered if this was her true destiny and just how much a role fate had played in getting her here.

Yet, despite her excitement and anticipation of the up-coming evening, it did not come without some minor concerns. She had not thought of it at the time, and Andrew never realized it, but she had no shoes to go with the gown. So, both reluctant and embarrassed to say anything to Andrew, she went out on her own to buy a pair of high heels that would complement her gown. She was shocked to see that her shoes would cost her nearly a week's pay, but she hoped that she would get much use of them in the future.

Of more concern were the hints and warnings she was get-ting from her co-workers about Andrew. At first, she thought it was from some petty envy on their part. But it was too consistent among most of the women who worked in the hospital. It should have raised some red flags on Cindy's part, but despite being told that he would never be willing to enter into a long-term relation-ship with any woman, let alone an "Okie," Cindy was willing to wait and see for herself. After all, she was not a "loose woman," and he did seem to be a perfect gentleman. Besides, she was no longer some wild-eyed kid from the Panhandle. Instead, she was an eighteen-year-old woman working to support herself and would soon be entering nursing school.

Her mother seemed to be more excited about tonight's date than Cindy was. Cindy never remembered her mother taking such an interest in her choices or activities in all her life. Still, today she was either advising or instructing her in just about everything. Yet, as enthusiastic as Eunice had been, Jake seemed just the opposite. Her brother had never met Andrew, but he admitted to having a strong distaste for him, as well as the class of society he represented. Cindy chalked it up to the fact that Jake was just an overprotective older brother. After all, it was he who went with her father to save her virtue at the roadhouse. At first, Cindy resented his interference, but now she found it reassuring. With Michael no longer there to look out for "his girl," at least she had Jake. Although there would be no need for him to protect her, it was nice knowing that he could be counted upon if necessary.

In an ironic turn of events, just as Cindy's mother had changed after coming to California, so too had Jake. The difference being that as their mother seemed to have gotten worse with her values and expectations, Jake had gotten better. He seemed more mature and had a plan for his life. He made the break from farming, just as Michael's brother Matthew had, and like Matthew, he was considering enlisting in the Navy. His and Cindy's relationships with their mother could have been better, but the fact that it had not been was through no fault of their own. As bad as Eunice had been attempting to control Cindy's life back in Oklahoma, she seemed even more determined to set out a course for Cindy that appeared to be more aligned with her interests rather than her daughter's. And with him seemingly having no set goals, she was constantly chastising Jake for not joining his brothers working on the farms up north. Then if Eunice was not extolling the virtues of Andrew to Cindy, she was criticizing Jake for not being more like Andrew.

Cindy checked the time. It was 5:45, and Andrew would be here in fifteen minutes. She looked at herself in the mirror and found it hard to believe she was looking at herself. Her gown fit perfectly, and it accented curves even Cindy did not realize she had. Never one for using or needing make-up, she did apply the perfect shade of lipstick to her smooth, moist lips. Even without the benefit of an expensive hair salon, her naturally curly auburn hair perfectly framed her pretty face. Being just eighteen had its benefits, and her perfect complexion required no face creams or powders. Even in the dim light, her bright hazel eyes seemed to sparkle.

Her mother was passing by and stopped to look at Cindy. She examined her as if she was inspecting a young foal to be bought and added to the stable. Then, approving, she told Cindy she looked beautiful. Never one to hold back on her opinion, Eunice said, "Now you have a chance to make something of your life, our lives. You be nice to Dr. Cauldwell and don't mess up this opportunity. You are, after all, a young woman." Eunice had purposely emphasized the word "woman."

Cindy disregarded much of what her mother had been saying lately, and this would be no different.

"Don't become like your brother, Jake. I don't know what's wrong with him. He didn't want to be a farmer. He doesn't have a job, and all he keeps talking about is joining the Navy. He's not even here to see his sister on her big night out. Instead, he's out gallivanting with some friends he made while hanging out by the navy base. If only your father were alive now. But we have that Johnson boy to thank for that."

"Ma, I just don't want to talk about it. And besides, there's nothing wrong with serving your country. Even Pa had been in the army during the Great War. Please, just let me enjoy myself tonight."

"It won't hurt to let Andrew enjoy himself also. I was just seventeen when I had Caleb. Your Pa was a decent man, but look where it got him. Look where it got me. I'm cleaning the home of rich people you could be married to."

At that time, Cindy heard the distinctive sound of Andrew's powerful convertible pulling up in front of their house. Disregarding her mother, she walked away and waited for Andrew to come to the front door. Shortly after that, Cindy heard two quick knocks against the old wooden door with its blistering paint. Taking a deep breath first, she opened the door to see Andrew smiling at her. Dressed in a black tuxedo, complete with a black bow tie, he held a corsage in his hand.

"Hi. This corsage is for you," Andrew said as he began to affix it to one of the straps on Cindy's gown.

"Thank you. The flowers are a surprise. I wasn't expecting

it."

"It's the least I can do. By the way, you look stunning."

Cindy was not quite sure what to say, so she smiled and thanked him with her eyes.

"Now, if you'll accompany me, we have a gala to go to," Andrew said as he walked Cindy to his car.

With light traffic, they arrived at the country club in less than twenty minutes. From the time they pulled into the large, curved driveway, Cindy was awed at the luxury of everything. First, the club's valet opened her door, while another opened Andrew's and replaced him in the driver's seat. When they were safely out of the vehicle, an attendant drove the car away until needed later. Next, another well-dressed and well-groomed employee opened the doors to the clubhouse. Cindy stared at the others inside the large room, almost as much as the male guests stared at her. While a string quartet was playing chamber music, a dozen servers, wearing tuxedos and expressionless faces, were carrying unlimited offerings of drinks and appetizers, each on silver serving trays and platters. Andrew took two narrow glasses and handed one to Cindy, mesmerized at the sparkling bubbles.

"This is champagne. You'll find it quite tasty, and it has other benefits," Andrew said without elaborating on what the benefits might be.

"Oh, it tickles my nose," Cindy exclaimed, having drunk it too quickly.

"Just savor it a little at a time, and you'll get used to it," Andrew said.

Andrew took Cindy's hand and began leading her through the maze of guests, introducing her to as many as he could. After the first few introductions, Cindy gave up on trying to remember the names of people she might never have occasion to talk to again. Cindy was amazed that Andrew knew all of their names, and they knew his name also. Despite all the glamour and glitz surrounding her, Cindy found herself not nearly as impressed by the guests. She felt that she was being paraded about by Andrew, who would seek their approval of her. Although they were more than polite when first introduced, sometimes she would glance back and see them now talking among themselves, as they would look disapprovingly at her. Probably because of her hard-working and straightforward upbringing, Cindy felt more of a connection with the service staff than the stuffy clientele they were tending to. Of course, she failed to realize that they shared no such bond with her, not knowing her background. She was also beginning to feel a bit uncomfortable as she noticed a group of three men staring at her. One of the men said something to the others, and they all began snickering among themselves while continuing to leer at her. On more than one occasion, she found herself under the watchful eyes of some of the wives. While some women seemed to be showing disdain at the approving glances of their husbands, the others almost seemed to be expressing pity for her as they would slowly shake their heads from side to side.

After several uncomfortable minutes of mingling with the other guests, the maître d'hôtel finally announced that dinner was now being served in the main dining room. As Andrew escorted Cindy to their seats, she watched as a small army of servers scurried about, filling glasses with water and delivering baskets of freshly baked bread to each table. Each table had its waiter, who was presently taking drink orders in addition to each diner's choice of tonight's entrees. Without waiting for Cindy's response, Andrew ordered another champagne while he ordered a dry martini. After she was seated, Cindy glanced about the large round table and the four other couples who would be her and Andrew's dinner companions for the evening. Once again, introductions began anew as Andrew was re-introducing Cindy to the other couples. When a few of them politely said Andrew already introduced them, she felt some comfort knowing that even he had forgotten that. Seated next to them on her left were Doctor Barnes and his wife.

"Hello, Cindy. I'm Robert Barnes, and this is my wife, Susan. You and I met briefly at the hospital the other day."

"Why yes, Doctor, I remember you," Cindy said, extending her hand.

"Please, call me Robert. I leave the doctor part out when I am getting together with friends."

"And you can call me either Susan or Sue. I'll answer to both," Mrs. Barnes said, smiling genuinely.

"And isn't she absolutely gorgeous," Andrew said, butting into Cindy's conversation with the Barnes.

Had Cindy's attention not been turned to Andrew, she would have seen the dismayed look Robert and Susan gave each other. But the atmosphere soon changed as a twelve-piece orchestra began playing. Clad in white dinner jackets and wearing black bow ties, their first song of the evening was a rendition of Glenn Miller's "Moonlight Serenade."

"Come. This song is a slow number. You shouldn't have a problem with it, and besides, the main course is still not here," Andrew said as he finished his martini.

As he took Cindy's hand, he passed their waiter and pointed to his empty cocktail glass. The waiter nodded his head, understanding Andrew's request for another martini. Then, despite Cindy's apologies for not being by any means an accomplished dancer, he led her onto the oak parquet dance floor, glancing about to take notice of the admiring eyes that were on Cindy.

"You look lovely," he said as he held her uncomfortably close to his body.

To Cindy's credit, she did move to the beat of the music, although it was more of a slow shuffling of feet than a proper dance step. Nevertheless, she could not stop thinking that this should have been with Michael instead of Andrew, wondering if Michael and Betty Miller were doing this same thing at Sonny's back in Oklahoma. She felt uneasiness from the tight hold Andrew had on her and tried to pull back for some separation. But Andrew was more powerful, and he just pulled her closer, as he would be able to feel her firm breasts up against his chest. Fortunately, the song ended, and Cindy was able to break free.

"Thank you for the dance. I think the waiters are serving our dinner now," Cindy said, being polite, as she began walking off the dance floor.

As they all sat and began enjoying their delicious and lavishly served meals, Susan Barnes leaned over to Cindy and said, "I think I need to visit the ladies' room. Would you care to join me?" However, something in the look she gave made Cindy think it was more than just that.

"Sure. I would be glad to," Cindy replied.

As they entered the spacious lavatory, Susan took Cindy aside and looked about to see if anyone else was there. Seeing there were none, other than a middle-aged female attendant whose job was to provide clean hand towels for the country club ladies, Susan spoke softly.

"It may not be my concern, but I feel I have to say something. It's about Andrew."

"What about Andrew?"

"He has a certain reputation with the women, and it's not good. So I don't know your expectations for this evening or with Andrew going forward if that should be the case, but I feel it necessary to warn you. He's handsome and charming, and he certainly has a way with the ladies, but coming from Oklahoma and with your country upbringing, all I'm trying to say is to be careful. Your values and his values may be at opposite ends."

Cindy stood there for a moment, thinking about what Susan said. She also thought about what the other women at the hospital had mentioned the other day. A warning bell should have been ringing loudly at this point, but Cindy still felt that all people were basically decent, and even Andrew should be allowed to prove the others wrong.

"I thank you for your concern, but I think that I am capable of making my own decisions. I don't know about any future Andrew, and I may or may not have going forward. But for all he has done for me, I owe him at least this evening as his date."

When she and Susan returned to their table, Robert looked over at his wife, only to see her sadly shaking her head. Meanwhile, Andrew had just finished another martini and ordered another champagne for Cindy, who had still not finished her second.

"Come on. Let's dance before the waiters bring out the next course. The orchestra's playing another slow number," Andrew said, as he was once again dragging Cindy back out onto the dance floor.

As he was holding her close to him, Cindy decided to take a risk and ask, "Andrew, where do you see you and me next year, or even next month for that matter?"

"Why does it matter, Babe. Let's just enjoy ourselves and make the most of it,"

It was not the best answer she was hoping for, and she was a bit taken back by his calling her "Babe," but the ever-optimistic Oklahoman continued dancing the best she could.

On the other side of San Diego, Jake Smith was celebrating a significant event in his life also. After several lengthy discussions over the past weeks with Chief Petty Officer Daniel Morrison, a local Navy recruiter, Jake decided to enlist. Jake had been sworn in along with three others and was now officially in the United States Navy. CPO Morrison had taken all four of them out drinking to a local bar frequented by sailors to commemorate the occasion. After downing several beers each and having listened to the assorted tales the veteran of twenty-three years regaled them with, they decided to call it a night. Not having a car, rather than have Jake take a couple of buses to go back home, the Chief offered Jake a ride home, which he quickly accepted.

At home, Eunice was daydreaming about the luxurious life that would soon be forthcoming as long as Cindy did not mess things up with Doctor Cauldwell. As their housekeeper, Eunice's values, as well as her goals for her family, had been slowly corrupted. She had been able to see, but not experience, the lifestyles of the wealthy elite. Now, that was all within reach. To her delight, her daughter was out on a fancy date with one of the richest and most eligible bachelors in San Diego. Tonight, she would try to stay up past her regular bedtime in hopes of hearing the results of Cindy's big date.

While everyone else seemed to be having a good time, Cindy was at the very least becoming disillusioned at the way the evening was progressing. As Andrew downed yet another martini, his actions and demeanor were no longer charming. Having first being enamored of his attentions toward her, she was now finding it annoying. When he would have Cindy out on the dance floor, his hand would slide down her backside until he let it rest on her buttocks, causing her to reach down and pull it back up. Even his charming way of talking was digressing into a roguish style more likely heard in a men's locker room. His now constant use of the word "Babe" was increasingly irritating, as was his now constant references to her anatomy. Feeling that Andrew's style of slow dancing was beginning to be just an excuse to grope her, Cindy said she wanted to go home.

"Why?. The night's still young," he asked

"I'm just not feeling comfortable. I just want to go home," Cindy replied.

"Are you serious? You want to ruin a perfect party because you're uncomfortable? You have no idea what uncomfortable is." The rage in Andrew's voice was matching the anger that was building up inside him.

"Please, Andrew. I just want to go home," Cindy said, pleading with him.

"Who do you think you are? Do you think I spent the money for your gown to share dinner with me and have a couple of drinks? Do you, for one moment, believe that I took you out tonight just to have a few crummy dances with you, trying to cop a feel? Half of the women here would jump at the chance to spend the night with me, and the other half are either too old or too stupid not to." As he said it, he pointed toward a group of women guests. His raised voice caught the attention of more than a few of them, who shot him back dirty looks.

Had Cindy been more experienced in matters like this, she would have sought an alternate way of getting home. But the prospect of traveling on unknown bus routes late on a Saturday night, while dressed to the nines wearing an expensive evening gown that she could not afford, limited her options. So, seeing no other way, Cindy did what seemed the simplest. She told Andrew to take her home. After all, her only true romantic partner had been Michael in her young lifetime, and Cindy had always trusted Michael to do the right thing. Even in the barn the night of her father's funeral, when Michael was driven by the heat of passion when she told him no, he listened and obliged her request. Why then should she not expect the same from a cultured, well-bred man such as Andrew?

When the valet brought the Cadillac to the front entrance, an unhappy Andrew got into the driver's seat as the valet opened Cindy's door for her after tipping him. No sooner had she sat into her seat, Andrew sped off. Unlike the start of the evening, this ride back was in direct contrast to the earlier one. At that time, Cindy's hopes for an enjoyable and memorable night were fresh in her mind. Now, she was counting down the minutes, waiting to just get out of his car. Cindy sat silent as Andrew grumbled to himself, occasionally speaking louder when he wanted Cindy to hear.

As they pulled up in front of her house, Andrew sat silently, staring straight ahead with the engine running. Cindy, not knowing what to say, said nothing. She opened her door and began walking away. By the time Cindy heard his footsteps, it was too late. Just as she was about to turn around, she felt Andrew's strong hand grab her shoulder and violently turn her around.

"Not so quick," he shouted as he forced his lips onto hers.

"No, stop," Cindy tried to say, her words muffled by the force of Andrew's mouth against hers.

Cindy tried to pull away, but Andrew was too strong.

"You like this gown? See how much you like it now," Andrew shouted as he grabbed it by the shoulder strap that held her corsage and yanked it down, partially taking Cindy's bra with it. Seeing Cindy's partially exposed breasts only incited Andrew's sexual desires more. Fueled by a combination of lust, ego, and several martinis, Andrew pushed Cindy onto the grass. She tried to cry for help, but Andrew covered her mouth with his hand as he was now straddling her, using his other hand to pull up her gown. Cindy bit down on one of Andrew's fingers, causing him to pull it away momentarily. But he quickly struck Cindy across her face with the back of his hand, his diamond pinky ring cutting her cheek. With blood running down her cheek and faced with his superior physical abilities, Cindy's prior attempts to cry for help were now her softened cries of anguish.

Emboldened by her apparent submission, Andrew reached up underneath Cindy's gown and ripped off her panties. Then, seeing her naked from the waist down, wearing just her stockings and garter, he began to unbuckle his belt. Looking around, Andrew saw that a large hedge afforded him all the privacy he would need. An occasional car would drive by, but the shrubbery blocked their view of what was happening behind it.

"Even an 'Okie' virgin like you must have learned a few tricks back on the farm. So let's see if this was worth all the bother," he said as he was about to open his fly.

As Cindy lay there, too stunned to do anything, she began thinking of Michael and the promises they had made to each other. She closed her eyes, regretting every decision she made that got her to this point in her life, waiting for the inevitable. Andrew was obsessed with one thing only, which affected his awareness of other events nearby. As he was about to rape an eighteen-year-old woman for the sole offense of not succumbing to his will, he did not hear the car door that had opened moments ago. But Andrew did feel the two strong hands that grabbed him and pulled him off Cindy. Before he could react, his attacker threw him into the hedge that had once given him the privacy he wanted. Recovering, Andrew charged at his attacker but soon found that playing golf at the country club did not build as much muscle as working on a farm, as Jake began to manhandle him. In what almost seemed comical, Andrew tried unsuccessfully to throw a punch at Jake, but he was off-balance and fell with his trousers falling around his knees. Jake reached down, picked up the stumbling doctor, and landed a solid right uppercut to Andrew's nose, breaking it instantly. With his nose now bleeding profusely and having to breathe only through his mouth, the stunned sexual predator was ripe for a quick succession of right and left jabs that staggered him. Barely able to stand, he took one more blow to his jaw, also breaking by the power of Jake's fist. The pummeled doctor fell to the ground. Before he passed out, he looked up at his unknown assailant and wondered what had happened.

Meanwhile, Chief Petty Officer Morrison had heard the commotion and had run to see what had happened. The entire fight took less than twenty seconds. Morrison saw Jake standing defiantly over his now unconscious opponent while a partially naked young woman stood quietly against the house. Her tattered clothes were partially hanging off her, and both blood and tears were running down her pretty but frightened face.

"What happened?" Morrison asked of Jake.

"This asshole was raping my sister," Jake replied, not yet knowing that his timely intervention made it an attempted rape.

"Do you know him?" Morrison asked, looking at the man who had now passed out from his ordeal.

"I know of him, but he doesn't know me. Well, at least not until now," Jake replied

"Well, lets' keep it that way. We don't need you the subject of a police investigation, especially having just signed up," Morrison added, as the distant sound of a police siren wailing in the night appeared to be getting closer. "Just leave him. Right now, get your sister inside and stay out of sight. He doesn't know you, so he can't identify you. If the police knock on your door, just say you don't know who did it. Better still, try not to talk to them. It's up to your sister if she wants to press charges, but try to stay in the background. I got to go."

As the sound of the siren was nearing, Morrison walked over to where Andrew's prone body was lying unconscious. Thinking of Jake's young sister and having nothing but contempt for any man who would stoop so low to do what he did, Morrison looked down at Andrew and said, "You goddamned, worthless piece of shit," as he kicked Andrew in his balls as hard as he could. Then, still benefitting from the high associated with the evening's earlier beers, Morrison said, "Go Navy," and began whistling "Anchors Aweigh," as he walked back to his car,

CHAPTER 23

Retribution

March 14-16, 1941

Taking CPO Morrison's advice, Jake stayed inside when the police finally arrived. A nosy concerned neighbor had seen the initial argument and called the police, not knowing what happened later behind the hedge. When the officers arrived, they found Andrew's car with its engine still running. Under normal circumstances, an expensive car such as this would have raised a few eyebrows in this lower-class neighborhood. However, as the officers searched the immediate area, they found Andrew lying on the grass, motionless with his face covered in blood.

"He's alive. Call for an ambulance," an officer shouted to his partner.

A third officer joined them, who took note of the trousers down around Andrew's ankles. "This guy is wearing a tuxedo, driving an expensive car in this neighborhood, and he's lying here, looking like someone beat the hell out of him."

Just then, the neighbor who called the police came walking from across the street, wearing slippers and a robe that she had hastily thrown over her nightclothes.

"I'm the one who called you, officers. The driver of that convertible got into an argument with a young woman. I couldn't see what happened next because of that tall hedge. Then it got quiet until another car pulled up, and two men eventually got out. One of them went back to his car and left. I never saw the driver of the convertible leave, nor the woman who was with him or the guy who got out of the second car. Are they all okay?"

The officers did not answer the neighbor's question but instead asked a few of their own.

"Did you recognize any of them?" an officer asked.

"It was hard seeing in the dark. The fellow with the convertible was wearing a tux, and the girl wore an expensive-looking gown. Their clothes were too nice for this neighborhood."

"What about the other two who got out of the second car that pulled up? Can you describe them?"

The first guy looked to be average size, maybe a little bigger, kind of muscular. His clothes were casual, but the guy he was with was in uniform."

"What kind of uniform?"

"Navy."

"Are you sure? You said it was dark and hard to see."

"Officer, I've lived here in San Diego all my life, and my late husband, bless his soul, was stationed at the Navy base here. So I know a sailor's uniform. And it wasn't just some seaman; he was either an officer or a non-commissioned officer like my Jim was, a Chief Petty Officer. Besides, I could hear him whistling "Anchors Aweigh" when he walked back to his car."

The officers looked at each other, thinking that what they initially believed to be just a routine domestic disturbance call turned into something much more bizarre.

"What do you know about the people who live across the street?" one of the officers inquired as he looked at Cindy's house and the large hedge beside it.

"Not much. They just recently moved in. There are three of them, the mother and her daughter and her son. They pretty much keep to themselves. "Okies," they are. Most mornings, the mother walks to the bus stop, as does the daughter, a pretty little thing. They probably have jobs somewhere. The son keeps strange hours. I don't know if he works."

"Thanks, you've been very helpful," the police officer said as he began walking back across the street. He stopped at Andrew's convertible and shut the engine off, just as a white ambulance pulled up, its rotating red light alternately illuminating the crime scene as it cast its red beam. Its crew paused briefly before taking their patient, looking at the odd crime scene and its victim.

When Andrew was in the ambulance, the officer who had spoken with the neighbor walked up to the Smith's residence. Inside the house, Eunice was asleep, having slept through the entire event, failing to keep her promise to herself that she would wait up for Cindy's return. Meanwhile, Cindy observed the scene, peeking out from under the window shade of the darkened living room. As she watched, she held a handkerchief to her face as she tried to stem the flow of blood from the cut Andrew inflicted upon her.

"Police," the officer announced as he knocked three times on the house door.

Heeding Morrison's instructions, Jake stayed in his room, leaving Cindy to answer for what happened. Frightened of what might happen to Jake, she reluctantly answered the door, disregarding the fact that she was the victim in all this. Yet, she could not help thinking that this was all her fault, and if she had not gone out with Andrew, none of this would have happened.

"Yes, can I help you?" she asked through the closed door as she tried to put her attire back together as well as possible.

"Yes, we need to talk to you. Please open the door."

"Certainly, officer. I will," Cindy responded as she turned on a living room light and slowly opened the door.

"Are you okay," the officer asked, seeing Cindy holding her bloody handkerchief and the disheveled look of her once exquisite gown. Then, quickly adding, "May I come in."

By now, Eunice had awakened and came into the living room. Seeing both the police and Cindy's condition, she exclaimed, "Oh my God, what happened?"

Seeing that Eunice could shed no light on what had transpired, the officer turned his attention to Cindy as her mother just sat down in disbelief and listened.

"There was a man outside your house near the hedge. He's beaten up pretty well. We think two men might have done it. Do you know the victim?" the officer asked, wondering if Cindy was the original victim.

Not knowing what to say and finding it hard to lie, Cindy said, "Yes. His name is Doctor Andrew Cauldwell, and he was my date for this evening." Just then, Eunice gasped when she heard who the victim of the assault had been.

"Did you see what happened?" he now asked.

Taking a moment to answer, Cindy tried to divulge as little information as possible without lying any more than necessary to protect Jake. "Two men, I think. It all happened so fast. They must have been driving by when it happened."

"When what happened? Did this Doctor Cauldwell assault you?" the officer asked, looking at Cindy still holding the bloody handkerchief and observing her ripped clothes.

"I'd rather not say. I mean, I don't want to get involved. It's complicated," Cindy answered, wishing that she could tell the whole truth, but it really was complicated.

"Well, that's up to you. But I can understand it. Seeing the car he was driving and the fact that the Cauldwell name is well known here, I appreciate your reluctance to press charges. The legal system sometimes has two sets of standards, one for people like him and the other for the rest of us. Are you sure you are okay? Do you need to go to the hospital?"

"I will be okay. The cut will heal, and those Good Samaritans kept things from getting too out of hand. Thank you, officer, for your concern," Cindy said sincerely.

"If it's any comfort, the beating that he took was probably far worse than any punishment the courts might have given him. Especially with a bunch of high-priced, fancy attorneys," the officer said in leaving, looking at Cindy and feeling sorry for her.

As he was walking out the door, the officer stopped and turned back to Cindy. "By the way, they are taking him to Pacific General Hospital." Then thinking about what the neighbor said about only the one Navy man leaving and suspecting that the other man who went to her aid might have been her brother, he added, "And when you see that Good Samaritan, make sure you tell him thanks. I have a feeling that he could show up at any time," as the officer looked toward the hallway that led to the other rooms.

Eunice sat there stunned the entire time. Her expression was blank, and Cindy did not know what her mother's reaction would be. Any chance it was concern for her daughter's safety and well-being would soon be put to rest as Jake emerged from his room. Seeing her brother, Cindy thanked him for the first time as she threw her arms around him.

"Thank you so much." She said, nearly crying. "If you hadn't shown up when you did, I don't know what would have happened." Although truth be told, Cindy knew what exactly would have happened.

As Cindy was still hugging Jake, Eunice saw Jake's bruised and bloody knuckles. Finally standing up from her chair, her face filled with rage as she began screaming at Jake.

"Have you any idea what you have done? You have ruined me. How can I go to work after what happened?"

Then, looking at Cindy, she shouted, "And you. All you had to do was be nice to him. Was that too much to ask? Now I have to get another job, and it won't be working for someone like the Cauldwell's."

Cindy was about to respond to her mother's outburst, but Jake spoke up first.

"You are a mean and insensitive excuse for a mother. Your daughter was about to be raped by that son-of-a-bitch whose family you obsess over. But all you care about is yourself. Well, I was going to tell you anyway, but I enlisted in the Navy. So I am officially in, and when I start basic training, it will be good riddance to you." Jake then went back into his room, slamming the door behind him.

Eunice was now looking at Cindy. "Well, are you going to leave also?" she asked sarcastically.

"My life now is no bed of roses either. I had a job at the hospital, and I was going to nursing school next month, but now that's probably not going to happen. But I'm sure you don't care about that. Jake is right. All you really care about is yourself. Maybe you never really were a great mother, but ever since Pa died, you've gotten worse. I'd leave here too if I could, but right now, I'm stuck. I'm stuck in this house, and I'm stuck living here with you."

Cindy returned to her room and started crying. The bleeding had slowed enough that she was able to put a bandage on the gash for now. She took the photograph of Michael from her dresser and looked at it as she sat on her bed. Seeing him made her cry even more. Holding the photo, she quietly whispered to herself, "Michael, why couldn't you have been here tonight? Why did you stop loving me? I hate you. I hate you. I hate you." She cried herself to sleep, not bothering to change out of her torn and tattered gown. Although the words said otherwise, in her heart, she fell asleep, knowing she could never stop loving Michael. It had always been so, and tonight she realized it even more.

That Sunday morning, Cindy was already planning not to go to work on Monday. It would be all too embarrassing. But, of course, that would be if she still had a job. That, along with her nursing future, would probably soon be ended by Andrew anyway. Meanwhile, Jake was preparing for his basic training to begin. Since he would be undergoing boot camp right here in San Diego, at least she would get to see him from time to time. She needed some normalcy in her life, which would help her get through the tough times she envisioned. She had gone to a local church of the same Baptist denomination she had gone to back in Oklahoma. She found some solace in the sense of community that the congregation provided, and the pastor's words provided some encouragement that her life was not over. But it would take quite a while to get over the memory of last night.

Her mother had left the house on Monday without saying a word to Cindy. Eunice had acted as if Cindy had been invisible. Nevertheless, Cindy had been able to say her goodbyes to Jake as he left for the Navy Base, thanking him once again for what he had done. She thought it ironic that they would wind up here because of him and her father unnecessarily attempting to protect her virtue from Michael. And because of it, he had to defend her virtue, this time for real.

Her thoughts were interrupted by a knock on the door. Opening it up, she was surprised to see a concerned Doctor Barnes standing there.

"Hello, Cindy. May I come in?" he asked, looking at the bandage on her head.

"Why yes, of course," she said, surprised to see him.

"I got your address from the hospital. We were worried when you did not show up for work today. Especially in light of what happened to Doctor Cauldwell."

"I can explain that," Cindy tried to say, but Doctor Barnes cut her off.

"I do not want to pry into your personal life, but some things are obvious. I don't know how Andrew got beat up, and I don't care to know. Although I am sure there was a good reason for it. What is important is whether you are okay?" he said, looking at her.

"This should heal quickly," Cindy replied, pointing to her head wound.

"There are other less obvious wounds that do not heal as quickly. I am also talking about you being okay besides the obvious injury. Forgive me, but I have to ask as a doctor and hopefully, as a concerned friend. Did he hurt you in any way, any way at all?"

"No, thank God. Two good people prevented that from happening."

"Good, I am grateful for that. My wife and I were very worried about you when you left the country club rather abruptly the other night. We would have been more than willing to have brought you home."

"Knowing what I know now, that would have been a much better option. But I thank you and your wife for caring. I also owe Mrs. Barnes an apology. She tried to warn me, but I disregarded her advice. I know now that it was also a mistake."

"I will give her your apology, but I am sure she would want you to call her Susan or Sue," he said with a smile.

"I will, when or if I get the opportunity," Cindy said, wondering how that might ever happen.

"Do you mind if I look at this?" Doctor Barnes asked, referring to her wound.

"No, not at all."

"It's not that bad, but it's not that good either if you don't get a couple of stitches. You'll also need to apply an antiseptic ointment on it until it heals completely. When you come into work tomorrow, I will have you see one of our plastic surgeons. It should heal with little or no scar."

"I still have my job?" Cindy asked, somewhat surprised.

"Yes, but only for two weeks. After that, you will no longer have the time to work since you'll be in nursing school full-time."

"How can that be? I was sure Andrew would not only have

me fired but have my name withdrawn from the program."

"I would not be too concerned about Dr. Cauldwell for the time being, or even beyond that. After what happened to him the other night, I am convinced he'll make sure to stay far away from you. He learned a lesson he will never forget."

"But why wouldn't he get back at me by canceling my application and admission?"

"As popular and influential he and his family are, Andrew had made just as many enemies over the years. Including the Dean of the nursing school, whose daughter he had once dated. Besides, I have already spoken to the Dean. And as a faculty member of the school, I can assure you that your admission is going through on schedule. And as far as Andrew goes, he has some serious problems from now on. His injuries raised many questions, particularly in light of his history. And those injuries will sideline him for quite a while. Of course, his broken nose is the least of his problems. The broken jaw is wired shut, and he'll be eating and drinking through a straw for the next six weeks or so. But besides his obvious injuries, when he fell the other night, he suffered a severe fracture of his right wrist. I was called into the hospital for his emergency surgery yesterday. It might take a while to know for sure, but there is the likely possibility that he may never fully recover one hundred percent of the wrist's movement. For a surgeon, that could be critical. Oh, one more thing. There's talk that the board of trustees is finally getting fed up with Andrew's antics, and even his father may not be able to save his seat on the board."

It took a few seconds for everything Doctor Barnes had said to sink in, but when it did, Cindy exclaimed, "Thank you so very much for everything."

"And I will see you at the hospital tomorrow, and Mrs. Barnes, Susan to you, told me that she would be honored to have you over for dinner next week. That is if you are feeling up to it."

"Definitely. Tell Mrs. Barnes, I mean Susan, I would love to." As she closed the door after Doctor Barnes had left, Cindy plopped down onto a living room chair, still not fully appreciating all that had just happened. Then she got up and walked into her bedroom. After taking out the picture of Michael, she said quietly, "I guess I don't hate you after all."

CHAPTER 24

Fate and Destiny

June 11, 1941

"So, what do you think? Blue or Brown?" Michael asked Paul as he held up two shirts.

"Blue, definitely blue."

"Yeah. But I'm thinking of going with the brown," Michael said as he put the blue shirt back down.

"Why bother asking? We both know that you are going to do whatever you want," Paul said, shaking his head.

"That's what big brothers are for, to get an opposing opinion," Michael said, grinning.

"Okay, now the big question. It's been nearly three months since you've been dating Betty. Are you over Cindy yet?" Paul asked, suspecting he already knew the answer.

"First, I've been seeing Betty for three months, but we haven't been dating, at least not until tonight. We're just friends. She's a sweet kid."

"And she's charming also," Paul interjected.

"Okay, we're both in agreement on that. But as far as Cindy, that ended when she stopped writing, and she was going out with that doctor she met. The one Matthew saw her with at the hospital. The one she was hugging in broad daylight, no less."

"You still didn't answer my question. Are you over her?"

"It's been three months, so I guess I am." Michael finally answered Paul's question.

"Then why do you keep her picture and look at it every night?" Paul asked.

"And just how do you know that? Are you checking up on me?"

"No. It's just that I've seen you looking at it numerous times, so I guess it's a safe bet that you do it even when I don't see you."

"Maybe I will always have some feelings for her. I just find it hard not to look at her picture," Michael admitted.

"Can I give you some advice?"

"When did you ever not give me advice," Michael said half-heartedly.

"Just don't go stringing Betty along. She deserves better than that."

"If I didn't know better, it sounds more like you've been dating her instead of me," Michael replied.

"So finally, at least you admit that what you've been doing has been dating," Paul exclaimed, as the two brothers were able to laugh together.

"Our first time going to the movies will seem more like a date than just hanging out and going for walks," Michael said.

"Don't forget the picnics you two have gone on either. I'm sure Betty likes you. But, I think the whole Cindy thing has both of you hesitant to become more involved. Have you ever kissed her yet?" Paul inquired, curious as to the answer.

"No, not yet. At least not in the sense you're asking. Sure, Betty's kissed me on the cheek, and it was nice. And the thought of kissing her has been on my mind. But to have done more, I just felt that it was not the right time. Not that I wouldn't like to. It's just...."

"Yeah, I know. It's Cindy. It can't be easy getting over her."

Maybe after tonight, things will be different," Michael said, wondering if that was possible.

"Which movie is it you're taking her to see?"

"Meet John Doe with Gary Cooper and Barbara Stanwyck."

"Well, in a darkened movie theatre, if you don't kiss her tonight, you never will," Paul replied, seeming almost melancholy that it was not him instead of Michael who was going out.

"Wish me luck, Big Brother," Michael said as he was finishing up buttoning his shirt.

At the San Diego home of Doctor Robert Barnes and his wife Susan, Cindy was helping to clear the table, having just finished eating dinner. She had become a regular at the Barnes' household, eating there once a week for the past few months. Cindy enjoyed the good home cooking. She also enjoyed their acceptance of her into their home, as well as their lives. Even more, with Cindy estranged from her mother ever since the incident with Dr. Cauldwell, Susan became someone Cindy could talk to about her problems. Susan would always take the time to listen to Cindy, and more importantly, she cared what Cindy would be saying. Susan would offer advice when Cindy sought it and even sometimes when she had not. Tonight's advice would be the latter.

"That roast was delicious. Unfortunately, eating here makes the food at the nursing school's cafeteria seem even blander than it is," Cindy stated as she brought the last of the dinner dishes into the kitchen.

"Thank you. We're glad that you can come for these dinners. Even Veronica enjoys your company. She said it's almost like having an older sister."

"She's a sweet kid. I like her also. Besides, like her, I never had a sister. I have five older brothers, but that's not the same. There are certain things you can't talk to them about."

Seizing that comment as an opportunity, Susan began to say what had been on her mind.

"About that, it's been three months now, and you haven't spoken about it. It had to be traumatic. Sometimes it's good just to let it all out."

"I'm fine, really," was Cindy's simple reply.

"Are you really, my Dear? I know I have no right to pry, but you do matter to us, and we are concerned for your well-being."

"I am doing fine in school. My grades are all good, and I have made many new friends. And that's not even including you guys who are like family to me. So I'm okay, really."

"I truly hope you are. But between the assault, your

mother's reaction to everything, and your break-up with Michael, it has to be a lot to deal with," Susan said with absolute sincerity.

The last part of her remark must have hit a sore spot with Cindy as a single tear began flowing down her cheek. She quickly wiped it away, hoping that it was unnoticed, but it did not escape the attention of Susan.

"I accept my lack of good judgment regarding Andrew, and I regret not listening to you in the ladies' room that night. His assaulting me was extremely unsettling, but I can take comfort in knowing that he got worse than what he did to me. Besides, if that never happened, I would not have you and Robert in my life. So some good came from the bad. Also, my relationship with my mother had not been great before all this happened. I could never open up and talk to her the way I can talk to you. So again, some good resulted from the bad. And as far as Michael, he...." Cindy had to stop talking as she was starting to cry. Struggling to go on, she continued, "He just stopped writing and got someone else and didn't even have the decency to tell me."

Susan put her arms around Cindy as Veronica walked in, asking what was wrong. Her mom said it was okay, and Cindy just needed some private time to talk about things. Then, sensing that it was a hint to leave, Veronica left her mother and Cindy alone.

"Do you still love him?" Susan asked, already guessing correctly what Cindy's answer would be.

"Yes, but I keep trying not to. It's painful to love Michael. Still, it's impossible for me not to. I don't know what I can do to stop it, to stop the pain," Cindy said, still crying on Susan's shoulder.

"Do you believe in fate?" Susan asked.

"Maybe, I guess?" Cindy replied somewhat curiously.

Susan walked over to a small table and invited Cindy to sit down as she handed her a tissue to wipe her eyes. As Susan sat down beside her, she began talking.

"I think that there are forces that cause our lives to play out the way they do. Think of the currents in the ocean. We have no control over them. If we were adrift, they would move us to places that we might never venture to on our own. We might find ourselves washed up on a strange and distant land, full of new adventures and opportunities. Sometimes, the currents might reverse themselves, and we find ourselves washed back onto the shore from where we started. You have your whole life ahead of you. What happens next week, next year, or even years from now is an open book. Much of it we cannot control. That is fate. But we each will have our final destiny, and as much as fate plays a role in determining it, we can still affect how we reach those destinies. There will be choices you will make along the way. Not all will be the right ones. Some will be wrong, and Andrew was one. But you will make many more correct choices than wrong ones. Michael had been an important part of your life. Fate had thrown you a curve, but that's not to say that fate might not yet bring the two of you back together again. You just have to continue with your life and try to make the best choices along the way. If you do, I am sure you will find the happiness that you seek, whatever that will be."

If Susan had been Cindy's actual mother, she could not have said anything better to settle her down. The tears flowing from Cindy's sad eyes had not yet stopped, but the beginning of a smile was appearing on her relieved face. Cindy had been suppressing her feelings and had not known how to deal with them. But, listening to Susan, Cindy had now received something that had been missing the past three months, hope. As eloquent as Susan had been, Cindy could say just two words in return. "Thank you," as she hugged Susan.

Having picked up Betty at her house, Michael drove to the movie theater in Guymon using his family's truck. Betty was looking especially pretty tonight, wearing a gingham dress that accentuated her fine figure. Despite their spending many hours together and having no difficulty finding things to talk about, there were awkward moments of silence, as they each appreciated the importance of this evening. Tonight would be the stepping stone to the next phase of their relationship. Betty had been very patient, knowing how difficult Michael's breakup with Cindy had been. But she felt the need to bring some degree of physical romance to their relationship finally.

On the other hand, Michael was still trying to come to terms with his breakup and his lingering feelings for Cindy. He had to admit he was physically attracted to Betty, and he felt the need now more than ever to move on with his life. But he could not stop thinking that he was somehow cheating on Cindy.

When the house lights dimmed, and the drapes covering the giant silver screen slid open, Betty, holding a box of popcorn in one hand, got comfortable and rested her head on Michael's shoulder. As was the case, before the feature film would begin, Movietone News filled up the screen with black and white newsreels of the ongoing war in Europe. Motion pictures of the recent evacuation of Dunkirk showed tens of thousands of British and French troops lined up on the beach. All of them were desperately awaiting a fleet of ships and boats of every size that would carry them across the English Channel and to the relative safety of England. Not receiving nearly as much coverage was the Japanese war against China and the possible threats to the United States and its allies in the Pacific.

When the screen was now showing coming attractions, one of the advertised future films was "Dive Bomber," starring Errol Flynn and Fred McMurray.

"That's the USS Enterprise, Matthew's ship. They had filmed it just before his transfer. Just think, he's on it right now," Michael proudly told Betty.

Finally, the musical fanfare of brass instruments announced the beginning of tonight's movie as the familiar "WB" shield of Warner Brothers Studios appeared before them. As the credits of the larger-than-life, black and white film emerged across the screen, Betty snuggled even closer to Michael. He, in turn, reciprocated by putting his arm around Betty's shoulder. About halfway into the movie, during a romantic scene between Gary Cooper and Barbara Stanwyck, Michael and Betty turned toward each other. Then, without saying a word, they kissed for the first time. It was brief, and it was sweet. Then, feeling encouraged by neither one objecting, they kissed again. The kissing occurred several times before the uneasiness of being seen in the crowded theater put a damper on their romantic exploits. They watched the rest of the movie with their bodies as close together as the theater's seats would allow.

After the movie was over and the house lights came back on, Michael and Betty joined the mass of moviegoers as they exited the theater. As they walked back to Michael's truck, he and Betty held hands as they had often done on their many walks together.

"That was a good movie," Betty said, speaking first.

"Yes, it was. But I think I liked you more," Michael said, referring to the kisses.

"They were nice," Betty said in reply, finally feeling satisfaction in the direction their relationship had taken.

Their truck was on a dark side street, just off the main road in town. Michael asked Betty if she would like to go for a soda, but she said not just yet and asked if they could sit in the truck for a while. Michael opened her door for her, and after she got in, he closed it and went around to the other side. Getting in, Michael asked if she was comfortable, and after once again snuggling up to Michael, she said yes. In the privacy of the truck, Michael began kissing Betty, who was gladly returning his kisses with her own. Unlike the earlier short and sweet kisses, Michael started kissing Betty as passionately as possible, much to her delight. But then something happened. His kisses began lacking emotion or desire. Betty instantly felt it and pulled back.

"Is something wrong?" she asked, realizing that there was.

"I don't know what came over me. Your kisses were great. You were amazing, but then I just lost focus all of a sudden."

"That's not exactly what a girl wants to hear from her boyfriend," Betty said with obvious concern.

"I think you're great, and I enjoy being with you. But is that what we are, boyfriend and girlfriend? Or are we just a boy and a girl who are good friends?" Michael asked, hoping Betty not only knew the correct answer but that she would also understand.

"Well, I had hoped that it was the first choice, but since you had to ask, I guess it's safe to assume it's the second," Betty said, as she was now sliding over to her side of the truck and sitting up straight.

"I'm sorry. I really am. I do like you. In fact, I like you a lot. Another time or another place and things would be different. But my heart's not in it, and you deserve better." Michael said, apologizing.

Betty was going to say it's Cindy, isn't it, but she already knew the answer. She should have been more upset than she was, but Betty respected Michael for his devotion to Cindy, hoping that she might be as fortunate to find her own Michael someday.

"I don't know how it could happen, but I sincerely hope that you are finally able to find the love and happiness that you deserve. Fate had brought you and Cindy together initially, and for whatever reasons it has, fate has caused you to be apart. When everything is said and done, I hope that your final destination in your journey through life is a good one. I had hoped that I would be part of it, although I know now that I cannot be. But I thank you for your honesty." Betty leaned over and kissed Michael on his cheek, wondering what her final destiny would be.

The ride back home, surprisingly, was not as awkward as either might have expected. Unlike the ride earlier, neither had any difficulty in finding things to talk about. It was almost as if an invisible weight was no longer on them. The romantic cloud that had hung over them had also cleared, allowing them to be good friends. But as that one had lifted, much more ominous and dangerous clouds were brewing thousands of miles away, as the storm clouds of war were increasingly casting their broad shadow across the Pacific.

CHAPTER 25

Day of Infamy

December 7, 1941

They were sleeping a little bit later than expected, but it was a typical Sunday morning in most other respects. With both the fall harvest and the planting of the winter wheat already finished, the daily chores of running a family farm were minimal at this time of year. For the Johnsons, it was one of the few Sundays throughout the year that would come close to being the day of rest mentioned in their family bible, prominently displayed on their living room table. Still, there were those chores they could not avoid or ignore. The farm's livestock could not read the bible, nor could they understand the meaning of the Sabbath. Life went on as usual for these creatures of God, and they did not abide by a seven-day calendar that originated nearly two thousand years ago in ancient Rome. The hens would still lay their eggs, the cows still required milking, and all of them, including the pigs, would have to be fed. But compared to the other six days, Sunday allowed the family to spend time together. There was nothing to indicate today would be anything other than an average Sunday.

Meanwhile, 3,400 miles west, the first rays of the morning sun had not yet risen above the eastern horizon of the Pacific Ocean. The Hawaiian island of Oahu was still asleep. Nevertheless, the light from a waning moon was still sufficient to illuminate the U.S. Navy's Pacific Fleet ships. Their massive, gray-steel exteriors were still visible in the darkness. The irregular shapes of their superstructures reaching into the dark sky towered over most land-based support structures and dominated the harbor's skyline. With most of their crews either asleep or onshore, only those necessary lamps were visible, their pinpoints of light helping to outline the ships' dark silhouettes. Most noticeable were the eight battleships that were docked side-by-side in the narrow channel or drydock. But just as with the rest of the fleet, with little or no discernible activity, these massive dreadnaughts looked to be asleep.

Across the harbor, the quietness of the night was evident at Hickam Field also. As one of the United States Army Air Corps' bases situated in Hawaii, Hickam was the headquarters for Bomber Command. Despite the war-like appearance of the aircraft assigned there, the base was essentially inactive at night and was resting just as peacefully as their naval counterparts. With no night flights either taking off or landing, other than the movement of the sentries assigned to base security, the airfield showed no activity. It appeared more like an expansive airplane museum rather than the bustling airbase it was in the daytime. Much of the same tranquility was evident at the Naval Air Stations on Fords Island, Kaneohe Bay, and the Ewa Marine Corps Air Station. Things would pick up later, as a squadron of B-17 bombers, flying in from San Diego, were due to arrive at Hickam Field sometime after eight o'clock this morning.

The peaceful calm that prevailed across Hawaii was not the case, just a couple of hundred miles to the north. A large carrier task force of the Imperial Japanese Navy had successfully evaded detection and was now within striking distance of Hawaii. Unlike the sleeping U.S. fleet, the six aircraft carriers at the task force center were bustling with activity. While their planes were being made ready on the flight deck above, their cockpit crews were below deck making their final preparations for their mission. As their aircraft were being fueled and fitted with their ordinance, their crewmen would begin the ceremonial practice of writing farewell letters to their families should they not return.

Additionally, the pilots would place small locks of their hair and fingernail clippings in the same envelope containing their farewell notes. Then, as the aircraft that would take part in the attack stood ready on the rolling decks of the carriers, their pilots would be making last-minute prayers for a successful mission at makeshift Shinto shrines. Finally, the airmen would stand in silence before making two sharp handclaps. Then, as a final gesture, they would down ritual shots of sake before going up to man their planes.

Of all the family members this Sunday morning, Sarah Johnson was the first to arise. Her day of rest would begin by having
to prepare breakfast. The advantage of living on a farm was that
you had fresh foods to eat. But these tasty meals did not appear
magically on the table. The bacon and the eggs had to be prepared
and cooked. The stacks of pancakes, as well as the homemade
biscuits, were made from scratch. Fortunately, the hand-churned
butter and the delicious jams spread on the biscuits and pancakes were previously prepared, thus saving Sarah precious time.
By combining her kitchen management skills and having had so
much practice to perfect them, Sarah would always manage to
have everything ready by the time the rest of the Johnson family
began gathering around the table. The sight of the food spread
out on the table, augmented by the aroma of the various cooked
foods, had no difficulty whetting everyone's appetite. As usual,
Sarah would lead the family in saying grace before her hungry
clan began partaking in the morning feast.

Grace and Rebekah would assist their mother in cleaning
up after everyone had their fill. Then, with the table cleared and
the dishes, pots, and pans all scrubbed clean and neatly put away,
there would be time for the family men to perform those farm
chores necessary before getting dressed for church services. Then,
as often as they did in the past, it was a comfortable walk to the
church with good weather. Along the way, they would join other
families that had remained on the Panhandle and also survived
the worst days of the prior decade.

With the cover of darkness long since gone, Army, Navy,
and Marine buglers on Hawaii would soon officially announce the
start of yet another day at each of the various military installations across the Islands. In conjunction with the musicians, other
servicemen performed the daily task of carefully unfolding the
American flag and attaching it to the lanyards of a tall flag pole or
mast. Then, standing rigidly at attention, with their brass instruments glistening in the glow of the morning sun, the buglers' call
to the colors would begin. As the buglers continued playing reveille, the flags continued rising until they came to rest at the top
of the masts. Those other service members who were starting yet

another day would also stand at attention, and if outdoors, they would render a sharp salute while facing the flag.

One of the eight battleships at Pearl Harbor was the USS Arizona. It was named in honor of the 48th state's admission into the union and put into service in 1916. With a length of 608 feet and displacing 29,158 tons, it carried an impressive array of weapons, including its main armament of twelve fourteen-inch guns. But the Arizona was also unique for something else it carried onboard, a band of musicians. Other large Navy ships also had bands, but the Arizona's band was different. The band was the only one in the U.S. Navy created and trained as a unit and assigned to a particular ship. Once there, it would compete against other Navy and Marine bands in the big "Battle of Music" competition.

The band consisted of twenty musicians and a bandmaster. Each highly recruited member was an accomplished musician, excelling in either high school or college, some of them winning their state competitions. Two had even formed their own professional dance bands before joining the Navy. They all had undergone basic training at Naval Station Great Lakes in Illinois. In addition, they all attended the Navy School of Music in Washington, D.C. They would play everything from military music to popular dance tunes, both in competition and to entertain their fifteen hundred crewmembers. In addition to their duties as musicians, they were all trained as ammunition handlers in the event of combat. On this Sunday morning, they all gathered on the ship's fantail in preparation for playing the National Anthem at eight o'clock sharp. As the time drew near, the Navy Band Unit 22, USS Arizona, began tuning their instruments. None of them knew that their performance of fifteen days ago, which earned them a spot in the competition's finals in two weeks, would have been their last.

The sight of the rising sun above the horizon was considered a good omen for naval aviators who came from the "Land of the Rising Sun." Having received the message, code name Niitakayama Nobore from Emperor Hirohito previously, which translated was, climb Mount Niitaka; the Japanese fleet had the authorization to proceed with its battle plans. Initially, the main worry for Marshall Admiral Mihashi Isoroku Yamamoto, the commander-in-chief of the Combined Fleet, and Admiral Chūichi Nagumo, commander of the task force, was whether or not they had maintained the element of surprise. Having received updated intelligence from intercepted U.S. Navy communications and Japanese spies at Pearl Harbor, it became clear that they would catch the U.S. Fleet off guard and vulnerable. Thus, upon Admiral Nagumo's flagship, the Akagi, the order for the fleet to turn into the wind and launch the aerial assault was given. Soon, the first wave of 353 aircraft lifted off the flight decks of the six carriers. As the pilots gunned their engines and raced towards the ship's bow, the encouraging shouts of the deck crewmen competed with the roar of the Mitsubishi and Aichi aircraft engines.

Just two months ago, she celebrated her fifth birthday, launched on October 3, 1936. She was a tad over eight-hundred feet long and was home to two-thousand, two-hundred and seventeen officers and crew. Among them was Seaman Second Class, Matthew Johnson.

She carried an impressive array of armaments. Although fitted with various defensive weapons, these were on a ship designed primarily for offensive purposes. The ninety aircraft she carried would be responsible for fulfilling that. The bombers and torpedo bombers that flew off her deck would take on that job if and when necessary. Her fighter planes could do double duty, providing a defensive shield should she be attacked from the air by an enemy's planes. Although built for fighting, she was already a movie star, having starred recently in the theatrical movie "Dive Bomber." That had taken place back at the Naval Air Station North Island in San Diego earlier this year. The ship was made available to the 150 actors and production crew members for an entire week. That was before President Roosevelt had ordered her to be forward-based, resulting in her deployment to the Pacific Fleet Headquarters at Pearl Harbor. She already had a nickname, "The Big E," and she would soon receive others. But for now, The USS Enterprise, hull number CV-6, a Yorktown Class aircraft carrier, had been tasked with ferrying a Marine Fighter Squadron to Wake Island to shore up that island's defenses.

Having completed her assignment, the Enterprise and the other escort ships of Task Force 8 headed back to Pearl Harbor. They were supposed to return to port yesterday. But as so happens at sea, bad weather can change schedules and itineraries. Thus, on December 7, 1941, when dawn would break above the picturesque island of Oahu, the Task Force would still be 215 nautical miles west of its destination.

Although hostilities with Japan had not yet broken out, the Pacific Fleet had been under heightened alerts. The possibility of running into the Japanese Imperial Navy in the middle of the Pacific Ocean was an ongoing concern. As a precaution, the order was given for the Enterprise to launch eighteen of her SBD Dauntless scout planes and dive bombers. Built by Douglas Aircraft, the SBD's official designation was "Scout Bomber Douglas." But later, the SBD, being battle-tested, would acquire the label "Slow But Deadly," as it would refer to its slow speed yet deadly performance in combat. The planes would search in an arc, covering an area northeast to southeast of the carrier task force. Assuming they made no contact with the Japanese fleet, they were under orders to return to Pearl Harbor, landing at the Naval Air Station at Fords Island, where they would await the return of the Enterprise.

As the carrier turned into the wind, flight and deck crews were busy preparing the planes for launch. One of those crewmen was Matthew Johnson. Matthew loved being a sailor, and he enjoyed his job, making sure the 1,000 horsepower Wright Cyclone engine would perform properly. Thinking back to his days on the farm, he remembered the enjoyment he had tinkering with anything mechanical, especially engines. The fact that not only did he get to work on such an incredible aircraft engine, but knowing his efforts had an impact on our national security, gave him a sense of satisfaction he had previously found lacking on the farm. Of course, now that their home port was Pearl Harbor, his wildest dreams had come true. One of the first things he planned to do tomorrow when he would be on liberty would be to just lie on the white sandy beach and look out over the beautiful blue waters of the Pacific. He pictured having a beautiful, well-tanned, young woman lying next to him, as a warm tropical breeze would cause a gentle swaying of a nearby palm tree. At the age of twenty-one, Matthew thought life could not get any better. Of course, there was always the Japanese, but he felt comfortable thinking that they would be too stupid to attack our forces so far from their homeland. All in all, life was good.

Their flight crews began climbing into the planes with their aircraft fueled, armed, and prepped for their mission. Matthew flashed a thumbs up to the pilot and his rear-facing gunner, seeing his crew taking their positions in the still open cockpit. Smiling back, they each returned the gesture. Soon, they received the go-ahead, and they began what they expected to be another routine mission. As Matthew watched the last of the SBDs take off from the Enterprise deck, the first waves of Japanese carrier-based aircraft were about to begin their attack on Pearl Harbor.

It would not be only the U.S. Navy caught off guard. A sizeable force of U.S. Army fighters and bombers capable of disrupting the attack and possibly attacking the enemy fleet became easy targets for the Japanese airmen. A newly installed radar facility had picked up a large number of planes inbound toward Hawaii. But, the Army had erroneously attributed it to the incoming group of B-17 bombers coming from the mainland. Without the warning that an attack was imminent, not a single U.S. aircraft from Hawaii would be airborne as the attackers would be flying over the American ships and airbases.

It was nearly noontime when the Johnson's were exiting the church. As they were exchanging greetings with the other congregants and thanking the pastor for his insightful and meaningful sermon, events were now underway that would alter the course of history forever. Even more personal to the Johnson Family, these events would change all of their lives forever. Then, on a day that also began both promising and hopeful, some three-thousand miles away, the terror started raining down from the clear blue skies over Hawaii. As impossible as it seemed, almost the entire U.S. Navy's Pacific Fleet was being savagely attacked by the Imperial Japanese Navy while anchored, defenseless at their base at Pearl Harbor. But for now, news of this Day of Infamy would not yet be forthcoming. So, for the time being, despite the world-changing event that was taking place, life would continue as usual for the next several hours, for not only the Johnsons but almost all the citizens of the United States.

As they would join the other families making the return leg of the trip back to their homes, they would still enjoy the simple pleasures that only a Sunday could provide. The stark differences between what was happening here, as the recent congregants were joking and laughing, compared to the horrific destruction and loss of life occurring at essentially the exact moment at Pearl Harbor, could not yet be appreciated. Yet, in time, this event's knowledge and resultant anger would significantly impact all of them. The Johnsons would be no exception.

The first wave of Japanese fighters and bombers was having tremendous success and faced almost little defensive opposition. The American airfields were under relentless Japanese attack while their planes were sitting either in their bombed-out hangers or in tight groups out in the open. They were sitting ducks from not only the bombs but from the strafing machine-gun fire. Eventually, a few planes would manage to get airborne, but they were way too few and far too late. To add to the confusion, as the attack took place, the inbound flight of unarmed B-17s was making their final approach to the airfield at Hickam. Despite facing both Japanese and friendly fire, most could land safely, although one B-17 had to use a now-empty golf course for a landing strip.

Meanwhile, stunned onlookers stood motionless, looking at the skies filled with Japanese planes, still not fully understanding the consequences of what was occurring. As the Japanese bombs were dropping and explosions shook the ground, there was still confusion about what was happening. Rather than acknowledge that the island was under attack, many thought it might have been the Army conducting bombing practice. Yet, even that happening this early on a Sunday seemed easier to accept than the actual attack.

While high-level bombers and low-flying fighters were devastating our airfields and air defense capabilities, our Navy was about to experience the full wrath of the Japanese Imperial Navy's aircraft. Dive bombers and torpedo planes were now targeting the closely moored fleet. The enemy's torpedoes, specially fitted with wooden flotation devices, allowed for their use in the relatively shallow water of the harbor. Much to their credit, the Imperial High Command had their pilots practicing these attacks for months. With no ability to escape, the U.S. Ships had no choice but to sit and take whatever punishment the Japanese were inflicting upon them.

As the realization finally sank in as to what was happening

throughout the harbor, the alarms sounded. The repeating blasts of claxon horns blaring and the shouts of "general quarters, this is not a drill, man your battle stations," coming over the ship's bullhorns, would be heard as the explosions of the torpedoes finding their underwater targets lent credibility to the statements. As crewmen began rushing to their assigned battle stations, many of them arrived only to find their guns either locked or unloaded without ammunition. If the torpedoes were not enough, aerial bombs dropped from the attacking bombers were also finding their targets. Even the Japanese fighters, having virtually no aerial opposition, used their wing-mounted machine guns to strafe both the ships' decks and any survivors who had jumped into the water. Many of those fortunate enough not to be strafed had to contend with the additional hazard of the burning fuel oils that were clinging to the water's surface.

Having completed their searches and seeing no indication of any Japanese threat, the eighteen SBDs from the USS Enterprise began to make their approach into Pearl Harbor. Arriving in pairs, they flew directly into the Japanese attack as they approached Fords Island. Being either bombers or scout planes, their pilots had little ability to take on the attacking aircraft, let alone provide for their own defense. They were caught between the Japanese and the defensive fire now coming from hastily activated, anti-aircraft batteries. Between both enemy and friendly fire, seven of the SBDs never landed safely. Among them were Matthew's pilot and gunner. Sadly, he would never see either of them or his Wright Cyclone engine again.

Aboard the USS Arizona, Band Unit 22 would never play the Star-Spangled Banner at eight o'clock as planned. So instead, all twenty-one band members rushed to their designated stations as ammunition handlers at one of the fourteen-inch gun turrets. Their actions were happening throughout the ship as hundreds of other crewmen, some still not fully dressed, rushed through crowded passageways. They bounded up and down narrow ladders, taking two steps at a time, desperately trying to reach their battle stations and do anything to help stem the attack. Finally, those able to secure small arms from the ship's armory would rush onto the decks, firing in vain at the passing planes speeding by. This scene would be replayed countless times on the other warships as well.

The Arizona was hit several times by aerial bombs, each time managing to survive the damage. But one well-placed strike by an armor-piercing shell caused a massive explosion on board the battleship. Then, the ship erupted in flames and rapidly sank, aided by the secondary explosions of large stores of black powder bags and artillery shells for its powerful fourteen-inch guns. Those officers and seamen who did not die from the initial explosions did not fare well either. Many others died, being unable to escape the blazing inferno. While others trapped inside would die from either suffocation or from drowning. All twenty-one members of Band Unit 22 died at their stations. In the end, of the 1,512 crew on board at the attack, 1,177 had died. Among them were sixty-three of whom were among sets of brothers. All of them to be forever entombed in the sunken battleship.

Having expended all their bombs and torpedoes, and before their fuel tanks started to run low, the Japanese planes began returning to their carriers. Staying any longer would not accomplish anything further, as all of their primary targets were either severely damaged or destroyed. As they departed, they left behind smoldering ruins of what had once been a powerful naval force. The future ability to project air power in this part of the Pacific or muster a strong defense was virtually non-existent, as most of Hickam Field and the other airbases were out of action.

Having received radio messages that Pearl Harbor was under attack, the Enterprise was under orders to attack a Japanese aircraft carrier and its escorts reportedly southwest of the Enterprise's position. The attacking force would consist of thirty aircraft, comprised of fighters, bombers, and torpedo bombers. At 5:00 p.m., with its bow facing into the wind, the Big E once again began launching its planes. As they took off, the hopes of those on both the aircraft and the ships were of sweet revenge. Unfortunately, their hopes were spoiled, as the location of the Japanese fleet remained a mystery. The bombers and torpedo bombers returned to the Enterprise, but the six F4F Wildcat Fighters received orders to divert to Hickam Field on Oahu. As can happen in the fog of war, panicked antiaircraft firing began despite receiving radio reports of their expected arrival as American guns targeted the friendly planes. Although the shooting at Pearl Harbor with the

Japanese had ended some ten hours ago, three of the six aircraft from the Enterprise were now tragically shot down by friendly fire.

As bad as things were, the Japanese had erred in their battle plans. The attacking forces had failed to destroy, let alone strike, both the tank farms containing the Navy's fuel oil reserves and its dry dock facilities. Of the eight battleships at Pearl Harbor, one of which was in dry dock for repairs, four had been sunk and the other four severely damaged. Yet only the USS Arizona would not see action later in the war. All the others were repaired and put back into service. In another instance of good fortune, none of the Navy's Pacific Fleet carriers, or their escort vessels, were harbored at the time of the attack. Admiral Yamamoto was fearful of his fleet being discovered and attacked by carrier-based aircraft knowing the U.S. carriers were out at sea. Thus, despite their over-achieving, initial success, he took a more cautious approach and decided not to launch a third wave of attack planes. Then, he ordered the fleet to head back towards more friendly and safer waters. But for the more than 2,400 Americans killed in the attack, this good fortune would mean nothing. Nor would it mean anything to the thousands of families who would be receiving telegrams from the War Department, regrettably informing them of the deaths of their loved ones.

Seaman 2nd Class Matthew Johnson stood stunned back aboard the Enterprise as he looked out over the dark Pacific. Since he woke up earlier this morning, his world had changed. Expectations that Matthew once held close to his heart were now in question. He was no longer in a peacetime navy. Matthew had experienced the loss of two friends. But more importantly, he realized that this would just be the beginning. There would be much more dying before it would end. He still felt comfortable in the conflict's inevitable outcome, although he knew there would be much pain and sorrow before this war concluded. He thought of what his father had told him when Matthew told him of his enlistment. Matthew wondered about Michael and if he would be drawn into the fray. He now felt relieved that Paul suffered that terrible injury at the hands of the hay bailer. At least Paul would be ineligible to serve and would be kept out of harm's way. As the ship's bow churned through the ocean's waves, he looked at the light of a waning moon as it reflected off the black water, wondering how that same moon looked back in Oklahoma. Then, he questioned if he would ever see Oklahoma again.

For most of the public, the first news of the shocking sneak attack came through bulletins interrupting the regularly scheduled radio programs. Although they were the farthest from the action, people in New York were among the first Americans to hear of the attack. Football fans were shocked hearing the news when the live, play-by-play radio broadcast between cross-town NFL rivals, the New York Giants and the Brooklyn Dodgers, was interrupted at 2:26 p.m. Eastern Standard Time. People everywhere were now hearing of the attack from either their neighbors or one of the nation's 45,000,000 radios. By the time Sunday evening came around, very few Americans would not be listening to their radios, anxiously awaiting not only the latest news of the war but also the official word from Washington. Ironically, the first acknowledgment from the White House did not come from the President of the United States, but instead, it came from the nation's First Lady. Eleanor Roosevelt would address the attack during her regular scheduled weekly radio show. However, the 133 million U.S. citizens, spread across the forty-eight states, would have to wait until tomorrow to hear from the President.

News of the attack took longer to reach the rural heartlands of America, but once it did, it spread quickly. Some of those families on their way home from church services, as were the Johnsons, came by way of twelve-year-old Billy Taylor. Billy had been listening to the radio when the first news broke into his regular program. Like Paul Revere announcing that the British were coming, Billy jumped onto one of his family's horses and rode off onto the dirt road that connected the many farms. As he would pass his neighbors, he would shout, "The Japs attacked Pearl Harbor. The Japs attacked Pearl Harbor." More often than not, he would receive inquisitive stares in return. Everyone knew who the Japs were, but not as many were familiar with Pearl Harbor. For reasons that they now wished did not exist, the Johnson family knew all too well of Pearl Harbor. Although her husband would be somewhat successful in trying to hide his concern, Sarah Johnson would have been a terrible poker player, as her expression gave a clear indication of her worry. No one said a word as the impact of the news started to sink in, but the concern on their mother's face was now evident to all of the Johnson children.

Desperate for more news, Sarah began walking as fast as she could to get home, hoping their radio would tell her more. Philip wanted to calm his wife's fears, but he realized that anything he might say at this time would be empty words. He alone of the group knew of the horrors of war. Memories of the death and suffering were still fresh in his mind twenty-three years later. He could only hope and pray that their son had not experienced first-hand what he had seen. More importantly, he prayed that God would spare Matthew and keep him safe.

Soon the entire family was keeping pace with Sarah, matching her every stride. As their house came into view, Michael broke off from the group and began running as fast as possible. His body, fueled with the adrenaline that the news had brought, seemed to make his strides quicker, longer, and faster. He was sprinting so quickly that the dust his shoes kicked up was caught up in his backdraft, trailing behind him like a small dust storm. Arriving at the house minutes before anyone else, Michael rushed into the living room and turned the radio on. He became impatient, waiting for the assorted vacuum tubes within the wooden cabinet to come to life. As if watching would make it happen faster, Michael peered into the vents on the back of the cabinet, quietly urging the cylindrical glass tubes to glow orange. Then he began adjusting the frequency dial back and forth until he found a station clear enough to be heard.

Had it been a typical Sunday, having attended church services and having had their traditional Sunday dinner, the Johnsons would have gathered around the Zenith radio that stood in the corner of their living room for an entirely different purpose. Although the reception would sometimes be disturbed by static, they would have sat and listened to their favorite Sunday evening programs. The family would often laugh aloud as they heard the on-air high jinks of comedy shows such as Jack Benny, sponsored by Jell-O. Another favorite would be Edgar Bergen and Charlie McCarthy, his ventriloquist dummy, hosted by Chase & Sanborn Coffee. Product jingles were also very popular, and some of the family members would sing along with the live radio performers during the show's commercial breaks.

There had also been a serious side to the radio, as the family would have taken advantage of the opportunity to get the most up-to-date news. Radio newscasters such as Edward R. Morrow became popular. His CBS radio show, airing live from London during the German bombing of that city, brought the tragic reality of war directly into people's living rooms. The ongoing conflict in Europe was obviously of interest, but it was more curiosity than a threat to life on the Panhandle. Europe was thousands of miles away, and the vast expanse of the Atlantic Ocean seemed to be more than adequate to isolate the nation from the threat of Germany. Local residents seemed to appreciate and understand the protection that it afforded us as a nation. However, most families in and around Goodwell and Texas County, Oklahoma, were less knowledgeable of the political and economic implications of that war and national alliances.

Of even less concern for most people of the Panhandle had been the ongoing war in Asia. Again, Japan had been waging war for most of the past decade, but again it was a foreign war among people who not only spoke differently but looked different. And like the war raging in Europe, there was an entire ocean separating us from that conflict. Besides, if you had conducted a survey just yesterday, most of the residents here had never even heard of Pearl Harbor, let alone knew of its military significance. Except, of course, for those few families who had relatives stationed there. However, by this evening, the entire nation had now heard of Pearl Harbor. As was happening all across the country, the members of the Johnson family would now sit attentively around the radio, awaiting further news of the attack. There would be no laughter tonight. Instead, there would be only fear and worry. Worry, not only for the nation but for Matthew.

By the time the rest of Michael's family arrived at the house, Michael had already found a radio station with a live telephone feed from Honolulu. With just audio and no video, the listening audience had to rely upon the descriptions given by people on the ground. They all quietly stood as they tried to picture the awful scene depicted by the news commentators. They could have sat, but somehow that did not seem appropriate considering the magnitude of what had happened. Sitting down somehow seemed disrespectful.

"The guy on the radio says there are fires and explosions everywhere," Michael was now telling his family as they gathered closer to the radio. It was as if being closer to the news could somehow give them more information.

The look of concern on his mother's face said it all. Although they would not know the full consequences of the attack for days, the strategic implications meant little to Sarah. All she cared about now was Matthew. Had she realized what ramifications the attack would have on Michael, she would have had even more reasons to worry. Hearing the eyewitness accounts, Philip could not get the image of Belleau Wood out of his head. It seemed like a lifetime ago, but the possibility that his son was now undergoing similar experiences pained him greatly. Philip knew how combat had scarred him, and he wished that Matthew would not suffer the same emotional scars that had plagued him all these years. But none of this would matter if Matthew had not survived.

Turning his attention to Sarah and saying it for the entire family, Philip tried to put everyone's minds at ease. "I'm sure Matthew is okay," he said, wishing he sounded more confident.

"If only I could be sure of that," Sarah said, looking to her husband for some sign of encouragement.

But for now, there would be none. Philip may have been in their living room listening to the radio reports, but his mind was back in time and at a place five thousand miles away. As the commentators would describe the horrific results of the Japanese aerial bombardments, Philip no longer heard the radio just a few feet away. Instead, he listened to the sounds of explosions. Philip was now back in another time, advancing toward heavily defended enemy lines, while German machine guns were ceaselessly firing across a field of death. He could no longer appreciate the scent of the apple pie that Sarah had earlier set out on the dining room table. Instead, he was now smelling the acrid odor of the hundreds of explosions and thousands of rounds of rifle and machine gun bullets coming from heavily defended German positions. It might have been December 7, 1941, in Goodwell, Oklahoma, but Philip was again with his 3rd Battalion, 5th Marines, at Belleau Wood. And now, half a world away, his son was probably experiencing the same horrific sights and sounds of battle. World War I was to be the war to end all wars. But now, a whole new generation of America's brave young men were facing death all over again. If Philip could understand the reasons why maybe it would make more sense. But throughout history, there had been battles and wars. And if people much more educated than him could not figure it out, then how or why could he.

"With all the reports about the various ships either hit or sunk, they didn't mention the carriers," Michael said. It was an observation, but it could have been just as easily a question.

"That has to be a good thing," his mother added hopefully.

"What do you think that means?" Michael was now asking the group but directed more at his father. Not getting an immediate response, Michael repeated the question, this time looking directly at him. Philip was finally brought back to the present. After not responding to Michael the first time, he did on the second attempt.

"I don't know. Maybe it's a good thing. Or maybe the government doesn't want to disclose the information," Michael's father answered, not knowing which was true.

Throughout this whole ordeal, Paul had said very little, while his sisters just stood in silence. Still, despite their unwillingness to join in the conversation, the looks on their faces showed the fear of not knowing about their brother's fate. Sarah, now aware of this, asked everyone to join hands. As they did, she offered up this prayer. "Oh Lord, our savior and redeemer, please grant onto Matthew your divine mercy and put him in the safety of your loving arms." The prayer might not have been perfect, but it was honest and sincere. Then, as an afterthought, she added, "And we pray for all those other brave servicemen and their families, that they too may be strengthened by your love and kindness." They all then unclasped their hands and lifted their heads. For the first time since hearing of the attack, the Johnson family held on to a glimmer of hope.

As more news came in, they would hear that not only had Pearl Harbor been struck by Japanese forces, but our military installations in Guam, Wake Island, and the Philippines had also come under attack. They would have stayed up all night listening to the radio, but they all had to get up early the following day. Despite the events unfolding in the Pacific Ocean, the family still needed to take care of the farm. So, one by one, the members of the Johnson family would say their goodnights until only Philip and Sarah remained by the radio. Turning the volume down not to disturb the others trying to sleep, Sarah took Philip's hand. Philip was a strong man, as well as a proud man. He was not one to talk at great lengths.

Instead, Philip felt that actions were stronger than words, and he felt confident that his efforts had always been sufficient to protect the family and their farm. But now, he felt that neither his actions nor his words were enough. There was so much Philip wished he could do. But realizing that he could not, tore at his insides. Sarah could see past the sad look on his face. In all their married life, she learned to understand her husband very well, especially when he did not speak what was on his mind. Still, having never been at a loss for words, Sarah could think of nothing to say. Instead, she turned the radio off and led Philip upstairs. None of the Johnsons would be having much sleep tonight as the events of the day would be replaying in their minds. Tomorrow would be a new day, but any hope that today was just a bad nightmare would not be forthcoming. Unfortunately, as bad as the events of today were, things were going to get much worse.

Earlier, eleven-hundred-miles and two time zones west of Goodwell, Cindy was in her dorm room at the nursing school when she first heard the news. She was reading one of her medical textbooks when she heard a commotion out in the hallway. A fellow nursing school student had been listening to her radio when the news bulletin broke into her regularly scheduled program of big band music. Hearing the reports, she began running down the hallway, announcing the news of the attack to each of the rooms she passed. Cindy soon joined the dozens of students as they now gathered in the noisy and busy hallway, each trying to sort out what had happened. As the sounds of the many concerned conversations filled the air, Cindy thought of Jake. After graduating from boot camp in San Diego, Jake was aboard a cruiser, the USS Indianapolis, part of the Pacific Fleet at Pearl Harbor. Someone had their radio tuned to a news station in one of the rooms trying to phone their affiliate station in Honolulu, but to no success. A sense of dread was now taking its toll, and Cindy felt the need to sit down.

She was not alone with her concerns, since being located near one of the Navy's largest bases, most of those trying to get more information were either related to or knew of someone in the Navy. Even her roommate was in tears, as her boyfriend had recently shipped out to join the Pacific Fleet stationed in Pearl

Harbor. But it was Jake's well-being that was preoccupying Cindy's mind. As more news became available and a shocked nation was slowly absorbing the extent of the destruction, she prayed that he had somehow survived.

Fate is a strange thing. It was fate that had The USS Indianapolis conducting gunnery drills and a mock bombardment at the Johnson Atoll, 750 miles southwest of Hawaii this morning. Had the ship been docked at Pearl Harbor, its fate would most certainly have been similar to the other victims of the air attack. It was also fate that somehow allowed the ship to evade detection from some twenty-five Japanese submarines sent to the waters around Hawaii. Their missions were to seek out and destroy any American naval vessels that survived the attack on Pearl Harbor. And it had to be fate that kept both the ship and Jake safe and out of harm's way. Yet fate can be fickle and can turn on you in a flash. But to Seaman Jake Smith, fully acknowledging the force and complexity of fate was a concept he had not yet mastered. As he stood on the deck of the USS Indianapolis, foremost in his mind was the realization that what had just hours ago had been simple target shooting would soon become the real thing. Yet, fate would still toy with the Indianapolis and Jake. Had Cindy known where he was and what he would ultimately be doing, Cindy would have been both relieved and terrified, as both the ship and Jake would play a significant role in the outcome of the war.

CHAPTER 26

Choices

January 3, 1942

Although the news reports made no mention of any attack upon the USS Enterprise at Pearl Harbor, neither were any reports of its current status. With Japan attacking targets throughout the Pacific and their Imperial Navy on the prowl to find and destroy United States Naval assets in the region, there was reasonable cause for the Johnson family to be worried for Matthew. Despite being thankful for the sincere concern and compassion shown to them by their neighbors and friends, most residents around Goodwell could only imagine the anguish of not knowing whether a loved one had survived. One family that could appreciate it was the Samuels, who lived about a mile down the road from them. Like the Johnson's, they also had a son in the service, a Marine assigned to Wake Island. When most of the other female congregants would hug Sarah after Sunday services, the most heartfelt hug came from Mary Samuels. Only she could share the anguish and concern that a mother would feel, knowing all too well what it was to worry constantly. Yet, even without saying a word, the two women shared a bond that neither one wished they had.

As would be expected, most of the Johnson family would spend hours each night with their ears glued to the Zenith radio that was their only source of information to the world outside the Oklahoma Panhandle. The exception was Sarah. Despite probably worrying more than anyone, she could no longer sit and listen to the fragmented and often censored reports that came across the airwaves. So instead, she would spend her spare time silently praying to her Lord that Matthew was safe. A decent woman, Sarah would feel guilty asking for special consideration for Matthew, knowing so many other exemplary service members were now at significant risk. But she justified her selfish concerns as a mother's privilege. Sarah carried Matthew within her womb for those nine months and nurtured him afterward until he no longer had to rely on her breasts for sustenance. She, along with Philip, had raised him and guided him as best as they could. Sarah was proud of the man he grew up to be, but like most mothers, Sarah had to allow him to be free, and she could no longer protect him from the evil dangers that lurked everywhere. Sarah had accepted Matthew's independence from her, but that did not mean she embraced it. But for now, all she could do was pray.

The most lively discussions about the war were between Paul and Michael. Because of his accident that cost him two of his fingers, Paul would complain about not enlisting, as many of his friends and former classmates were doing. Michael would try to show the bright side of Paul's situation, only to have it fall on deaf ears. Meanwhile, their father would sit there quietly, absorbing both the latest news reports and the conversation of his two sons. Although it was Paul who complained about not enlisting, Philip was more concerned about his youngest son. It was not from any words that came from Michael, but more from the look that he recognized on Michael's face, especially his eyes. While Paul would speak of enlisting, Philip would look into Michael's eyes. It was as if there was a window into his mind, as well as his soul. Philip was correct because Michael was running his options through his mind, as well as doing some serious soul searching. Philip was sure of it since he recognized it as what he had experienced twenty-three years earlier. He stayed silent for now, realizing that soon he might have to break his silence, giving Michael the same talk he had given to Matthew.

The following day it was Rebekah who saw him first. She had been out near the barn when she saw him coming up the road that led to their farm. Crying, she went running to the house, drawing the attention of all three Johnson men who were working in the barn. As she ran up the steps to the porch and threw open the door to the house, Rebekah ran into the arms of her sister. A startled and scared Grace was attempting to console her sobbing younger sister. But she found it difficult to fight back her concerns, still unsure what prompted Rebekah's reaction. First, the commotion in the living room caused Sarah to step out of the kitchen, still holding one of the morning's breakfast plates in one hand as she held a dishtowel in the other to dry it. Then, as Sarah looked out the living room window, she saw him also, causing her to drop the plate as it shattered to a dozen pieces upon hitting the hard wooden floor.

By now, Philip and his two sons were nervously watching as he drew closer. Finally, with an unemotional face, the Western Union telegram employee approached the entrance to the Johnson farm. Out here on the farms, everyone knew there was just one reason to receive a telegram, and it would not be good. The possibility of bad news from the War Department drew the attention of some of the neighboring Miller family. Now, Betty and her mother and father looked on at a distance with obvious concern. Betty's appearance had not gone unnoticed by Paul, but he was now focused on the young man from the telegram office as he continued riding his bike in the cold morning air. As he was now looking at the Johnson's, he tipped his cap as he passed their entrance and continued pedaling down the road. All those watching breathed a collective sigh of relief, knowing that at least for now, there would be no gold star hanging in their living room window.

As she was now attempting to clean up the mess from the broken dish, Sarah said a prayer of thanksgiving to God. She thanked him for sparing Matthew and their family from dealing with what would have been a tragic and horrible loss. But then it struck her as she thought of the telegram's final destination. Sarah thought now of Mary Samuels and her family, hoping and praying that they too would be spared from the inevitable pain and suffering that would come with the notification. But knowing there was just one other family in the area with a son in the military, Sarah thought of the inevitable sadness about to fall upon them despite her prayers.

That following Sunday at their church, a memorial service was held for Corporal William Samuels, USMC. Befitting the occasion, it was cold and gray with some light snow. There would be neither a funeral nor a burial today. Instead, their twenty-three-year-old son remained on Wake Island, his body buried along with forty-eight of his fellow Marines. After the obvious difficulty in extending their condolences to the Samuels family, it was a quiet ride back to the house, as no one knew how to express what they were feeling in their hearts. Except for one. Michael knew now, more than ever, what his destiny might be. Had Cindy still been a part of his life, maybe things might have been different? Or perhaps he might have felt the same, but he was going to do what he knew he needed to do. Michael would feel bad for any anguish this would place on his mother and his siblings, but Michael dreaded most having to tell his father what he was about to do. He would have been relieved of his last concern had he known that his father had already been aware of Michael's intention for the past few weeks. Like father, like son, Michael would soon be the latest member of the Johnson family to have been a United States Marine.

CHAPTER 27

Transitioning

January 17, 1942

The bus finally pulled into the asphalt parking lot at the Marine Corps Recruit Depot, San Diego. It had been a long journey for most, and this was the farthest from home that Michael had ever been. The stately palm trees that seemed to be everywhere were so foreign from the landscape he used to see back on the Panhandle. Nevertheless, the air smelled fresh, and despite the intense sun and bright blue skies, the temperature felt comfortable, aided in no doubt by a strong onshore breeze coming off the yet-to-be-seen Pacific Ocean. Awaiting patiently and seemingly annoyed were two Marine NCOs. NCO was the acronym for a non-commissioned officer. It referred to a category of enlisted members of the Corps. By nature of exemplary performance and demonstrating leadership skills, they have been delegated leadership or command authority by a commissioned officer. In simpler words, they were sergeants.

After it picked up recruits arriving at the San Diego train station and the local bus terminal, the bus had broken down on the way here, and because of it, they had arrived two hours behind schedule. By the stern and unhappy looks on the faces of the two sergeants, they did not appreciate its tardy arrival. The sergeants stood ramrod straight, with their arms behind their backs and their hands clasped together. These recruits would soon learn this was known as "parade rest." The two drill instructors watched with observant eyes as Michael and the other forty-one former civilians piled out of the bus. Peering out from under their wide-brimmed campaign hats, proudly displaying the eagle, globe, and anchor insignia, they appeared to look with disdain at the disheveled crew that was attempting to assemble before them. Carrying all their worldly belongings in an assortment of bags, satchels, and suitcases, the band of recruits began looking about at what would be their home for the next two months.

One of the drill instructors walked to the point that he probably used many times before and barked out the order, "Form up on me, two straight lines," then to add emphasis, he shouted, "Now!"

As the recruits began trying to line up in two straight lines, the sergeant standing in the background tried hard to suppress a smile, as the recruits became a mess of entangled arms and baggage as they nearly knocked each other over. When they finally came to rest in two uneven and wavy lines, the sergeant giving the order began walking in front of the first row, eyeballing each recruit as he passed.

"I am Sergeant Landon. The other fine gentleman you see standing behind me is Sergeant Randolph. For the next few weeks, you will address us as "Sir." When we decide you have achieved the right, you may then address us as Sergeant. After that, it is our job to turn you into Marines. But make no mistake about it, just because your service record has you listed as a Marine, that is not the case. Your mamas and your girlfriends back home might think you are Marines, but you will need to earn the right to be called that here. And whether or not that will ever happen depends on you. Because right now, you are without doubt the most half-ass, sorry excuse for Marines I have ever seen," he stated as he continued walking down the line. He finally stopped in front of Michael, who was standing at the end of the first row.

"Do I make myself clear?" he asked.

As a few of the recruits simply nodded their heads and the rest murmured something resembling yes, the sergeant's face grew red, and the vein on his neck began to bulge out. Then, shouting louder, he asked, "I said, do I make myself clear?"

The sergeants heard a better response of "Yes, Sir" from the group of recruits.

Still not satisfied, the sergeant shouted even louder, "I can't hear you!"

A loud, "Yes, Sir," finally came from the forty-two voices.

"What's your name, recruit?" Sergeant Landon asked as he

looked at Michael.

"Michael," he answered.

"Do you have a last name recruit, or were you born without one?"

"It's Johnson."

"I will ask you again, What is your name, recruit?" the Sergeant asked, now shouting in Michael's face.

"Michael Johnson," Michael shouted back.

"Michael Johnson, what?" the Sergeant demanded.

"Michael Johnson, Sir!" Michael shouted back, now remembering what the Sergeant had just told them.

Now looking directly into Michael's eyes, the sergeant demanded, "Starting with you, I want each man to count off to twenty-one."

"One," Michael said in a normal voice.

"I can't hear you," the Sergeant shouted back.

"One!" Michael replied, this time much louder.

Soon each man began counting off until one of the recruits faltered when it came to his turn to shout his number. Within seconds, the drill instructor was in his face shouting, "If you cannot count to fourteen, maybe you should go back to school and learn how. Now, let's try it again, starting with number one," as he was once again looking at Michael.

The Sergeant made an abrupt about-face with the count now successfully completed and began walking back down the line.

"If you aren't one to twenty-one, then form up in the row behind you," he ordered, as he looked at the last two without a number in the first row.

Having succeeded in having the recruits lined up in two equal rows of twenty-one each, he ordered them to drop their bags and line up in two straight lines. As he stopped at the end of the first row, he looked down the row and said, "I want to see just one person and no part of any other body sticking out. Do you understand?"

Hearing a few weak answers from the assembled group, he

again shouted, "I can't hear you!"

"Yes, sir!" this time, the group shouted back much louder in unison.

When the recruits were able to approximate what the Sergeant wanted and knowing that at this stage, this would be as good as it gets, he ordered the men to attention. Taking a clipboard with all forty-two names printed on a sheet of paper, Sergeant Randolph walked to the front of the group and began conducting roll call. One by one, each recruit answered, "Here, Sir."

Turning to Sergeant Landon, Sergeant Randolph stated, "Recruit class all present and accounted for."

Then, after acknowledging Sergeant Randolph, Landon told them to pick up their bags and suitcases. Anticipating what would happen from past experience, he shouted, "Column, left face." Thirty-six of the recruits turned to their left, four turned right, and the remaining two did not move. Sergeant Randolph was now unable to keep a straight face and tried hard to suppress an audible laugh.

"Your other left," Sergeant Landon shouted at the four facing the wrong way. Then, looking at the two who did not move, he asked, "What are you two waiting for, an engraved invitation? Again, column, left face!" he shouted even louder. With all forty-two lined up and facing the same way, the Sergeant was satisfied that this group had accomplished something as a unit for the first time. It would be his job and the other drill instructor to take forty-two individuals and turn them into a cohesive unit that would follow orders in combat without questioning them. They had seven weeks to achieve their goals. If unsuccessful, some of these men might die needlessly when in battle.

Marching together for the first time, with Sergeant Landon upfront counting the cadence and Sergeant Randolph bringing up the rear, their first stop after dropping off their belongings would be the mess hall. As the group would try to keep marching in step with each other and the Sergeants, inevitably, some would have trouble remembering their right foot from their left. They passed other platoons that were also marching to the staccato cadence of "left, left, left-right-left."

With the recruit's bellies satisfied, under their drill instructor's orders, they fell back into formation outside the mess hall, and once again, they would march as a unit to the camp's barbershop. There, standing in ankle-deep piles of hair of every shade and color, were several barbers, smiling broadly at the recruits as they held their electric clippers in their hands. After receiving the standard recruit buzz-cut, the forty-two men looked even more like a unit with a single purpose, as they began looking more and more alike.

The rest of the first day was a whirlwind of events. Still wearing their civilian clothes, or "civies" as they would learn to call them, they proceeded in a single line passing a row of Marines standing behind stacks of assorted uniforms. With their arms outstretched in front of them, each recruit received everything from utility trousers, shirts, underwear, socks, and boots to helmets and caps, officially referred to as utility covers. The piles of clothes continued to get progressively larger, heavier, and higher as they moved down the line. Talking among the ranks was not permitted unless asked a question. When asked what size, often the recruit would receive a size other than the one he requested. If brought to the Marine's attention that it was not the recruit's correct size, the typical response would be, that's your size now.

Another essential piece of equipment each recruit received was his "dog tags." Although they were all to be issued paper identification cards, these IDs would not fare well in extreme conditions compared to the two metal tags connected by a ball chain that would hang around their neck. Imprinted with their name and service number, it also included other vital information such as blood type and religious affiliation. The last two would be of importance on the battlefield. One for those wounded needing a blood transfusion to survive, while the other was for those who would not survive. In the latter case, the deceased's command would make efforts to find a chaplain of the same faith to pray for his soul.

Loaded down with everything the recruits would need to wear during the next seven weeks, they would now double-time it. So rather than marching in columns, they would jog in a single file to their squad bay where they would be living during their time here. Along the way, it would be inevitable that at least one member of the group would have some article or articles of clothing fall off. This action would disrupt the smooth flow of the line of recruits, as he would have to stop and retrieve the fallen items.

When finally able to rejoin the line, he would have been subject to the less than flattering comments of either of the two sergeants. Detailed instructions would later describe the proper wearing of their uniforms and how and where to store everything issued to them. But for now, they would just place everything on their racks, also known in civilian life as bunk beds.

The processing and equipping of the recruits were not over. Each man still had to receive their rucksacks, along with their entrenching tool, bayonet, knife, sheaths, shelter-half, blankets, canteens, cartridge belts, compasses, first-aid kits, and aluminum mess kits. Then, filling up their arms once again, Michael and the other members of his platoon would once again double-time back to their squad bay to drop off their loads. But, of course, what good was a Marine without his rifle, so the day would not be complete without a trip to the armory, where each man would be issued his M1903 Springfield rifle. However, by the war's end, the five-clip, bolt-action M1903 would be replaced by the newer, semiautomatic, M1 Garand rifle, with its larger clip holding eight rounds of ammunition.

Having received everything they needed, the recruits could wind down and converse among themselves for the first time since eating in the mess hall. One of the first orders of business was to acquaint yourself with your bunkmate.

"Hi, I'm Michael Johnson," he said, extending out his hand.

"Yeah, I know. I heard you earlier telling the Sarge. I'm Stanislav Meidzwiecki," he said in reply, shaking Michael's hand in return.

"Damn. That's a mouthful," commented the recruit in the rack next to theirs. "Where are you from?"

"Brooklyn. The Greenpoint section, to be precise, but Brooklyn born and bred," Stanislav proudly answered.

"I'm Pete Dawson from Wichita, Kansas. Why are you here instead of Parris Island on the east coast?"

"My family moved to Los Angeles two years ago, but I'm still all Brooklyn. Go Dodgers, both baseball and football."

"Well, from now on, you are simply Brooklyn. That's a whole lot easier than calling you whatever it is you call yourself." Dawson replied.

"It's easy. Just say, Stanislav Meidzwiecki."

"Like I said, you're Brooklyn from now on."

"What about you, Johnson? Where are you from?" Dawson asked as all eyes turned to Michael.

"Goodwell, Oklahoma," Michael answered.

"Hey, we got an Okie," Brooklyn said, seeming to enjoy the contrast to his upbringing.

"What about you, Pete? What are we going to call you?" Brooklyn asked.

"You can call me Pete, just plain Pete. I don't need no damn nicknames," Dawson said as Michael and Brooklyn were taking note of his robust six-foot, three-inch frame.

Just then, all conversation stopped as "Ten-hut" was loudly heard from the booming voice of Sergeant Landon, as a Marine officer wearing two silver bars on his collar walked into the squad bay, followed by Sergeant Randolph. Then, as all forty-two recruits stood at attention next to their racks, the captain began to speak.

"As you were. I am Captain Wilcox, your company commander. I want to welcome you to USMC Recruit Depot, San Diego. I expect each of you to perform your duties to the best of your abilities. If you do, with the training you will receive from your exceptional drill instructors, I do not doubt that you will succeed. Our country is fighting for its survival, and our nation depends upon us to right the wrong we suffered from our enemy. You are joining the finest fighting force the world has seen, and I look forward to your graduation."

Then, after looking over the assorted recruits standing before him, the Captain said, "Carry on," and he began to leave the squad bay.

"Ten-hut!" was once again shouted out by Sergeant Landon as the Captain exited the squad bay.

With Sergeant Randolph standing by the entrance, Sergeant Landon began walking down the center of the large open room, eying the men as they still stood rigidly at attention at their racks. Not saying anything for effect, he continued walking until he reached the other end. Then, after turning around, he spoke.

"Today was the first, and the last easy day you will have had during your forty-nine days with us. In each of your lockers is a copy of the Marine Corps Manual and the Rifleman's Creed. They will be your companions, your source of knowledge. Everything you need to know about the Corps is in there. If it isn't, then the Corps does not consider it to be important. Read them. Study them. Then, read them again. Learn your general orders. Memorize them." Then stopping, he paused and looked around at the men still standing at attention before continuing.

"Reveille will be at 0600 hours tomorrow. For you former civilians who do not yet know what that is, that is 6:00 a.m. Do not concern yourselves with setting your alarms since you have no clocks in here to do so. However, if your sorry asses are not yet up, Sergeant Randolph and I will be more than happy to assist you in waking up."

"You will be lined up outside in the company street by 0610. The uniform of the day will be tee-shirt, utility trousers bloused at your boots, and of course your boots. If we have anyone here not accustomed to wearing socks, let me add that in for their benefit. You will wear socks. We will then double-time in ranks with the rest of the company, eventually joining up with the rest of the battalion at the exercise field. There, we will introduce you to your daily dozen calisthenics. If you are not in shape, then you will have wished that you were. Then, as your reward for completing your morning exercises, we will proceed to the grinder, where we will work up a hearty appetite for breakfast by running eight laps around it. If anyone's doing the math, let me save you the trouble. It's two miles. Then, just for fun, you will have your first crack at the obstacle course. Get used to it since this will be your normal routine each morning as long as you ladies are our guests."

"Oh, before I forget. When we return here before breakfast at the mess hall, you will have thirty minutes to complete your three S's before changing into your class b utility uniforms. Do not bother looking them up for those of you who do not know the three S's. You will not find them listed in your manuals. However, I will advise you now of what they are. It is shit, shower, and shave. Not necessarily in that order, as there are but eight latrines in the company head for nearly two hundred men. Any questions?"

One brave but also naive recruit from Denver asked. "Sir, when do we get to shoot our gun?"

Hearing that question, Sergeant Landon walked over to the recruit, as Sergeant Randolph was wincing at what was next.

"What is your name, recruit?"

"Andrews, Sir."

"Andrews, strip from the waist down."

"What, Sir?"

"Are you having difficulty hearing, Andrews?"

"No, Sir, no."

"Good, then do it and get your rifle," Landon ordered.

Now naked from the waist down and holding his Springfield M1903, Landon ordered him to take three steps forward, putting Andrews in the center of the squad bay.

"Now repeat after me. This is my rifle, this is my gun, one is for shooting, the other is for fun," Landon said as he pointed to Andrew's genitals for the latter part of his rhyme.

Embarrassed, Andrews repeated what the Sergeant had said as laughter and snickering came from some other recruits.

"You think this is funny? Sergeant Landon asked. Then, not thinking that it was, he gave the order, "Platoon, at ease. Now everyone drop down and give me thirty pushups."

As they began their punishment, groaning was heard, with not everyone completing the thirty required.

"For those of you wondering why you're doing pushups because you weren't one of the ones who laughed. This is why. You are one unit. In the field, you live or die together. What one does affects each of the others. You will enjoy the spoils of victory together, or you will suffer the pain of defeat together. But at least you will have done it together with your brother Marines."

As the last of them struggled to complete as many of the thirty that they could, Sergeant Landon turned to the men before walking out and said, "Lights out in forty minutes. I suggest you do what you need to do. Any more questions?"

Just then, a resounding, "No, Sir," was heard from all forty-two.

Brooklyn looked over to his new friends and said, "I guess we're not in Kansas anymore," referencing Dorothy's famous line from the film of two years ago, "The Wizard of Oz."

CHAPTER 28

Progressions

Winter 1942

True to their words, Sergeants Landon and Randolph did help anyone who was still asleep at 0600 and had missed reveille. Grabbing the lids from the metal trash cans at each end of the squad bay, they began banging them against the cans, creating enough noise to have awakened the dead. Those recruits still not out of their racks would find themselves jumping out, unaccustomed to this type of alarm clock. Those not used to sleeping on the upper part of a bunk bed would take a while to get used to the safe dismount from their racks.

Even the gruff-sounding Sergeant Landon would allow some leeway to the recruits in their first few days, especially when making their beds with military corners. But for now, it was more about the speed than the style, as forty-two young men were trying to square away their mattresses, sheets, and blankets while dressing for the required assembly outside in just ten minutes. Some forward-thinking recruits had slept wearing their uniform of the day to save time. They were not unnoticed by the two drill instructors, who wondered whether they should be complimented for their ingenuity or punished for trying to beat the system.

As they fell into ranks outside, the sun in the east had not yet risen, and the darkness of the night was still minutes from being displaced by the morning's dawn. Despite the relatively warm climate of Southern California, the chilly morning air could be evidenced even without a thermometer, as many of the assembled recruits stood shivering while at attention. Unlike the previous day, today's formation had changed to four columns instead of two. Finally, after taking the roll call, the platoon began double-timing over to the exercise field. After completing the daily calisthenics and the two-mile run on the grinder, which doubled as an asphalt parade ground, the platoon made its way to the obstacle course. The obstacle course, or "O course" as it was known, was the most demanding of the morning's rituals. Each recruit had to overcome various obstacles and climb over wooden walls, often requiring a team effort to help those struggling to get over. After completing the course, each recruit would attempt to climb up a thick rope hanging from a wooden beam twenty feet above the ground. If successful in getting to the top, they would ring a large brass bell.

With the platoon members finishing up at different times, rather than wait in formation to head back to the squad bay, the recruits were allowed to run back to the company head on their own. As tired as they might have been, the prospect of reaching the showers first, or finding an unoccupied toilet, provided an added incentive to push themselves further physically, thus finding the strength to run back as fast as they could, beating the others.

For Private Michael Johnson, taking a shower in the company's head was something that he looked forward to each day. His enjoyment had not gone unnoticed by his newly made friends.

"What's so great about having to shower in a room with a bunch of other naked guys passing around a bar of soap? Brooklyn asked.

"I guess you never had a shortage of water back where you lived. But as a kid growing up during a drought lasting nearly a decade, standing under unlimited water is a luxury," Michael responded.

"Watch out if you drop the soap and have to bend down to pick it up. I'm not sure if I trust all of these guys," Pete said, laughing as Michael looked perplexed at his statement.

Each day was busy from reveille to lights out. Today after breakfast, it was a trip to the base hospital for yet another physical exam. They would line up to walk through a gauntlet of hospital corpsmen, each holding a large and threatening hypodermic needle. Michael and the other would winch in pain as they watched the sharp needles going into their arms. The vaccines they contained were for diseases that were generally not known or discussed in either the urban or rural areas of the country. They used any free time at night to study the Marine Corps Manual or break down and clean their rifles. They would also learn and memorize the "Rifleman's Creed," also known as "My Rifle and the Creed of the United States Marine."

Surprise inspections would occur often, and having a dirty weapon after a day at the firing range would not go unpunished. One such recruit from Albuquerque, New Mexico, Pvt. Louie Amato found out the hard way what that might entail. Having his rifle declared dead because of it not having a clean and pristine barrel, the sergeant held a funeral for the weapon. As Sergeant Landon instructed him, he emptied his footlocker and ordered him to use it as a coffin for the burial. With his rifle interned inside, it was carried out to an area just off the grinder as the whole platoon joined in the procession. Under the watchful and annoyed eyes of his fellow recruits, using his entrenching tool, the recruit proceeded to dig a grave. Finally, having dug deep enough to bury his footlocker with the rifle inside, he began covering it with the dirt he had just removed. Having succeeded in doing that, Sergeant Landon ordered the platoon to observe a moment of silence. Then, like Lazarus rising from the dead, the Sergeant ordered the recruit to recover the buried weapon and return it to the squad bay, where it would undergo the thorough cleaning it should have had in the first place. The desired effect of the platoon losing an hour of precious free time and the peer pressure resulting from it gratified Sergeant Landon. It would be enough of a deterrent to prevent Amato, or any other platoon member, from being caught with a dirty rifle the remainder of their time in boot camp.

If asked, Michael, or any of the others, would say after each day that their basic training would never seem to be any closer to ending. Yet, with the seven weeks of training drawing to a close, they would all wonder where the time had gone. During this time, the strenuous physical training left each one in better shape than when they first arrived. Those who did not grow up in an environment that required firearms for hunting were now familiar with using a rifle and other small arms. They had learned how not to blow themselves up when tossing a grenade. And they learned how to crawl on their bellies, staying low enough under barbed wire as not to get shot by the live rounds whizzing by above their heads. They became as proficient as one could be, not being in actual combat, in how to evade an enemy's bayonet attack while sticking your own into his chest. They had learned other offensive and defensive tactics in hand-to-hand combat that would prove helpful. They also discovered that their entrenching tool could not only dig out a foxhole to provide cover but was also available as a weapon of last resort. They had acquired basic first-aid skills and recognized and identified the ranks of the various service members. But the most important thing they learned was the value of teamwork and working not as an individual but as part of a fighting unit. They had come to understand that all the dreaded time they spent doing close-order drills and executing sharp turns and abruptly halting had a purpose besides looking sharp on the parade grounds at graduation. The forty-two Marines could be able to act as one. There would be much additional specialized training beyond what they learned in boot camp, but they proudly earned the right to be called Marines.

Unknown to Michael, less than ten minutes away on the other side of San Diego Harbor, someone else had been undergoing what was essentially her basic training. Cindy was several months into her schooling at Pacific General Hospital's nursing program. If she thought it would be all the glamour portrayed in the movies, she would have been very disappointed. As with most professions where you start at the bottom and work your way up, this was also true of becoming a nurse. Before Cindy could proudly earn the title of a registered nurse, she would have to perform all the lowly tasks that provide for a patient's care, including those least desirable. Whether it was sponge bathing an elderly patient, changing the sheets of a patient with bedsores, or cleaning up after a sick person who could no longer control their bowels, she had to do it all. At times, having had to clean up the vomit of a critically ill patient, Cindy had found herself having to leave the hospital room, as she would find it necessary to throw up. But as Michael was getting used to his challenging routines, she also would begin to take these events in stride.

A few of her fellow students had discovered a USO club nestled between the Marine base at Camp Pendleton and the San

Diego Naval Base. Finding it an excellent place to unwind from the pressure, as well as the sights and smells of their training, they had asked Cindy to join them this coming weekend.

"I don't know if I want to," said Cindy.

"Why not? Come on. It'll be fun," Helen said, trying to convince her.

"I'm just not ready for the dating scene," Cindy said, trying to defend her position on the matter.

"Who said anything about dating. You go there for fun. We let a few of the sailors or the Marines buy us drinks, get to dance, and maybe have a little smooching before we all call it quits for the evening. Nobody gets hurt, and we'll probably never see each other again. That's definitely not dating."

"It's also the patriotic thing to do for our servicemen," another student named Carol said, winking her eye.

"It's been about a year since that incident with Doctor Cauldwell, and you haven't dated anyone since. It's time you put yourself back out there. You're not getting any younger, you know." Helen was again trying to convince Cindy to go with them

"First off, I'm still just nineteen years old, in case no one noticed. And I am over that whole incident. I just don't feel comfortable being with anyone right now," Cindy replied.

"If you ask me, it's not that bastard Cauldwell who got you like this. It's that guy in the photo you keep looking at each night. You must have fallen for him big time. Was he really that special?" asked Carol.

"I certainly thought he was. I probably still do. There's a whole story to the day we got our halves of the photo, but it's a long story. Maybe one day I'll tell you about it. I wonder at times if I look at it more of a habit than a hope that I'll ever see him again."

"Well, if it's just a habit, then why not come with us. Face it, the guy in the photo will never know, and he probably no longer cares," said Helen, as she rejoined the conversation.

"Maybe I should go out. But no promises. If I feel the least bit uncomfortable, I'm turning around and walking out. Deal?"

"Deal!" both Helen and Carol said simultaneously.

Had Cindy known where Michael was now, she might have had different expectations, but fate was still playing out its hand. Michael, meanwhile, was planning his future after graduating from boot camp tomorrow.

"Where do you think we'll wind up?" Michael asked to no one in particular.

"Scuttlebutt has it that they're forming that 3rd division right nearby at Camp Ellis," Brooklyn answered.

"Maybe we'll all go there as a group," Pete offered, hoping it would be true. They had all bonded during their seven weeks of training, and they became good friends also.

"Well, whatever and wherever it is, I'm planning on blowing off some steam this weekend. The USO has a place not far from here, and from what I hear, that place is jumping. Good food, good drinks, and broads, lots of broads. And not the skanky kind. Nice ones, and they're all hot to trot," Brooklyn said, rubbing his hands together.

"Were you this way back home also?" Pete asked.

"No. I was worse," Brooklyn replied, laughing.

"I'm in. What about you, Okie?" Pete asked.

"I don't know. I didn't have much luck with girls the last two times, and the last one didn't work out because of the first one."

"Is that the broad whose picture you sneak a peek at each night," Brooklyn asked.

"Yes, and she's not a broad. She's a lovely girl, or at least she used to be," Michael responded as he began reminiscing.

"Well, what's her name?"

"Cindy."

"Well, do you think Cindy will be sitting home alone this Saturday night? Of course not, Then why should you. Hey, we only graduate from boot camp once. Besides, we're like the "Three Musketeers." All for one and one for all," Brooklyn stated proudly.

"Hey, Brooklyn. You amaze me. I didn't have you pegged for reading the Alexandre Dumas classic," Pete said.

"Who said anything about reading. I saw them in the movies

a couple of years ago, the one starring Don Ameche. But what about you, Okie? Are you coming?"

"Since you put it that way. Who am I to break up the Three Musketeers." Michael said, smiling.

The following Saturday evening, two taxis picked up passengers from two different locations, but each received instructions to head to the same destination. Cindy and her friends arrived first. Dressed nice and looking very attractive, they were already collecting stares from the scores of servicemen hanging about. As they walked into the club, the sounds of big band music filled the air, adding to the festive atmosphere. Michael and his buddies arrived a few minutes later. As the two groups were mingling in the crowded dance hall, Helen caught Brooklyn's eye, and he immediately made a note of her and her friends. As the three women sat down at one of the large, round tables, Cindy excused herself, saying she needed to find the ladies' room. While Helen and Carol were taking in the eye candy of so many handsome servicemen in their well-pressed uniforms, Brooklyn had brought Michael and Pete with him to meet the girls.

"Hi, I'm Stan," Brooklyn said, surprising both Michael and Pete, who had never heard him called that.

"Stan?" Pete asked, whispering.

"Tonight with the ladies, I'm Stan. Who'd want to go out with a guy named Brooklyn," he whispered back.

"Hi, I'm Helen, and this is Carol," she said, continuing with the introductions.

"This is Pete, and this fellow over here is Okie, I mean Michael," Brooklyn said, quickly correcting himself. If he did not want a less than flattering nickname, then neither should Michael.

Looking at the empty seat that had been Cindy's, Brooklyn asked Helen, "Wasn't there a third in your group?"

"Yes. But our friend had to go to the ladies' room. She should be back soon."

"That's good. We'd hate to have our buddy here feel left out," Brooklyn said as he looked at Michael.

Michael sat down next to the empty seat as the band began

playing a rendition of Artie Shaw's "Stardust."

"Hey, this is a great number. Do you want to dance?" Brooklyn asked Helen.

"I'd love to." She replied as Brooklyn took her hand and led her onto the dance floor.

"Would you care to join me?" Pete asked Carol as she was admiring his tall and fit body.

"I sure would," she said as she stood up and took Pete's extended hand.

As they joined Brooklyn and Helen on the crowded dance floor, Michael watched the two couples slowly dancing as the two women were being held close by his two buddies. Seeing this brought back memories of when he and Cindy wanted to go dancing. Memories that he did not need at this time. Michael got up from the table with no sign of the missing third woman and walked to the dance floor, stopping by Brooklyn.

"This isn't working for me. Sorry guys, but I got to go. I'm going to catch a cab and head back to the base."

Brooklyn may have protested his friend's departure more had he not enjoyed having Helen in his arms as they were dancing. When the music stopped, the two couples returned to their table, finding Cindy sitting there alone, wondering what she had missed.

"Oh, they had a friend with him, but for some reason, he must have lost interest and left," said Helen.

Just great, Cindy thought, now seeing her two friends cozying up with the two Marines. She sat there for a while, beginning to feel sorry for herself. She had wished that maybe someone nice like Michael could have been there, but instead, she felt alone and abandoned.

"I'm sorry, but my supposed partner lost interest without even seeing me. I thought this might be good for me, but maybe it is too soon. I'll take a cab back to our dormitory," Cindy said, excusing herself.

Michael had stopped to say hello when he met another member of his platoon. As they were finishing their conversation in the crowded entrance, someone was jostled into him, as he felt a shoulder brushing against his back. Michael could barely hear the words "excuse me" above the din of the crowd and the music, as Cindy quickly apologized, not seeing the face of the person she had bumped. By the time Michael could turn around, he only saw the back of a woman walking hastily out the front door. As Cindy approached a line of cabs at the taxi stand out front, she entered the next one in line. Facing the driver to give him her destination, Cindy overlooked the Marine who just walked up to the front of the line. As she pulled away, Michael was getting into the cab that took over the vacated spot.

For each of them, it was a lonely and disappointing ride back. When Michael returned to a now-empty squad bay, his loneliness was much more apparent, as he was currently the only one there. Lying in his rack, he pulled out Cindy's picture and could not stop wondering how it all went wrong. He realized he had to move on, but Michael did not know how it was possible without having the answers he needed.

Just a few miles away, Cindy returned to her dormitory room and began wondering the same thing. She wanted to break free from the invisible hold that Michael had on her, even though she believed that he somehow no longer cared about her. Cindy was angry at him, wondering why, but Cindy also asked herself if it was something she did or perhaps did not do. Looking at his picture, she too wanted answers, but they would not be forthcoming.

Meanwhile, in another part of town, a bitter and lonely Eunice Smith had returned from working her second job. Her previous hopes for ascending the economic and social ladders of San Diego were over. If forgiveness was a virtue, it had escaped Eunice, as she still blamed Michael and her daughter for what happened. Unable to recognize her responsibility for her current situation, she had but one pleasure in her life. She had not known why she decided to save them at the time, but Eunice was glad that she did. Standing on a chair she brought from the kitchen, Eunice began pushing aside various items in the hall closet until she retrieved the shoebox containing the stack of envelopes that she had hidden in the back of the top shelf. Untying the string that bound them together, Eunice retrieved one of the envelopes. As she sat down on the chair, she opened it up and removed the letter. It was the last letter that Cindy had written to Michael. Rather than feel empathy for her daughter's broken heart, a malevolent smile appeared on her aged and wrinkled face. As undeserving as it was, Eunice would take pleasure in knowing that at least she was the one responsible for breaking them up. When she had finished reading, she placed the letters back on the shelf. Living alone, she no longer needed to hide them in the shoebox, as she would look at them often.

As all three of them would ultimately fall asleep tonight, even Eunice had no idea of the enormous impact that her actions would have on each of them. It would have seemed unlikely that fate would have had anything to do with her devious acts, but nobody ever knows what fate has in store for them. And fate was far from being finished in influencing their ultimate destinies.

CHAPTER 29

The War

1942-1943

As the nation was now fully involved in a two-ocean war, the early results were not looking good. The German juggernaut had rolled across most of continental Europe with little resistance and was driving deep into Russia. At the same time, England remained free from invasion by the German army, its ability to survive as a nation was taking place in a desperate air battle high above London and its other major cities. The German successes did not stop on the European Continent, as the shadow of the Third Reich fell across northern Africa as well. In our Army's first encounter against the Germans at the Kasserine Pass in Tunisia, the inexperienced and poorly led U.S. forces were no match against the battle-hardened Afrika Korps commanded by Field Marshall Edwin Rommel.

Meanwhile, the U.S. and its allies suffered a string of losses in the Pacific and Southeast Asia. Allied airpower all but eliminated; Japanese planes could fly almost non-contested and were making bombing runs over Australia. As nearly 130,000 British, Australian, and Dutch military personnel became prisoners of the Japanese, Singapore fell. The combined naval forces of the British, American, Australian, and Dutch navies suffered defeat at the Battle of The Java Sea. The Philippines were lost, as 80,000 United States and Philippine soldiers had no choice but to surrender. Combined with the earlier losses of Guam and Wake Island, the airbases now in Japanese hands helped to provide an air shield for the seemingly unstoppable Japanese Imperial Navy. Even the threat of an attack on the U.S. Pacific Coast had not abated. From a combination of genuine fear and underlying racism, President Roosevelt signed Executive order 9066. His order resulted in the internment of 117,000 people of Japanese ancestry into reloca-tion camps, most of whom were American citizens whose loyalty was never in question.

Sacrifices were being made on the home front as well. Gold Star Mothers would both proudly and sadly display the evidence of their loss, as all too many gold stars were now hanging in the windows of these grieving families. Aletta Sullivan of Waterloo, Iowa, would hold a record that, fortunately, would not ever be broken or sought after. Mrs. Sullivan had lost five of her sons in a single day as their ship, the light cruiser USS Juneau, was the tragic victim of a Japanese torpedo during the Naval Battle at Gua-dalcanal. In addition to Mrs. Sullivan, unfortunately, 682 of her son's shipmates would have also made their mothers eligible for membership in the American Gold Star Mothers.

But there were some encouraging signs in the war against Japan, as the nation desperately needed some good news. In what would be a one-way mission, sixteen U.S. Army B-25 bombers did what had never happened before. Stripped of all defensive weap-ons to keep the plane's weight down, they would try to launch from the short runway that an aircraft carrier provided. Led by Lieutenant Colonel James Doolittle, the aircraft successfully took off from the USS Hornet and made it to Japan. They dropped their bomb loads over Tokyo in a more symbolic gesture than a stra-tegic attack. Knowing that they would not have enough fuel to return to the Hornet and land the heavy bombers on the carrier's deck even if they had, they would try to make it to the China Main-land. Once over China, they would try to land and hopefully team up with friendly Chinese troops. Of the sixteen planes, fifteen had managed to crash land in China, and fourteen of those crews could get out safely. Eight airmen were captured and brought to Japan for trial. Of those eight, three suffered execution as war criminals.

Unfortunately, the fortunes of war are often not intended or anticipated. Since every action has a counteraction, the conse-quences for the Chinese people for having aided the American at-tackers would result in horrific reprisals. As punishment for their actions, some 250,000 civilians and 70,000 soldiers would lose their lives at the hands of their Japanese invaders. Oddly enough, the sixteenth plane, and the only one not to crash, landed safely at an airfield in the Soviet Union. The crew members were detained for a year until they managed to escape through Iran with the help of Soviet Interior Ministry Officials.

On the other hand, Doolittle, whose idea it was for such an attack, was expected to be court-martialed for losing all sixteen of the Army's bombers. Instead, he found himself to be the hero of a grateful nation. He would receive the Congressional Medal of Honor and be promoted two grades to brigadier general.

Besides making good newspaper headlines and boosting the morale of the American public, the attack would play a significant role in pushing up Admiral Isoroku Yamamoto's plans to attack Midway Island in the Central Pacific. One month after a major naval engagement in the Coral Sea, where the Japanese won the early decision based on numerical losses, but the U.S. won a strategic advantage going forward, the Battle of Midway would prove more decisive. In the largest naval battle fought entirely by aircraft, Japan would lose four of its major aircraft carriers. It was a defeat they would never recover from, and it would be the beginning of the end of Japan's offensive advantage.

In the Johnson family farm in Goodwell and a hospital dormitory room in San Diego, family members anxiously awaited letters from their loved ones. Despite the generally good feeling reading those letters would provide, the delay from when they were written to when they would be received and read could give no guarantee of the sender's current well-being or status. Equally frustrating were the many redacted words and sentences that military censors would blackout from the letters. The fear that enemy spies would intercept the correspondence and glean valuable information had led to this practice. Soon, posters would appear advising of the dangers of having "loose lips." Post offices in both Goodwell and San Diego displayed posters with the warning, "A slip of the lip can sink a ship." On the sign was the image of a drowning sailor, set against the backdrop of his burning and sinking ship.

In Goodwell on this day, they were huddled around the large kitchen table when Philip finally opened the envelope. They all looked forward to reading the letters that they would receive from Matthew and Michael. Michael's letters came more frequently and more on time because they came from peaceful San Diego, whereas Matthew's would come from somewhere in the hostile and battle-torn Pacific Ocean. Later, each family member would take their turn rereading it. Being able to hold the letter in their hands somehow made them feel closer. But for now, as head of the household, Philip would read Michael's letter out loud for all to hear.

September 16, 1942

Hi everybody,

I finally received my orders for my permanent assignment. We were initially assigned to the 2nd Marine Division, but we will be part of the new 3rd Division they're forming right here in San Diego at Camp Elliot. When I say we, I mean my buddies from Boot Camp, Brooklyn, and Pete will be coming with me.

How is everybody doing? I am doing okay. Have you heard from Matthew? I was glad to hear that Paul and Betty are finally dating. They make a lovely couple, and she's perfect for him. Is Grace still seeing her boyfriend? I still feel bad that I missed Rebekah's high school graduation. I can't believe that she's going to the local state college right there in Goodwell. At least she's still living at home. There is so much to say and so little opportunity to say it. Please keep your letters coming. They mean so much to me. I love the weather here in San Diego, but I must admit I miss not being back on the farm.

I don't know if I will take advantage of my leave and try to come home for a visit. There are rumors that the division might be shipping out in the next few months. They don't tell us where, but the scuttlebutt is that it could be either ▮▮▮▮▮ *or* ▮▮▮▮▮▮*. Can you imagine that? Me, finally getting to see those places I dreamed about in school. They say that their summer is in the winter and vice versa. So when we get there, it'll be summer all over again. That would be pretty neat.*

I know the reports coming out of our bases in the Pacific don't sound good, but we will take them back and show the Japs that they can't push us around.

Don't worry about me. I will be fine. I got the best training possible, and I'm with a swell bunch of guys. We look out for each other. I wish Ma could send me one of her delicious apple pies, but it would probably be no good by the time it got here. I also wish you could see me in my dress uniform. Pa would be especially proud.

That's it for now. I will write again soon.

Your loving son and brother, Michael

It was not only the Johnson family that looked forward to receiving those letters. A thousand miles away in California, a former resident of Goodwell was happy to see her letter in the mail. Cindy was excited as she carefully tore open the envelope. She had immediately known it was from Jake. Cindy sunk lightly into the bed's mattress, sitting with her legs crossed as she shifted positions until she was comfortable. Hearing Billboard's number one hit for the past eight weeks playing on her roommate's radio, Bing Crosby's crooning of "White Christmas" added to the happy but somber mood as she began reading the letter.

November 26, 1942

Hi Sis,

I don't know when you will receive this, but today is Thanksgiving out here in the Pacific Ocean. We had a nice Thanksgiving dinner, at least as enjoyable as one might expect, being ▇▇▇ miles from home. This past ▇▇▇▇ we joined up with the ▇▇▇▇ and the ▇▇▇▇. We are all heading to ▇▇▇▇▇▇ where we hope to do some damage to the Japs.

How are you doing with nursing school? It must be hard. I still can't picture my kid sister as a nurse. Back in port, they have nurses in the base hospital. Some of those Navy nurses are pretty good-looking. We enlisted men can't touch them, but a guy can dream. Now that I think of it, you'd look pretty nice in a Navy nurse's uniform. Bet you'd get the attention of a lot of the officers. They get all the breaks.

We don't get the mail on time, so Christmas will probably be over when you write back to me. We all hope that this war will be over soon. Since we really handed it to them at Midway back in June, we're all hoping that we got them on the run. Maybe next Christmas in '43, we'll all be able to celebrate together. Well, at least most of us. I wrote one letter to Ma, but I never heard back. Have you seen her? Probably not.

You probably don't go back to the house that we had moved into anymore. But if ever you do, could you look for my whittling knife. I left in such a rush I hadn't brought it with me. I think it must be either in my old room or up in the hall closet. It's not a big deal, but Pa had given it to me a couple of weeks before he died. It had been his. I'd like to have it, although right now, in the middle of the ocean, there's not a whole lot of wood to whittle.

There's scuttlebutt going around that five brothers died on the ███████ *at* ███████████ *a few weeks ago. Had you heard anything back in the states? They play "White Christmas" a lot over the ship's PA system. I'm sure you heard it. The guys kind of like it, because it reminds them of home, but it's sad also knowing that we can't be home for Christmas. Besides, there's no snow out here, and there's probably no snow back in San Diego either. I bet Goodwell has some, though.*

They just rang seven bells. I go on watch at eight, so I have to end this now. Stay safe and well.

Your "youngest" big brother, Jake

Letters went both ways. As much as family and friends back home wanted to hear from their loved ones in the military, even more so did those away from home, especially those in harm's way. Cindy, more than most, knew the importance of staying in touch, especially receiving letters. She would write as often as possible, not knowing when Jake would receive her letters. Getting mail to any troops overseas was an enormous undertaking. Getting it to a ship in the middle of the ocean was even more challenging.

April 18, 1943

Dear Jake,

I hope you are okay. We hear a lot about the various sea battles going on in the Pacific where you are. Of course, we have no way of knowing if you and your ship were involved. And you can't tell us even if you tried. It probably wouldn't matter, since by the time I would get your letter you would probably be hundreds of miles away already.

I can't believe how fast this year has been going by. Does it seem fast for you also? It will be Easter in one week, and it will be another Easter without our family being together. Hopefully, we can all enjoy it next year.

I still haven't been able to get myself over to Ma's house. Even though it's just across town, I just can't do it. There's still too much hurt at that house, and unfortunately, Ma was the cause of it. Maybe one day I'll have the courage to go there and face her, but I have no interest in doing so right now. And I haven't forgotten about your whittling knife. If I ever get there before you do, I will look for it. I would just go ahead and buy you a new one and send it to you, but I know it's special because Pa had given it to you.

Can you believe I am starting my second year of nursing school? As fast as the time has been going, it won't be long before I graduate, and I will be a registered nurse. I could easily stay here at Pacific General, but I want to do something different, something more meaningful. Who knows, maybe I'll sign up to be a Navy Nurse.

The Barnes have been very supportive of me, and they treat me as if I were their daughter. I see them often, and we have Sunday dinner together most weeks. Their daughter Veronica will be eighteen soon, and she's getting all grown up. She's adorable, and she treats me like her older sister, which is nice, having grown up with five brothers. By the way, we were all able to get together a while back, and we're all proud of you.

Caleb said he had heard from cousin Bertha's daughter that the talk around Goodwell was that Matthew Johnson was on the USS Enterprise. He was always nice to me back then. Wouldn't it be funny if you two bumped into each other? That would be something. There was no word about the rest of his family. Not that I care. Well, maybe I do care a little. It's just that I can't stop wondering about Michael. I just don't know why or how it happened. That's the troubling part. Was it anything that I did that made him stop writing? I guess I'll never know, and I will probably never see him again in my lifetime or come within 1,000 miles of him. At least I'll have you to write to me, so you better not stop. Do you hear me?

I sent you a package for Easter. I hope you like it, and I hope you get it in time. Stay safe and be well.

Love, your favorite sister, Cindy (ha-ha)

As Cindy was sealing the letter, she thought about what she had written. She once again took out Michael's photo with a heavy heart, and after looking at it, she lay down on her bed. Still clutching the picture, she quietly cried herself to sleep. At the same time, somewhere in the hostile waters of the Pacific Ocean, both Matthew Johnson and Jake Smith were aboard their ships.

Their fate and those of their fellow crewmates would remain unknown. Meanwhile, asleep in his barracks at Camp Elliot in San
Diego, Michael was unaware of either his brother's current role on
the other side of the Pacific Ocean or Cindy's heavy heart just a
few miles away.

CHAPTER 30

3rd Division

1943-1944

Michael and his buddies enjoyed the New Zealanders' friendliness ever since the division had been deployed there since the beginning of the year. But as with all things in life, especially in the military, nothing good is ever permanent. With the decision made to move the 3rd Division to Guadalcanal for additional training, the task of moving an entire division would begin. As the Marines were loading nearly 20,000 men and their equipment onto the transport ships that would take them to their next temporary home, Michael glanced back and took a mental photograph of Auckland. These images would have to take the place of an actual picture. In his limited time in the Corps, Michael had already seen people and places he might have thought impossible just a few years ago. Now, New Zealand would add itself to his collections of memories of the world outside of the Oklahoma Panhandle. Still, the only actual photograph he possessed would go with him everywhere. Safely nestled in his billfold, he would look at it every night, still wondering what went wrong.

As they were making the five-day, 2,095-mile journey, the Marines would try to find ways to pass the time. Besides giving them something to do besides gripe about the cramped sleeping quarters or having to endure the smell of vomit that hung heavily in the stale air below deck, it helped take their minds off the torpedo threat from an enemy submarine. For some, it would be playing cards, while for others, it would be shooting dice. Although the intent of both games was to win, winning a large sum of cash before going into battle was considered a bad omen to many. For those not inclined to gamble, often a Marine might just lie on his rack, one of the hundreds stacked four and five high, thinking of places other than this. Rumors, or scuttlebutt as it was commonly known, ran rampant in situations such as these. Everyone knew someone, who knew someone, who had the inside scoop. Most often, they were wrong. But every now and then, the information was spot on.

"Hey, I just heard that we're getting a new platoon sergeant when we get to Guadalcanal. A guy from the 2nd Platoon had heard our captain and the colonel talking about it when they passed by him on deck. The guy's supposedly a real piece of work. A real hard ass. Gunnery Sergeant Richard O'Neill. And get this, he comes with a nickname, Big Dick," Brooklyn was excitedly telling his friends.

"I heard about him. He had been with the 2nd division, and then he was with the 9th regiment before coming over. Supposedly, he was shot at Belleau Wood back in '18. A few years ago, they said he had been a Sergeant Major before they busted for threatening some shavetail lieutenant over how to discipline his men. They say he's about six-foot-five and tough as nails," Pete chipped in.

"He sounds like someone you'd want on your side when the going gets tough," Michael offered.

"Hey, Okie, didn't you say your dad had fought at Belleau Wood also?" Brooklyn asked.

"Yeah, he did. He never talked about it much. I don't think he ever got over it."

"That would be hot stuff if Big Dick knew your dad," said Brooklyn.

"If I were you, I would not let him hear you call him that," said a sergeant who was walking by. "I had been with the 9th Marines, and he was the real deal, but only his friends could get away with calling him Big Dick. But don't get me wrong, there's no one better to be with when the shit hits the fan. And from what I hear, that could be happening sooner than later."

"More scuttlebutt," Pete said as the sergeant walked away.

"It's only a matter of time that we see action. That's why we're moving to Guadalcanal. There's something brewing," Michael added.

"Well, anything has to be better than being on this damn

ship," Brooklyn said as it continued to roll from the heavy seas. As he finished talking, another Marine, just twelve feet away, began throwing up from being seasick.

With the entire division on Guadalcanal, training began in earnest for the first combat the new division would see. It was soon apparent that it would consist of an amphibious landing and jungle fighting, neither of which was a surprise considering the narrow choice of possible targets. Even the 1st Marine War Dog Platoon, consisting of twenty-four Dobermans, German Shepherds, and their handlers, took part in the training. Employing the special K-9 unit, using the dogs to sniff out hidden snipers and machine-gun nests further supported the jungle fighting notion.

Soon after arrival on Guadalcanal, Michael, and the rest of the men of the Fourth Platoon, Foxtrot company, were assembled in front of their tents when a larger-than-life figure approached them. Standing every inch of six-foot-five-inch, with shoulders broad enough to provide shade at the beach, Gunnery Sergeant Richard O'Neill was introduced by the company captain. Already a twenty-five-year veteran, O'Neill had first enlisted as an eighteen-year-old when the United States had entered the First World War. Billed as "The War to End All Wars," O'Neill had served at Belleau Wood, where he would receive a purple heart for having been shot by a German soldier. After spending time in a hospital in France, O'Neill found himself back in the States, where he fully recovered, ultimately deciding to stay in the Corps. He rose through the enlisted ranks during times of relative peace, but he was always expecting to once again be in combat. His combat experience caused him to drill and train his men hard, but it also earned him his reputation as tough and always prepared. Now twenty-five years after the end of World War I, that training and preparation would serve both him and his men well. After addressing the men and informing them of what he expected from them, he dismissed the platoon. As they dispersed into small groups, they all began wondering what was lying ahead.

After many weeks of intense training, O'Neill walked to where his platoon had been gathered, spotting Michael and his buddies.

"Private Johnson, can I have a word with you?" O'Neill asked.

"Yes, Gunnery Sergeant," Michael replied.

"It's Michael Johnson, isn't it?" he asked.

"Yes, that is correct," Michael answered, somewhat surprised by the Gunnery Sergeant's less than usual blustery mannerism.

"Where are you from, Private?" O'Neill asked, but suspecting that he already knew the answer from Michael's twang.

"Oklahoma, Gunny."

"I heard that your father was in the Corps. Belleau Woods back in '18. Is that so?"

"Yes, Gunny. That is correct."

"Come walk with me, Michael," O'Neil said.

"Yes, Gunny," Michael responded, now more confused than ever by not only the gunnery sergeant's casual demeanor but by being called by his first name.

"You probably have heard the story many times that the Germans shot me at Belleau Wood. Frankly, after all these years, I am tired of hearing it myself. But you may not know is that when I was lying on the ground and afraid of bleeding to death, and yes I was afraid, I was carried to safety by a fellow private who threw me over his shoulders and risked his own life to save mine. He became my brother. All of us here are brothers. We may not be blood relations, but the bond between us is just as great, maybe even greater. I never really got a chance to thank him properly. In fact, I never saw him again. All I know is that his name was Johnson, and he was from Oklahoma. I never forget a face. When I look at you, I see him in you. I will never know for sure if it was your dad who saved my life, but I'd like to think that he was. If you ever get the opportunity to ask him about this, I would like to know if he remembers carrying that scared, skinny kid to safety. And yes, back then, I was skinny." O'Neill had now been smiling as he put his arm around Michael's shoulder. The Gunnery Sergeant added, "If it was him, tell him I owe him a proper thank-you."

"Knowing my Pa, it could have easily been him. If it were him, then I'm glad that he did it. I guess that it was just not your day to die back then. Maybe fate had a reason for you being here now. Thanks, Gunny, for sharing that story."

"That's okay, Kid. You're alright. But one day, you have to

tell me the story of that picture of that girl you carry around with you. I've seen you looking at it, but you never speak of her."

"There's a reason I never talk much about it, but for you, Gunny, I will," Michael said as they continued walking with Michael telling O'Neill all about Cindy.

The scuttlebutt had been right all along regarding both Gunnery Sergeant O'Neill and the division's soon-to-be seeing action. At dawn on November 1, 1943, elements of the 3rd Division began landing on the island of Bougainville, coming ashore at Empress Augusta Bay. An estimated 40,000 or more Japanese troops were on the Island, and intelligence reports had incorrectly believed them to be stationed mainly around the Island's airfields. Aerial reconnaissance photos failed to disclose the extensive system of bunkers located in the dense jungle just above the beaches. As a result, many of the first to come ashore came under heavy fire from the hidden and heavily armed Japanese.

Bougainville was the largest island in the Solomon Islands archipelago. Since the turn of the century, it had been under the control of three different nations, beginning with the Germans who claimed it in 1899. During the First World War, Australian troops had occupied the island, wresting control of it from Germany. Under a mandate from the League of Nations, it became part of the Australian Territory of New Guinea in 1920, which it remained until Japan invaded it in 1942. As part of the Allies' Operation Cartwheel, it was strategically important because of the Japanese constructed airfields. If control of the island and its air bases were to fall, then the U.S. Forces could threaten Japan's ability to protect its major naval base at Rabaul. Then, rather than attempting to invade and capture the port city of Rabaul, Allied forces could simply isolate it and render it useless.

Having moved off the beach, Gunnery Sergeant O'Neill had just stood and was about to lead his men forward when heavy rifle and machine-gun fire erupted from within the dense jungle. O'Neill was the recipient of two Japanese bullets as he was directing his men to take cover from the withering hail of bullets. The first hit was a clean through-and-through in his left shoulder, the shot coming from an unseen Japanese soldier firing his Arisaka Rifle. As O'Neill was recoiling from the impact, he instinctively raised his Thompson submachine gun to a firing position and began squeezing the trigger. He quickly fired into the jungle when he was hit a second time, this time to his right thigh by the same shooter. As the bullet from the 6.5x50mm cartridge tore into his flesh, it severed his femoral artery as bright red blood began spurting out. Collapsing to the ground, the Gunnery Sergeant continued to bark out orders to his men.

While return fire from his fellow Marines was now firing at their unseen adversaries, Michael had crawled across the exposed terrain, going to the aid of his stricken comrade. He grabbed O'Neill and began pulling him to safety. Seeing the nature of his wound and knowing that he might bleed out anyway, O'Neill told Michael to save himself and rejoin the platoon.

"No way Gunny. It ain't your day to die," Michael told him as he began applying a tourniquet on his leg.

"That's not your decision to make, Private," O'Neill yelled as bullets were whizzing overhead.

"I'm sure my Pa would not have left you at Belleau Wood if he had the chance, so I'm sure as hell not going to leave you here either," Michael responded as he kept the tourniquet tight and was wondering if history was repeating itself.

As reinforcements rushed to the platoon's aid, two M1919 Browning .30 caliber machine guns began raking the enemy positions. Soon, the "whoomph" sound of Marine's M1 mortars fired in response to the Japanese attack was heard, followed shortly by the explosion of their 81mm projectiles as they blew apart sections of the dense jungle undergrowth with its Japanese defenders. With most of the defenders either dead or wounded, their remaining comrades fled deeper into the jungle.

"We need a corpsman," Michael shouted as an appreciative O'Neill thanked him. Then, staying true to form, he threatened to have him court-martialed for refusing to obey his order to leave him and take cover.

O'Neill was treated by a corpsman and loaded onto a litter to be carried by two stretcher-bearers who briefly stood there, wondering how they were going to carry the massive Marine. Before leaving, O'Neill winked at Michael and gave him a thumbs up.

"I owe you a big one, Okie." He said as they began the task of bringing him to an aid station in the rear.

"Do you think we'll ever see him again?" Pete asked.

"He's one tough son-of-a-bitch. I don't think we've seen the last of him yet," Michael said, not knowing just how true his statement would be.

The 3rd Division returned to Guadalcanal in January 1944, its combat role at Bougainville now over. However, mop-up operations by mainly Australian troops would continue throughout the war, as stubborn pockets of half-starved Japanese soldiers would refuse to surrender. But despite the desperate efforts of those remaining Japanese, the 3rd Division had been victorious. With the Solomon Islands back in Allied hands, the 3rd Division would begin readying for its next offensive.

"Hey guys, guess who's coming back? Big Dick himself," Brooklyn shouted, not allowing anyone to guess who it was.

"Hey, that's not surprising. It was only a flesh wound," Pete offered.

"You call a severed femoral artery a flesh wound?" Michael asked.

"Well, it went through his flesh, didn't it. Besides, you keep playing up his wound, so you have a better story to tell your grandkids when they ask you about that medal they gave you," Pete responded as he grabbed Michael's utility cover from his head and began tossing it to the others in the group.

"You're just jealous," Michael said as he attempted to recover his eight-point, sage green cotton twill cap.

"Jealous of what? A Bronze Star. Now, if it were gold, then that would be a different story. Besides, what's the deal with the story going around. They're saying that your dad had done the same thing with Big Dick back in 1918." Pete was now more serious, as the rest of the men standing around were now listening.

As Michael finally grabbed his utility cover, and after placing it firmly back on his head, he said, "I wrote to my Pa and asked him about it. He never spoke of it, but I guess he felt that he had to now. My Pa did carry a young Marine to safety who the Germans had shot. He said it could have been O'Neill, but unlike the Gunny, he never got a name. He just went back about his business.

He said there was a lot of that going on, and it could have just as likely been someone else. O'Neill suspects that it was my Pa, but that's just a guess."

"Well, in any event, it sure makes a great tale to tell. I'd say that if nothing else, the gunny owes you big time," said Brooklyn.

"What kind of sorry ass excuse for Marines do we have here," as the booming voice of Gunnery Sergeant O'Neill interrupted the conversation.

"Hey Gunny, welcome back," was spoken in unison by those gathered.

"Thanks. It's good to be back. It'll take more than being shot to keep me away. I would have been back sooner if not for the case of Malaria I must have caught there also. I think I'd rather get shot again than have to suffer through the fever and the delirium that comes with Malaria. But they say I'm good enough to be able to break your balls again," O'Neill said with a laugh. Then, becoming serious, he looked at Michael and added, "The other news is that Private Johnson will no longer be a member of the platoon."

As all looked around, wondering what was going on, none was more puzzled than Michael.

"Why? What gives, Gunny?" Michael asked.

"It's because you're now Corporal Johnson. Private Johnson no longer exists. Apparently, a medal was not enough. I guess the brass thought you should get rewarded for saving this cranky old Marine's ass. Congrats, Corporal," O'Neill stated as he handed Michael his new chevrons.

"So what's next, Gunny? They had us training constantly while you were gone. Scuttlebutt is it could be Guam," the new corporal asked.

"Well, although being a gunnery sergeant doesn't make me privy to what the top brass is planning, all these years of service count for something, and the word is definitely Guam. Probably by the summer."

"We go ashore. We fight. We win. Then, we rest, only to train some more. Then it's another island, and we do the same thing all over again. Why don't they just give up and get it over with?" Brooklyn asked.

"If you ask me, it won't end until we kill every one of them.

And that includes invading Japan itself. A few of them are still holding out on Bougainville, and we beat them months ago. You better get used to this island-hopping because there's a lot of Jap held islands between here and Japan," said O'Neill.

CHAPTER 31

Graduation

April 1944

Cindy had been anxiously awaiting this day for three years. Even she would have had to admit that graduating at the top of her class was more than she could ever have hoped. Despite the excitement of her achievement, it was also a bittersweet moment for her, as she watched the parents of most of her fellow graduates waiting to congratulate their daughters. Cindy thought of how proud her father would have been, which brought moistness to her eyes. However, her emotion had suddenly changed from sadness to irritation when she accepted her mother's absence. Although they barely had contact with each other during the past three years, Cindy did send her mother an announcement of the graduation ceremony when she felt somewhat sympathetic and was in a charitable mood. Not seeing her made Cindy more grateful for the Barnes family, as Robert, Susan, and their daughter Veronica were coming forward to congratulate her.

"Cindy, we are so happy for you. Thank you for making us proud," Doctor Barnes exclaimed as he was the first to greet her.

"Honestly, it is I who should be thanking you. Without you, I don't know where I would be or what I would be doing," Cindy replied, as now Susan and Veronica were each taking their turns to hug Cindy.

"Dear, we are pleased with what you have achieved," Susan remarked while looking at Cindy's white nurse cap.

"Top of your class. Hey, not too shabby," Veronica added.

"I expect you to do even better when you take your premed courses," Cindy replied, smiling at the future college student and future doctor.

"I hope you have an appetite because I made reservations for us at the best steakhouse in town," Doctor Barnes enthusiastically proclaimed.

"I hope she does also," Susan said, speaking directly to Cindy. "Look at you. I don't think you were eating enough at the hospital's cafeteria. You need to put on a few extra pounds."

"I'm fine, really. I'm just three pounds less than I was when I started nursing school. Maybe it's the uniform that makes me look thinner."

"Well, whatever it is, you can certainly afford to indulge yourself with a big well-deserved dessert tonight. The restaurant has the best apple pies there, and add a little ice cream on top, and it's heavenly," Susan answered.

Although Cindy's mother was a decent cook, when it came to baking, the thought of one of Michael's mother's delicious home-cooked, deep-dish apple pies immediately came to mind. She was thinking of the many times when she and Michael would argue over who would get the last slice. Then, to no surprise, Cindy began experiencing that melancholy feeling she would get despite there being something positive in her life. Cindy could never get over the hurt that came with not sharing the happiness with Michael. Other than the picture she still kept of him, she had not seen his face, nor had she heard his voice in over three years. Yet, in her mind, she was picturing him standing there before her, beaming proudly at what she had accomplished. And despite the voices of the other graduates and their families filling the auditorium, as well as the Barnes discussing their dinner plans, she imagined Michael's cheerful voice telling her that he was proud of her and how he still loved her. If only that could be true, she thought.

"Now that was a great dinner. Perfectly fitting for a great occasion," Doctor Barnes said, feeling the need to loosen his belt.

"Yes, it was, and thank you again for everything," Cindy replied.

"Now, I know you said you had made up your mind, and I respect your career choice but are you sure you don't want to reconsider? Pacific General is a great hospital, and they can certainly use someone of your caliber," Doctor Barnes had asked, hoping for Cindy's reversal of her decision.

"Robert," Susan said sternly, "You know we have talked about this. It's Cindy's choice, and I applaud her for it."

"And I think it's neat," Veronica said, attracting a disapproving look from her father.

"You all know how grateful I am for all you have done for me. More importantly, not just getting me into nursing school but accepting me as one of your family. I would love to be working here in San Diego at Pacific General and to be able to be close to all of you. But, I feel, rather I know, that my calling is somewhere else. I want to do my part in this war. My brother Jake is putting his life on the line as our boys fight the Japanese, and they are just that, boys. If I can do anything to help them make it back home, then I would have succeeded as a nurse. I could always go back to civilian life after the war, but right now, being a Navy nurse is something that I need to do." Cindy was now looking across the table, hoping to see acceptance on Doctor Barnes' face.

"Cindy, you know I will always support you and whatever you decide to do, but I just want to make sure that you are doing it for the right reasons. With that whole Cauldwell episode, and especially your boy back in Oklahoma breaking up with you, I just hope that you're not running away from your problems," Doctor Barnes asked, hoping it did not hit a sore spot.

"I know you have my best interest at heart, and I love all of you for that, but this is the best thing for me. Maybe I need to move on, but that's not quite the same as running away. What's important to me now is having your support and knowing that I have your love to get me through any tough times that may lie ahead."

"That, you will always have," Doctor Barnes replied as his wife and daughter were nodding their heads. Then, as if on cue, all three stood up and went to hug Cindy.

Back at her dormitory room for the last time, Cindy was packing up her belongings. She looked at the picture of Michael, as she did every night, and wondered how his life had turned out. Cindy had told the Barnes that she needed to move on, and in a sense, that was true. But as long as she clung to that half of their photo, she could not truly move on. Part of her wanted to rip it up once and for all, hoping to erase all memories of Michael. But the other part wanted to keep it and cherish it, with all the fond memories of the first eighteen years of her life that it represented. She would wonder what the reason was that fate had in mind for her and Michael to break up. She had even considered going back to Goodwell and confronting Michael once and for all. At least, then she would get answers and perhaps closure. But deep down, Cindy did not want closure, nor did she want to give up hope that somehow she and Michael would once again be together. It would be scary not knowing what fate had in store for her, but even more frightening to know what that future might be. As long as there was the slightest glimmer of hope, she felt that nothing was impossible. And if nothing else, Cindy had hope. Whether that would be enough would soon become apparent.

CHAPTER 32

Balboa Park

May 1944

Having spent the past three years living in a dormitory while attending nursing school at Pacific General Hospital, the transition to the Navy and its sparse accommodations at Balboa Park came relatively easy for Cindy. The fact that she was still living in San Diego further eased the change in her life. But it was not the physical trappings of military life that concerned her. Despite excelling at her nursing duties back at Pacific General, Cindy had hoped that she would be mentally and emotionally tough enough for the tasks that lied ahead. Although she had seen her share of accident victims and the occasional victim of a brutal crime, much of what she had to deal with were the sick and often elderly patients that came from a non-violent environment. Now, seeing so many sailors and Marines suffering from the severe damage inflicted upon their young bodies would be hard to take. She worried if she would be up to the task of dealing with the daily care of those so seriously wounded on the battlefield. Yet, it was for this very reason that Cindy wanted to serve. She felt the need to challenge herself to perform at this level, and that could only be satisfied by taking this journey. She would pray that Jake would never need such care, but she would hope that someone would take care of him as well as she would treat others. Now, as a Navy nurse and having been assigned to the Naval Hospital at Balboa Park, Cindy would have an opportunity to prove to herself that she was capable of living up to that challenge.

Balboa Park had initially been named City Park, but the name was changed in 1915 when San Diego hosted the Panama-California Exposition. After much public discussion, the park's commissioners, appropriately enough, chose to honor Spanish-born Vasco Nunez de Balboa, the first European to see the Pacific Ocean while exploring Panama. The Navy's presence dated back to 1914 when they acquired land in the park to establish a field hospital for the 4th Regiment, USMC, under the command of Colonel Joseph Pendleton. Subsequent expansions resulted in the creation of the expansive naval hospital facility. By January 1942, The hospital had already begun receiving the first victims of the attack on Pearl Harbor to continue their recovery. At that time, the sprawling complex consisted of 56 buildings and a total of 1,424 beds. Because of the war, the hospital would expand to 241 buildings and 10,499 beds by next year. In addition, many of the original Spanish-Renaissance buildings from the 1915 exposition were in use by the Navy. The former House of Hospitality and the California Building served as dormitories for the nurses assigned to the massive facility.

Having lived in San Diego, Cindy had seen the "Pink Palace," as the main hospital building was nick-named. But to be actually living and working there as a Navy Nurse would be a life-changing experience. As she was walking to the building that would probably be her home for the next one-hundred-eighty days, the realization of what she had signed up for began to settle in. Even the largest civilian hospitals paled in comparison to the enormity of Balboa Park. Further evidence that she was now in the military came by way of a group of thirty-six nurses, impeccably dressed in their "ward whites" uniforms, standing three abreast and twelve deep. Cindy watched as they stood motionless and silently at attention as a Marine drill instructor inspected their ranks. She watched with interest as the instructor began shouting orders to the women to start marching. As they began stepping off as a single unit, Cindy took note of their serious faces, realizing the importance that the Navy put into this part of their training. It was so unlike the crowded and noisy halls at Pacific General, but the camaraderie of the women was evident, and it was something that Cindy found appealing.

Walking further among the complex of buildings, she finally entered the building formerly the House of Hospitality at the 1915 Exposition. She then walked into the large dormitory room, which she would share with twenty other young nurses. Spotting an empty set of bunkbeds, she walked over to them and placed her bags on the lower bunk. She had begun to put her things away when a friendly voice announced its presence.

"Hi. I guess we're going to be bunkmates. I'm Irene, Irene Kelly. I'll flip you to see who gets the upper," the fellow nurse said as she extended her hand, speaking with a heavy New York City accent.

"Nice to meet you. I'm Cindy Smith. And I don't mind, I can take the upper bunk," Cindy said as she extended her hand in return.

"Nope, fair is fair. Heads I win, tails you lose," Irene said laughing as she tossed the coin, waiting for Cindy's reaction.

"Oh, now I get it," Cindy said after a few moments, thinking that this matchup with her new bunkmate was definitely going to be interesting.

"Pay no attention to me. It's just a little bit of New York humor. I'll take the upper. That is unless you want it?" Irene asked while shaking Cindy's hand.

"No, that's okay. The lower will be just fine. Back home, I was lucky to have my own room, as the only gal among us kids."

"Wow, that's quite a twang you got there. Where are you from?"

"Right here in San Diego for the past three years, but Oklahoma before that. On the Panhandle, a little town named Goodwell."

"How little?" Irene asked.

"Don't know for sure, but maybe a few hundred. We had more, but many left in the '30s. Things got pretty bad back then," Cindy answered.

"Wow. I had more than that just living on my block back east."

"And where back east was that?" It was now Cindy's turn to ask a question.

"The Bronx, East Kingsbridge Road to be exact," Irene answered proudly.

"I'm not sure exactly where that is," Cindy stated honestly.

"It's part of New York City, one of the five boroughs."

"What's a borough?"

"It's like a county. Brooklyn, Queens, Manhattan, and Staten Island are the other four," Irene said, beginning to sound more like a geography teacher than a nurse.

"I heard of Manhattan. Isn't that New York City?" Cindy offered.

"It is, but so are the rest."

"Then wouldn't it be easier to say New York City. Besides, what makes the Bronx different from the rest of the city?" asked Cindy.

"Really? We have Yankee Stadium with those "Bronx Bombers." How about "The Babe?" Nobody was ever better than Babe Ruth. And Lou Gehrig, "The Iron Horse." If he hadn't died from that horrible disease, who knows how long he would have played. Now we have Joe DiMaggio. You must have heard of them. How about Fordham University and their football team, the Rams? They had that great offensive line, the "Seven Blocks of Granite," with Vince Lombardi and that wild 1936 season? I could see the university from my living room window. How about The Grand Concourse? Doesn't any of this ring a bell?" Irene asked, somewhat skeptical of Cindy's lack of knowledge in this regard.

"I'm sorry, I've never been east of Oklahoma, and we don't have those types of sports teams here in California, nor did we back home in Oklahoma. But I have heard of Babe Ruth, and Oklahoma University had its football team, the Sooners." Cindy replied, amused by Irene's rapid-fire way of talking.

"Well, at least that's a start. I never understood why this part of the country didn't have professional sports teams," Irene proclaimed as she was putting her bags on her bed.

"I grew up on a farm. I never saw a big city until we moved here to San Diego. What is it like living in a place like New York?" It was now Cindy's turn to ask a question.

"Well, compared to New York, even San Diego seems small. I went to nursing school at Bellevue Hospital on the lower east side of Manhattan, near the East River. Although technically, it's not a river. They just call it that. It's actually a saltwater tidal estuary. Now that's a mouthful, isn't it? I could look out the hospital's windows facing west and see the Empire State building.

Now that's a skyscraper. Tallest in the world. They built it during the height of the depression in just thirteen months."

"How do you know all this?" Cindy asked, amazed at the facts Irene was stating.

"My dad used to read all about New York, and he was constantly retelling it to my brother and me when we were growing up. He especially enjoyed reading poems by Edgar Allen Poe. Poe lived in a cottage that is still there in Poe Park, right across the street from my apartment. I could see it out my bedroom window. My mom used to say that's why they moved to that building," Irene said with pride.

"I grew up with five older brothers, but most of what our father quoted to us was from the bible. As far as skyscrapers or sports teams go, there's not a whole lot to tell about Goodwell, but it was a nice place until the draught and the dust storms came. That's how I wound up here on the West Coast. So how did you wind up here? Weren't there Navy hospitals out east?" Cindy asked.

"Yeah, there are some big ones up and down the coast. But I wanted to serve out here, in the Pacific. I had a brother who was part of our fleet at Pearl Harbor. He was on the USS Lexington, but they were out at sea when the attack came. He survived Pearl Harbor, but an explosion on the Lexington killed him during the Battle of The Coral Sea. For me, the war in the Pacific is personal." For the first time today, Irene's voice turned serious

"I am so sorry for your loss. I have a brother on the Indianapolis, and it's a cruiser. I guess I'm here for the same reason," Cindy said, realizing that she and Irene, as different as they were, shared a common bond.

"Have you got a guy here, or maybe one from back home?" Irene inquired, quickly wanting to change the subject.

"That's a long story, and it's complicated, but the short answer is no."

"Well, I love long and complicated stories, especially when it comes to guys and romance, so I'm all ears whenever you're ready to start talking."

"Maybe later. As I said, it's complicated. What about you? Do you have anyone special?" Cindy inquired.

"No, I'm not ready to settle down. Besides, I don't want my love life to be complicated like yours," Irene said with a mischievous grin.

"Maybe complicated is a good thing," replied Cindy.

"Listen, if we're going to be bunkmates, you are going to wind up telling me the story anyway, so why not do it now and get it over with," Irene insisted.

Remember, you were the one to ask," Cindy said as she pulled out Michael's picture.

"Well, how about us. You, a country gal, and me, a city girl bonding like this. Who would've thought?" Irene said, smiling, as she sat down on the edge of her bed, listening to Cindy's tale of Michael and Doctor Cauldwell.

"Now that's a story. I'm glad that son-of-a-bitch doctor got a good beating. But maybe it's time to give up on the other guy. If he couldn't wait for someone like you, then maybe he's not worth it." Irene remarked, having listened to Cindy's laments.

"But it's hard to understand. Michael really was that nice. Maybe it's me that should wait for him," Cindy replied, wondering if she believed what she just said.

"That's up to you, country gal, but this city girl wouldn't be wasting my time on a guy who just gave up on me. There's plenty of other fish in the sea if you catch my drift," Irene commented, happy to use nautical terms since they were now in the Navy.

As Cindy was lying in her bed that night, she looked up at the bottom of Irene's bed frame and mattress. This image was in stark contrast to her thoughts of the seemingly endless expanse of the Pacific Ocean and her brother Jake aboard the Indianapolis. She had thought about what Irene had told her about her dead brother, feeling bad that she never asked her his name. She thought it would somehow feel more meaningful if there were a name attached to his sacrifice.

The former civilian nurses soon became indoctrinated into the military ways. One aspect of that would be marching under the watchful eye of the Marine Drill Sergeant that Cindy had seen earlier. Learning the various ranks and the bars and insignias that identified them would also become a job skill, unlike civilian life. The rapid influx of nurses into the Navy would be a scene that would be repeated often, both here at Balboa Park and other naval hospitals throughout the country. Before the attack on Pearl Harbor, there was a total of just 1,700 nurses, both active duty and reserve status. By next year, the number actively serving in the Navy Nurse Corps would increase to over 11,000.

They were all trained nurses, and medicine was generally the same everywhere. But military patients, especially combat patients, would require a new skill set that they would soon all acquire. Treating wounds, amputations, inserting IVs, blood transfusions, and caring for burn victims would happen at much greater frequencies than usual in civilian hospitals. The nurses would also be responsible for training hospital corpsmen.

The nurses' ongoing training was intense, but there would still be time for leisure and social activities. The Navy encouraged a buddy system for enlistment into the Nurse Corps, and additional bonding among the recruits would often result in lifelong friendships. Unlike the draft, all of these nurses were volunteers. Like Cindy and Irene, some enlisted to serve their nation for personal reasons, while others were the result of recruiters who had gone to the major hospitals and nursing schools. But in the end, no one had forced them to be here, and they were all serving their country. Hospitals, for obvious reasons, ran twenty-four hours a day, seven days a week. As a result, the nurses would find themselves working with the same crew as part of a team. This work closeness would lead to even further bonding. Temporary duty assignments would occasionally separate a nurse from her regular group, even while at the same hospital, especially one as large as Balboa Park. But more often than not, when they were free from their hospital duties and taking advantage of any granted liberty or off-duty time, they would do things together.

"Hey, Cindy. Did you get a glance at the new work schedule? They have you down for SOQ next week. I hear that can be a pretty good assignment," Irene said as she was reading the list posted on the wall.

"SOQ? What is that?" Cindy asked.

"Sick Officers Quarters. It's a plum assignment. Your patients are all officers. Some high-ranking, which could be good for your career in the Navy. While, some of them are young, good-looking eligible bachelors, who could also be good for your career outside of the hospital if you catch my drift."

"By now, I think everyone catches your drift. Besides, I don't know if I'm ready for a serious relationship," Cindy replied.

"Who said anything about serious. If it turns out to be serious, all the better. But you need to have some social life, even if it's just temporary."

"I think you're forgetting that they are in SOQ for a reason, and that reason would make it hard for them to include dating at this time. And can't their wives be patients there also?" Cindy answered with a question of her own.

"Yes, some wives might be. But as far as the bachelors, most do fully recover, and you never know. Listen to me, Country Gal, this city girl knows what she's talking about. It wouldn't hurt to be extra nice to them. There's nothing wrong with having friends in high places.

"First off, I'm nice to all my patients, regardless of rank. I'm not going to do anything different. I take care of all of my patients the same, whether they're a seaman or an admiral. But I guess you do have to respect the higher rank and the position it holds. You may be correct that knowing someone up high couldn't hurt." Cindy responded as she was now thinking about her new assignment.

"Let's get back to the romance issue. Just promise me that if some handsome Lieutenant is there recovering from something minor, like a stomachache, and he should ask you out, at least you'll consider it. And please, don't bring up that whole Michael and Doctor Cauldwell thing again. Not all guys are like that."

"I promise you I will consider it," Cindy said smiling.

"Why do I feel that considering it is the only thing that you would do?" Irene asked, shaking her head.

There would be other perks to living in Balboa Park, and silk stockings would be one of them. The war was now in its third year, and like everywhere else across the nation, the needs of the military had created shortages of essential items. Some were more essential than others. But to a woman, silk stockings were considered more of a necessity than a luxury. Unfortunately, silk was a product that was rarely available to the general public. Much of it was because of the demands of the nation's Army and Navy. The Army used it for the parachutes needed by both the airborne divisions and the flight crew members of the Army Air Corps, whereas the Navy used it for the bags containing the explosives that powered their large guns. Since the silk disintegrated completely when the bags exploded, it left no damaging residue.

Before the war, Japan had been the sole supplier of silk to the United States. But on August 2, 1941, with trade talks deteriorating with Japan, the Office of Production Management (OPM) seized the nation's entire supply of silk as a precaution. That decision proved to be foretelling when, four months later, Japan attacked Pearl Harbor. Fortunately for American women, a substitute would save the day as nylon stockings were available, a product first introduced at the 1939 World's Fair in New York. But soon, this option would also disappear. With nylon needed in the war effort to supplement rubber in short supply, the former OPM, now the War Production Board, seized the nation's entire nylon supply on November 15, 1942. Once again, women across the country had to contend with bare legs. But just across the border from San Diego, silk stockings were available in Tijuana, Mexico.

Cindy and Irene were still debating the merits and logistics of finding eligible officers to date. Just then, their conversation was interrupted when a few of their fellow nurses had come over.

"We're all going down to Tijuana tomorrow. We heard that they have the black silk hose that we need for our dress blue uniforms. Do you girls want to come? We're planning to make a day out of it," one of the group asked.

"Sure, count us in," Irene responded before giving Cindy a chance to answer.

Cindy, Irene, and a half-dozen other Navy Nurses on their day off went into Tijuana, finding the silk stockings that made them the envy of women not fortunate to be living on the border with Mexico. Someone took a picture of them sitting in a cart that a mule was pulling. Copies were made and distributed to all those involved. Cindy looked at the simple photograph and added it to her growing collection of photos at Balboa Park. She thought how ironic it was that with all these photographs of her current life, the only picture she cared about was from her past life.

With thoughts of her past with Michael at least temporarily gone, Cindy began thinking of her future. Despite already doing her part in serving her country, she felt that she could still do more. She could have had no way of knowing it then, but her assignment to SOQ would have ramifications well beyond the time she would spend there. Fate was funny that way. Seemingly small events in Cindy's life could turn into unknown changes that could alter her destiny. Not knowing what they were could be a blessing in disguise.

CHAPTER 33

An Ocean Apart

Summer 1944

It came as no surprise that Guam was the next target for the 3rd Division. It had been among the first U.S. Territories in the Pacific to fall to the Japanese, as it came under attack just a day after Pearl Harbor. Two days later, the lightly defended Island surrendered to the superior Japanese forces. Now, on July 21, 1944, it was the Americans having the superior numbers. An invasion force of some 48,000 Marines and the Army's 77th Infantry stood ready to wrest control of Guam from its 19,000 Japanese defenders.

Having learned from their losses at Saipan just last month, the Japanese attempted to dig in deeper, but the combined effect of nearly 45,000 artillery shells, fired from a fleet of 274 U.S. ships, wreaked havoc on the shore defenses. Adding to this were the bombing sorties from the thirteen aircraft carriers that took part in the attack. By the time the first elements of the Third Marine Division came ashore, they must have been encouraged by what they saw. Navy and Marine pilots dropped 4,283 bombs on the island, burning or destroying every palm tree and building within sight. Further inland, however, Japanese artillery sites protected by caves, or the dense tropical jungle, would become a source of serious resistance for Michael and the rest of the men from the 3rd Division. Added to their difficulties were the numerous Japanese counterattacks, staged mainly at night under cover of darkness. Although the Japanese attacks would ultimately prove futile, significant U.S. casualties would still result. By the end of hostilities, seventeen Marines from Michael's company would have breathed their last breaths in Guam.

All in all, total U.S. Casualties were 1,783 killed and 6,010 wounded. However, the Japanese had suffered much greater retribution for their previous victory, as only 1,250 soldiers surrendered. The remaining 18,337 died in the three-week battle.

With Guam back in U.S. hands, aside from some mopping-up operations, the division remained in Guam to retrain, refit, and replace personnel and equipment lost in the battle. Meanwhile, at Apra Harbor on the western side of the island, the cruiser USS Indianapolis had the honor of being the first U.S. ship to enter the port since the Japanese had taken the island earlier in the war. Michael had watched as the cruiser had sailed past his company's position. He had not known that standing on deck was Seaman First Class Jake Smith, his former neighbor and nemesis, who was equally unaware of Michael's presence on the island. Ironically, 6,183 miles away in San Diego, someone important to both of them was taking the first steps that would ultimately put her in harm's way also.

As the U.S. forces were retaking the Pacific piece by piece, rather than being weakened, Japanese resistance and determination grew stronger the closer the U.S. forces got to Japan. The 3rd Division's next objective would prove to be its hardest and deadliest, as they would not be attempting to retake a captured Allied territory. But, instead, they would be attacking the enemy on Japanese soil for the first time. Not looking like much on the map was one of the Japanese Volcano Islands, lying 750 miles due south of Tokyo. With its Mount Suribachi, rising 554 feet above the Pacific Ocean, Iwo Jima would forever go down in the annals of the United States Marine Corps. The significance it would have on Michael's life would be just as meaningful.

While both Michael and Jake were across the Pacific Ocean, each serving their country, Cindy was doing her part back at San Diego. The huge Naval Hospital had been expanding ever since Pearl Harbor. While growth is usually a good thing, the need for its growth was not. There were reasons why all those additional naval hospital beds were necessary, and the reasons had names. Thousands of Marines and sailors from previously unheard-of places, such as Leyte Gulf, Coral Sea, Saipan, and Guam, needed medical care. As was always the case, the bulk of the day-to-day care of these wounded warriors would fall to the cadre of nurses working in the various Navy hospitals.

Navy Nurse and Ensign, Cindy Smith, had lived up to her top-of-the-class nursing school reputation. By summer's end, despite having been a Navy nurse for just five months, Cindy had excelled as both an operating room nurse and as a floor nurse. She would have been recognized for her excellent performance for these reasons alone, as her fitness reports would confirm. But sometimes, just being good, or even great, is not enough. Many times to be genuinely recognized takes more than raw talent. Some might call it luck, or being in the right place at the right time, or maybe just fate, but whatever it was, the stars were aligned for Cindy this one summer morning.

"Hey Cindy, they have you assigned to SOQ again. It's too bad you weren't there yesterday. Eleanor Roosevelt was there. Just think, the wife of the President, and you could have met her. She was visiting patients, and she made a special visit to see Colonel Evans Carlson." said Irene excitedly.

"I had heard about it. I had Colonel Carlson as a patient briefly the last time I had been at SOQ. From what I hear, there's quite a story about his Second Marine Raider Battalion, "The Carlson Raiders." He suffered wounds in Saipan going to the aid of an enlisted Marine radio operator. They said it was his second Purple Heart. He was very humble and modest, actually quite different from a lot of the officers. It's because he probably started as a private and worked his way up."

"You know, with all the big brass you treat at SOQ, do you think maybe this time you could latch on to some high-ranking, good-looking Marine or Navy officer? It wouldn't hurt, you know," Irene said, silently wishing it had been her working there instead.

"We've been through this before. You keep forgetting that there's a reason these senior officers are in Sick Officers Quarters. They're not really in dating condition, you know. Besides, the top brass are older and are usually married anyway," replied Cindy.

"They can't all be old and married. There have to be some eligible bachelor types, like a handsome Lieutenant or maybe even a young Lieutenant Commander. Also, you're a nurse, and isn't your job to make them better?" Irene said as more of a statement than a question. Then, to follow up on what she had just said, she started to say, "If it were me, I'd make them really better, if you...."

Before Irene could complete her sentence, she was interrupted as Cindy and several nurses standing nearby all shouted, "...catch my drift," finishing Irene's statement.

After they all had a good laugh, Cindy said, "I'd rather be in the O.R. doing surgeries, but the change isn't all that bad, and you do get to meet some interesting people. And they're not all high-ranking male officers; some of them are their wives."

"Well, if they need someone else, I'm always available," Irene advised Cindy.

"I think everyone knows you're always available," Cindy said with a mischievous smile.

"Wow. The sweet, innocent country gal goes one up on this city girl. I'm impressed. Maybe there's hope for you after all," Irene responded, now her turn to smile.

"Ten-hut," someone shouted as the laughter ceased, and the group stood at attention as the Commander in charge of the nurses unit came into the room, accompanied by a Rear Admiral dressed in his summer white service uniform. While the other nurses were impressed by the distinguished-looking officer and his glistening, gold shoulder boards, Cindy seemed almost underwhelmed by the appearance of such a high-ranking officer in their nurses' quarters. As "at ease" was directed to the assembled group by the Commander, The admiral smiled and added, "As you were," as he walked over to Cindy.

"May I have a word with you, Ensign," he said, talking directly to Cindy.

"Yes, of course, sir," Cindy replied.

"Walk with me, Ensign," he said as he guided Cindy to a private area of the dormitory.

As Cindy accompanied the Admiral, all the eyes in the room were affixed on them as he continued his conversation. When some of them attempted to lean in closer to hear better, the sound of their Commander loudly clearing her throat and her cold stare was an unspoken order to stand down.

"It's so nice to see you again. Since we have already met, no further introductions are necessary," the Admiral stated cordially.

"It is a pleasure to see you again also, Admiral." It was now Cindy's turn to be cordial.

"I have to fly out to Pearl Harbor on the next flight. Admiral Nimitz and the others at CINCPAC have a staff meeting that requires my attendance, so I'll be brief. I just wanted to personally thank you for the excellent care and compassion you showed my wife while she was recovering from her ruptured appendix. She said that all of you nurses were great, but she said she liked you the most. I saw how professional you were the day that I was in her room visiting her. I think you are an excellent nurse, and I believe the Navy can make good use of your qualifications."

"Thank you, Admiral. I was just doing my job as best as I could."

"Well, your best is the best that I have seen in a long time. And I've been around this Navy for nearly thirty years. I see that you and your bunkmate, Ensign Kelly, have requested a transfer to a hospital ship. I can help to expedite that if that is still something you wish to do. I believe you would be an asset in that capacity."

"Thank you very much. It is certainly something I would look forward to doing."

"Then consider it done. It will still take a while for all the paperwork to catch up. It would be before your normal 180-day rotation ends here in San Diego, but I believe you have earned the right. Besides, if I cannot grant a favor, then what good were all these promotions I got over the years," the Admiral said laughing.

"Again, thank you so much, on behalf of Ensign Kelly also," Cindy said, now beaming proudly.

"Oh, and one more thing. It's only in its preliminary discussions, but Admiral Nimitz has been looking at the other service's flight nurse programs. We could use it here in the Navy, especially with all the future campaigns that will be coming. It might be something to think about in the future."

"I will definitely do that, Admiral."

"Once again, on behalf of my wife and I, we want to thank you."

"It was my pleasure, Admiral," Cindy said sincerely.

As they walked back, Cindy and the admiral were under the watchful eyes of the other nurses. When the admiral had cleared the room, the other nurses began huddling around Cindy, wanting to know what that was all about.

"He just wanted to thank me for taking care of his wife," Cindy said honestly.

When all the others went back to their regular routines, Irene looked at Cindy and asked, "Is that all he said?"

"Actually, no," was Cindy's short reply.

"So tell me more," Irene asked curiously.

"I'll tell you more later, but for now, don't make any long-range plans for here in San Diego," said Cindy, as Irene responded with a puzzled look on her face.

CHAPTER 34

Choices

September 1944

It started as just another day at the vast hospital complex, but before it was over, things would be set in motion that would forever change Ensign Cindy Smith's final destiny. But for now, she was happy in her life as a Navy Nurse. Ever since Cindy was a young girl, she had a strong desire to help people, especially those who could not help themselves. Although she always wanted to be a nurse, it took an act of war, ruthlessly perpetrated against her country, that led her down the path to join the Navy. Like so many of her fellow nurses, it was the combination of their compassion for the sick and wounded and their staunch patriotism that made them voluntarily enlist. Unlike men, they were not subject to the draft, and no one forced them to sign up. They did so because they wanted to help those brave, primarily young men who had given up so much of their time, talent, and lives. This dedication was true of all the women in the Naval Nurse Service, but for Cindy and her friend Irene, their desire to do even more would soon become a reality. They would allow themselves to be put in harm's way to maximize what they could contribute to help those who could not help themselves.

Cindy and Irene had just finished their shifts at the hospital's surgery unit. Each was highly proficient at their jobs, and their current assignment would prove to be beneficial in preparing them for their next mission. By now, they both had known that their transfer to a hospital ship was as good as done, and it was just a matter of the Navy's paperwork catching up to make it official. They both were looking forward to their new assignments and the challenges they would be facing. Although their hands-on experience in the surgical unit here at Balboa Park would be beneficial, the types of surgery they would now be dealing with would be entirely different. Here at the Naval Hospital San Diego, most of these patients had already been through the initial trauma surgery and were either recovering or would be requiring follow-up surgeries. Aboard a hospital ship, the surgeries would be for recent and often gruesome battlefield wounds. The urgency of the surgeries would be different, as it would often result in life-or-death scenarios. But it was a challenge that both Cindy and Irene acknowledged and were ready to accept. They realized that they would be seeing the worst of what war could do to a fragile human body. They understood the difficulty of seeing those Marines and sailors suffering from horrendous wounds of all kinds. And, they realized the emotional strain they would have to endure, as they would not be able to save them all. Yet, despite all this, it was something that they still wanted to do. Even more so, it was something they knew they had to do. So it came as no surprise when their commanding officer advised each of them that their transfer to a hospital ship had come through. They each had earned the right, and the helpful push by that Rear Admiral, whose wife Cindy had taken care of in SOQ, certainly did not hurt.

"Ensigns Smith and Kelly, your transfers came through. You will be serving on the USS Bountiful. It's currently at Manus Island, Papua New Guinea. The ship's current duty status is a floating hospital, but it should soon be given orders for its next duty station, most likely in an active battle zone. You will join the ship as soon as your transportation is confirmed."

"Manus Island?" Irene Kelly asked curiously.

"It's part of the Admiralty Islands, north of New Guinea. We have a large naval base there at Seeadler Harbor. You will receive your travel orders separately. Good luck to you both and fair winds and following seas."

"Thank you, Commander," they each said simultaneously. Then after the Commander had left, they gave each other congratulatory hugs. Soon, the other nurses who were in the room came to congratulate them also.

"We're going to miss you both. Whether we'll miss hearing Irene saying "if you catch my drift" might be a different story. But I have to admit I'm a bit envious. I wish it could have been me. Maybe next time," said one of the nurses whose bunk was next to

Cindy and Irene's.

"For all our sakes, let's hope that there will be no need for a next time," Cindy stated solemnly, causing a temporary suspension of the celebration, as everyone knew the significance of what she had said.

"Wow, we'll be stationed aboard a ship in the middle of the Pacific Ocean. We really are in the Navy now," Irene stated, as the reality of what they would be doing was setting in.

With their transportation arranged, Cindy and Irene were preparing for their upcoming journey. Despite only having been here at Balboa Park just five months, they both fostered great friendships with so many of the other nurses, some of whom they would remain in contact with for many years to come. Although they were excited and enthusiastic about the next stage of their nursing and Navy career, leaving here would turn out to be more challenging than either one would have thought. It was not just about changing addresses; it was about changing their lives and leaving a part of their lives forever behind. As nurses, they put their hearts and souls into providing the best care possible for their patients. They would continue to do so at their new assignment, and knowing that you had made a difference in peoples' lives would be very gratifying. But for Cindy, there was another lingering issue. It was Michael. Despite not having seen or heard from him for over three years, she had never really gotten over him. When she looked at Michael's picture, she would wonder where he was and what he was doing. A part of her still hoped that one day she might see him walk through the door and embrace her in his strong arms, telling her that he still loved her as much as she still loved him. It could have happened here, she thought, but now being on a ship somewhere in the Pacific Ocean would make that scenario impossible.

"Here, this is the last mail we'll probably see for a while," Irene said as she handed Cindy a letter.

"It's from my brother, Jake," Cindy said as she was opening it.

"Is he still on the Indianapolis?" Irene asked.

"Yes. The letter was from last month. Jake was actually in Guam. I'm surprised that information made it past the censors. I haven't seen him in over three years. It's unlikely that he'd still be there. There is a large naval base at Manus. It would be great if he were, and we had the chance to see each other."

"Hey, you never know what could happen," Irene said optimistically.

Back in Guam, with no enemy to fight at the moment, the men from Foxtrot Company had focused on complaining about life's everyday gripes in the Marine Corps. Whether it was about the food, the lack of any mail, or the weather, sometimes it just felt good to let off some steam.

There is hardly anything positive about being in combat. It is both physically and mentally challenging, as well as emotionally draining. If you are one of the lucky ones to survive that day, you only wonder what tomorrow might bring, and there could be a heavy sense of guilt that you survived, but your best buddy did not. Staying alive requires your complete and undivided attention. Failing to do so could not only get you killed but your fellow marines also. It was a concept that could not be understood by those fortunate enough never to experience it. But if there were one benefit, it would be that it distracted you from all other day-to-day concerns. For Michael, the thought of Cindy was never far from his heart or his mind. However, at least during the times of battle, he would not, nor could not, focus on it as much. But now she was back on his mind, probably more so than ever. Unfortunately, the more he thought about her, the more depressed and agitated he became.

"What's your problem now, Brooklyn. I can hear you bitching from fifty feet away," Gunnery Sergeant O'Neill demanded to know as they were completing yet another training exercise.

"If it's not the damn mosquitos, it's the damn rain and the mud. How can you keep your socks dry when you have to wade through this crap constantly? At least back home, we had concrete sidewalks to walk on." Brooklyn replied as he was sinking into nearly a foot of mud.

"Quit complaining. Back home in Oklahoma, we would have loved to have this rain when I was a kid growing up. All we had was dust. Dust in your hair, dust in your shoes, dust in your eyes, and dust in your food. You name it, and it had dust on it or in it." Michael said as he walked behind Brooklyn, trying to step in the depressions created by his buddy's footsteps.

"We had our share of that dust back in Wichita also. Maybe not as bad as you, but it was still pretty dry. Maybe I don't remember it being that bad, but right now, I'd take the dust and dryness over this slop," Pete added, as his boot was sinking into the muddy quagmire.

"Are you ladies going to be worrying about the rain and mud when an enemy machine gun starts opening fire on you?" O'Neill asked, not expecting an answer.

"No, but if I have to get shot, I'd rather be on dry ground instead of mud. I'd want a clean face to look good for those pretty Navy nurses while I'm resting up in the hospital. There's something special about a nurse, if you know what I mean," Brooklyn said, forgetting that the last thing Michael knew about Cindy was that she worked in a hospital and she wanted to be a nurse.

Maybe it was the rain and the mud, or perhaps it was the thought of yet another battle. But this war lasted longer than anyone expected, and nerves were getting raw, even among friends.

"Can't you just shut up for more than a few seconds? Nobody wants to hear your bullshit anymore," Michael yelled as he scooped up a glob of mud and threw it at Brooklyn, hitting him squarely in his face.

"Hey dumb ass, that hurt. Maybe you'd like to see what it feels like," Brooklyn shouted as he began to advance threateningly towards Michael.

"Hey guys, cool it. We're not the enemy," Pete said as he stepped in between the two of them.

"Do we have a problem here?" asked a now aware Gunnery Sergeant O'Neill.

"No, Gunny. Just a minor disagreement," Pete answered, still standing between the two.

"Good. That better be all that this is. Save your fighting for the Japs. Now, let's keep moving," O'Neill ordered.

"I'm sorry, Gunny," Michael said as he looked at the mud on Brooklyn's face.

"He's alright. You only hurt Brooklyn's pride," Pete offered, trying to keep things light.

Suddenly, Michael stopped abruptly and froze in place as his thoughts were transported back to Goodwell fifteen years ago. It was then when he was the surprised victim of a snowball thrown at him by Cindy, giving him a bloody nose.

What's wrong, Corporal?" O'Neill asked Michael more formally, seeing a distant look on his friend's face and sensing that something was on his mind other than the training exercise at hand.

"Nothing, Gunny. Nothing at all," Michael replied, less than honest as he started moving again.

"Nothing, my ass," O'Neill muttered to himself, not believing Michael's statement.

That evening, O'Neill walked over to where Michael was sitting. "Hey, Okie, do you mind if I join you," The Gunnery Sergeant asked, knowing that he did not need permission.

"Nope, be my guest," Michael responded, trying to be cordial.

"You know it's only a matter of time before we leave this place and storm the beaches somewhere else. Then before you know it, we'll be back in the thick of things. I need your head to be in the game. I've seen that look you had on your face earlier today after your dust-up with Brooklyn. If you lose focus in combat, you could get yourself killed. What's more, you're a corporal, and you could get your men killed also. You want to tell me about it?"

"There's not much to talk about. I was just thinking about something from my past when I was a kid. It won't happen again," Michael answered, avoiding mentioning it involved Cindy.

"Well, for everyone's sake, I hope so," O'Neill said as he patted Michael on the back and walked out of the tent.

When Cindy and Irene finally arrived at Manus, it finally felt good to have their feet on the ground. However, the sensation would be short-lived since they would soon be on the Bountiful. But for now, they marveled at the number of vessels and massive floating dry docks that filled the harbor. Having defeated the Japanese earlier this year, the gigantic Seeadler Harbor was a hub of naval activity. It had become a large U.S. Navy base and staging area for continued Allied operations in New Guinea and the Philippines. But for now, the two nurses were more interested in spotting the ship that would be their home and workplace for the foreseeable future. Scanning the harbor, they both set their sights on a twenty-eight-year-old World War I transport ship.

Launched on June 17, 1916, at the Philadelphia Navy Yard, the USS Henderson (AP-1) was put into service transporting units of the American Expeditionary Force to France. The ship was capable of carrying 1,500 men and 24 mules in her holds. During the war, she made nine voyages to France, carrying both troops and supplies. In what would be a precursor of the ship's future purpose, the Henderson established two large base hospitals in France. However, she almost did not make it through the war as a nearby convoy ship was the victim of a torpedo from a German U-boat. She escaped a further attack from the prowling submarine by hiding in a smokescreen.

The ship had not finished thumbing its nose at fate because a severe fire broke out in one of her cargo holds during her seventh voyage. The ship was listing so severely that its entire troop load and equipment had to be transferred to another transport while rolling heavily in the rough seas. On another voyage, while carrying wounded soldiers back to the United States, the ship was inadvertently rammed by another troopship whose steering gear jammed. Although the Henderson suffered a hole below the waterline, her crew could repair the damage, and the ship was able to complete its assignment. On another occasion off the coast of New Jersey, a German U-Boat had sighted the Henderson. The submarine started to dive in preparation for a torpedo attack upon the Henderson. However, seeing the threat, the Henderson rammed the submarine, damaging the U-boat's conning tower and periscope, causing it to break off its attack.

Still, the USS Henderson's good fortunes continued. Just one day before the Japanese attacked Pearl Harbor, the ship had been right next to Battleship Row. With both troops and their families on board, the vessel had left Pearl Harbor on December 6 and was outbound from Hawaii when the attack took place. Yet, she was still not out of harm's way. As a slow-moving transport without any escort, the Captain ordered radio silence to avoid detection through seas that might contain enemy ships. Unable to contact the Henderson after repeated attempts, the ship was presumed to have been missing in action. Only when she safely arrived at San Francisco Harbor several days late had her fate been revealed. On her last voyage as the USS Henderson, she was transporting 71 much-needed nurses to Noumea, New Caledonia, once again as an indication of her next role. On October 13, 1943, the Henderson and its role as a transport ship were over. After being refurbished as a hospital ship, she became the USS Bountiful (AH-9).

"That must be it over there," Cindy said, as they each were looking at the same ship.

"I know it's too late to ask, but have you ever been on a ship before?" inquired Irene.

"No. Have you?" Cindy said, still looking at the ship.

"I was on the Staten Island Ferry once. Other than that, not really," Irene replied.

"I don't know if that counts. What if we get seasick?"

"You're just asking that now? Way to go, Country Gal."

"There weren't a whole lot of opportunities to find that out back home in Oklahoma. Goodwell wasn't exactly a port of call for the Queen Mary. Besides, what makes you immune from getting seasick?" Cindy snapped back.

"Hey, I've been on the Cyclone rollercoaster at Coney Island. If that didn't get me sick, then I don't think that ship will either."

"Well, I'm hoping that surviving the bumpy roads back in Oklahoma in an old Model-T with a broken spring suspension counts the same as your rollercoaster. If not, this could be interesting in ways we hadn't given much thought. But if not getting seasick is hereditary, then maybe I'll be okay because Jake said it didn't bother him at all.

"Well, Country Gal, we both got what we wanted. Let's see what this is going to be like," Irene declared, as a new chapter in their lives was beginning.

For the most part, grudges among men, especially in the military, tend to be short-lived. And fortunately, the men holding those grudges have short-term memories. So it was not unusual that Michael, Brooklyn, and Pete would all be together and looking forward to having a day off from training. Besides, the rain had stopped, and with a clear blue sky, it was an excellent day to check out Agana and Apra Harbor. On the way back to camp, the sun was beginning to set below the western horizon of the Pacific Ocean, turning the distant Navy ships into dark silhouettes against a painted orange sky. Finding a good vantage point alongside the road, the three buddies stopped to admire the view.

"It's nice to look out at the ocean and not see ships firing their guns," Pete said.

"Yeah, why can't people just live in peace with one another and enjoy the view," Brooklyn added, sounding unusually philosophical.

"Even the sky is peaceful. No planes dropping their bombs or making strafing runs," said Pete, as the three sat and watched the sun go down.

"Hey guys, close your eyes and listen," Michael requested.

"I don't hear anything," declared Brooklyn, after listening for a few seconds.

"Me neither," Pete added.

"That's just it. It's quiet. No guns, no explosions, and none of the noise of the battlefield. It's just the way God had created it to be," Michael said, breaking the silence.

Meanwhile, plans were being made for the division's next Pacific Island amphibious assault. This one was an operation conducted by the Fifth Amphibious Corps, consisting of the 3rd, 4th, and 5th Marine Divisions and the 147th Regiment of the Ohio National Guard. As odd as it would seem to have an independent National Guard regiment as part of a Marine operation, it would not be the first time, nor would it be the last. Besides fighting with the Marines on Guadalcanal, Saipan, and Tinian, the 147th would join them once again on Iwo Jima. Soon, other members of that same regiment would play a small role in the most important event of the twentieth century, if not in the history of humankind. Ironically, the same event would have the USS Indianapolis forever secure its place in U.S. Naval history.

The training in Guam would continue for several more

months as Michael and the rest of the 3rd Division were having mixed feelings about their role in the war. To say that the men were not happy to be no longer shot at or be blown apart by the Japanese soldiers so willing to die would be inaccurate. After having fought at Bougainville and on this same island they now called home, it was comforting to know that they could get a good night's sleep. It was good to be on a cot and not have to worry about either a Japanese banzai attack or having their throat slit as they curled up in a hastily dug foxhole.

Yet, there was a restlessness. It came with doing nothing while the rest of the world seemed to be engaged in continuous combat. In the Philippines, the largest surface naval battle in history was taking place in the Leyte Gulf. As part of the irony that occurs in war, three of the battleships of the combined U.S. fleets had been victims of the Pearl Harbor attack. The USS West Virginia and the USS California were sunk by Japanese torpedoes and bombs, while the USS Tennessee was damaged. Now three years later, after being repaired, refitted, modernized, and rearmed, these three battleships were able to play a part in finally ending the ability of the Imperial Japanese Navy to be an effective offensive force. And while the 3rd Marine Division was starting to appear more like a garrison force in Guam despite all the training, the U.S. 6th and 8th Armies under General Douglas MacArthur were fighting a ten-month long campaign to take back the Philippine Islands.

Across the world in Europe, General George Patton's 3rd Army was racing across France and Belgium as it squeezed the German Army from the west. At the same time, Germany's Eastern Front was collapsing, as it was no longer able to stop a vengeful, rejuvenated, and reinvigorated Russian Red Army as it drove into Poland from the east. The tide had finally turned against the Axis powers, and it now seemed like only a matter of time before the war would be over. But Michael and his fellow Marines knew that before they would finally be able to return home, they would have to defeat Japan. It would not be easy, but that was what they had trained to do. And if that meant going back into battle sooner rather than later, then so be it. In very short order, they would be allowed to help control their destinies.

Cindy and Irene's time at Seeadler Harbor in Manus had been

cut short as a combined Army and Marine offensive was underway at Peleliu, about 800 miles southwest of Guam. The Bountiful would spend most of the year transporting casualties from Peleliu to hospitals in the Solomon Islands. In what would be a break from its normal hospital duties, the Bountiful even briefly returned to its original roots as it transported veterans from the fighting at Leyte to rear bases. This new assignment gave Cindy and Irene, and the other medical staff onboard a respite from the need to provide acute care for the wounded. It was during this downtime that Cindy was doing a self-reflection of her role in the war.

"I'm not complaining about not having a constant influx of wounded coming onboard. I think we all could use the break. But somehow, I wonder if I am doing enough. I signed on as a Navy Nurse to be able to help as much as possible. Now, I'm not sure if this is all I can contribute," Cindy revealed to Irene.

"It sounds like maybe you are complaining, but we are doing our part, and we can only do what the Navy allows us to do. I feel satisfied that at the end of each day, we did our part," Irene replied.

"I do too. But I feel that I should do even more. Remember what the Admiral had told me that day back at Balboa Park about Nimitz wanting to possibly set up a Naval Flight Nurse program like the other services. He told me to consider it. Well, they started the program, and the first class of twenty-four will graduate in January. So I think I'm going to apply for the program."

"If that is what you want to do, then you should do it. I know this much. If you get in the program, you will do great."

"Getting in will not be easy. And if I do, I hope it's not just because of the Admiral's help."

"Hey, if that's your destiny, then that's what you need to do. But for now, let's just enjoy what we're doing, even if it isn't much. I'm sure it's going to get busy again," said Irene, not knowing how right she was.

Two months later, the USS Bountiful would set sail from its homeport of Manus to the off-shore waters of an insignificant-looking volcanic island. At the same time, a massive convoy would be heading from Guam to that same island. The goal of the hospital ship was to save as many lives as possible. While the Marines' plan on the convoy was to stay alive while taking as many enemy lives as possible. As disparate as their goals would seem, they both were noble in their ways. Although neither one would know it, Cindy and Michael would be in close proximity to each other. But before the forthcoming event would be over, their lives would never be the same. How these changes would happen would be in ways neither one would have thought possible.

CHAPTER 35

Iwo Jima

February 1945

"I don't know what's worse. Being on this stinking transport ship or being on the stinking island," Brooklyn asked as he was wiping the sweat off his brow.

"Which stinking island is that? The one we are going to or the ones we had been at," Michael asked

"All of them. Take your pick. In the end, they're all the same," Brooklyn answered as he continued to strip down and clean his rifle.

"At least here on the ship, there's no Japs trying to blow us to bits or cut our throats at night," said Pete, as he instinctively covered his throat with his hand.

"Yeah, all we have to worry about is a Jap sub commander looking at us through the crosshairs of his periscope," Gunnery Sergeant O'Neill exclaimed as he walked in on the conversation.

"Thanks, Gunny. I needed that encouraging thought," Brooklyn remarked sarcastically.

"Glad to be of service," O'Neill replied, with a wide grin that was in stark contrast to his hardened and weathered face.

"Tell me, Gunny, what is so important about this piece of rock sticking up out of the ocean anyway?" Pete asked.

"Supposedly, its airfields and its proximity to the Japanese mainland is what makes it so important. At least that's what they're telling us. In any event, the Navy's big guns and the airstrikes will have hopefully softened them up by the time the first units go ashore. Besides, it won't be us going in first since our division is being held back in reserve, so you better get used to being on this ship. We could be here for quite a while." A slight unease was noticeable in Gunnery Sergeant O'Neill's voice, only reporting what was said to him and not what he felt in his gut. He had seen too much in his career not to have concerns before going into combat. But, unfortunately, his apprehensions would soon prove justified.

"That's great. We're stacked in here like a can of sardines, but I guess it's better than fighting our way through stinking jungles once again," Brooklyn remarked.

"From what I hear, there are no jungles on Iwo Jima. It's just a big volcanic rock sticking up from the ocean," Pete added.

"If that's the case, then where are the Japs going to hide?" Brooklyn asked.

"Dug in deep, in caves and tunnels. That's why we need the Navy's big guns to blast them," Gunnery Sergeant O'Neill offered as he turned his attention to Michael.

Oblivious to the conversation, a melancholy Michael sat quietly on his rack, his legs dangling over the side, as he eyed the photo of Cindy he had carried throughout the war. Then, sighting his friend, O'Neill walked over to Michael.

"I'll say this much, Corporal. You're not one to ever give up hope," O'Neill said, looking at the photo.

"Have you ever been in love, Gunny?" Michael asked.

"Once. And that was a long time ago. She was a cute little nurse I met when I was convalescing at a hospital in France. You got to love those nurses. But I was sent back to the states soon after I recovered, and I never saw her again. The most important thing I learned from all that was that you have to move on. If you stay stuck in the past, you'll never have a future. Still, there are times when I think of what could have been. I get where you're coming from, but you have to face reality. In a couple of days, we'll be attacking yet another island, and you'll need to have your head clear and focus on the present. Otherwise, if you let your guard down, you'll be dead."

"I'll be fine. It didn't bother me at Bougainville or on Guam, and I won't let it bother me here either." Michael responded, still holding Cindy's photo.

"Good. I can't be bothered having to train some new, god-damned corporal," O'Neill said, half-joking.

As the invasion force moved closer to Iwo Jima, the preliminary bombing had already begun in earnest. As a result of a string of devastating losses to the combined U.S. fleets over the past three years, the Japanese defenders could not depend on the Imperial Navy to prevent an amphibious landing on the island. In addition, having acquired virtually complete control of the skies, American Navy, Marine, and Army planes had been able to bomb Iwo Jima with minimal opposition for the past nine months. Despite these aerial attacks, the island had remained in Japanese hands, necessitating the inevitable ground assault to wrest control of Iwo Jima from its nearly 21,000 determined defenders.

Despite it being a joint effort of the Navy and Marine Corps, an inter-service difference of opinions was evident as arguments would take place over the length of the naval bombardment. Major General Harry Schmidt, commander of the Marine landing force, had wanted a ten-day, heavy shelling of the island. In contrast, his counterpart, Admiral William H.P. Blandy, commander of the Amphibious Support Force, insisted on only a three-day bombardment. Blandy and other naval brass were concerned about re-supplying their depleted munitions and believed that the combined firepower of the 450-ship task force would be sufficient. The fact that General Schmidt would be proven correct would bring no comfort to him, nor the 60,000 marines under his command.

In June of 1944, Lieutenant General Tadamichi Kuribayashi had assumed command of the island's defenses. His assignment was essentially a suicide mission, as he knew too well that his forces could not withstand the sheer magnitude of the overwhelming numbers and firepower of the American invaders. But his objective was not to save Iwo Jima. Instead, it was to conduct a defense that would inflict the maximum casualties on the U.S. forces before ultimately losing the battle. His hope, and that of his superiors in Japan, was that if the attackers paid so high a price for gaining a small volcanic island, the U.S. and its allies would reconsider attacking the Japanese mainland. Their thought process might have been correct had they not fully understood the U.S. Military's resolve and the Americans' desire to right what was considered an unforgivable wrong. A wrong that was inflicted upon them nearly four years ago by an overly ambitious and over-confident Japan. Regardless of what would happen at Iwo Jima, world-changing scientific breakthroughs taking place in the New Mexico desert would ultimately change all this.

Still, Kuribayashi had hardened his island's defenses against the constant aerial and naval bombings. His soldiers had built eleven miles of tunnels deep within the hard volcanic rock when the invasion had begun. These tunnels connected a series of bunkers and command centers as much as seventy-five feet below the surface, making them essentially bomb-proof. Supplies, ammunition, and gun emplacements were also either dug in or camouflaged. Artillery, tanks, mortars, and machine-gun nests had been pre-sighted and locked-in to create killing fields for the unsuspecting Marines as they would land on the beach. Some Kamikaze pilots were also made available to inflict damage to the larger ships of the task force.

Of great concern to the Marines would be the defender's access tunnels and the ability of the Japanese to crawl out of their hidden positions and counterattack, often at night and under cover of darkness. If this was not bad enough, most Japanese soldiers knew, as did their commander, that theirs' was also a suicide mission. Nevertheless, with surrender considered to be a disgrace and dishonor to their families back home, they would fight to the death rather than give up.

At a relatively safe distance from the fighting, the hospital ship USS Bountiful was already preparing for the influx of wounded coming from the island. Although hospital ships were exempt from attack by an international agreement of the belligerent nations, the agreement provided no shield against an enemy attack. The truth was that the thin coat of white paint on the hull of the ship, as well as the color of its large red cross, would not provide it any protection from an enemy shell, bomb, or suicidal Kamikaze attack. Since the start of the war, twenty-three hospital ships in both hemispheres had been struck and sunk by enemy fire. Whether the threat was intentional or accidental, the vessel was in harm's way and would continue to be so as long as it was in an active war zone. And to be effective in treating the mass casualties that would result from the fighting on the island, it had to be close enough to receive its patients in a timely matter.

With the continuous naval and aerial bombing having ended, the first units of Marines began landing on the island. With little or no resistance from the Japanese defenders, a sense of optimism pervaded the high command that the Navy's three-day bombardment had been sufficient. However, the actual physical act of crossing the beach and moving inland proved to be quite tricky. The first Marines to have landed had been advised that they would find excellent beach conditions. Instead, they saw fifteen-foot-high slopes of soft black volcanic ash after having made it across the beach. The soft ash made it difficult to climb over and provided minimal protection should they come under enemy fire. With the advance inland slowed due to the ash, both troops and equipment began piling up on the beach. Believing the landing of more men and equipment could proceed unimpeded, scores of landing craft made continuous drop-offs of men and equipment for the next hour. As the lead elements of the 5th Marine Division inched their way forward, an eerie silence was broken only by the sounds of American tanks and amtracs, their engines straining as they would unsuccessfully try to climb over the ash slopes.

With the beach overcrowded with men and equipment, Kuribayashi ordered his forces to open fire and engage the Americans. At once, all hell broke loose. Kuribayashi's strategy and the protected placement of hidden bunkers, pillboxes, and artillery, resulted in the first wave of Marines coming under withering machine-gun, small arms, mortar, and artillery fire. Attempts to return fire by the Marines were useless, as there was no enemy in sight and were nothing more than an invitation to have your head blown off. With nowhere to go and no place to seek cover, the beach became a killing field. Those fortunate to have made it off the beach were soon stepping on land minds the defenders had placed below the soft soil. Covering the battle for Time and Life magazines, correspondent Robert Sherrod reported the scene as "A nightmare in hell."

Among those standing on deck, watching the smoke from thousands of explosions billowing up from the mountainous island, were Cindy and Irene.

"All those explosions cannot be a good thing since our Navy stopped the artillery barrage right before our forces landed. They must be from the Japanese on the island." Cindy said aloud for anyone to hear.

"They thought that all that bombing and shelling would eliminate any serious resistance. I guess the admirals were wrong," Irene replied, shaking her head in disbelief.

"It's only a matter of time before we see just how bad it is on the island. Right now, all we can do is pray," Cindy said, still watching the explosions and hearing the blasts seconds later as if it were the distant thunder following a summer lightning storm.

"Here's where we get to earn our big salary and find out just how good we really are," Irene said, wishing that she didn't need to.

"We need to scrub up and get ready. The first ones will be arriving shortly," Cindy stated, as an announcement was made over the ship's intercom system confirming what she had just said.

As Cindy turned from the island, she began to think about Jake and wondered where he was at this time. She had no way of knowing that his ship, the USS Indianapolis, had been part of Vice Admiral Marc Mitscher's Fast Carrier Task Force that attacked enemy air assets on the Japanese Mainland several days ago. Although losing 49 of their carrier planes in the raids, the task force had claimed 499 enemy aircraft. Those lost Japanese planes were no longer available to attack the U.S. Fleet supporting the ground invasion of Iwo Jima. Nor did she know that Jake's cruiser had joined the invasion fleet and provided close-in artillery support to the Marines on the island.

Cindy also thought of Michael and wondered where he was at this time. Had he enlisted? "Had he been drafted? Was he still dating Betty Miller, or even worse, could they have been married? All these questions and more were rapidly popping up in her mind. The thought that he would be in one of the transport ships that were just visible off her ship's bow was not one of them. It was probably best that it had not been.

With nearly ideal weather, the transports ever so slowly rose up and down in the gentle seas. Michael and his friends went topside and looked out over what would otherwise be the peaceful waters of the Pacific. Although their division was still being kept back in reserve, the threat from a sudden Kamikaze attack kept everyone aboard the ship a bit jumpy. Soon Iwo Jima would appear in the distance, but it was not yet visible, hidden beyond the horizon. Around him were hundreds of ships, including the landing craft that would take him and his other Marines into yet another battle on yet another island. Fate had delivered him here, and unknown to him, fate had delivered other people from his past to this same place in history. Joining the operation was the USS Enterprise. As it was now known, the "Big E" was launching its planes to continue the assault on the island. Helping to keep its aircraft flying was aircraft mechanic and Seaman First Class, Matthew Johnson. The two brothers had each correctly assumed that they were both involved in this action. But despite not having been this close to one another in over three years, they would not see one another, and there would be no guarantee of when, or if, they would ever see each other again.

How Michael would have felt had he known would forever remain a mystery. Still, just a few nautical miles away, the USS Bountiful was setting up to receive a large number of expected wounded now that the invasion began. Onboard the hospital ship was Nurse Ensign Cindy Smith. Fate, played through the devious actions of Cindy's mother, had dealt them cards that neither Cindy nor Michael would have ever wanted or deserved. Once again, the two childhood and high school sweethearts were so agonizingly close. Yet, neither of them would know how close, nor would they understand the reason for their separation. Worse yet, fate had not finished dealing them more bad cards. Had they been playing poker, they might have wanted to call Fate's bluff, but unfortunately, what was going to happen was no bluff.

The fighting was now on its second day. The men of the 3rd Division, although eager to fight, were grateful that their division had been held in reserve. If the naval and aerial bombardments had been as successful as everyone hoped, the island should have fallen already. But the Japanese defenders were unaffected despite the thousands of artillery shells and bombs pounding the island. Now, the information coming in was of heavy resistance by the outnumbered Japanese. Even more ominous were the reports of high casualties from the initial landings. Despite their reserve status, it was soon evident that some elements of the 3rd Division would be needed to join the battle. With officers scurrying about and the concerned looks on their faces, it came as no great surprise when Gunnery Sergeant O'Neill walked into the hold below deck, where the men of the 4th Platoon, Foxtrot Company, were billeted.

"Okay. Let's mount up. Grab your gear and make any last-minute preparations you haven't made already. We're going ashore," O'Neill shouted.

At once, forty men began to move as one, preparing for battle and checking their equipment as the hundreds of hours of intense training were once again showing its effect.

"I knew it was too good to last. But at least we'll get to get off this ship, and I won't feel like a sardine anymore," said Brooklyn.

"As long as they don't send us back in a can like a sardine, I'll be happy," Pete said.

"Don't worry about it. They'll just bury you in the sand," Michael added, trying to use some gallows humor. Before Pete could reply, the billowing voice of Gunnery Sergeant O'Neill took command of the room.

"Okay, men, listen up. For those of us who have been together a while, we've done this before. It's the same enemy, same shit, different island. From what I'm hearing, the tactics will be different because the conditions on the island will be different. No dense jungles or thick undergrowth. Nor will there be mud or rain. But the island has a lot of soft ash, and the island stinks. It stinks of sulfur, and it stinks of Japs. They're dug in and hidden everywhere. The casualties were bad on day one. That's why we got the call. It won't be easy, but as long as we stay together and watch each other's backs, we'll get through. For you newbies, stay close, pay attention, and don't do anything stupid. Our officers hate having to write those letters to your families. That's all. May God bless you, and may God bless the Marine Corps."

Before walking on deck to disembark onto the landing craft that will take them ashore, Michael took out his picture of Cindy. He looked at the date he had written on the back, 9/20/39. Then Michael looked at the photo. He saw Cindy's sweet face and pretty smile. That was over five years ago, and it had been over four years since he last saw Cindy. He wondered if he was nothing but a fool, not only to have carried her photo all this time but to have let her steal his heart also. His mind agreed that he was a fool, but he trusted his heart, and his heart was okay with his feelings. He looked at the photo again and then safely folded it and put it back into his billfold. He wondered just how many more times he would be able to see her face. As he started to join the rest of his platoon, he could not help but wonder if it even mattered.

As Michael and his buddies watched the explosions on the island, the announcement came over the ship's loudspeaker that it was time to disembark. Michael had been through this before. But this time, something about it was different. It certainly would not be the walk in the park as so many of the top brass were predicting. If it had been, then why would so many men be needed. And why so many ships and planes. Maybe they just wanted to put on an overwhelming show of force to force the Japanese to surrender. But previous experience showed that scenario to be unlikely. And there was no denying the troubling reports of the first-day casualties. But it was still only the second day, and maybe things would improve. Even Admiral Nimitz had suggested that the Japanese might surrender rather than face the onslaught of the forces coiled to spring at them. But Michael and the other veterans of Guam and Bougainville knew better. Maybe the newbies believed that stuff. If so, then just as good, as it might reduce the "pucker" factor that came with facing combat for the first time. Had they known what was ahead of them, they might lose the edge that all these months of training had been honing. But as green, as these newbies were, by the time the battle for Iwo Jima would be over, they would be hardened veterans.

As Michael looked around at his platoon getting ready to climb down onto the landing crafts that would take them the final miles to the beachhead, he wondered which of them he might be seeing for the last time. He did not disregard the possibility that there might be a bullet with his name on it, but like his comrades, he felt more concerned for the loss of the others. Just as important, as a corporal, Michael had to set an example for the men of his squad. He did not expect to fall short in this endeavor, but he would always wonder if what he would do would be enough. Once aboard the LCI, Michael again took out his picture of Cindy, and as he looked at her pretty face, he wondered if he would ever see her or her photo again.

Not only were Admiral Nimitz and the top planners of the invasion all wrong in their estimate of how long it would take to secure the island, but so was Michael for hoping that maybe they would have been right.

"Does anyone know what day it is?" a newbie asked.

"Why? Does it really matter?" Pete asked the newbie in return.

"I'm keeping track by making a mark on my belt for each day that we're here on this island. I just want to make sure I didn't miss a day."

"If you ask me, that's not only stupid but bad luck also. Just keep away from me. I don't need to share in your bad karma," Brooklyn told the newbie.

"By my calculations, it's March 11[th,] and we've been on this rock nineteen days for anyone who's counting. However, it seems like it's been forever. And by the way, it probably is bad luck to be counting," answered Michael.

"If it's bad luck, then why have you been counting," Pete asked of Michael.

"Just a dumb habit, I guess, but I still think it's probably bad luck."

The resistance of the remaining Japanese was still strong as they would climb out of their hidden caves and tunnels at night and silently slit the throats of any Marines foolish enough to fall asleep in their foxholes. Lack of enemy rifle ammunition or mortar shells did not appear to be a problem either, as the men were under constant threat of both. For more than a week now, the Marines would clear out enemy bunkers using flamethrowers and grenades. Then, believing that no one inside could survive that, they would walk past what was assumed to be a safe bunker. It was then that they would be ambushed from the rear by other Japanese soldiers. The Japanese used their extensive underground tunnels to reuse the bunkers once the fires burned out. Gunnery Sergeant O'Neill and the rest of the 4th Platoon were taking no chances now, but they had lost three good men before they caught on to what the Japanese were doing.

With Mount Suribachi behind them, Michael was leading his

squad away from the beach when they approached an area that was not yet fully secured. They were about to move up the contested hill when a group of about twenty Japanese soldiers popped out of their hiding places and began shooting at the Americans. Three of his squad went down instantly from a hail of bullets from two hidden machine-gun nests, while a sniper's bullet to the head took out a fourth member of the squad. The sniper's victim was the newbie keeping track of the days, who would never get to make his twentieth mark on his belt.

The remaining Marines began returning fire and taking whatever cover they could find. Brooklyn started tossing grenades while Pete did the best he could do with his Browning Automatic Rifle. But it was no match against the two Japanese Type 92 heavy machine guns, fired from within two fortified concrete pillboxes. Currently outnumbered by three to one and running low on ammunition, Michael's only hope was to be able to hold out until the other squads of his platoon could reinforce them.

As one of the enemy machine guns was beginning to sight-in on his poorly defended position, Michael attempted to move to a better position behind a large lava rock. As he darted out from his previous location, A shell from a 50mm, Juteki Type 89 mortar exploded about thirty-five feet in front of him, the concussion of the explosion instantaneously knocking him to the ground. As he lay there, his eyes stung from the effects of the blast. But much more importantly, a large steel fragment from the mortar shell was embedded in his chest. As bad as it was, the only reason it was not worse was that the same soft volcanic ash that made the sand black absorbed much of the shell fragments. He tried to reach for his rifle, but he was unable to move. Before passing out, his last conscious thoughts were of Cindy.

As the surviving members of his squad were desperately short of ammunition, things began to look bleak. Finally, Michael's squad heard the sound of reinforcements firing their weapons as the other platoon members began rushing to their aid. Then, the platoon heard the ominous sound of an M-4 Sherman Tank, its metal tracks grinding against the rocky surface. Gunnery Sergeant O'Neill and his men engaged the heavily protected Japanese positions as the tank approached the enemy pillboxes. Specially equipped with a flame-thrower instead of the standard 76mm gun, these tanks proved very effective against the Japanese pillboxes and bunkers. As the tank opened fire with its flamethrower, the distinctive "whooshing" sound of its pressurized stream of ignited gasoline and napalm instantly drew the attention of both the Americans and the Japanese. With great accuracy, the tank poured the burning liquid into the narrow openings of the pillboxes nearly 150 yards away, incinerating anybody or anything inside. With the insides of the pillboxes now glowing an intense orange and with dense black smoke pouring out, the threat was over. And having learned the hard way from the past, the platoon would make sure that it stayed that way.

Meanwhile, an unconscious and gravely wounded Corporal Michael Johnson, USMC, would never see day twenty on the island.

CHAPTER 36

Salvation

March 11, 1945

"There's another one over here," a Marine shouted as he hurried to the side of the gravely wounded corporal. "We need a corpsman. He's still alive," he added, seeing the shallow rise and fall of Michael's chest.

A Navy Corpsman, his uniform soaked with the blood of the many Marines he had previously tended to this day, knelt to where Michael was lying. After the initial battle that wounded Michael, reinforcements had driven the relentless Japanese forces back into their underground maze of tunnels. Although the relative calm would only be temporary, it at least provided an opportunity for those not dead or seriously wounded to tend to those casualties that unfortunately were.

"He's not going to make it," the corpsman said while shaking his head.

Limited resources and too many casualties made triage decisions on the battlefield all too cold and calculating. The hospital corpsman looked like he should still be in high school. But a closer look into his eyes revealed a different maturity. The anguish, the suffering, and the horrors of the battlefield were taking their toll. War had the unique ability to either make young men old or prevent young men from ever having the opportunity to grow old. For some, even death seemed to be the better of the two alternatives.

"He's not dead until I say he's dead," Gunnery Sergeant O'Neill bluntly stated as he looked at his friend. The chevrons on his uniform may have given him authority, but his aggressive and intimidating manner was even more persuading. Of course, his six-foot-five-inch frame towering over the kneeling corpsman did not hurt in pressing his argument.

"Load him up and get him down to the aid station," barked the Gunnery Sergeant at the stretcher-bearers, as the corpsman was still stuffing gauze into Michael's wound in an attempt to stem the loss of any more blood.

As they were preparing to lift Michael's body onto the canvas litter, O'Neill knelt beside him. Looking at his unconscious friend, he drew his face closer to Michael and whispered into his ear, "Hang in there Okie. Today's not your day to die."

O'Neill watched as the stretcher-bearers began to hurriedly carry Michael to the aid station while the hospital corpsman kept pace at his side, holding a bag of plasma whose IV he had placed in Michael's arm. O'Neill then began wondering if he might have finally repaid Michael's father for his actions at Belleau Wood.

Despite the beach no longer being the target of enemy fire since the initial days of the invasion, there was still much evidence of the carnage continuing in the attempt to drive out the last of the island's Japanese defenders. But unlike day one, when Marines fell from the intense enemy fire directed at the beach, the dead and wounded bodies now spread across the blackened sands are from other parts of the island where the fighting continued. In a way that mimicked military formations on a parade ground, these new casualties were now arranged in neat rows as they awaited evacuation or burial. This orderly grouping contrasted with those killed and wounded just weeks ago, their bodies haphazardly filling the beach where they fell in battle.

Just five days ago, with much fanfare from the press, Admiral Nimitz's vision of Naval Flight Nurses had come to fruition. The first Navy Nurse to set foot in an active combat zone arrived on the island. Twenty-two-year-old Jane Kendeigh, and other dedicated nurses like her, would eventually evacuate thousands of wounded Marines and sailors from Iwo Jima, taking them safely to hospitals away from the battle zone. However, considering the grave nature of Michael's wound and his need for immediate surgery, Michael would not have been a candidate for this type of evacuation. He would have needed surgery first, or he would not have survived the eight-hour flight. Michael's only hope would be to make it to the hospital ship offshore before he died of his wounds.

As a team of Navy doctors was walking between the rows of stretchers, they would attend to the wounded. Every so often, one of the doctors would pronounce a patient to be deceased. Not being able to help anymore, the remains of what was once a proud Marine would become the responsibility of the Graves Registration Service. One of the deceased's dog tags would be removed for record-keeping and notifications, while the other would remain with the body. The matter of any weapons the victim may have had with him would also fall to this unit. If it were still serviceable, it and any ammunition would be removed and redistributed to other Marines to continue in the battle. Ironically, a lifeless piece of steel and wood would survive the once-living Marine who had initially possessed it. However, before this would happen, a Navy Chaplain would kneel beside the deceased, saying a prayer for his soul. It would not matter whether the dying or the dead were of the same religion as the chaplain or if the deceased had no faith at all. At this time in a person's life, God made no distinctions.

A Navy doctor was walking among the wounded, attempting to assess the severity of their wounds. It was a form of battlefield triage, which meant deciding who was worth saving. From a purely unemotional and pragmatic view, it prioritized the limited medical resources to those wounded that had a better chance of surviving. As heartless as it seemed, the sad truth was it made no sense to take up space transporting a gravely wounded Marine to the hospital ship if he had no real chance at survival. The doctor, who before the war had been a pediatrician whose practice used to be on Manhattan's prestigious east side, was about to make another life or death determination.

The men of the 4th Platoon were mopping up when Gunnery Sergeant O'Neill received orders from Battalion Headquarters to pull back from the front line. Unfortunately, it was not to give his men a break from the fighting that they well deserved. Instead, it was a tactical decision. Their ranks had suffered so many casualties they were no longer effective as a cohesive fighting unit. Finally, after getting much-needed replacements, they would soon be seeing action once again. But for now, the dying would end. Tired and dazed from the endless fighting and lack of sleep, those that were able walked back down to the beach. Their uniforms, showing the effects of blood, sweat, and grime, clung to their bodies from the oppressive heat of this volcanic island as they plodded their way down. As they walked silently, they passed new replacements heading in the other direction. Although most were probably of similar age, with their clean-shaven faces and untarnished uniforms, they looked so much younger than the men they were relieving. They stared at the men from the 4th platoon, Foxtrot company, wondering if this would be their fate also.

Finally reaching the beach, most of his men took the opportunity to either grab a smoke or have some hot food from a mess tent set up nearby. Before them, the offerings set out were the first hot food they would have eaten in nearly two weeks. It was also the first meal that they would have eaten without the constant worry of being shot at or hit with mortar fire. Further down the beach was the temporary aid station where Corporal Michael Johnson had been brought. Satisfied that his men were being taken care of, Gunnery Sergeant O'Neill began walking parallel to the ocean, not concerning himself with the occasional incoming surf that would flow over the suede leather uppers of his combat boots. As he approached the aid station, he saw wounded Marines being carried one by one onto an amphibious landing craft, their litters carefully secured onboard. Meanwhile, ten miles offshore, the hospital ship, USS Bountiful, AH-9, stood ready for the ensuing influx of patients.

When O'Neill finally reached the aid station, his hawk-like eyes began scanning those casualties left onshore. His gaze stopped when he recognized Michael as one of them. A Navy chaplain was kneeling beside his wounded comrade and was making the sign of the cross. Michael's eyes were still open, and although he was not conscious, he was still alive, if only barely. Hearing the landing craft's diesel engine revving up, O'Neill quickly approached the chaplain.

"Where's the doctor?" O'Neill demanded, not caring about any momentary lack of respect for a man of the cloth.

"Over there," the chaplain responded, pointing to an olive-green canvas tent twenty yards away.

With marked determination, the Gunnery Sergeant stormed into the tent, searching for the doctor. Spotting him, he interrupted the doctor, who was conversing with one of the medical corpsmen.

"What about that one?" he shouted, demanding an answer while pointing at Michael.

Showing his annoyance of not only being rudely interrupted but having been done so by someone of lesser rank, the doctor took his time to answer. "He's not going to make it. There's nothing more that we can do. So if you don't mind, I have more important things to do than explain my decision to you."

His face now turning beet-red, O'Neill grabbed the officer by the arm and pulled him out of the tent. The other corpsman stood there in shock, but they failed to do anything but watch as the hulking Gunnery Sergeant continued dragging the protesting doctor outside.

"I am a Lieutenant and a doctor. I will have you court-martialed," the doctor yelled to no prevail as O'Neill finally stopped in front of Michael.

"Now listen to me, you damn son-of-a-bitch. He ain't dead until I say he's dead. You are going to put him on that landing craft before it leaves, and you better make damn sure that he doesn't die before he gets to the hospital ship." Then, if the angry tone of his voice was not forceful enough, O'Neill drew his Colt .45 caliber pistol and stuck it into the doctor's ribs.

"So that we understand one another. I don't give a rat's ass about any goddamned court-martial. I should have been dead already. You want to court-martial me, go right ahead. You'll be doing me a fucking favor. It'll get me off of this damn excuse for an island and out of this fucking war."

Looking over at a few of the stunned corpsman and stretcher-bearers, the doctor, still shaking from what he thought was a near-death experience, ordered Michael to be brought onto the craft before it departed. He finally breathed a sigh of relief as O'Neill removed the sidearm and re-holstered it. They both silently stood as Michael was put onto the landing craft, just moments before it pulled away from the beach. Then, as if nothing had happened, O'Neill looked the doctor straight in the eye, smiled, and said, "It's your call."

Between the fear of what this madman might still do and feeling somewhat compassionate for the Gunnery Sergeant's concern for his men, the doctor said nothing. Then before turning to leave, O'Neill snapped to attention and saluted the doctor. As he walked away, he passed the shocked chaplain who had just witnessed everything.

"Pray for us, Padre. We're all going to need it," O'Neill asked the chaplain, but the priest could not be sure whether it was a request or a demand. Either way, he nodded his head and made the sign of the cross, happy that there was not one more unnecessary casualty today.

As O'Neill was walking back to rejoin the rest of his platoon, he turned towards the ocean. Slowly making its way toward the horizon, the increasingly smaller image of the landing craft was visible, bobbing up and down in the choppy blue waters. Were it not for the sounds of war coming from his rear, the view would have made for a serene and peaceful image. O'Neill tried to block out the distant sounds of rifle fire and explosions, as he wondered if his efforts earlier made any difference in Michael's outcome. For all his bluster and toughness, he realized that whether or not Michael survived, the chances were that he would never see him again, and this made him sad. Taking a knee, he prayed openly to God.

"I haven't been much with prayers lately, but if you can, could you please not let this be Michael's day to die." As he stood up, a single tear began flowing down his gruff unshaven face. Then, standing straight as a ramrod, he rejoined his men. But, unfortunately, for some of them, over the remaining days of combat, it would be their days to die.

CHAPTER 37

Irony

March 11, 1945

"Look, over there. There's another one coming," Ensign Irene Kelly said to her friend, pointing to the approaching landing craft.

"They'll be making the announcement soon, so we might as well get ready," Fellow Ensign Cindy Smith said in reply.

"I wonder which will end first. The Japanese resistance, or the non-stop arrivals of wounded Marines?" Irene said pensively.

"With God's help, I pray that it's both," Cindy said remorsefully as they began moving to the reception area for the incoming patients.

The trip took about twenty-five minutes, but for those gravely wounded who were unfortunate not to survive it, it was an entire lifetime. As for Corporal Michael Johnson, USMC, it was still too early to know just how much life he had left. The steel shrapnel of the mortar shell that impaled his body was the cause, but now it was more about the consequences. Michael's concussion resulting from the explosion would diminish over time. The flash burns to his face and eyes would heal and have no adverse or noticeable impact. Fortunately, most of the other small multiple fragments that struck his body were survivable. But the single large piece of jagged steel that ripped violently into his chest was having its effect upon his survivability. Michael had lost a large quantity of blood before the corpsman found him. Administering plasma to him on the battlefield had bought him time, but his time was running out. Whether he would make it to and through surgery would make the difference of having a Purple Heart commendation to show his grandchildren years from now, or having his family receive the dreaded telegram from the War Department. Of course, the medal would still come later, post humorously, and his mother would be able to display a gold star in their home's window. But that would be of little comfort to his family.

One of his last thoughts before passing out was of Cindy. Had his mind been able to think clearly, he would have thought how sad it would be for him to die and have her never knowing of it. Even worse would be if she did not care anymore. Since that day at the fair when they had it taken, he faithfully carried her picture for over five years. It helped him get through the toughest of times. Michael was not overly superstitious, but he considered it something of a good luck charm. But more importantly, he carried it as a remembrance of his only true love. Michael never gave up hope that someday he and Cindy might be reunited, and their photos could become one, as would they. But if there were any luck in that photograph, he would need every bit of it today.

As the ship's loudspeaker announced the imminent arrival of new patients, U.S. Navy Ensign Cindy Smith immediately began preparing for the influx of newly wounded Marines. Wearing her hospital scrubs, she joined her team of surgeons and nurses, awaiting those lucky enough to have made it this far. Cindy watched as other crewmembers were carefully lifting the wounded, still in their litters, onto the hospital ship. She watched intently as one by one, the stretcher-bearers placed the litters containing the wounded down on the blood-stained wooden deck. Having done this many times, she acted instinctively, readying herself to move down the line, assisting the doctors as they selected those most in need of surgery. Just a few feet away from her was Michael. He was lying there, unconscious and shirtless. His uniform trousers were bloody and torn and shredded in places, the result of the mortar blast. A large blood-soaked bandage was covering the wound on his chest. Cotton gauze that a hospital corpsman had put on Michael's face to protect his eyes was still in place. One of the surgeons knelt to assess Michael's condition, as well as his chances for survival. Doctors, as well as operating rooms, were an invaluable resource. But like most resources, they were limited. Having examined the wound and seeing the shrapnel embedded in his patient's chest, the doctor shook his head. Michael's chances had gone from slim to near zero. Cindy had been looking the other way as the doctor lifted the bandage covering Michael's eyes. Replacing the dressing, the doctor stood up.

"I don't know how this one made it this far, but he came too far for us to give up on now. So, Ensign, I need you to prepare this patient for immediate surgery," the doctor ordered, looking at Cindy.

She signaled to a pair of hospital corpsmen standing by and had overheard the doctor's instructions. They picked up Michael's litter and carried him to one of the ship's operating rooms as she followed closely behind. As they placed Michael on the operating table, she began cutting away his trousers, carefully removing the bloody fabric that had already started to adhere to Michael's leg. Seeing no other life-threatening wounds, she stated that fact loudly for all to hear, as one of the other operating room nurses began applying liberal amounts of iodine to the area around his chest wound.

As the doctor was about to have the bandage removed from Michael's face, Cindy spotted a small billfold that had fallen out of his pocket while she was cutting off his trousers. Michael's blood was partially covering it. She picked it up, holding it by one of its dry corners. Before she could examine it further, she was interrupted by the familiar voice of her commanding officer, a veteran of twenty-two years' service and himself a well-respected surgeon.

"Ensign Smith, Ensign Kelly will relieve you of your duties. See me in my wardroom when you are properly relieved. Your transfer came through for Naval Flight Nurse School. You will leave immediately," the Captain said, trying hard to suppress his happiness for her as he left the busy operating room.

As the other nurses and medical personnel were making final preparations for Michael's surgery, and with her back to the operating table, Cindy turned and greeted her friend.

"Congrats, Country Gal, you got what you wanted. Now go and give them hell, and don't forget to write," Irene said, showing a wide grin.

"I'm going to miss you," Cindy said, still holding the billfold in her hand.

"Me too," her friend replied as they gave each other a brief hug.

Cindy started to walk away when she realized she still had the billfold. She stopped and turned back to Irene.

"Here, I almost forgot. This wallet was in the patient's pocket. It's kind of messy."

"No problem. I'll take care of it," Irene said as they once again said their goodbyes.

Cindy walked out of the operating room, initially thinking more about her future than that of the poor Marine she had to leave on the operating table. Ironically, his life or death would depend upon a group of total strangers and God's will. She had seen too many similar instances, and she knew well enough not to get caught up in the hope for a nameless, and in this case, face-less Marine. Yet, there was something slightly different about this one. She was experiencing sadness, thinking that should he not survive the surgery, he would die alone, thousands of miles away from any family or loved ones. She learned early on not to get emotionally connected to the recovery prospects of those gravely wounded, as it would just make their unfortunate demise all the more painful to accept. But she stopped briefly to say a prayer for this one. The thought that his last vision of this life might have been the cotton gauze covering his eyes was disturbing in ways she could not comprehend.

When she reached the Captain's wardroom, she knocked on the metal frame of his open door, awaiting permission to enter. Sitting at his desk, he told Cindy to enter. Still wearing her hospital scrubs, she said, "Yes sir, you wanted to see me," stating the obvious.

"Ensign Smith. You are a damn good nurse, and I would be less than honest if I said I would not miss you, but you will have an opportunity to do even better things in your new assignment. Although, I must say that the nature and timing of your transfer are somewhat unusual. But, it came directly from CINCPAC head-quarters, and it carries the signature of one of Admiral Nimitz's top staff officers. So, something tells me that this might not be that much of a surprise to you."

"It's been no secret that I applied for Flight Nurse School. I hope that it was because of my skills and capabilities and what I have accomplished in my time as a Navy nurse, but sometimes simply doing the best that you can do pays off. Especially if the right people recognize it," Cindy said with a slight smile, partially explaining the Captain's curiosity.

"Well, whatever it was, it certainly paid off. You'll be leaving on the landing craft that just arrived when it departs in twenty minutes. Although, with orders directly from Admiral Nimitz's office, I think we can hold the craft for you if you need a few extra minutes. You'll land on a secure beachhead, and from there, you will go directly to the airfield on Iwo. There's an inbound Naval Air Evacuation Service flight coming from Guam. It's due to arrive at 1500 hours. You will be on that plane when it leaves, bringing you to Agana, Guam. Once there, you will hop on a series of flights that will eventually take you to Naval Air Station Alameda, where you will begin your training. Then he added, "Oh, and by the way, good luck. We'll all miss you."

Now, sharply standing at attention, she replied, "Aye, aye, Sir!"

The surgical team had begun the extensive surgery necessary to give Michael any chance of surviving. Despite most of them having come from civilian medical fields that might never see trauma such as this in their lifetime, the doctors and nurses were now veterans dealing with battlefield injuries. Their surgical expertise was saving countless young lives. Yet, despite their valiant efforts, they could not save everyone. Although probably no one gave Michael any real chance of surviving, they did everything possible to provide him with that ability. It would be two hours before they would know if they were successful. They would have done all they could do. It would be up to a power greater than them to decide if they had done enough. Much would also depend upon the patient's ability to fight the constant threat of infection and his ability to will his body to heal.

Earlier, Cindy had gathered up her belongings and thrown them all into her sea bag. A move like this in civilian life would be unheard of and impossible to do on such short notice, but this was the Navy, and with the war going on, it was not all that unusual. Besides, she had packed lightly coming here, so it would be no surprise that she would pack lightly leaving. With no stores to shop at, she certainly did not add anything to her wardrobe. As a last-minute check, she had looked once more in her locker, and to be sure she had everything of importance, she had opened up her handbag and looked inside. Seeing that she had Michael's photo, she looked at it quickly, again wondering why he stopped writing and pondering where in the world he might be and what he was doing. Her thoughts of him were promptly interrupted as the ship's loudspeaker had announced the last call for boarding the landing craft that would take her away. Grabbing everything, she walked out of the wardroom she shared with Irene and the other nurses. Stopping briefly, she had looked back on the past year and said her goodbyes to the USS Bountiful, looking forward to the next phase of her life.

She had walked past the spot where the most recent wounded had been brought aboard. She had experienced a sense of Deja Vue, which she immediately attributed to having seen and done that so many times. Yet, like her thoughts back in the operating room, there was something odd about it. As she had approached her transportation to the island, a sailor took her bags and helped her down onto the waiting landing craft. Then, she would be on her way to the airfield where she would board the flight that would be the first step in beginning her new assignment. Despite this exactly being what she wanted, she was experiencing some unease in having left the operating room so abruptly. Although she understood that her absence would have had no bearing on whether or not that Marine survived his surgery, she felt as if she had somehow failed him. Despite having taken care of hundreds of patients, this one seemed different for some reason. Maybe it was because of how she had left him. Having to leave a patient about to undergo surgery was not something she was used to doing. Trying to provide the best personal care and not becoming attached emotionally to a patient was a constant challenge for any nurse. Yet, this one disturbed Cindy, and not knowing the outcome was beginning to weigh heavily on her. But she was able to take some consolation in believing it was what fate probably had in store for her.

As she stood in the landing craft as it bobbed up and down in the choppy sea, she had reflected upon her life and wondered if she would ever again experience true love. It gave her comfort knowing that she still had Michael's photo and the memories that went with it if nothing else. But it pained her just as much that he stopped writing to her with no explanation. Maybe he had a good reason, but that did not make her feel any better. But if he had no reason at all, the thought of that would make her feel even worse.

With Michael's surgery completed, Irene and the other medical personnel went about the task of cleaning up and getting the operating room ready for its subsequent use. She remembered the billfold Cindy had given her and was about to give it to one of the corpsman to put it away with the patient's other belongings. Just then, a small folded photograph fell out. Retrieving it, she took note of its jagged edge, thinking it was an odd coincidence. It was similar to one Irene had previously seen numerous times with a comparable edge. Curious, she carefully unfolded it, wiping away the blood covering what appeared to be a young woman. As more and more of the picture became recognizable, Irene shouted, "Oh my God," attracting the attention of the others in the room. As she continued to stare at the picture in disbelief, it was evident that she was looking at a photo of her friend. Had she had the other half of the photograph that Cindy carried with her, she was sure the two sets of jagged edges would match perfectly.

Irene was trying to come to terms with what she just discovered. If Michael had forsaken Cindy all these years as Cindy thought, then why would he be carrying her picture with him into battle nearly five years later. The irony that Michael had initially been Cindy's patient, yet Cindy had not known it, just seemed cruel. Now, with Cindy on the island and not contacting her, it just added to the heartlessness of fate. Still holding the photo, she gave the billfold to the corpsman and headed to the wardroom she had shared with Cindy. When she arrived, one of their other roommates was there, a night nurse sitting cross-legged on her bunk. Seeing that something was troubling Irene, she asked, "Is something wrong?"

"This photo is all wrong," she answered as she showed it to her.

"Where did you get it?" she asked, recognizing both Cindy and having seen the matching half previously, as Cindy would take her half out and look at it each night.

"It was on one of the recent arrivals. The Marine had it in his pocket. He must be her Michael. And he was briefly her patient," she said, shaking her head at the irony of it all.

"But why do you have it and not her?" the other nurse asked, seeming confused.

"She doesn't know. She left before I found out."

"But she didn't leave, at least not yet. Her transport was having engine problems. She had to get off it and reboard the ship. They are sending a replacement. Cindy was just here ten minutes ago. If you hurry, you might be able to catch her," the roommate said excitedly.

Without wasting time to respond, Irene began running, still clutching the photograph in her hand. Cindy had to know what she had discovered before it was too late. Running through several passageways and up several sets of ladders, Irene reached the outside deck where the landing craft had previously moored to the hospital ship. As she arrived, the landing craft was just pulling away. Irene looked frantically for Cindy, finally seeing her looking out towards the distant island. She yelled out Cindy's name, but the sound of the landing craft's noisy engines muffled her desperate call, rendering it impossible to hear.

The slow-moving craft was still less than fifty yards away, but she could not get Cindy's attention. Finally, Cindy turned and faced Irene as she continued yelling out to her, waving her arms desperately. Seeing her friend waving to her, Cindy waved back in reply, thinking it was just a nice farewell gesture since she missed seeing her just minutes ago at their wardroom. Irene stood there helplessly as the boat moved further away until it was just a speck on the horizon. Her thoughts went back to Michael as Irene looked down at the photo, and she wondered if he would survive his wounds. Dejected, Irene slowly walked back to her room. It would take quite a while before she would get her answer.

As Cindy got onboard the R4D-1, she received her first look at what life as a Navy Flight Nurse would be. The plane's interior had 32 litters, each containing a wounded Marine except for two Seabees from the Navy's 133rd Construction Battalion involved in fighting on Iwo Jima. What surprised her most was the general good spirits of these seriously wounded men and their sincere gratitude for the care being afforded them by the sole Naval Flight Nurse and her Pharmacist Mate assistant. She observed the professionalism of the nurse onboard and wondered if people had thought the same of her. Cindy graciously offered to help in any way she could. The Flight Nurse just as graciously accepted her offer while saying that hopefully, it would not be necessary and she should enjoy the flight as best as she could. She also warned Cindy of some of the more difficult challenges she would be facing when she was at Alameda.

If she had any lingering doubts, seeing the nurse in action put them to rest as she realized that this was her calling. Of great importance to Cindy was that she would now be able to do more as a Navy Flight Nurse. She would be able to assist in getting so many more wounded Marines and sailors safely evacuated out of harm's way and to a land-based hospital than she could do on the Bountiful. So as the sight of Iwo Jima slowly disappeared behind her, she took out a notepad and began writing a letter to Jake, advising him of her transfer. As the plane gained altitude and the loud humming of its engines penetrated the plane's cabin, she thought of Michael and all the letters she had written to him. Then, with no one to share her thoughts, she pulled out the picture she carried of him and stared at it. Unfortunately, for now, her excitement of receiving her transfer was suppressed by the sorrow of what might have been.

CHAPTER 38

Frustration

March 1945

Although the surgery had successfully repaired the organ and tissue damage, the outcome was still very much in doubt. Michael's body had suffered severe trauma, and the effects of post-operative infection were still an issue. His minor shrapnel wounds and the flash burns from the explosion would heal over time, but the severe injury to his chest was causing the problem. Despite the plasma the corpsmen had given him previously and the subsequent transfusion of whole blood on the ship, Michael's body had already weakened to near death before his operation. While convalescing after surgery, Michael would pass in and out of consciousness as his body's temperature would rise to dangerous levels. Even when conscious, he would often be delirious and was not capable of holding any meaningful conversation. These issues were a concern to not only his doctors and nurses who were caring for him but especially to Irene Kelly. As much as she cared about his complete recovery, she also desperately wanted to be able to speak with him about the photo of Cindy he had carried with him.

Each day, Irene would stop by after completing her other duties to check on Michael's status. By now, the nurses involved in Michael's care knew of the photo and the mystery that came with it. When Irene would come into Michael's ward, the heartbreaking look of the nurse on duty would tell her all she needed to know of Michael's condition.

The good news was that the fighting on Iwo Jima had now ended, and there would be no further casualties. The Naval Air Evacuation Service and its Naval Flight Nurses had evacuated 2,393 seriously wounded Marines and sailors from the island from March 6 through March 21. With the USS Bountiful filled, many of those evacuated would not have survived the long trip to the hospital on Guam by surface transport ships. Unfortunately, the bad news was that taking control of the island from its Japanese defenders came at a terrible cost. Total U.S. casualties were 6,821 killed and another 19,217 wounded. Having served its job, the USS Bountiful set sail for Guam to off-load its patients before going to its next station off the coast of Okinawa.

It was increasingly frustrating for Irene as the USS Bountiful drew closer to port. Time was running out. If she could not talk to Michael before leaving the ship and being transferred to the base hospital at Agana, she might never know about the photo. Each day, she would check in on Michael, only to be again disappointed by his inability to converse. At least, his condition had stabilized, and his doctors said that his prognosis for a full recovery was good. But they also advised her that he probably would be off the ship by the time that had happened. Often, she would sit at his bedside, talking to him as if he were partaking in the conversation. She would sometimes look again at the photo that she had put back with his other belongings into his billfold. She would ask him about the picture and why he stopped writing to Cindy. Without waiting for or hearing his response, Irene would sometimes speak for Michael, coming up with possible answers. She would wonder if he heard any of this. More importantly, she hoped that somehow he would remember the conversations. But if he had, his expressions showed nothing to indicate that either of these hopes would come to fruition.

The last night before pulling into port, Irene could not fall asleep. She tossed and turned restlessly in her bunk, unable to accept the fact that she was unable to talk to Michael. She wanted desperately to be able to tell her good friend that Michael still cared for her, as much as she still cared for Michael. But there was still the question of why he stopped writing to her. She also wanted to let Michael know that Cindy still carried his picture faithfully and never stopped loving him. He deserved to know that. Maybe there was a reason the good Lord allowed Michael to survive his wounds. But if she could not find out from Michael what happened to their relationship, all of this would be nothing more than a cruel tease. He would never know any of this, and Cindy would forever wonder what had happened.

Still not able to fall asleep, Irene threw on a robe and walked out on deck. She stood and looked out over the now peaceful waters of the Pacific as she enjoyed the feel of the balmy ocean breeze on her face. As the ship steadily churned its way through the waves, Irene looked up at the countless number of stars that shone brightly in the otherwise darkened sky. She spotted one exceptionally bright star, thinking back to when she was a young child; she decided to make a wish upon it. It was not for herself, but instead, it was for Cindy and Michael. It developed into more of a prayer as she was making it, as she prayed for them to both find their true loves, whoever they might be.

Walking back to her wardroom, she decided to first stop by Michael's bed, not to question him, but instead to say a quiet good-bye to the person she had previously hoped would have been able to answer all her questions. Entering the usually quiet hospital ward, she heard someone talking as she acknowledged the night duty nurse.

"He's restless again tonight. He's still running a fever, but his other vitals are good. He sometimes has been rambling on, but it's mostly incoherent talk, nothing that makes any sense," the night nurse said, knowing why Irene was here.

"Thanks. I couldn't sleep, so I thought I'd stop by to say goodbye to Michael before the mass exodus tomorrow. I won't be long," Irene said as she walked over to Michael.

"No problem. Take as long as you need," replied the nurse.

As Irene pulled up a chair and sat next to Michael, she took a cool damp cloth and began gently patting his forehead with it. Other than her previous one-way conversations with him while he was non-responsive, she never spoke a word with him. Yet, having listened to Cindy's stories over the past ten months about her and Michael growing up together as best friends, then becoming childhood and high school sweethearts, she felt like she had known him personally. When she and Cindy first met at Balboa Park, she could not understand why Cindy dragged his picture around. Irene also was critical of Cindy's laments about her failed relationship with Michael, questioning why she did not just move on. But now, looking at Michael's face, Irene wondered what it would be like to have someone like Michael, who, after all these years, would still be carrying her picture with him.

She was ready to leave when Michael started tossing about as he lay in his bed. His face took on a look of distress as he began shouting Cindy's name.

"Cindy. Why? Why did you stop? I never stopped. Why did you?" Michael said while his eyes were still closed.

Irene moved closer to Michael and asked, "Stopped what? What is it, Michael?"

"You just stopped. Why? You never answered; you just stopped," he said, as his face took on a sadder and less stressful appearance.

"It's okay. It's all going to be all right," Irene said as the night nurse came over to see what was going on.

"Cindy, is that you? Did you come back to me?" Michael asked as tears began flowing from his eyes.

"Yes, Cindy's here," Irene replied, taking Michael's hand and thinking this is what Cindy would have wanted her to do.

"I wrote every day until you stopped writing. Then I still wrote to you. But you never answered. Then, my brother Matthew saw you with that doctor in San Diego." With that, Michael was becoming more agitated as he continued to hallucinate.

"We need to calm him down," the night nurse said to Irene.

"He'll be okay. Let him finish," Irene said as she began stroking his head.

"Cindy, I still love you. Do you still love me?" a much calmer Michael now asked as he began to drift off to a more peaceful sleep.

"Yes, I do," Irene said. Now she was the one with tears in her eyes.

Irene had toyed with the idea of writing Michael a letter and leaving it with his personal belongings when he would leave the ship. Then, when he was able, he could read what she wrote. But still not knowing what his medical condition would be at the time, she did not want him to get depressed, upset, or otherwise emotionally excited in any way that might affect his recovery. Besides, trying to explain all this in a letter without knowing the whole story would prove to be difficult at best. If Michael were to find out, it would have to be some other way. She just wished that she knew what that different way would be.

Irene was there when Michael was taken off the ship and transported to the base hospital. She had hoped that by some miracle, he would have awakened at the last minute, and fully conscious, he would have been able to tell her the whole story. And just as important, Irene would have been able to tell Michael of Cindy. But this would not be forthcoming.

Irene watched as Michael went into the ambulance that would take him away. She realized that despite her hopes of having a meaningful conversation with him during the past week, she had something more to tell Cindy, at least after last night. The problem confronting her was that the letter she would have to write to Cindy would torment her more. Although it would provide Cindy with some of the facts Cindy needed to know, Irene also knew that the letter would be heartbreaking. Cindy would have to live with the knowledge that not only had Michael still cared for her, but she had been with him in the operating room that day she left. She would be shocked to find out that she had physical contact with him. Plus, Cindy still would not know why the letters had stopped. How fate could be so cruel gave Irene cause for concern. Also troubling was what Cindy's reaction would be to receiving her letter and not being able to do anything about it. But Irene knew that she had to do it, and later that night, she began composing what would be the most challenging letter she ever had to write.

The next day, Irene dropped the letter off in the outgoing mail. Typically, it would take no more than ten days to be processed, read by censors, and make its way to Alameda, California. But nothing in war is normal, and this piece of mail would be no exception. Because of a snafu in the mail operation, the Navy would forward all of Irene's mail to Cindy at the Naval Hospital San Diego, Cindy's last command. As this, and other letters from Irene, were traveling back and forth across the Pacific, Cindy would not know about the transpired events. A frustrated Irene would sometimes find her letters to Cindy were somehow coming back to the Bountiful, which would soon be receiving its first patients from Okinawa. But it would be a wounded Marine from Okinawa who would not be brought to the USS Bountiful that would significantly impact Cindy's life. Fate had not yet finished teasing her.

CHAPTER 39

Flight Nurse School

March 14, 1945

Mary Ellen O'Connor was not your typical flight attendant. It was not that she had been a registered nurse since that had been an existing prerequisite to becoming a flight attendant in the early years of commercial aviation. What made O'Connor special was how many flights she had during her distinguished career with United Airlines. She had already racked up 2,500,000 miles in the air. That was the equivalent of circumnavigating the earth one hundred times or flying to the moon and back five times. She had also received the distinction of being named the "flyingest woman in the world." So when the Navy, especially Admiral Chester Nimitz, decided to establish its School of Air Evacuation Casualties, it came as no surprise that someone with O'Connor's credentials would oversee its operation. So, in December 1944, the first class consisting of twenty-four nurses and twenty-four pharmacists mates started their training.

With the success of the Flight Nurse program, more volunteers were necessary, and the school located at Naval Air Station Alameda in California began additional eight-week classes. To be considered, a candidate had to be highly recommended and of good character. Something that Cindy checked off all the boxes. Besides graduating from nursing school at the top of her class, her high fitness reports at San Diego and her superb performance onboard the Bountiful did not go unnoticed. A strong letter of recommendation from her commanding officer, as well as the backing of an admiral who had initially suggested to Cindy that she apply, went a long way. In all aspects, she seemed perfectly suited for the role.

Cindy was finally glad to be on the ground, which might seem odd for someone who wanted so much to be a Naval Flight Nurse. But having flown the 6,100 miles by island-hopping aboard three different planes, she felt good to have finally arrived. Her training would not begin until Monday, so Cindy had almost the entire weekend to explore nearby San Francisco. But first, she would have to get settled in at the base housing, where she would spend the next eight weeks. Carrying her seabag with her, she found a friendly sailor parked in a jeep who offered to take Cindy to her quarters.

"First time to Alameda, Ma'am? The seaman asked. Although her uniform bore the single gold bar of an ensign, having had no formal military training, nurses' ranks at that time were considered a "relative rank," and as such, did not rate a salute from an enlisted man.

"Yes, it is," Cindy said, looking about as they drove to the base housing.

"You'll find that it can get chilly at night, especially when the winds blow in off the ocean. But it beats where I come from."

"Where's that?"

"Billings, Montana," he said proudly.

At first, Cindy thought it odd for someone from a state with no coastline to be in the Navy, but she quickly remembered that Oklahoma did not have any ocean on its coast either.

"I grew up on the Oklahoma Panhandle where we could get some bad winter weather also, but the past few years, I've been living near San Diego."

"I've never been there, but I hear it's nice. We have a big base down there, and your summers are a lot milder than what we get here. Of course, it gets pretty darn chilly here at night during the summer."

"I don't suspect I will still be here to experience that. I should be shipping out at the end of my eight-week training."

They continued driving as they passed rows of buildings that seemed to date back to the early part of the century.

"Here you go, Ma'am," he said as he pulled in front of a two-story building with clapboard siding that seemed in need of a fresh coat of paint.

"Thanks, Sailor," Cindy said as she grabbed her bag and exited the jeep.

"Good luck," he shouted as he put the jeep into gear and began to drive away.

As she walked into the building, she was eager to report for duty and put her limited belongings away. Then she could get acclimated to her new surroundings. She would appreciate the added space and that the building did not rock from side to side or end to end as her ship had done. But it would take time to get used to not seeing the horizon from the deck of a ship. Yet, a short walk to the ocean would provide her with a similar vision should she find herself longing for that particular view.

Not surprising, one sight she would not miss was the constant arrivals of gravely wounded Marines and Navy personnel, their once young, muscular bodies ravaged by the horrific effects of war. It was much different for those personally involved than those fortunate enough not to be affected. Seeing the censored Movietone Newsreels of the war at your local movie theater was a far cry from actually experiencing it as either a victim or their nurse. But wanting to do something to help these proud young men is what had her join the Navy's Nurse Corps. Cindy thought of the many she and the other nurses helped save, but she also thought of those they could not. So, although not seeing their anguish, Cindy missed doing something to help them ease their pain. She looked forward to graduation and then once again being as close to the front lines that the Navy would permit. It was what she wanted to do as a nurse, and she realized it was one of her life's passions.

Her mind flashed back to the last battlefield casualty she saw. As the young Marine was being prepared for surgery onboard the hospital ship, she thought of his bloody trousers, his coagulated blood bonding them to his skin. As she had cut away the trousers, Cindy remembered the billfold that fell from his pocket. What clues to his life before the war might it have contained? Perhaps he had a girlfriend somewhere. If so, would he have carried a picture of her, and would she have even known of his fate? Cindy wondered how she would feel if that had been her boyfriend. Of course, Cindy had no boyfriend now, but she still had the memories of the one true love of her life. Thinking of what it would be like if Michael were in a similar situation sent a brief chill up and down her spine. She felt sad, knowing that because she had to leave before his operation had begun, she would never know if that Marine on the operating table had survived.

Cindy's remembrance of the recent past was quickly interrupted as a strong male voice announced his presence.

"Welcome to Naval Flight Nurse School, Ma'am, or as the Navy officially calls it, the School of Air Evacuation Services at Naval Air Station Alameda. I am Chief Petty Officer Thomas Willet, and I will be one of your instructors during your eight weeks with us. You must have just come in on that flight from Pearl," the Chief Petty Officer said, now speaking cordially.

"Yes, I did. I'm Cindy Smith, that is Ensign Cindy Smith," as she quickly corrected herself, still forgetting to use her relative rank from time to time. "I was looking to get settled before checking out the area this weekend."

"I would be glad to offer some suggestions, Ma'am, if you don't mind."

"Not at all. That would be great. By the way, what will you be instructing us on?"

"Swimming. Rescue swimming in the event of a crash landing at sea, to be precise. Hope you like the water, Ma'am; you'll be seeing a lot of it."

"Well, after all, this is the Navy, Chief."

"Yes, Ma'am, that it is. Did they advise you that you'll be billeted at the BOQ, Ma'am?" the chief asked.

"I was curious as to why we females were staying at the Bachelor Officers' Quarters," Cindy said, emphasizing bachelor.

"Soon after the war started, they also started housing female officers who were WAVES at that facility. Since then, it has been for all unmarried officers, including those nurses like you in the Flight Nurse program. So you'll be sharing your quarters with two other Flight Nurse candidates. I hope you find it satisfactory." The chief stated, knowing that even if it was not, the young nurse had no choice.

The chief's words stuck in her head as Cindy realized that she really was still just a candidate and had not yet proven herself.

"I'm sure it's an upgrade to the quarters we had on the USS Bountiful," Cindy said, believing that to be the case.

"Is there anything else I can help you with, Ma'am? Lieutenant Mary O'Connor will officially meet you and the other candidates Monday morning at 0700."

"No, Chief. Thank you. I will look forward to your tips about what to see and where to go."

"One of your bunkmates had already checked in ahead of you and has the list. So apparently, you're not the only one wanting to check out the area," the chief said smiling.

The chief was right about three things. First, the accommodations were satisfactory. Second, he provided good information that Cindy and her bunkmates put to use that weekend, and Lieutenant Mary O'Connor was there to address her new class at 0700 promptly. She told them that she would be overseeing their advanced first aid training as it pertained to the specific and unique challenges they would encounter during flight, most significantly the treatment of patients in non-pressurized cabins. She also advised them that they would receive instructions in the latest methods of dealing with shock, splinting, and the redressing of wounds.

As the class sat listening to her describe their eight-week curriculum, Cindy was impressed not only by O'Connor's knowledge and demeanor but also all that the former flight attendant had accomplished in her lifetime. It was no wonder that Admiral Chester Nimitz had hand-picked Mary O'Connor to head up the program. She advised the class that although these aspects of their advanced training would take up most of their time here, it would not be the most challenging part of their training. Finally, she told them of the physical demands that each would face in the coming weeks.

Cindy was fully aware of the emphasis this training would have on being physically prepared for all outcomes, none of which had to do with the usual administering of first aid or tending to the needs of her patients. Totally unlike her previous training, this would have more to do with her survivability and the patients in her charge. There would be classes on different subjects that pertained explicitly to flight, such as learning about artificial horizons and altitude. In addition, she and the other candidates would participate in various flight simulation exercises. Since the cabins of the planes she would be flying in were not pressurized and carried no oxygen on board, Cindy had to experience what the effect of loss of oxygen would have on her body. So, she and the other nurses would sit in a hyperbaric chamber that altered the oxygen and pressure, waiting until the first nurse would pass out. They would also undergo intensive training in how to survive a crash landing at sea.

Perhaps the hardest and most challenging part of the physical regimen was the swimming. Cindy had virtually no opportunity or reason to swim when growing up on the Oklahoma Panhandle. The first time she ever swam, or at least attempted to, was after she and her family had moved to California. Her first experience was less than ideal, as it required the efforts of a young and well-tanned lifeguard who had to rescue Cindy when she waded out too far into the Pacific Ocean. She felt more embarrassed than anything, apologizing to the lifeguard, who was more than happy to be carrying an attractive young woman in his arms. She managed to learn how to swim after that incident, but what was required of her now was entirely different from recreational water sports. She would have to learn not only to swim underwater but to be able to swim one mile, a far cry from doing one or two laps in a pool. Yet, what would probably prove to be her most demanding task was to tow a victim 440 yards in ten minutes. This requirement attempted to simulate the need to rescue an incapacitated patient in the event of a crash-landing at sea. In the end, thanks to both a strong will to succeed and possessing a body in excellent physical shape, Cindy would go on to pass her training with flying colors.

After graduation, she and the rest of her classmates would receive their assignments. Most of the thirty-two Flight Nurses found out they were going to the Naval Air Station Agana in Guam. They had not known it at the time, but they would soon face their biggest challenge to date, the invasion of Okinawa.

CHAPTER 40

Okinawa

May 15, 1945

Okinawa had become the largest invasion to date of the war against Japan. An invasion force consisting of both U.S. Army and U.S. Marine Corps units began attacking the series of islands on April 1, 1945. Naval bombardments from the massive U.S. Fleet and help from the British Pacific Fleet would pummel the island's fortresses. But as they had successfully done at Iwo Jima, the Japanese forces avoided much of the brunt of the explosions by hunkering down safely in elaborate underground caves and tunnels. The ferocity and fanaticism of the Japanese defenders were unlike anything seen up to this point. Suicidal Kamikaze attacks, in which Japanese pilots would attempt to fly their planes into our Navy's ships, were deployed in massive numbers. The battle was an indicator of what might lie ahead when a full-scale invasion of the Japanese mainland would begin. The top military leadership fully expected that the only way for Japan's capitulation would be to attack the country and bring it to its knees. To do so would require the destruction of their military, their industrial capacity to make war, and the will of their civilian population to carry on. To accomplish this mission, it would require a massive invasion force. A task so daunting, it would make the D-day invasion at Normandy pale by comparison.

It was a common belief that there would be high casualties among the civilian population. However, there was no indication of how the civilians would react to their homeland coming under attack until now. Distant as it was from the main Japanese archipelago that lay five hundred miles to the northeast, Okinawa had been officially part of the Japanese Empire since 1879, when it was declared the Okinawa Prefecture. Japan's ties to it went back even further. In 1609 it was unofficially annexed after Japan had invaded the Ryukyu Kingdom. As a result, its approximately 300,000 inhabitants were Japanese citizens and not just some conquered people who would welcome the American forces as liberators.

Complicating matters was the gross misinformation that the Japanese authorities were telling its citizens. With their husbands and fathers having been conscripted into service with the Japanese Army and falsely believing that the American invaders would rape and torture their females and their children, countless families would commit suicide. Often an entire family would hold hands as they jumped to their death from the island's many cliffs, incorrectly fearing the retribution they mistakenly believed would come at the hands of the American invaders. If projected onto the entire Japanese population of some 73,000,000, the extent of civilian casualties invading Japan would be staggering. By the time hostilities would end next month, nearly half of Okinawa's civilian population of 300,000 were either dead or missing. Many were suicides, but many were simply victims in the middle of a raging battle between opposing forces.

Now seven weeks into the battle, the intense fighting would continue for another four weeks before officially being declared over. However, by that time, U.S. forces would suffer over 75,000 casualties, including over 20,000 dead. Additionally, during the combined land and sea battles, U.S. losses totaled 768 aircraft and 368 ships, either damaged or sunk, primarily by suicidal Kamikaze attacks. Among those severely damaged was the hospital ship USS Comfort, the victim of a Kamikaze pilot who crashed his plane into the ship's operating rooms. Among the twenty-seven killed were five doctors and six nurses. The Japanese would pay dearly, however, sustaining over 110,000 killed in action. An alarming footnote to the statistics was that only 16,000 Japanese soldiers were either captured or surrendered, many of those conscripts whose dedication to service was less than commendable. These numbers would catch the attention of the policymakers as they would begin to make projections for the forthcoming invasion of Japan. As damaging as the Kamikaze attacks were, with a loss of 1,430 Japanese planes, it dramatically reduced what remained of Japan's air forces, as well as its pool of trained pilots.

Besides being strategically important, Okinawa was also a

window into what an even more extensive invasion of the Japanese mainland would entail. As the battle assessments worked their way back to the decision-makers in Washington, it would impact major military and political decisions in the next few months. Unfortunately, while the top echelons of the U.S. Military were learning of the consequences of fighting Japan on its home ground, so did Gunnery Sergeant O'Neill. Although his 3rd Marine Division was back on Guam to train for the expected invasion of Japan, after fighting on Iwo Jima, O'Neill, as always, found himself in the thick of things. Accompanying a group of officers sent to Okinawa to get a first-hand look at what the 3rd Division could expect when they would invade the mainland, O'Neill once again found himself in harm's way.

Although their job was to observe, the front lines on a battlefield were often very changeable. Despite being in a relatively safe rear area, they were still close enough to hear the distinctive whooshing sound of a flame-thrower being deployed against the Japanese, hiding deep beneath the rocky surface in well-constructed tunnels and caves. Those yet to be eliminated Japanese, safe in their fortified positions, would prove to be a constant threat. Thus, it should not have been a tremendous surprise that O'Neill might find himself the object of that threat. At a forward observation post, watching the fighting through his binoculars, Gunnery Sergeant O'Neill felt the impact a full second before he heard the shot. A round from an unseen Japanese sniper had entered into O'Neill's left arm near the radial notch, where his humorous and ulna bones came together, essentially fracturing his elbow. He would later debate whether he or his binoculars hit the ground first, but needless to say, his participation in the remainder of this war had ended. The rest of his team would fly back to Guam the same way they flew here. But for Gunnery Sergeant O'Neill, his flight back to Guam would be different.

The twin-engine Douglas, R4D-5 landed on the secure airfield in the central portion of the large island. The military version of the C-47 had to pass through clouds of smoke before the pilot could safely land. Then, with all three of its tires now firmly on the ground, the plane rolled to a stop near the end of the paved runway. Although the airfield fell into U.S. hands early on from its Japanese defenders, fierce battles still raged on the island. Until the entire Island would be secure, the enemy could still rain mortar or artillery shells onto the Army and Marine positions. Onboard the plane was Ensign Cindy Smith, USN, on her inaugural assignment as a Navy Flight Nurse. As ground personnel began offloading boxes of badly needed medical supplies and whole blood, Cindy was preparing to receive her first group of Marines evacuated off Okinawa and flown to the U.S. Navy Hospital in Guam. Among her patients would be a gruff-looking Gunnery Sergeant, his large and muscular body still looking intimidating even as he lay prone on a litter.

As the pilot and navigator stepped off the plane, other ground-crew personnel began preparing the aircraft for its next flight. As the ground-based medical personnel carefully lifted the patients into the plane under the watchful eye of Cindy, she was handed the patient manifest from a Navy doctor. On it were the names of the thirty-two patients confined to their litters, as well as six ambulatory patients who would also be able to fit in the plane. Alongside each name were brief descriptions of the patient's injuries and specific medical needs. While the last of the patients were being placed securely into the aircraft, Cindy and the other crewmen took advantage of the brief lull to walk outside and hopefully get some much-needed fresh air. The standing order was to be on the ground no longer than an hour, but that could not always be the case. Its non-compliance would be neither unusual nor enforced.

The III Amphibious Corps consisted of the 1st, 2nd, and 6th Marine Divisions and many of the Navy's smaller Underwater Demolition Teams, or UDTs for short. They had been fighting since landing in force on the western coast of Okinawa on April 1st, six weeks ago. Although having the upper hand by sheer numerical advantage, overcoming the stiff Japanese resistance did not come without a price, as casualties continued to mount. For those Marines suffering from severe wounds, the luckier ones were sent to Navy hospitals to recover before finally being sent home. Those not so fortunate would remain buried in makeshift graves on a hostile island, thousands of miles away from their homes and loved ones. Gunnery Sergeant Richard "Big Dick" O'Neill, USMC, was one of the luckier ones.

Checking the next patient in line to be put aboard the plane, a Navy Corpsman saw that the Gunnery Sergeant was from the Third Marine Division.

"What are you doing here, Gunny? I thought you guys were being held back for the big invasion of the mainland," he asked.

"We are. I was here with some high-ranking muckety-mucks to assess the situation. Just my luck, I get hit by some Jap sniper."

"Well, that sucks. But, at least you get to go home."

"Yeah, that's what they keep telling me," O'Neill replied, sounding less than enthusiastic and experiencing some deep breathing, the result of a recent flare-up of his previous bout with malaria.

Still having time before their return flight to Guam, Cindy and the other crew members walked across the runway to a building housing airport operations. The simple structure provided little creature comforts, but it at least had basic bathroom facilities. It was nothing fancy, but it was more than what was on the R4D-5. They would also have time to grab some chow from the mess tent nearby. As they were walking, a reminder of the ongoing battle made itself known. The artillery fire from a U.S. Navy destroyer's five-inch guns reverberated throughout the surrounding hills and across the airfield. At times Cindy could feel the ground vibrating as the ship's guns pummeled enemy positions near the shore.

With their plane refueled and loaded with its wounded who were hoping to leave this island forever, it was time for Cindy and the others to prepare for lift-off. With its parking brake set, the pilot gunned the engines to maximum RPMs. The plane strained to lurch forward as its twin Pratt & Whitney, fourteen-cylinder radial engines generated a combined 1,600 horsepower. Finally, with the go-ahead given by the control tower, the pilot released the brakes, and the plane began rumbling down the runway. Taking advantage of every inch that the runway provided, the pilot pulled back hard on the control yoke. Slowly, the R4D-5's nose began to rise, and those on board would no longer hear the rumbling as the plane became airborne.

The plane continued to gain altitude as it banked its wings and turned southeast. Looking out one of the windows, Cindy could see the smoke and flashes of artillery fire on the hills and cliffs that ran along the coastline. As Okinawa slowly disappeared from view, the job of attending to those thirty-eight Marines and sailors who they were evacuating became the primary concern of her and the Pharmacist's Mate who assisted her. With the noise from the powerful engines, it was not easy to carry on a conversation inside the spacious cargo area. But since keeping the patients' spirits up was an essential part of their recovery, the nurses would do their best in this regard. Cindy, with her warm and genuine smile, exceeded in this category.

"How are you feeling, Gunny?" Cindy asked of O'Neill, addressing him by the informal name for his rank.

"I've been better, but I've also been worse. So not bad overall, I guess."

"Well, it looks like you got the million-dollar wound, and you'll be finally going home," she said, looking at his elbow, fractured by a sniper's bullet and thinking that this was a good thing.

"The Corps is my home and has been for the past twenty-seven years. So I'm not sure what that means, going home. I've been all over the world and stationed at so many bases; I'm not sure where home is anymore."

"At least you won't be going back to Okinawa," Cindy said, not knowing quite how to have responded to the Gunnery Sergeant's statement.

"If it's not Okinawa, then it'll be someplace else if there even is a next time for me. The names change, but it's really all the same. Death doesn't care about a name in some world atlas. And a bullet doesn't give a damn about some name on a map. I've fought at Iwo Jima and Guam, and at Bougainville, I nearly died after being hit twice. Now I get shot in Okinawa, and I shouldn't have even been here. When I was just an eighteen-year-old kid, I was fighting the Germans in France. And I got shot there too. This war will eventually end, but there'll always be the need for people like me. We don't start the damn wars, but they expect us to finish them." As O'Neill finished talking, he had to cover his mouth as he began coughing.

At first, Cindy stood in silence. Then, hearing him cough and knowing his medical records and history of malaria, she went to get something from the medical supply locker.

"It sounds like your malaria is acting up," she said as she

removed a pill from its container.

"This arm wound will heal. But it's the damn malaria that won't seem to go away," O'Neill said, beginning to sweat and looking jaundice.

"Here, maybe this will help," as she gave him an Atabrine pill and some water.

"The side effects of this are worse than malaria. I may not be such a good patient after taking this."

"I'm sure you'll be your usual charming self," Cindy said, smiling.

O'Neill began looking more intently at Cindy, which was not unnoticed by her.

"Do I know you?" he asked.

"Well, other than the fact that we just met, I don't think so," Cindy replied.

"I never forget a face, and you certainly look familiar."

"I used to be assigned to the Navy Hospital in San Diego. Were you ever stationed at Pendleton or Camp Elliot? We could have crossed paths there," she said, offering a possible explanation.

"I was there up until 1943. That's when my unit shipped out."

"Maybe that was it. I got there in '43."

"No, I don't think that's it. But your face is familiar. Of course, you look a little older than I remember, and your hairstyle is different, but I definitely recognize you."

As O'Neill lay there trying to figure it out, he began sweating more profusely and continued to have difficulty breathing. Finally, Cindy put her hand to his forehead and knew a fever was setting in. Eventually, the Atabrine would have some effect on his symptoms, but she had seen cases like this before, and she knew it might get worse before it got better. Still, O'Neill was stubbornly trying to remember how he knew Cindy.

"Where are you from?" he asked.

"Before here, I was in California. I moved there in '40."

"Yeah, but you aren't from there. Not with that twang. I'm

guessing Texas."

"Close, but not quite. Good guess, though. I was born in Oklahoma on the Panhandle, not far from Texas. Ever been to Oklahoma?"

"Nope. I can't say that I was." But then, suddenly, it all became clear. His buddy, Michael Johnson, aka Okie, was from Oklahoma. Cindy was the girl in the photo that Michael carried with him constantly. So many times, he would proudly share her image with his fellow Marines. She was younger then, but that same sweet face and smile had not changed. Besides, the name on her uniform was the same name that Michael would speak of constantly.

"Oklahoma. That's it!" he exclaimed between taking deep breaths.

"What's it?" Cindy inquired.

"You're Cindy Smith."

"Gunny, if this is some kind of parlor game, you're going to have to do better than that if you want to impress a girl," she replied, pointing to her name on her uniform.

"Listen, the Japs shot me, and I have malaria, but I'm not blind. I knew what your name was when you first came by. Hell, the greenest recruit in boot camp could have figured that out. But you're not just any Cindy Smith; you're Michael's, Cindy Smith." O'Neill said, struggling to get the words out as he was getting worse.

"Which Michael?" she asked, not fully understanding the implications of what he had just said.

"Michael Johnson," the Gunnery Sergeant managed to say before passing out.

"No. Stay with me Gunny. How do you know Michael? And how do you know me?" Cindy asked, but she would have to wait for his answer, as the fever made any chance of him talking further not possible at this time. As she began doing what she could for his malaria attack, her mind was racing. She was trying to assess what just had happened, but all she got were more questions but no answers.

As Gunnery Sergeant O'Neill was finally able to sleep more comfortably during the rest of the eight-hour flight, Cindy could not get his words out of her head in between caring for him and her other patients. She thought back to those good years in Oklahoma when she thought she and Michael would be together forever. Cindy remembered the day that they got that photo. And despite Michael failing to write and never answering her letters, she still kept half of the picture with her. It had become not so much a good luck charm but a symbol of hope. A hope that one day she and Michael could somehow be together again. But now, here in the middle of the Pacific Ocean, the thought of him some-how reentering her life was playing heavily on her mind. Was he here somewhere? But would it even matter if he has lost interest in her? Was he in harm's way, or worse yet, what if he had been here on Okinawa? Then, she felt a chill, wondering if Michael may have laid dead, buried not far from where she had just been.

She thought how cruelly ironic it would be if she and Michael had somehow crossed paths without knowing it. Had she understood just how often that happened, it would have made her last thought seem tame. The Gunnery Sergeant lying just a few feet away from her might be able to provide the answers to all her questions. But until that happened, it would all remain a mystery.

CHAPTER 41

Trinity

July 16, 1945

For the past two years, 109 East Palace was an innocuous adobe-style building in the middle of Santa Fe, New Mexico. It dated back to the 1600s, but it now served a different purpose than when it was a Spanish hacienda. Although it was just off the main square, it was not a large building by any definition, and most visitors could have easily overlooked it. But to the thousands of unique guests who would pass through its doors, it was a must-stop for their arrival in New Mexico.

Seated as usual at her desk was forty-six-year-old Dorothy Scarritt McKibbon. Looking more like a friendly librarian, only a select few knew of her unique position at the small office where she worked. Dorothy's journey to her place in history was not easy. Born in 1897 to wealthy parents in Kansas City, she had attended college, graduating in 1919. However, her future took some dramatic turns for the worse. Soon after graduation, she contracted tuberculosis. Needing both treatment and a dryer climate to recover in, her parents sent her to the Sunmount Sanitarium in Santa Fe, not far from where she now worked.

Dorothy eventually recovered, and after moving back home, she married Joseph McKibbon. With the couple finally settling in Saint Paul, Minnesota, she gave birth to Kevin in 1930. Unfortunately, tragedy struck again, as her husband died one year later of Hodgkin's disease. Now, a thirty-three-year-old widow with a one-year-old son, she made a decision that would change her life forever and play a role in what would be the most important event of the twentieth century. She packed up all of her belongings that fit in her Model-A Ford, and with young Kevin with her, she moved to Santa Fe.

She got a job as a part-time bookkeeper working for the Spanish and Indian Trading Company that represented local artists, many of whom would sell their works at the local street market just down the block. However, with the outbreak of the war, tourism suffered, as did the business. Finally, the company had to close, as it became an unintended economic casualty of the war. Now, without her job and any other viable means of support, Dorothy needed help. Fortunately, during her years here in Santa Fe, her genial demeanor made her many friends. One of them arranged an interview with a newly arrived physicist by the name of Robert Oppenheimer. Oppenheimer had the task of overseeing a top-secret government research facility at Los Alamos, about thirty miles northwest of Santa Fe, code name, "The Manhattan Project." Oppenheimer instantly became impressed with Dorothy, and he hired her as a secretary, albeit one with top-secret clearance.

On her first day of work, she asked an official with the project if she needed any special instructions. She received the answer never to ask for a name to be repeated and never ask a question. Thus, she began her job of processing the thousands of civilian workers reporting to the top-secret project. The project's officials would tell the workers that they were to report to her at the East Palace address. Once there, she would issue them credentials. And, although entering through the office's front door, they would be whisked away through a rear exit to awaiting transportation. That transportation would take them to Los Alamos, often referred to as "The hill." Dorothy was also responsible for the flow of all non-military supplies to the facility. On any given day, these trucks might be carrying anything from household supplies such as toilet paper or the essential scientific equipment necessary to develop the project's goal.

On July 16, 1945, the fruits of the labor of so many talented individuals would result in the United States winning the race to produce a weapon so terrifying, even some of its creators would have second doubts about its use and creation. Then, at the Alamogordo Bombing and Gunnery Range in southern New Mexico, the world would change forever. Finally, at 5:29 a.m., under the code name "Trinity," hanging from a steel tower one-hundred-feet above the desert, the world's first atomic bomb was successfully detonated. The magnitude of the explosion would not only silence skeptics forever, but it even exceeded some of the most optimistic expectations of the scientists.

Within hours of the successful test, at the Hunter's Point Naval Shipyard in San Francisco, the USS Indianapolis would depart on a top-secret mission. Carrying nearly half of the world's remaining supply of enriched uranium-235 and other parts of a second atomic bomb, code-named "Little Boy," the cruiser raced across the Pacific. When it finally reached Tinian Island, where physicists and engineers would assemble the bomb, the Indianapolis had set a new speed record for the first leg of the trip as it arrived at Pearl Harbor. Yet, so secret was its mission, the ship was under orders to engage in radio blackout, and it was unaccompanied by any support or escort vessels.

The most critical decisions, both militarily and politically, would be made in less than a month. These decisions would impact the future of the war still raging in the Pacific and that of the world's future.

While Seamen 2nd class, Jake Smith knew nothing of the top-secret components his ship was ferrying across the ocean, he was not alone in his unawareness. Like most of the world, neither Cindy nor Michael would know what was going on onboard the Indianapolis or behind the scenes of that small office in Santa Fe. More important to Jake would be how his ship's top-secret mission would adversely affect the Indianapolis and its entire crew. Especially for 879 fellow crew members who would never know the results of that mission.

CHAPTER 42

USS Indianapolis

July 30, 1945

With the fighting finally over in Okinawa, the daily flights that evacuated the wounded to and from the naval hospital in Guam were no longer needed. With the Philippines finally being also liberated, for the first time since Japan had attacked various American interests across the Pacific, all major land battles and invasions had ceased. The Allied Forces had recaptured every island or territory that the Japanese Army and Navy had seized in their earlier successes. Japan had rightfully paid a steep price for their aggressions, as the number of their dead decimated the ranks of their invading armies, as well as the continued diminishing of their once-powerful naval and air assets. It was clear that Japan's capability to wage war against its neighbors successfully was no longer viable. Yet Japan was far from conceding defeat and the Allied Forces were not interested in allowing Japan to go unpunished for their acts.

Despite the absence of U.S. ground forces engaging the enemy, the war was far from over. Regular bombing raids of Japanese cities were extracting a heavy toll on the civilian population, in addition to the stated objective of eliminating their once-powerful industrial production. But despite the non-stop bombing, it was clear that nothing less than an outright invasion of the Japanese mainland would result in Japan's total surrender. And although their offensive capabilities were nearly non-existent, as a defensive army defending their homeland, their capacity was formidable. Accepting that they no longer stood any chance of winning the war, Japan hoped to extract such a terrible toll on the invading forces that the Allies would seek an armistice with terms much more satisfactory to Japan. And the fanatical and suicidal defense of Iwo Jima and Okinawa gave a clear indication of how many casualties would result on both sides from such an invasion. Still, any chance for a diplomatic end to the war was lacking, so plans were in place for the attack to begin in November.

While the planning, training, and preparations for the impending invasion were ongoing, Cindy and her fellow Flight Nurses found themselves in a temporary lull, having no casualties to evacuate from active war zones. Instead, to use their skills and training, the Navy found another use for their talents. They began assisting in transporting repatriated prisoners of war from the Philippines to Guam, many of whom were suffering health and medical issues from the effects of their harsh captivity at Japanese hands. Still, they all knew that once the fighting began again, they would be back to their regular tasks of evacuating the wounded. Despite that this was what they had trained long and hard to do, they all wished that the need for their services would no longer be necessary.

As Cindy was logging many miles in the air making flights back and forth to the Philippines, she had been able to meet up with her brother Jake last week. After its top-secret assignment of delivering the atomic bomb components to Tinian, the USS Indianapolis had arrived at the naval base in Guam, where members of the crew who had completed their tours of duty would be relieved. Seaman 1st Class Jake Smith would have been eligible, but he decided to stay and extend his tour on the cruiser. At least he had the opportunity to have seen his sister for the first time since he had enlisted four years ago, even if it were just briefly. But now, the ship would be heading to Leyte in the Philippines for crew training before joining a task force stationed off Okinawa.

Once again, the Indianapolis would set sail without an escort and still under confusing orders about maintaining the radio silence necessary for its previous voyage to Tinian with its secret cargo. Despite being highly unusual for a ship of this size and class to make the voyage across open seas alone, since the Indianapolis had just crossed most of the Pacific Ocean unescorted, its 1,195 crew members were not overly concerned. The ship and its captain would have been more worried had they been advised that there had been enemy submarine activity in the area. But the information that a destroyer, the USS Underhill, had been attacked and sunk just four days ago was never relayed to the ship.

Shortly before midnight on July 29, after being at sea for two days, the Indianapolis was detected by a Japanese submarine. Unaware of the impending danger, the Indianapolis continued cruising on a straight course at a leisurely seventeen knots, not taking any evasive action. At 00:15 on July 30, two of the six torpedoes fired at the Indianapolis struck their target. The first one exploded near the bow of the ship, blowing away most of it. The second torpedo exploded amidships, instantly igniting fuel stores and causing a massive explosion that rocked the cruiser. With the ship on fire and taking on water, it sank within twelve minutes of the attack. Before beginning its three-mile descent to the bottom of the ocean floor, the ship managed to send out three distress calls despite the perceived notion of radio silence. With an estimated 330 crew members dead or still trapped inside, the ship slipped under the ocean's surface, forever entombing those onboard.

Approximately 860 men initially survived the sinking by abandoning ship and jumping into the dark, fuel oil-coated waters. None of the survivors would have suspected it at the time, but the terrible fate that was facing most of them would be as bad, or worse, than those others who died quickly. A few were lucky enough to be on life rafts, but the majority were floating, many without having had time to secure their life jackets. One of those was Cindy's brother, Jake. Those swimmers who were strong enough would spend the night swimming until the break of dawn would allow them to find something amidst the debris to hang on to stay afloat. Those too weak would have drowned during the night. Many of the survivors would form human circles and chains, supporting one another to stay afloat. Their skin and clothing coated with fuel oil filled the air with a nauseating smell. Any initial hope of a speedy rescue soon faded, as time would pass with no aircraft or ships in sight. Unknown to those in the water, despite three separate naval facilities having heard the distress calls, no action was underway to dispatch a rescue operation. Later investigations would reveal that the personnel in charge of each facility, or their procedures, were at fault or grossly negligent in verifying the calls for help.

To compound errors, the Navy at that time assumed a large ship such as the Indianapolis would have arrived safely at its destination unless notified to the contrary. But still operating under radio silence with no escort ships to report its sinking and the failure to acknowledge its distress calls, there was no notification to the contrary. Had it not been for the accidental discovery of the survivors floating in the water by anti-submarine patrol planes, the tragedy would have been even greater. But after four days of no fresh water to drink, no food to eat, and no protection from the intense rays of the sun reflecting off the water's surface, the number of survivors had rapidly dwindled. When the rescue ships finally arrived, 544 of the original 860 who had escaped the sinking ship had died. Although most of the deaths were due to exposure, dehydration, and salt poisoning, an untold large number resulted from shark attacks. Whether individually or in groups, the floating survivors were easy picking for mostly oceanic whitetip sharks. Initially feasting on the corpses floating in the water, they soon turned their attention to the defenseless survivors whose only hope would be that the sharks picked someone else other than himself for their next meal. By the time the recovery efforts were over, 879 members of the Indianapolis had died. Of these, more than half died while waiting to be rescued.

It wasn't until Cindy had returned to Guam with yet another planeload of former POWs that she would be aware of the news. All Navy hospitals in the region were on alert for providing medical care and treatment for those 316 who miraculously survived their ordeal. Returning to the hospital, her first indication that something terrible had happened was the added sense of urgency that the staff exhibited. Her second, and more disturbing clue, were the looks on the faces of the people she knew. She saw their expressions of concern and sympathy, as they would try to avoid eye contact with her, each knowing something dreadful that she did not. But none of them wanting to be the first to tell her.

When she finally learned of the sinking, her heart sank as she collapsed down to the floor on one knee. Quickly supported back onto her feet by a nearby Pharmacist's Mate, Cindy was both discouraged and encouraged at the same time as the number of dead and those who survived were made known to her. She took comfort knowing that more than three hundred had survived, but she could not avoid the fact that for everyone who had survived, more than twice that number had not. Indeed the odds were not good as far as Jake was concerned.

As Cindy had retreated to the relative privacy of her quarters, she sat quietly on her bunk thinking about how things had turned out since moving from Goodwell and her prior life on the Oklahoma Panhandle. Of immediate concern was the condition of Jake, if he had been fortunate enough to survive. She would spend the next several days trying to glean any information that she could about Jake's status. After the blow-up with their mother, Jake had made Cindy his next-of-kin. That would make her the one to receive notice of him either being killed or missing in action. But having never been through this before, she had no first-hand knowledge of how long that would take. Besides, notification of injuries did not automatically trigger correspondence from the War Department. She also remembered that she still had not heard from Irene ever since the day of her transfer. Assuming that Irene had written to her as she promised, her failure to receive her letters was another example of a bureaucratic failure.

Cindy also wished that there was someone there to comfort her in her time of need. She appreciated the support and kind words from her fellow nurses and other hospital personnel, but the help she needed was for someone like Michael to be there to support her. Then, reflecting upon what she had just thought, Cindy corrected herself. She did not need someone like Michael; she needed Michael. Little did she know that within a five-minute walk, all that she ever really needed was recuperating from his injuries. Even more frustrating would be knowing that although it was in different capacities, they had both been at the same hospital ever since Cindy was assigned here out of Flight Nurse training at Alameda.

As Corporal Michael Johnson was waking up this morning, he felt no lingering pain in his chest. That, in and of itself, would not be anything special. But for Michael, it was the first time since he was wounded on Iwo Jima that he could say that. Despite the apparent good news, it also seemed to be just another long day in his long road to recovery. A patient at the Naval Hospital at Agana, Guam, for almost four months, he had recovered from most of the serious hurdles that he faced after his life-saving surgery. Although it was no longer a question of whether or not he would survive, he still had to battle the difficulties associated with a severe chest wound, as well as the fevers and hallucinations accompanying it.

Nevertheless, his doctors had advised him that he would soon be well enough to be transferred back to the states. As well as he was treated by the Navy's nurses, between the time he spent in the hospital, plus the time he spent fighting and later training on this island, Michael felt that he had enough of Guam for a lifetime. But, of course, he might have felt entirely different had he known that Cindy had been stationed here also during the past couple of months.

In another part of the sprawling hospital, recovering from his wound, was Gunnery Sergeant Richard O'Neill. Between the several surgeries necessary to reconstruct his elbow as best as possible, and the resurgence of his malaria that was plaguing him, O'Neill had not been able to find out what happened to Michael, nor was he able to track down his whereabouts. Soon, however, O'Neill would be able to do both, but not without dire consequences for Michael and Cindy.

Since both O'Neill and Michael were patients here, and Cindy had been transporting patients to the hospital facilities in Agana, it would have seemed that their paths should have crossed by now. But actually, the opposite had been true. Because the main hospital building had been destroyed last August during the liberation of Guam from the Japanese, the hospital now consisted of Quonset huts spread out in different locations that provided medical care not only to the wounded but to the 100,000 U.S. Military Personnel stationed there. Still, fate would always seem to find a way to affect the course of people's lives in the strangest ways. That the heroic actions of a law school graduate in the western Pacific would impact Cindy and Michael hundreds of miles away was just one of those ways.

CHAPTER 43

Decisions

August 2, 1945

The USS Cecil J. Doyle, a destroyer escort, was the first of seven rescue ships to arrive at the scene of the sinking of the Indianapolis. Upon its arrival, the vessel and its crew saw an incredible sight. Using its searchlights, in the darkness of night, it spotted a U.S. Navy PBY-5A Catalina, a twin-engine, top-wing, amphibious patrol bomber floating next to the survivors. Lashed to its wings with parachute cords were the overflow of the fifty-six survivors the Catalina picked up but could not fit in its limited cabin. Earlier, the plane had been one of several dispatched to investigate the reported sightings of men in the water by land-based patrol bombers. Coming upon the scene and realizing the dire consequences the survivors were facing, the Catalina, piloted by Lieutenant Commander (Robert) Adrian Marks, a law school graduate before the war, knew he had to do something. After taking a vote of its crew, Lt. Cmdr. Marks decided to land his craft on the choppy ocean, despite the twelve-foot swells and standing orders not to do so. Lt. Cmdr. Marks and his crew retrieved as many of the Indianapolis' crew as possible and waited for the surface ships to arrive.

As the dark of night shrouded the scene in blackness for the fourth consecutive night, The USS Cecil J. Doyle used its searchlight as a beacon of hope for those still in the water awaiting rescue. When the other ships finally arrived, all the remaining survivors were located and were brought safely on board. This included the fifty-six from the Catalina, as well as its crew of eight. With its wings damaged, the PBY-5A Catalina was no longer capable of flight. Rather than have it fall into enemy hands and allow some Japanese submarine the enjoyment of blasting it out of the water with its deck gun, the Doyle fired its guns into the plane. Lt. Cmdr. Marks and his crew watched as it sank, its final resting spot on the ocean floor, not too far from the Indianapolis.

Despite disobeying orders and having his plane sunk by a ship of the U.S. Navy, a unique distinction, Admiral Chester Nimitz personally awarded marks the Air Medal. If the hero pilot and Cindy ever had the opportunity to have met, he would have also earned her gratitude since one of those successfully rescued that night was none other than Seaman First Class, Jake Smith.

Back on Tinian, under tight security, top scientists were doing the final assembly of the atomic bomb, code name, Little Boy. They used the parts and the enriched uranium that the Indianapolis had delivered just days before its tragic demise. A B-29 Superfortress sat parked in a secure area of the airfield to deliver the payload to its final and unfortunate destination. Guarding the plane and its secret weapon were members of the same Ohio National Guard regiment, the 147th, which had operated as an independent regiment alongside Michael and the 3rd Marine Division back on Iwo Jima. With orders to shoot anyone not authorized to be there, the citizen-soldiers from Ohio did not know what they were guarding. Yet, what would be on that plane would result in not only the end of the war but the saving of countless American lives, albeit at the expense of the Japanese. But the final decision to authorize its use would have to be made at the highest level of the government.

Back in Washington, D.C., the President of the United States had awoken this morning, still not knowing of the tragic event that took place three days ago in the Pacific Ocean. Had he known, he probably would have thought what an odd coincidence that the Indianapolis was a factor in the dilemma that undoubtedly caused him many sleepless nights. It was partly through the efforts of the USS Indianapolis before its tragic sinking that President Harry S. Truman would soon make the most significant decision confronting any American President. And it would be his decision alone to make. But, of course, President Truman would prefer not to have to make this decision. If given a choice, he would have chosen not to be President. But as fate would have it, in 1944, the least likely Vice Presidential candidate became the official running mate of three-term President Franklyn Delano Roosevelt. Winning the November election easily, Roosevelt began his fourth term in office in January 1945. Despite attempts to hide his ill health from the public, the increasingly frail president fatally succumbed to a stroke on April 12, 1945. Shortly after that, Harry S. Truman became the 33rd President of the United States.

To suggest that Truman hit the ground running after being sworn in would be completely inaccurate. Despite being the Vice President and just a heartbeat away from being the President and Commander-in-Chief during a world war, Truman was out of the loop concerning many major military and diplomatic issues. When he became president, they rushed to brief him on the Manhattan Project and its development of a functional atomic bomb. With the war in Europe coming to an end, the threat of Nazi Germany developing their atomic bomb was no longer a concern. And although Japan had been in the very early development stages, it had not even been close to achieving that goal. That left the United States as the only nation to possess a weapon capable of mass destruction. The fateful decision to whether or not to employ such a weapon, especially against hundreds of thousands of civilians, would fall on just one person, the President of the United States. And that unlikely person was a piano-playing, former bankrupt clothing store owner from Missouri, who had never owned his own house, nor had the advantage of having gone to college.

It all came down to the numbers. Projections vary, but an invasion of Japan could result in as many as 500,000 U.S. combat deaths. If that high-end estimate held, and there was no reasonable argument to dispute it, that would be near twice as many as the current total of 291,000 killed in action so far in the entire war. If the current ratio of dead Japanese soldiers to their American counterparts remained consistent, the number of Japanese soldiers who would die would be many times that number.

Yet, the most disturbing truth was the death and destruction that would inevitably fall upon the civilian population. If Okinawa were any indication of civilian casualties, between conscripts forced into military service, the collateral damage of war in general, and the possibility of mass suicides, the Japanese mainland would be awash with dead bodies. With just the massive conventional bombing of Japanese cities, hundreds of thousands had already perished under the daily onslaught of the B-29 bombers. The fire-bombing resulted in tens of thousands of buildings to have gone up in flames, very often with their inhabitants still inside. The alternative to all this future death could end the war and the dying on both sides. But to do so would cause instant mass casualties, the likes of which the world had never seen. The ultimate decision would come down to which choice was the lesser of two evils.

Despite all the high-level discussions of the pros and cons, the military assessments, the casualty projections, the geopolitical ramifications, and the moral considerations, the choices were simple. Either yes, or no. In the history of the world, no more significant decision would ever be made. Never before would a simple yes change so many lives. And never before had one man changed the course of history, just not for now, but for years to come.

In the early morning hours of August 6, Colonel Paul W. Tibbets, Jr, and his crew of eleven lifted off from the runway at Tinian. The plane took off with two other B-29s, one carrying instrumentation to measure the blast and the other cameras to photograph it. They flew separately to Iwo Jima, where they once again rendezvoused in the air. Earlier this morning, while the plane and its payload were still on the ground at Tinian, Col. Tibbets had the name Enola Gay painted on the fuselage beneath the cockpit. It was in honor of his mother. The mission commander, Navy Captain William S. "Deak" Parsons, was the weaponeer and the one who would arm the bomb.

In Guam, Corporal Michael Smith was sleeping peacefully as the Enola Gay was approaching its target. On the stand next to his hospital bed was the picture of Cindy. In another part of the hospital, Gunnery Sergeant O'Neill was sleeping restlessly. Whatever it was he was dreaming about must not have been agreeable to him, as his face showed signs of distress. In yet another part of the hospital grounds, Ensign Cindy Smith, Nurse, USN, must have been dreaming about something pleasant, as she had a slight smile on her face. It was a welcome change from her daytime consternation and worry about Jake's status. None of them would have realized that by the time they would be getting up, the destruction of a city, whose name was not recognizable to most people, would bring them all one step closer to the end of the war.

Hiroshima was an industrial city that had avoided the bombings that were taking place in other locations throughout Japan. Although it could have been a military target, it lacked any aircraft manufacturing facilities, which were the primary targets for the U.S. Army Air Corps, XXI Bomber Command. Fortunately, Hiroshima had also been spared the fire-bombing wreaking havoc on Tokyo and other major Japanese cities. For whatever reason, its 350,000 residents were grateful. Still, Hiroshima was a viable target. It was the headquarters of Field Marshal Shunroku Hata's Second General Army. Their 400,000 soldiers were responsible for the defense of Southern Japan, which would soon be the focus of the anticipated Allied invasion. Hiroshima was also the head-quarters for Japan's 59th Army, its 5th Division, and 224th Division, with as many as 40,000 personnel believed to be in the city.

At 8:15 a.m. local time, from a height of 31,000 feet, the Enola Gay released the world's first atomic bomb to be used against an enemy. As the bomb was descending upon the unsuspecting city, Colonel Tibbets gunned the plane's four powerful engines to full throttle and began racing away at the plane's top speed of 350 mph. In less than a minute, the device exploded as planned at an altitude of 1,900 feet above the ground. As the Enola Gay was speeding away from the detonation, a blinding flash of light was visible. Despite being more than ten miles away, the B-29 Superfortress shook violently when the shockwave eventually caught up with the plane.

A towering mushroom-shaped cloud filled with debris, smoke, and super-heated gases was billowing up from the ground, the result of the equivalent power of 16,000 tons of TNT exploding nearly two thousand feet above the city. Even though the bomb was considered inefficient from a scientific perspective, it had still destroyed 4.7 square miles of the city. Although impossible to ever know the actual number, an estimated 70,000-80,000 of the city's population were killed instantly by the blast and its resultant firestorm. Another 70,000 were injured. Just three days later, the city of Nagasaki would suffer a similar fate, as the world's second atomic bomb to ever be used as an offensive weapon, code name Fat Boy, was dropped upon it. With the threat of more cities destroyed and no way to stop it from happening, on August 12, Emperor Hirohito informed the Imperial Family of his decision to surrender. On September 2, 1945, aboard the battleship USS Missouri in Tokyo Harbor, the Japanese authorities finally signed the formal articles of surrender for all the world to see.

Had Emperor Hirohito not decided to surrender, other Japanese cities would suffer the same fate. A reluctant President Truman had approved Tokyo and others as the next targets, a decision the President did not take lightly. With the war finally ended and no longer the need to invade Japan, life for most Americans would slowly return to normal. Whether fate would ever allow that to be true of Cindy and Michael was very much in doubt. Even more troubling would be the role Jake and Gunnery Sergeant O'Neill would have in that outcome.

CHAPTER 44

Finally Moving On

August 14-15, 1945

Little did he know as a child growing up in Wake County, North Carolina, that he would deliver the news of an event so emotionally powerful that it would cause massive celebrations all across the United States. But at seven o'clock p.m., on August 14, 1945, from his CBS radio studio in New York City, Robert Trout did precisely that, as he was the first person to announce to the country that Japan had agreed to the surrender terms imposed on it by the Allies. With that news, millions of joyous men, women, and children flooded the streets of every town and city in America. As horns honked and church bells rang, exuberant young men, many of them in uniform, would kiss anyone wearing skirts who happened to pass by.

Because of the International Date Line that runs down the middle of the Pacific Ocean, it was 9:00 in the morning on August 15th in Guam when the news broke in New York. Although there had been much hope and optimism as the news spread of the powerful new weapon the United States had employed against Japan, the day started uneventfully. Sentiment against Japan, being what it was, created minimal sympathy for the civilians killed. Just a casual walk around the hospital seeing all those seriously wounded sailors and Marines, many of them maimed forever, would show why. Besides, the prevailing opinion was that Japan had started it, and now they were getting what they deserved. The reported atrocities committed by the Japanese Army added to that belief. All that mattered now was a possible end to the war and the tragic loss of the young lives it caused.

Although Michael was ambulatory, the severity of his chest wound had made his recovery slow, and he would tire quickly.

In addition, he was still undergoing therapy to help increase his breathing. Although the treatment would not raise his lung capacity, the exercises would strengthen his muscles, inflating and deflating his lungs. Because of this, when he would be out on the hospital grounds unattended, the nursing staff made sure that he would be in a wheelchair, something Michael detested. But it would only be a short time before he would leave Guam and the wheelchair forever. When Michael was out for a spin with his set of wheels, the news began trickling in. At first, there was a noticeable murmur among the patients and staff, which ultimately grew to a loud roar as more and more people heard of the surrender. Soon, people were showing their pleasure by shaking hands, hugging, and even kissing one another. Sitting by himself beneath the shade provided by the dense foliage of a flowering flame tree, Michael suddenly felt alone as he watched the celebration from a distance. Despite having no one with whom to celebrate, Michael felt a sense of satisfaction in that maybe something good was finally coming from all the pain and suffering he and so many others had to endure. Yet, he still longed for Cindy and wished she was here to share in the celebration.

On another part of the hospital grounds, Cindy received two pieces of great news this day. She shared the first news with her fellow nurses and medical staff, as small celebrations spontaneously broke out throughout the hospital grounds. The second would shortly come after a flight came in with a new transfer of patients from the U.S. Naval Base Hospital at Peleliu in the Palau Islands. But for now, Cindy was rejoicing with the news that the war was finally over. She was happy, but a part of her missed not having that special someone with whom to celebrate. Soon, as the euphoria subsided, more serious thoughts about the future would play in her mind. Her time as a naval flight nurse would be drawing to a close with no further need to evacuate the wounded. The Navy would keep some of them, but since a reduction in force would result in most of them facing discharge, she began to realize that she might soon be going home. Whether that home would be San Diego, she was not sure. However, she could not stop thinking that her decision would be much easier if she had Michael to share it with her.

Gunnery Sergeant Richard O'Neill was able to find someone to grub a cigar. As he lit it up in celebration, he realized that he had not taken a drag on either a cigar or a cigarette since his bout with Malaria. He held the cigar with his right hand, as his left arm was still in a sling, the result of what was hopefully his last and final surgery. O'Neill strutted about the hospital grounds. His large chest was sticking out with pride at the job his Marines had done.

O'Neill also had dual reasons to be glad today. First, a chance conversation with a corpsman from the 3rd Division revealed that a member of O'Neill's Foxtrot Company was convalescing from a serious chest wound in another part of the spread-out hospital grounds. The corpsman spoke of the fact that the Marine would often look at the blood-stained photo of a pretty young girl that he carried with him. A huge grin was on O'Neill's face as he murmured to himself, "Well, Okie, I guess it really wasn't your day to die."

Among the Navy personnel getting off the plane from Peleliu was Jake Smith. Happy to be anywhere on the ground after his ordeal, Jake was pleased because he knew that Cindy was assigned here in Agana. With no more casualties to evacuate from battlefields, the likelihood of her being here to surprise was almost a certainty. Jake had been one of the luckier ones to have survived the sinking, but his face and arms still showed some blistering from the severe sunburn he received during those four days in the sun. He had also suffered dehydration, as did most of the survivors, but all-in-all, he felt fine. Jake had no idea what plans the Navy might have for him with the war coming to an end. But having signed recently up for another tour of duty just before his ship was sunk, he hoped there would be a place for him in the new peace-time Navy. For now, though, his primary objective would be to locate Cindy and surprise her. He would be successful on both counts.

Walking to the area that Michael had been in for the past four months, O'Neill began to think about how he would break the news about Cindy. Because of his Malaria, there were times that O'Neill was not even sure if he saw Cindy on that plane, thinking that maybe it was just another one of his wild and feverish dreams. But she was real, and he did see her. However, his actual conversation with her was fuzzy because of the Malaria. Yet he remembered her asking him about Michael. And even though he never saw her on Guam, he knew that this was her base of operations since she attended to him on the flight to the base hospital here from Okinawa.

As he got closer to the area Michael was in, O'Neill debated whether to be serious or funny as he would tell Michael what happened on the plane. But whichever he chose, he could not wait to break the news that Cindy was probably somewhere near at this very moment. Even the crusty, old Marine started to get misty-eyed thinking about it. Finally, after five months, the two buddies who had saved each other's lives were to be reunited. More importantly, after no news about Cindy after more than five years, Michael was about to hear something that would fulfill his prayers. He had no way of knowing, but his former Gunnery Sergeant was about to change Michael's destiny.

Spotting Michael under the ornamental shade tree, O'Neil shouted, "Hey Okie, "I didn't think they let riff-raff from the Oklahoma Panhandle into a swank place like this." O'Neill was speaking with a smile as he ground out the ashes on his cigar against the trunk of an adjacent coconut palm tree.

"Gunny, I heard that you bought it on Okinawa. What the hell were you doing there?" Michael asked, happy that the scuttlebutt about O'Neill's demise was wrong.

"That's a long story, but you should know better that it's not that easy to kill off an old Marine like me. Or even a young one, just ask your Dad," O'Neill responded, extending his good right arm around Michael as he stood up from his wheelchair.

"I'm sure you heard about the surrender. I was going home next week anyway, but now there's no need to keep most of us here," said Michael, looking at the sling and bandages on O'Neill's arm and elbow.

"Yeah, I'm sure the whole world knows about it now. I just hope that the Japs know about it," O'Neill stated while rubbing his surgically reconstructed elbow.

"Are you going out on disability?" Michael inquired.

"I don't know, but I don't know anything else to do," O'Neill answered truthfully.

"Well, after two world wars and getting shot three times, I

think you've done enough."

"Yeah, maybe. But what about you? What are your plans?" O'Neill asked, thinking that this would be an excellent lead-in to tell Michael about Cindy.

"Don't know. I haven't really thought about it. I'm sure my Marine Corps career is over with a damaged lung. But hell, at least I'm still breathing. I hear that you had a lot to do with that," said Michael as he sat back down in his wheelchair.

"Let's just say I owed you one, Okie." But then O'Neill quickly added, "But there's something important I have to tell you."

"What's that?" Michael asked, wondering what it might be.

"When I was on the plane flying out of Okinawa, one of the nurses...."

Just then, O'Neill was interrupted by one of Michael's nurses. "Excuse me, Gunny, but it's time for the corporal's physical therapy," she said as she began to wheel Michael away.

"Wait. I haven't seen my friend since he was an evacuee from Iwo Jima, and there's something important I have to tell him," O'Neill told the nurse.

"I'm sure if you had waited that long, you could wait another sixty minutes," the nurse announced authoritatively.

"Listen, Ma'am; you don't understand, I need to...." O'Neill said before once again being cut-off as he stood in front of Michael's wheelchair.

"No, Gunny. You don't understand, So please get out of my way, or I'll have to roll this wheelchair right over your foot. Then, looking at O'Neill's sling, she added, "I'd hate for you to get laid-up with a bum foot to go with your bad arm.

As the tough Marine stepped aside, it was Michael's turn to speak. "It's alright Gunny. Meet me outside the PT building in an hour. You can tell me about your news then. Besides, we have a lot to catch up on," Michael shouted to O'Neill as the nurse was pushing him further away.

"Will do," O'Neill shouted back, thinking that he was glad it was not this nurse he had to contend with back on Iwo Jima instead of that doctor. Then, after wondering if all this time in the hospital had made him soft, O'Neill re-lit the stubbed end of his cigar and wandered off.

With the news of the surrender no longer new and the celebrations slowly ending, Cindy resumed going about her regular routine. Trying to obtain any updated information about the casualty lists of the Indianapolis, Cindy was on her way to the building that housed the operations office of her unit. At the same time, with nothing to do for the next hour, Gunnery Sergeant O'Neill decided to take a stroll around the hospital grounds and enjoy the nice weather. Neither he nor Cindy could have imagined what fate had in store for them. As she turned the corner, she was in direct sight of O'Neill, who stopped dead in his tracks. He had seen her just that one time on the flight out of Guam, but he knew it was her. Although the Gunnery Sergeant saw her instantly, Cindy's attention had not yet turned to him. O'Neill, grateful for the good fortune to have found her by chance, began thinking of how this would all play out. Not only would he be able to tell Michael about Cindy, but he might be able to surprise him with her presence. Of course, that would depend upon Cindy wanting to see Michael also, but now he would have the opportunity to talk to her about him. From his fuzzy recollection of their conversation on the plane, she seemed interested in hearing of Michael. O'Neill was feeling more and more confident that he would be able to have a hand in reuniting them after all these years.

Cindy began to look in O'Neill's direction and started smiling broadly, her bright hazel eyes beaming with anticipation. O'Neill was surprised that she reacted so excitedly to seeing him. But he quickly realized that she had just as many unanswered questions about him and his relationship with Michael as he had about her and Michael's relationship. As Cindy began walking quickly towards O'Neill, a broad-shouldered sailor passed by him, quickly closing the distance between him and Cindy. O'Neill stood in shocked silence as the two embraced, utterly oblivious to him standing there just twenty-five feet away. As Cindy kissed and hugged the sailor, a shocked O'Neill began to slowly back out of the area. He was still watching the reaction on Cindy's face as she held tightly on to the mystery seaman, overhearing her tell him how glad she was to see him once again. As he turned away, the last thing O'Neill heard was the sailor telling Cindy how he was happy to see her once again also. Just before he left the area, O'Neill looked back one more time, catching a glimpse of Cindy and the sailor walking away with their arms around each other. O'Neill was silently cursing the damn "Squid" that somehow bested a "Leatherneck" and won Cindy's heart. Unfortunately, the possibility that the sailor was Cindy's brother, who she thought might have died during the sinking, would have never occurred to the Gunnery Sergeant.

O'Neil had spent much of his adult life making life or death decisions. He was trained well by the Corps to handle almost any situation that anyone might throw at him. But for the first time in his nearly twenty-eight years of service, he was stumped. Michael needed to know the truth, but maybe it was better not to hear the truth. It would sadden him greatly to have to break Michael's heart. But perhaps that's what Michael needed to move on. O'Neill looked down at his watch. He would have forty-three minutes to decide.

Cindy and Jake sat down on a bench that had a view of the Ocean. It was then that Cindy noticed it. When looking out across the open waters, Jake appeared to be transfixed. Cindy was talking, but Jake was not hearing.

"Jake, are you alright?" Cindy asked, concerned for his well-being.

"Yeah, I'm sorry. Seeing the ocean look so peaceful contrasts with what it was like when the ship went down and having to watch your buddies dying during the next four days. The worst part was not being able to do anything about it. I sometimes wonder why I was one of the lucky ones that survived."

"You shouldn't think like that. Yes, you did survive, and there has to be a reason for that. Maybe we don't know why just yet, but there's always a reason for everything. With Pa gone and Ma out of the picture, you are my closest relative, and right now, I'm glad to have you back. I have only seen our brothers once since we moved to California. Other than you, I have no one special in my life anymore. I wish I did, but I don't."

"There has to be someone out there waiting for the opportunity to meet you. Just look at you. You're pretty, you're smart, and you have a great personality. I see the way all the men look at you. I know that look because it's the same look I have when

I see an attractive woman. Could it be that you have just closed yourself off to the possibility of meeting someone new? Someone other than Michael? After all, it's been more than five years." Jake realized he hit a sore spot, but he also realized that it had to be said.

"All I can say is that my brain says you're right, but my heart says something else. I thought I was moving on with my life back in San Diego, but that night when you saved me, it made me realize that I wasn't ready yet."

"Be honest, Sis, not just with me, but more importantly with yourself. Do you still love Michael?"

Cindy took a moment to consider the question, then she answered, "Yes, I do. I always have, and I probably always will." As Cindy said it, a tear slowly rolled down her cheek.

Jake had no magic words to say that would make Cindy feel better. So instead, he put his arm around his sister and kissed her on her cheek. Then she rested her head on his shoulder as the two of them sat silently looking out over the ocean. Each one deep in their thoughts, wondering what their futures would be.

O'Neill had been walking forty minutes with no clear idea of what, if anything, he would say to Michael about Cindy. Even a walk down to the water provided no help. All it did was provide a safe place to flick what remained of his cigar. As he approached the Quonset hut where the nurse had taken Michael, O'Neill had finally decided what he would do. He would tell Michael about Cindy. O'Neill would tell him about seeing her on the plane and the parts of the conversation they had that day that he remembered. But he would also tell Michael about what he saw earlier. Michael had to know if he could ever have the opportunity to put all of this behind him and move on. Maybe it would be hard to take, but if Michael could survive his ordeal on Iwo Jima, he could survive this. He had to.

The same nurse from before had pushed Michael and his wheelchair back under the shade tree as O'Neill walked up.

"Delivered as promised, Gunny," the nurse said, realizing that she held the upper hand in their earlier standoff.

"Much appreciated, Ma'am," O'Neill replied, also knowing that she had.

"So, Gunny, what is the important thing you couldn't wait to tell me?" Michael asked.

O'Neill was careful as to how he would choose his following words.

"Do you still carry that half a picture around with you? The one of that girl, what was her name?" O'Neill asked, wanting to sense Michael's reaction.

"Cindy," Michael proclaimed proudly. Then he reached into his pocket and removed the billfold that contained the photograph. He took out the photo and handed it to O'Neill.

"About the girl in the photo...." O'Neill started, but before he could finish, Michael cut in.

"Did you know this photo is why I cheated death? It was what made me want to keep fighting to stay alive. After my surgery, they didn't give me much chance of surviving. There were terrible times when the pain was so bad I could have easily given up and just let go. But it was the hope that this picture offered that kept me going. I know it's my past life, and I may never see her again, but everyone needs a reason to get up each morning and live their lives the best they can. This picture represents that. Cindy is the real reason why I'm able to be here today to talk about it."

"Sounds like that's powerful stuff," O'Neill said, trying hard to understand Michael's undying devotion to someone who's been out of his life for five years and had broken his heart.

"It is, but now it's your turn. Fill me in on the important news about that nurse on the plane you had started to tell me about earlier."

"You're not going to believe it, but that nurse was no other than...." O'Neill paused, looking at the anticipation in Michael's face, realizing how the truth would destroy everything Michael had hoped and believed in these past years.

"...the same nurse I had back when they shot me at Bougainville," O'Neill quickly lied, unable to tell Michael the truth. Trying to substantiate the falsehood, O'Neill threw in more fabrications, "You must remember her. She was the cute one who thought you were cute also. I had thought that maybe the two of you might be able to hook up. But I found out that she was back at San Diego."

O'Neill was hoping that his made-up story adequately substituted for what he had initially intended to say.

"Thanks, but that's okay. Besides, I should be back at the Naval Hospital in San Diego soon anyway. Then I'll probably get my medical discharge. After that, I'll probably go back home to Goodwell. I don't know what I'll do, but the GI Bill they passed last year provides for college, so I'll have a whole lot of employment opportunities available after that."

"Promise me that you'll move on with your life. And I don't just mean with your education and employment," O'Neill sincerely asked his friend.

"You're asking me to promise something that I don't know if I can. But I will say this; maybe it's time that I at least try. But no promises, at least not yet," said Michael honestly.

They spent the rest of the day catching up on everything else that happened since that fateful day on Iwo Jima. Finally, when it was time to say goodnight, O'Neill was glad that he didn't tell Michael the truth. But, unfortunately, what O'Neill thought was the truth, was not.

Ironically, across the hospital grounds, Cindy and Jake would also soon be saying their goodnights. But, unlike Michael and O'Neill, there was no need not to tell the truth.

"If they discharge you, what would you do after getting back?" Jake inquired.

"Being a nurse, I can get a job just about anywhere. So I won't be limited to San Diego. But I really don't know. Years ago, Michael and I always dreamed of traveling and seeing far-off places. Now, I've seen far-off places, and all I do lately has been traveling, whether it's been by ship or by plane. Maybe it's time to settle down, but that would be easier if I had someone to settle down with. I've been very fortunate, but my life hasn't exactly turned out the way I thought it would."

"You have always known what you wanted, and I'm sure you will eventually get what you want, wherever and whatever that might be. But, you're only twenty-three years old, and you have your entire life ahead of you," Jake reminded Cindy.

"Actually, I'm still only twenty-two. Although, of course,

I won't be twenty-three until November, but who's counting," Cindy said with a smile.

"I'll only be here for another day or two; then they'll probably be sending us to Pearl Harbor, at least that's the scuttlebutt. With the Indianapolis gone, I don't have a ship or a home anymore. If the Navy decides to keep me, I have leave time due me. Maybe I can get back to California and look up the rest of the clan. If they don't keep me, then I'll probably head back there anyway," Jake said as he pondered his uncertain future.

"I don't know which one of us gets back home first, but if it's me, I will look for the whittling knife you thought you left at the house. I know how much it meant to you. I do not want to see Ma, so hopefully, I can do it while she's out working. The only reason I know she still lives there is because I got a letter from cousin Bertha, and she said so," Cindy said, thinking it odd that she can get a letter from her cousin, but not any from her friend Irene.

"Thanks, Sis. That would be great."

Later that evening, with Michael reuniting with O'Neill, and Cindy with Jake, all four would count their blessings. Each thanked God that the war was finally over. Gunnery Sergeant O'Neill was also grateful to have discovered that Michael survived his wounds from Iwo Jima. While Seaman 1st Class Jake Smith was thankful to be alive after the ordeal at sea, he still questioned why he lived, and so many others had not. Cindy was glad that Jake had survived and he would remain a part of her life. As for Michael, he was happy to be alive and have a future ahead of him, as uncertain as it might be. And despite their separation and the hurt that came from not knowing the reasons, Both Cindy and Michael were grateful for at least having had the opportunity to not only have been in love but to have had someone to love them in return.

But the two of them might not have felt so grateful had they known how fate, through the workings of a vindictive and ambitious mother, had turned their lives upside down and denied them the life together they each truly deserved.

CHAPTER 45

Discovery

September 22, 1945

As expected, Corporal Michael Johnson, USMC, had been sent home last month to continue his recovery. His first stop was at the Naval Hospital in San Diego, where the doctors medically evaluated him as to his ability to no longer require care at an inpatient facility. When the Navy's doctors felt confident that Michael could safely be discharged from the hospital, it coincided with his separation from service. For the first time in nearly four years, Michael was once again a civilian. It would take him a while to not write Corporal before his name and get accustomed to not dropping flat on the ground every time the old John Deere tractor back-fired, but the adjustment was proceeding well.

The entire Johnson family had cause to celebrate. Last year, after two years of courtship, Paul finally gathered up enough nerve to ask Betty Miller to marry him. Next year they will be expecting their first child. Grace had been seeing a nice gentleman and former Marine who lived in nearby Guymon. Last week, after dating for just six weeks, he proposed to Grace. To everyone's surprise except Grace, her answer was an enthusiastic yes. His loss of two fingers during the battle of Iwo Jima earned him an early discharge and an instant bond with both his future brothers-in-law. He and Paul would trade tales about the loss of their fingers, while he and Michael would simply silently respect each other's service and wounds, preferring not to talk about it.

Rebekah was now entering her final year of studies to be a teacher at the Panhandle Agricultural and Mechanical College right here in Goodwell. When she graduates with her degree next year, she will be the first member of the Johnson family to have done so. And although he would not be here today, Chief Petty

Officer Matthew Johnson was still aboard the USS Enterprise. The "Big E" had recently returned 1,141 servicemen due for discharge to Pearl Harbor. His ship was to sail for New York in three days, going by way of the Panama Canal. After serving with distinction, Matthew had decided to remain in the Navy. He would soon be taking advanced courses involving the new jet engines under development.

Michael was glad to be home with his family, but everyone sensed what was missing in his life. It was the eight-hundred-pound gorilla in the room that everyone avoided, and it was Cindy. After the initial week or so, every family member tried to speak to him about her, but Michael just politely shut each one down in their efforts. Even his mother and father would have no success. Still, things were much better here than what was soon to happen some thousand miles west in San Diego.

As Cindy expected, as successful as the Navy's Flight Nurse program was, the need for all of its qualified and dedicated nurses was predicated on evacuating the wounded. With no new numbers of wounded coming from active battlefields, the inevitable reduction in force occurred. Consideration for being offered the opportunity to stay was based not only on performance but length of service also. For some, the current policy of not allowing nurses to marry was incentive enough to leave the service. Had Cindy and Michael still been together after all these years, this rule would have made the decision to go much easier, as they had always talked of eventually getting married. But as it turned out, the decision was not Cindy's. She and most of the original "Angels of the Airfields'" would no longer serve on active duty and begin the transition to civilian life. In addition to any discharge papers they would receive, as members of the Navy Hospital Corps, they were the recipients of a commendation from Secretary of the Navy, James Forrestal, for their exemplary service during the war. In the citation for the commendation, he had written, "Out of every 100 men of the United States Navy and Marine Corps who were wounded in World War II, 97 recovered. That is a record not equaled anywhere, anytime."

But before she would no longer be wearing the uniform

of a Navy Nurse, the Navy would have to return her to the United States. In Cindy's case, that would be San Diego, where her life took a dramatic turn after leaving the Oklahoma Panhandle. While still officially on active duty, she would be staying once again at Balboa Park until her separation would be final. Her stay here would be busy, as she would need to secure housing for herself and employment. She was hopeful that her friends, Doctor and Mrs. Barnes, might be of some assistance. They had corresponded regularly during Cindy's service in the Pacific, as their mail had no trouble finding its way to Cindy as she changed duty stations and assignments. Maybe it was because the war was finally over, or perhaps it was just because someone finally figured it out and got it straight, but at today's mail call, Cindy would receive six months' worth of previously undelivered mail. All of it was from Irene Kelly.

Cindy was unsure whether she should be amused or angered at the unnecessary delay. Still, she looked forward to finally catching up with Irene and her other experiences on the USS Bountiful. But first, Cindy had to fulfill a promise she had made to Jake. So, she proceeded to head to the house that she and Jake once shared with their mother.

The ride to the house brought back old memories, none of which were good. Besides the attempted sexual assault by that doctor, it was here that Michael had finally stopped writing to her. Something that, despite her still loving him, she never forgave him for doing. When the driver pulled up to the front of the house, it looked even seedier than Cindy had remembered. She still had her old key, and Cindy had hoped that her mother had not changed the lock. Inserting the key into the lock, she breathed a sigh of relief as the tumbler turned, and Cindy heard the distinctive click of the door unlocking. Pushing the creaky door open, Cindy looked about at the sparsely furnished rental. The furniture had not held up well during her absence, as it showed excessive signs of wear and tear. The house had a musty smell, so Cindy opened one of the windows to let in some fresh air. Seeing the squalid conditions in which her mother lived, a part of Cindy was actually feeling sorry for her.

After a brief tour of the other rooms, Cindy set about to do what she came here for, looking for Jake's knife. After checking the most obvious places without success, she remembered what

Jake had written once in a letter. He had suggested that it might be up in the hall closet. Grabbing a chair from the kitchen, Cindy stood up on the chair and searched the closet's top-shelf. Reaching in the dim light, she felt something hard and retrieved it. It was the old whittling knife that had been given to Jake shortly before their father had died. Cindy felt satisfied that at least some good would come from her short visit. She was about to step down when a stack of letters at the rear of the shelf caught her attention. Curious, Cindy grabbed the bundle, neatly tied up with a string, and carefully stepped down from the chair, holding the knife in one hand and the letters in another. Despite the poor lighting conditions, she immediately recognized the two different sets of handwriting on the envelopes. One was hers, while the other was Michael's.

Eunice Smith's attitude towards her daughter had not changed much since Cindy last saw her. Although her relationship and feelings towards her were no different, her appearance had changed dramatically over the past four years. Part of it may have been due to the natural aging process of a middle-aged woman getting on in her years. But much of it probably had to do with working several different jobs cleaning houses rather than the posh job she once had as the housekeeper for the Cauldwell family. The bitterness that she kept in her heart did nothing to improve her physical appearance or personality either. The raw edge of that bitterness that was soon to be exposed was the furthest thing from her mind as she got on the bus to go home.

Cindy sat at the kitchen table staring at the envelopes but not fully understanding what this all meant. As she untied the string that bound them together, she noticed that someone had opened each one. Spreading them out on the table as if they were a deck of cards, Cindy took note of the postmarks. She singled out those latest ones that were written to her by Michael. Each of their dates was before the time that Cindy stopped receiving his letters. As she read each one, a flood of emotions swept over her. Cindy initially felt outraged, betrayed, and anger at her mother, but then she was overwhelmed by sadness and guilt, as she thought of what Michael must have thought of Cindy as he never received her last letters either. Then, a feeling of optimism emerged, as she realized that Michael never stopped loving her. At least not at that time.

　　She sat at the table, rereading all of Michael's letters to her. Then, having finished, she read them once again. Her optimism was replaced by sorrow, as she realized all the time they had lost, time that would have been their time together. Sitting alone in the dingy kitchen, she thought of all the times she had looked at his photo and could only pray that Michael had done the same. Finally, her pent-up emotions found release in the only way possible. First, Cindy let out a loud cry of, "No," that passersby could have heard outside. Then, she began sobbing uncontrollably as a flood of tears began cascading down her smooth face. Eventually, as her tear ducts dried up, Cindy just sat there at the table, her eyes transfixed at the opened envelopes before her. Soon, her face tensed up as a wave of pent-up anger was quickly growing inside her. The object of her anger would soon face Cindy's rath.

　　Michael was on the porch of his family's house, looking out towards the winding country road that he walked on countless times growing up. More often than not, it had been with Cindy. All of the others had been inside when Grace came out. Seeing Michael, she walked over to where he was standing. An unusually silent Michael glanced at her direction, minimally acknowledging her presence by the slightest nod of his head.

　　"You've been especially quiet today. Is everything all right?" Grace asked Michael.

　　"I don't experience any shortage of breath if I take things easy, and the doctors said I should do okay eventually," Michael answered, knowing he was evasive.

　　"That's not what I'm asking, and I think you know that," Grace shot back.

　　"I never could put one over on you," said a melancholy Michael.

　　"Why don't you try to track her down and find out why she stopped writing and never answered your letters. Even though Matthew had seen her with that doctor in San Diego, that doesn't mean she's still with him. After all, even you were dating Betty before Paul did. You and Cindy both had an incredible connection. Something that special deserves a second chance."

　　"First, I'm not even sure I would know where to start. But

even if I did, I couldn't."

"How about the hospital in San Diego for a start? And why can't you if you still love her?" A curious Grace wanted to know.

"It's because I'm scared. There, I said it. I'm afraid of finding out the truth. As long as I don't know for sure, there's still hope. That hope is what kept me going all through the war years. I don't know how I could get by if I lost that hope. I don't know how I would be able to accept the fact that it is over. I just can't find out," Michael said dejectedly, finally admitting not just to Grace but himself also what was his greatest fear.

"I wish I had an answer for you, Little Brother," Grace said regretfully as she put her arms around Michael.

Cindy had been sitting in silence for about twenty minutes when she heard the sound of the front door opening. She had rehearsed in her mind what she would say and how she would say it. But now that her mother was here, Cindy's well-prepared and thought-out response to what her mother had done was wasted, as pure emotion would now drive her words. But in the ensuing clash, it was Eunice who fired the first salvo.

"You have some nerve being here," she shouted at Cindy before noticing the envelopes on the table.

"Don't you dare lecture me about nerve? How could you?" Cindy shouted back, picking up the envelopes and waving them in front of her mother's face.

"I did it for you, but you were too much in love with a worthless farmer from Oklahoma to realize it. He would have never amounted to anything. And you would have been stuck in a life like mine, poor and lonely."

"Don't lie to me. You did it for yourself. Just like you trying to hook me up with Doctor Cauldwell. All you cared about was increasing your social and financial status at my expense." Cindy's face was now flush with anger.

"That boy killed your father and made me a widow. How can you defend someone like that," Eunice proclaimed, not showing the slightest bit of remorse.

"Pa died of a heart attack. He was wrong what he did, but he did it out of love for me. That's a whole lot more than I ever got from you."

"How dare you talk to your mother like that," Eunice hollered as she smacked Cindy hard across her face.

Recoiling from the impact, Cindy put her hand to her red and already swollen cheek. Then, composing herself as she stared directly into her mother's cold and impassive eyes, she calmly said, "You are not my mother. You are just some nasty and cranky old bitch who happened to give birth to me."

As Eunice stood there silently in shock, Cindy picked up all of the envelopes, as well as Jake's knife. Then holding up the knife, Cindy said sarcastically," This belongs to Jake. I'm sure he would have wanted to extend his heartfelt thanks to you in person also, but he would never care to set foot in this house ever again."

Cindy then turned her back to her mother and walked out the door, symbolically slamming it shut behind her. Just as she was slamming shut this portion of her life.

Later that night, as Cindy was back in her temporary quarters awaiting her final discharge, she carefully put the envelopes into her sea bag. It had been a draining day emotionally, and she thought that at least things could not get any worse. But, unfortunately, she could not have been any more wrong.

Seeing the stack of letters from Irene, she decided to read what she had missed out on for the past months. Being a logical and well-organized person, Cindy sorted the letter by postmarks, starting with the oldest ones first. This way, she would get a chronologically correct storyline of what her good friend had to say. So she opened the oldest one first, taking note of the date it was written. Then, sitting on her bunk, Cindy began reading.

March 11, 1945

Dear Cindy,

I don't know how to tell you this in a letter, but I could not tell you in person before you left the ship. I feel terrible knowing that it's too late now for you to do anything, since by the time you receive this letter, you will be at your new assignment stationed in Guam, but here goes.

That Marine you were prepping for surgery, the one that I replaced you when you were ordered to leave, had the other half of your photo in that billfold you had handed me. I did not know right away, and by the time I found out, you were leaving for the island on that landing craft.

I checked him out after the surgery and discovered that he was Corporal Michael Johnson. Your Michael Johnson. He survived the surgery, but his long-term prognosis is just 50/50 at best. I will try to speak to him after his recovery if that's possible. If I can, I will write you about what I find out in future letters. If he can pull through, he'll probably be transferred to the Naval Hospital at Agana, where you will be stationed. Then you should have the opportunity to talk to him and find out why he still carried your picture after all these years. Maybe there's still hope after all.

Love,

Your good friend, Irene

Things had suddenly gotten worse as Cindy put down the letter in disbelief. At first, she was shocked at what Irene had written, but then realizing what she had written set in. She had been with Michael that day. More incredible was the fact that she had touched him. He could have died right there on the operating table. But, just as disconcerting was the fact that he still may have died, and she would be unaware of it. If Michael had died, not only would he be out of her life forever, but he would have never known the reason why he stopped getting her letters. The thought of a suffering and dying Michael, thinking that she no longer had loved him, was too much for Cindy to take. Crying inconsolably, Cindy collapsed on her bed. She would later fall asleep, still clutching the letter in one hand while holding Michael's picture in the other.

CHAPTER 46

Homecoming

September 23-25, 1945

By the following day, Cindy had recovered from the physical effects of her disturbing discoveries. The tears were no longer flowing, but the emotional scars from the recent revelations were fresh and nowhere close to healing. But at least the clinical approach to problem-solving instilled in her from her nursing school training and hands-on experiences had kicked in. Like an accountant adding up assets and liabilities, Cindy began assessing the available options and the potential problems associated with each.

From reading the rest of Irene's subsequent letters, Cindy could fill in some of the missing blanks concerning Michael. First, Cindy felt reassured that Michael most likely did survive his injury, but Cindy could not know the degree of any disability he might have suffered. Second, Cindy knew that Michael had been a patient at the same Naval Hospital in Guam where she was assigned. Something that she wished she had known about previously while she was also there. Cindy also knew with certainty that he did not forsake her after she moved to California. Instead, the end of their writing back and forth was an evil and vindictive orchestration perpetrated by her mother. Finally, Cindy was also becoming more comfortable with the possibility that he could still be in love with her based on him carrying the photo.

Of some lingering concern was Michael's relationship with Betty Miller. Cindy only knew the lie her mother had told her. Eunice had falsely told Cindy that the information came from their cousin Bertha back in Goodwell. Ironically, Eunice had not known that Michael and Betty had briefly dated when Michael rebounded from the false belief that Cindy stopped writing to him.

However, Cindy, only aware of what her mother had lied about, could not know that there had never been a serious romantic connection between Michael and Betty, and she could not know that they had long ago parted as friends. With only the lies from her deceitful mother, Cindy was concerned that Michael might fall into Betty's waiting arms upon returning home. Worse yet, she could not entirely ignore the possibility that Michael could have even gotten married. But despite these concerns, Cindy would now begin taking the necessary steps to determine her next course of action.

Although still officially in the Navy, Cindy's status was pending discharge, a status she was sharing with millions of other returning servicemen and servicewomen. Accordingly, she was free to travel back to her former hometown in Oklahoma. But before she could do that, she still needed to learn more about Michael's status. A simple phone call to him, or his family, would not be that easy, even if the Johnson's had a telephone, which they did not. She realized that she would have to obtain the information she needed through official government sources.

Her first stop was the admissions office at the Naval Hospital in San Diego. A friendly hospital corpsman was able to confirm that not only had Michael been transferred here from the Naval Hospital in Agana, Guam, but that he was discharged last month and was sent back home to Goodwell. But, unfortunately, the next information she needed would not be that easy to obtain, his marital status. Still worried about Betty Miller, Cindy went to the nearby Marine base at Camp Elliot, Michael's former 3rd Division home. Going to what remained of the division's headquarters, she encountered a Marine Yeoman at his desk.

"Excuse me, Corporal, I need some information about one of your Marines. His name is Michael Johnson."

"Do you have his service number?" he asked.

"No, I'm afraid that I don't," Cindy replied.

"Well, Ma'am, there are several problems with that. First, I'm guessing that there are probably a dozen or so Michael Johnsons in the 3rd Division, if not more. Besides, as you can see, there are not a lot of us left here. The headquarters staff transferred out to Guam with the division, and with the war over, the entire division is being disbanded within the next few months. Sorry, but I really can't help you."

"Are you sure you cannot help me.? I need to know his marital status, or at least who he has listed as his next-of-kin. Or even who's the beneficiary on his GI life insurance policy," Cindy pleaded.

"What you're asking me to do is nearly impossible. And even if it were possible, it would take nearly forever to obtain that information unless you were either some high-ranking general or admiral."

Cindy was about to walk away dejected, but then it struck her. "Thanks. That was a big help," Cindy said sincerely to the now puzzled Yeoman.

When Cindy returned to the Naval Hospital, she made a series of phone calls, at each level dropping the name of a particular, appreciative Rear Admiral at CINCPAC, who finally returned her call.

"Ensign Smith, or is it just Cindy now? What is it, a year since we last met at the hospital? My wife and I were just talking about you at dinner the other night, wondering how you were doing. How can I help you?" the Admiral asked.

"It is still Ensign, Sir, at least for the next few days. I hate to impose, but I need a favor, Admiral."

"Go on," was the Admiral's simple reply.

Cindy went on to explain what she needed and why she needed it. The Admiral listened carefully, and when Cindy had finished, he spoke, "That's easy. Let me make a few phone calls, and I'll get back to you. Let my staff know how to reach you."

"Aye aye, Sir, I will. And thank you so very much, Admiral."

"You are very welcome, Ensign Smith, and soon to be just Cindy Smith, and good luck," he said with a laugh as the Admiral ended the call.

True to his words, Cindy received the information she needed. As far as the Navy Department knew, Michael was not married, and the Navy still had his parents listed as next-of-kin. This news encouraged Cindy, but her enthusiasm faded somewhat, realizing that this did not preclude the possibility that Michael could have married after he left the service. But with nothing else to draw hope from, Cindy would embrace this knowledge as she made the final preparations. Within a few days, she would finally know the answers, once and for all.

That evening, Cindy needed to reflect upon all that had happened. Receiving so much news about Michael in such a short time felt overwhelming. Yet, she understood that there was so much more that she didn't know. Having always felt at peace looking out over the ocean, she walked down to the beach and found a spot to sit as she watched the sunset. She thought of that Marine at Iwo Jima who nearly died being just inches from her, not knowing at the time that it was Michael. She looked to the west, thousands of miles beyond the distant horizon, thinking of Guam and how they were both there, so close, yet not knowing of it. As the sun went down, Cindy wondered what the reason for all this could be. Now she would finally have the opportunity to set things straight. This time it would not just be another ironic twist of fate. Even fate could not be that cruel, she hoped.

Back in Oklahoma, things there were also beginning to get back to normal. Many returning sons, husbands, fathers, and boyfriends were finally returning home. Mixed-in were a few women who, like Cindy, had valiantly served their country. But the vast majority were men who would now be either returning to work the farms or readjusting to civilian life, as they would seek employment in the new post-war economy. For Paul Johnson, and his pretty wife, Betty, there would be no need for readjustment. While Michael and Matthew had been away fighting the Japanese in the Pacific, Paul had helped his dad run the family farm. He felt terrible not being able to serve due to his hand injury, but he was happy to have been able to assist his father. With Michael now back at home, the question would be if Michael's plans included the farm. Even Michael did not know the answer to that question.

Cindy had packed light, just as she had during her time in the Navy. It would be a long trip for several reasons. First, having to take two different trains that made multiple stops, the trip would take nearly two days. But sitting in the passenger coach for that long and not knowing what to expect when she would get off, it would seem even longer. Second, Cindy did not expect or anticipate the emotional aspect of the trip. When the train pulled out of San Diego's Santa Fe Depot, it left full of returning service members anxious to get home. The train would have a festive atmosphere as each of them would be excited at the happy future that lied ahead. Just before reaching their destinations, wide grins would break out on the faces of those about to get off. Cindy would stare out the window at each stop along the way as eager wives or girlfriends would run into the welcoming and open arms of their male companions, many of whom they had not seen for three or more years. She would watch with envy as the returnees were showered with hugs and kisses, often with tears of joy freely flowing down their faces.

With each subsequent stop, the scene would replay itself over and over again, with no shortage of happy reunions. As the once crowded train was gradually emptying, Cindy would look out the window at the passing countryside, seeing the landscape beginning to look more and more like the flat Oklahoma Panhandle she once called home. Often, as the train negotiated a curve, she would be able to see the large black locomotive steadily moving ahead as large clouds of dark smoke billowed from its exhaust stack. But despite the train moving on, Cindy was beginning to doubt whether she could. As excited as she was when leaving San Diego, her joy was now replaced by a foreboding of what-ifs. What if Michael was not happy to see her? What if Michael did not believe her story of what her mother had done? Or what if he did not care?. What if the war had changed him, and he was no longer the Michael she had known and loved? Or the worst-case scenario, what if he was now with Betty Miller? Would she feel like such a fool, traveling two days to surprise someone who just did not care about her anymore? Cindy was probably more scared now than at any other time in her life.

She was lost in her thoughts when the loud blast of the train's whistle announced the arrival at yet another station. As the train's conductor walked down the aisle, Cindy finally heard the words, "Goodwell, Oklahoma, next stop. Next stop, Goodwell." Cindy looked out the window, seeing the town she grew up in for the first time since her family left nearly five years ago. She was surprised at how little things had changed. But then she realized that although the town had not changed much, she and her life had. The question confronting her now was whether or not Michael had changed.

When the train lurched to a stop, she almost did not get up

from her seat, frozen in fear. It was only under the curious eye of the conductor who knew it was her stop that she summoned enough strength to get up. Stepping down from the train, she realized now that she could not turn back.

Unlike the happy reunions she had witnessed during the past two days, there was no one there to greet Cindy. Not that she expected anyone to be there for her, but standing on the empty station's platform all by herself, Cindy felt both alone and disheartened. She began to feel anxious and nervous, not knowing what lied ahead at the end of her journey. Still, having come this far, Cindy knew that whatever fate had in store for her, it would be up to her to find out. She would finally know her destiny at the end of a fifteen-minute walk.

Leaving town, she stepped foot once again on the gravel road that connected her and Michael's farms. Carrying her bags in her arms, she walked past the two-story schoolhouse that she and Michael had attended all those years. Pleasant memories began flooding her mind until she remembered Betty Miller had also been there in the early years. Undaunted, Cindy continued walking as she recalled more memories from her childhood. Passing her old church, Cindy thought of Black Sunday, when a violent dust storm quickly came upon them, and how a courageous Michael shielded her with his body. She stopped briefly at the mailbox, where she threw the snowball at Michael that bloodied his nose as a young child.

Soon, Cindy could see her family's old farm in the distance. Now it was owned by the Miller family. She hoped that Betty Miller was still living there and not with Michael. Then, her thoughts went back to her father's funeral and that night in the barn with Michael. Then walking closer to the Johnson's farm, a brief smile appeared on her face as she remembered how Michael's brothers and sisters had helped him intercept her family's convoy when they were leaving Goodwell forever. Knowing that it meant so much to Michael to have that last kiss warmed her heart. Then, realizing it was the last time they had kissed and she was in Michael's arms, she hoped that soon that would no longer be the case.

As Cindy passed her former house, the Johnson farmhouse was now just several hundred yards away. Her pulse and breathing had quickened, as her anxiety level was quickly creeping up. Already a bundle of nerves, she paused to compose herself. Then, when she felt able to continue, she began walking again while praying to God that all of this was not in vain.

Just out of sight, Michael was sitting on an old rocker on the front porch of his family's house. At his feet was Shep, the family's dog, who, upon Michael's return last month, had sensed his coming and ran out to greet him after a four-year absence. His mother was in the kitchen preparing this evening's dinner with the assistance of Grace and Betty, who was now living with Paul in the Johnson's farmhouse. Michael's father worked in the barn with Paul, their old pick-up truck parked in its usual spot.

Michael was not the rocker type, but he spent much time languishing in it after returning home. At first, his mother and father thought it was due to his war injury. But it was not due to his healing chest wound that made Michael seem tired and depressed. Instead, it was another of Michael's organs that needed healing; only this one was not capable of being healed by conventional medicine. Grace was the first to realize it was Michael's heart, and Cindy had broken it. And despite everyone's best efforts, they all knew there could be only one cure, and that cure was someone named Cindy.

Shep was the first to sense it. His head lifted from the porch's wooden floor as he began sniffing the air while his ear was cocked, listening to the distant sound of someone walking.

"What is it, Shep?" Michael asked as the dog became increasingly restless.

Shep was now barking louder and jumping up onto Michael's lap, the commotion drawing the attention of those inside the house. By now, Michael was out of the rocker and standing at the porch's railing, straining to see what got Shep's attention. Of course, Shep would bark if a stranger walked by, but he had a more excited tone to his bark if it were a friend or someone he knew. As the person drew closer, Michael recognized something familiar in the way the person walked.

Cindy had spotted Michael first, probably helped because she was seeking him, whereas her arrival would come as a complete surprise. Her heart was now racing as she picked up the pace, wanting to be with Michael as soon as possible. Shep had now left the porch and began running towards Cindy, his tail wagging and his tongue hanging out, eager to greet his missing friend. Hoping, but not believing that it could be her, Michael softly asked himself, "Cindy?" When he finally recognized who it was, Michael shouted Cindy's name so loudly that it drew the attention of everyone. Then, not believing his eyes, he quickly stepped down from the porch and ran towards her.

Cindy, not wanting to wait any longer, dropped her bags and began running to Michael. In past times, Michael could always outrace Cindy, but still recovering from his chest wound, it would be Cindy this time that closed the distance. As she neared Michael, she leaped into his arms and began kissing him. Still surprised but definitely obliging, Michael started to kiss her back, their lips clinging to each other's, not wanting to separate. He spun her around, thrilled to have her in his arms once again. Despite the happiness they were now sharing, tears of joy were flowing down both their faces.

"I'm so sorry. I never stopped writing to you. It was all my mother's doing. I never stopped loving you," proclaimed a happy but crying Cindy.

"I never gave up believing that we might one day be together again. I have always loved you, and I always will. I still have your picture, and I looked at it every night," declared Michael, elated at being together again.

"I carried yours also. Deep in my heart, I knew you loved me, despite all the curves fate threw at us. It helped get me through some tough times."

After several more minutes of long overdue and well-deserved hugging and kissing, the two former high school sweethearts began to reflect upon the past five years.

"I have missed you so much. But now we're together again, and I will never let anything or anybody cause us to be apart. We have so much to catch up on," Michael said, thinking of everything that had happened but glad to have finally gotten to this point in their lives.

"I came to know a little more about you than you might imagine. It's a long and interesting story, but we'll have the rest of our lives for me to tell you, "Cindy said, as she rejoiced to be with Michael.

As the happy couple continued their embrace and the

kisses that each had missed the past five years, Michael's family looked out at the two life-long friends and lovers, glad that they were finally together again.

That night, Cindy and Michael each took out their halves of that photo taken at the Tri-State Expo years ago. They joined the two jagged edges together, as the separate pictures were now one. Then, Cindy took out the frame that Michael had given her as a Christmas present when she first moved to San Diego. Michael was surprised that she had still managed to have kept it all these years. Putting the completed photo into the frame, they looked at the two of them, happily standing side by side with their entire future ahead of them. "True Love is Forever" was inscribed on the frame. Then they remembered what the woman who cut the jagged edges had told them of the photos. "Not only will you each have a permanent reminder of the other, but should circumstances ever occur where you are to be apart, just as these two pieces will only match up with the other, so shall the two of you."

AUTHOR'S NOTE

◆ ◆ ◆

Fate's Final Destiny is a novel inspired by the period of American history that "Our Greatest Generation" helped to make famous. It begins on the battlefield of Iwo Jima during World War II and goes back in time to the Oklahoma Panhandle. The story chronicles the lives of two young friends from Goodwell, Oklahoma, growing up during the turbulent times of the Great Depression and the Dust Bowl. One of the book's goals was to have accurately set the stage as they grow into young adults full of hopes and dreams, only to have those dreams shattered by world events.

Goodwell had initially been chosen by simply looking at a map of Oklahoma. It seemed to be as logical a choice as any, and it became the setting for the novel. As the story progressed, it became apparent that Goodwell was the right choice. Besides the correct geographic location, it possessed the people of that generation that endured tremendous hardship and exemplified the American Spirit. They were hard-working and family-oriented. They had great faith, and they used their faith to help them persevere through the toughest of times.

Although the plot is about fictitious people, the story's framework is about actual historical events. Much research was needed to represent the era and the characters as accurately as possible, but written publications can only provide facts. What was needed was the human perspective. Gaining this viewpoint would require talking to people from the Oklahoma Panhandle who not only lived there but were also able to impart their recollections of the past. Thus, what began as an attempt to write a historically based drama became a journey of discovery. Besides justifying the selection of Goodwell for the novel, the friendliness and cooperation of the residents of Goodwell and the surrounding area were impressive. Their efforts to help a perfect stranger trying to fill in the missing bits of local history were note-worthy. The acknowledgment section that follows will mention who they were. But more importantly, having been able to talk with them reinforced the belief in the American spirit. It is alive and well in Goodwell, as I am sure it is in similar small towns across our great nation.

Perhaps, the most significant, enlightening, and emotional experiences of this endeavor came from researching our Navy Nurses' role in the Pacific during World War II. Once again, nothing could provide as much insight into the real thing as much as speaking with someone who experienced it firsthand. Through the generous help of the Navy Nurse Corps Association, I was fortunate to interview one of the last remaining U.S. Navy Flight Nurses from World War II. Lieutenant Jacqueline (Jacquet) Melvin was one of the original "Angels of the Airfields" and was on the ground in Okinawa evacuating severely wounded Marines and Sailors while the fighting was still going on. It was an honor and a privilege to have been able to speak with her. It was an experience of a lifetime. Sadly, Jacqueline (Jacquet) Melvin passed away shortly after, three months shy of what would have been her 100th birthday.

As with the enthusiastic and helpful people of Goodwell, there were others from the Navy Nurse Corps Association who were of great assistance. They, too, will be mentioned in the acknowledgment section of the book. An added benefit was developing friendships with the people who were instrumental in providing the information needed to accurately portray the life and times of one of the central characters. Besides the oral histories provided, the copies of photographs, letters, personal notes, and log entries made writing the novel easier and more insightful.

It was vital to have accurate facts as well as a precise timeline. Therefore every effort was made to ensure that the dates involving the characters' actions correctly corresponded to the real-time historical events. This exactness meant checking minor events such as the release dates of any movies mentioned in the book. And although the characters in the novel are not real, the other stories and people they interact with are. Therefore, the challenge was to make it difficult for the reader to separate the story's fiction from real-life events. If the characters seamlessly blend into those times and events, these efforts will have been successful. Finally, to keep the dialogue authentic to the times and situations, apologies are extended to anyone or groups that might have taken offense for the necessary choice of words. Although not considered politically correct today, any derogatory terms or expressions were historically accurate and used commonly three generations ago when this story takes place.

Finally, although the story is by no means a reference work, great effort was made to infuse as many fascinating facts of that era as possible. That included searching for the lesser-known stories behind the better-known events of that period. Often it required searching multiple sources to both understand and confirm those stories. By the conclusion of the research, the result was having a better understanding of how important it is never to forget that crucial period of American history and the people who lived it. They indeed were the "Greatest Generation."

ACKNOWLEDGEMENT

I want to acknowledge all those people who had a role in helping to make this book possible. With sincere apologies to anyone I inadvertently omitted, these individuals provided much-needed information and contributed many valuable ideas and suggestions. I especially want to thank those individuals and organizations who have provided the relevant and historical information needed to make this novel as authentic as possible. Although the characters and some establishments were fictitious, the events and locations were genuine representations of our nation and the events at that time. Without their aid and assistance, it would have been impossible to accurately describe the authentic atmosphere and sentiments of those times and places in American history. Of course, any errors and conclusions are the responsibility of the author.

First, I want to thank my family for their continued encouragement and support. Thank you for believing in me and offering helpful suggestions during this process. This was especially true of my wife, Donna.

For sharing her literary expertise, a special thank you to Jeanie Prall, Program Director of Middle & Secondary Education, Keystone College, LaPlume, Pennsylvania.

Many thanks are due to Seth Hammond of the No Man's Land Historical Society and curator of the No Man's Land Museum in Goodwell, Oklahoma. Seth was of great assistance, allowing me to understand better the setting of Goodwell for the story. For my specific questions of the area, Seth either knew the answers or knew who to ask.

A tremendous thank you is necessary to Nichole Bourne,

Town of Goodwell Court Clerk. If it were not for her constant and selfless efforts to provide me with the information I could not find elsewhere, the novel's authenticity would have suffered. In particular, Nichole's assistance connected me with long-time residents of the area. These residents provided their first-hand knowledge and insight into what life in Goodwell had been in the 1930s.

One of those residents was Johnnie Davis, who is the town's unofficial historian. Ninety years of age, he provided excellent background information on Goodwell during the period of the story. His knowledge of the area's history was extremely helpful in getting a feel for what life was like on the Oklahoma Panhandle three-quarters of a century ago. It was no surprise that most people in town would point me in his direction to get the facts I needed. If Johnnie did not know it, he knew who did. One of those persons he found was Jolene Strong, who, although now living in Oklahoma City, provided much-needed information about the history of Goodwell High School's policy regarding dancing.

Thanks also to the following individuals who took the time to help me find the necessary background information for the book's settings.

Gaby Ojeda, Goodwell Public Schools, Goodwell, Oklahoma

Dr. Katy Levings, Assistant Librarian of the McKee Library, Oklahoma Panhandle University, Goodwell, Oklahoma.

Virgil Bartlett, General Manager of the Tri-State Exposition, Amarillo, Texas.

Shay Martin, Guymon Daily Herald, Guymon, Oklahoma

Christy Kelso, Postmaster, Goodwell Oklahoma Post Office

The Navy Nurse Corps Association was extremely valuable in providing insights into the Navy Nurses' role in the Pacific during World War II. The insights they offered were far beyond what was available in books, articles, or online publications. Several of their members were extremely helpful in this matter.

I want to acknowledge Captain Mary Mahony, USN (retired), the Executive Director of the Navy Nurse Corps Association, and a veteran of thirty years of service to our country, including Operation Desert Storm. Captain Mahony was of great help, and her generous offer to arrange for me to talk to an actual World War II Naval Flight Nurse and her daughter would prove to be invaluable. These provided a glimpse into the life of World War II Navy Nurses and Naval Flight Nurses that were not available from other sources.

Special thanks are a must for Maureen Christopher, Commander, USN (retired) with twenty-one years of service and another Navy Nurse Corps Association member. Maureen was also the daughter of an original World War II Naval Flight Nurse. Maureen's vast knowledge of these brave women helped me to fill in more than a few blanks in the history of their great service to our nation. Allowing her mother to be interviewed provided the opportunity to gather first-hand knowledge of these incredible women. In addition, Commander Christopher provided a treasure trove of information from her mother's notes, letters, aviator flight logbooks, and photographs. I will long remember her genuine friendliness and willingness to answer my many questions.

Finally, no acknowledgment would be complete without honoring and thanking Lieutenant Jacqueline (Jacquet) Melvin, Naval Flight Nurse, USN. Jacqueline Melvin was one of the original one-hundred-eight World War II "Angels of the Airways." She flew in and out of Okinawa, where some of the war's fiercest fighting in the Pacific took place. Her assistance in evacuating hundreds of severely wounded Marines and Sailors undoubtedly saved countless lives. My conversation with her as she approached the celebration of her 100th birthday provided me with first-hand knowledge of what these remarkable women had accomplished. Her recollections of Balboa Park, Alameda, Guam, and Okinawa helped make this novel more authentic. Sadly, Jackie, as she was known to her friends, died before the publication of this book. When we speak of that "Greatest Generation," Jacqueline Melvin was one of their best ambassadors, showing why they were just that. She was and will always be an American treasure. To Jackie and those like her, this book is dedicated.

BOOKS BY THIS AUTHOR

The Puzzle Pieces

This is the story of a young woman who struggles to save her past life, as well as her future, when it is mysteriously turned upside down as the result of an accident. Hoping that love will enable her to set things straight once again, she sets out on a mission to restore her life as it had once been, and in doing so, to win back the true love she once had. But first she must overcome the many obstacles blocking her from achieving her goal. With the help of her family and her best friend, she tries to discover the difference between what is real and what is not. A series of twists will keep readers guessing right up to the very end.

Made in United States
Orlando, FL
27 February 2022

15193874R00221